THE COPPER CLUB

Patrick Bell

MINERVA PRESS
ATLANTA LONDON SYDNEY

THE COPPER CLUB
Copyright © Patrick Bell 1998

All Rights Reserved

No part of this book may be reproduced in any form
by photocopying or by any electronic or mechanical means,
including information storage or retrieval systems,
without permission in writing from both the copyright
owner and the publisher of this book.

ISBN 0 75410 319 6

First Published 1998 by
MINERVA PRESS
195 Knightsbridge
London SW7 1RE

Printed in Great Britain for Minerva Press

THE COPPER CLUB

For my mother and father

About the Author

The author established himself as a successful commodities trader before the age of twenty. By the age of twenty-four he had worked as a senior commodities dealer with three of the world's most prestigious securities firms. His experience includes stints at U.B.S. in Sydney, Goldman Sachs in New York, and Merrill Lynch in London. At twenty-five he decided to write a book and pursue a career as a private investment manager.

Author's Note

The 13th June, 1996 is a day that I will never forget, for more reasons than one. For on this day, the chairman of Sumitomo Corporation, Tomiichi Akiyama, announced to the world that his company had lost 1.8 billion U.S.D. trading copper. He attributed the losses to the rogue activities of a trader in their metals department, Yasuo Hamanka. This loss was later officially revised to 2.6 billion U.S.D., although in reality it was probably a lot more. In October of 1996 Yasuo Hamanka was arrested in Tokyo and pleaded guilty to charges of forgery. It smelled like a typical Japanese cover-up.

Everybody has their theories as to what happened at Sumitomo. What really happened? We will probably never know. It is unlikely that Hamanka acted alone or was a fool like Nick Leeson. Too many people made money on the back of Sumitomo's business for it to be the work of a single man acting alone. As a senior trader on a base metals desk in London at the time of the copper debacle, I was in a better situation than most to see what was happening. For me it was simple. The writing was on the wall for a long time before it unfolded in the public domain. It was plain to see that the situation would blow up eventually. I have my own ideas on the subject which I would be happy to share with you over a beer or two.

But this book, although inspired by the Sumitomo debacle, is purely a work of fiction. The characters, companies and events depicted are entirely creations of the author and stem from a very fertile imagination. Any real companies that have been featured are incidental to the plot and I hope they have been shown in a favorable light. Any factual inaccuracies or errors in the text, and there are sure to be some, are entirely the fault of the author.

At this point I would like to thank everyone who played a part in bringing this project to fruition. Special thanks go to my family and friends, traders and non-traders alike, who were my sounding boards and army of readers. In the dark hours, it was your support and encouragement that kept the project alive, especially when skiing or bumming about in the Greek Islands seemed a better use of my available time. A special note of thanks to all my friends around the world who put me up in London, New York, Tokyo and L.A. Also to the people in cyberspace who place random stuff on the Net, I say thanks. Without the use of the Internet, the research I needed to do for the book would have taken forever.

When you've finished the book, I'd love to hear your thoughts. Any feedback would be appreciated. You can e-mail me at 'thecopperclub@yahoo.com'. I will reply to everyone personally. I hope you enjoy it!

Regards
Patrick Bell

January 31st, 1995

Ten million dollars was not a lot of money in the big scheme of things. So thought David Green to himself as he lounged back in the oversized padded leather chair in his study, and besides, it was a small price to pay for his silence.

Smoke filled the air as he leant forward to fix himself another double shot of vodka from a bottle of Smirnoff black label, his second of the evening. He returned the bottle to its post, a position precariously close to the edge of the mahogany desk. He normally took his vodka on the rocks, but the effort needed to remove himself from the comfort of his chair at this point was by far greater than the incremental pleasure he would derive from the ice. At this time in the morning he was way beyond caring. In fact he cared little for anything these days though there had once been a time in his life when he had. In those days he had had it all, the great job, the wife, the two beautiful children, the house in affluent and leafy Greenwich, Connecticut and a summer home in the Hamptons. But that had all evaporated when his wife had left him. Now all he had was mortgage payments, alimony and every other weekend with his kids. Sure, he had kept the house, but at what cost? Paying off the bitch had cost him everything he had stashed away for retirement and then some.

Now all he felt he had left was his precious Russian mistress. How much had he grown to love her since the divorce was finalized, he mused to himself as he pursed his lips, sinking yet another double shot. Yes, all he had left was his drink and enough information to sink what was probably the greatest fraud to which the world would ever bear witness.

He stared out of the window and pondered his future. Somewhere outside a dog barked that annoying bark that all neighbors hate at two in the morning. Ten million dollars would be spare change to these men, but it would be enough to ensure his silence and provide him with an income for his ever graying years. He leant forward to pour yet another drink from the bottle on his desk.

A reflection in the computer monitor on his desk caught his glance. It was too late. His reaction time impaired, he was a stationary target. The impact of a powerful forearm across his chest thrust him back into the confines of his armchair. Simultaneously, a second hand shot forward covering his nose and mouth with a cloth soaked in chloroform. His body slumped limply in the chair. His heaving chest the only sign that he was still alive.

The first man placed his arms under Green's armpits and linked them around the chest of the unconscious man, the second grabbed his feet, and the two men struggled through the doorway and up the stairs with his overweight frame. Carefully maneuvering the body along the upstairs corridor, making certain that they did not bump or scrape their cargo, they carried Green into the master bedroom. Here they dumped his body, watching it bounce lifelessly onto the covers of the queensize bed that filled the room.

The first man stayed in the bedroom to arrange Green's body face-up in a semi-starfish position, to look as though he had passed out. Legs almost spread-eagled, right arm outstretched and clasping the covers of the bed, left arm outstretched towards the small wooden bedside cabinet which housed an alarm clock, a bedside lamp and one of the ubiquitous ashtrays which had dominated the interior landscape of Green's house since his wife had left. She had never let him smoke in the house.

Meanwhile, the second man worked furiously downstairs. He pulled open the top drawer of Green's mahogany desk, carefully removing each and every one of the floppy disks that he found. Then, by waving a high-powered magnet across the surface of each of the floppy disks, he erased the data that each disk contained. Next he reformatted the hard drive on Green's computer, erasing every bit of data that it contained. His job done, he quickly exited the room, grabbing the liquid leftovers of Green's evening alone.

He returned from the study carrying the half full bottle of Smirnoff, the tumbler from which Green had been drinking, and the still-burning cigarette gripped tightly between the fingers of the surgical gloves that both he and the other man were wearing. He poured the vodka across the top of the bedside cabinet making sure it pooled well and started to run down the back of the cabinet towards the curtains. He then lay the empty bottle on its side, on top of the cabinet, so as to look as though it had been knocked over. Beside it he placed the tumbler. Then he placed the cigarette that Green had been puffing away at (before he was rudely interrupted) in the pool of white spirit. A light blue flame plumed from the surface of the pool and a soft-sounding whump filled the room as the spirit ignited. Flames rushed up the highly flammable curtains giving off plumes of toxic smoke. The two men in black disappeared into the shadows just as quickly and as silently as they had come.

The price of David Green's silence was a lot less than ten million dollars.

*

Around the time the fire crews were arriving at David Green's house, James Hayward was surfacing from a restful night's sleep. At 7 a.m. in a wintry London it is still dark, which made it all that much harder to arise on this particular morning. He was going to be rather late for work on this crisp morning, but he didn't really care. He ambled into the bathroom of his Holland Park apartment, turned on the shower, quickly tested the temperature with his hand before stepping under the full force of the water gushing in front of him. He grabbed the bar of Imperial Leather soap and started to lather up.

The 31st of January was bonus day for many of the bankers in the city of London, particularly those with a December year end. It marked the first day of the game of musical chairs that is played annually in the City by those disgruntled workers who believe they have not been sufficiently compensated for their sweat and toil in the previous year. Hayward would be among these itinerants by day's end.

Hayward had worked for Smith Brothers of London for fifteen years. Starting as a junior in the back-office, doing all the basic confirmations and settlements for the traders, he had worked his way up to the trading desk. Here, he flourished in the mediocrity that was encouraged on the desk by the then head of trading, Clive Palmer. For Palmer, the bottom line would never be as important as being able to sink a few pints with your mates and have a good laugh. If the natural business that flowed through the doors of Smith Brothers enabled them to cover the costs of their six figure salaries and pay the other overheads, they were in great shape. That meant shorter working hours and a great team atmosphere that could only be enhanced by the boozy three hour liquid lunches at the pub. This was a recipe for inefficiency, incompetence and a thoroughly unsophisticated business. Hayward was a master of the four quick pints at lunch before going back to the office for the afternoon trading session, and Palmer had rewarded him handsomely for his talents, making him a senior trader on the base metals desk. But all this soon changed after the Big Bang.

The bastions of British banking were being gobbled up by foreign predators. The Union Bank of Switzerland had devoured Philips and Drew; Deutsche had swallowed up Morgan Grenfell; and Nelson Prescott Securities, the U.S. giant, had acquired Smith Brothers. The newly formed Nelson Smith Securities was now one of the largest securities firms in the world, a behemoth, second only in size to the colossal Merrill Lynch.

The massive changes to the landscape of the City brought sweeping changes to the management of the firms that had been devoured. For Smith Brothers it was such a culture clash that many of the executives resigned and took up the golden parachutes that had been guaranteed at the time of the merger. Nelson brought in younger, more aggressive investment bankers to fill the void. These young Turks did the job that had needed doing for some time. They remedied the malady of the London operation in the classic American, corporate re-engineering style of the Nineties, slashing the all-important head count by twenty-five percent. There was even the tale of the newly appointed head of European Bond Trading, Ivan Kowalski, firing everyone who worked for him on the Monday he arrived to take over. They were all perfectly welcome to apply for positions on his desk tomorrow, he told them, for that was when he would begin hiring. It was no wonder he was referred to by his subordinates with some fear and loathing as 'Ivan the Terrible'.

For Hayward, the change had not been that extreme. Well, not at first. Six weeks after the merger, Clive Palmer had been fired for reasons that were never properly explained to the staff on the trading desk. His replacement, Simon Anderson, had come from the foreign exchange desk in New York. Anderson was a gung-ho, thirty-something, no-nonsense kind of guy who would have been as much at home commanding a platoon of Humvees in Desert Storm as running a trading desk. His closely cropped brown hair, barrel-chested physique, and the impeccable fit of his Armani uniform meant he looked more like a drill sergeant at an army boot camp than a trader. He had a reputation for action, discipline and results, which was what mattered most in the trading arena. But Anderson was a trader first, a trader with no experience in commodities whatsoever, let alone base metals. This was deeply resented by those stalwarts on the desk he had been sent to manage in London.

The advent of the Anderson era on the base metals desk marked the beginning of pronounced changes in the day to day lives of those around him. Instead of the cushy nine-thirty to five existence that most members of the desk had enjoyed under Palmer, a strict seven till seven routine had been instituted. Gone were the long lunches, in fact, gone were the lunches altogether, as Anderson made them all eat lunch at their desks. This was intolerable for many of the old crew on the desk, and one by one they resigned to go elsewhere. As they left, Anderson replaced them with fresh young guys who were intelligent and hungry for success. In Anderson's opinion the desk was over-staffed anyway and he would have fired each and every one of the old crew had it not been for an archaic clause in their contracts that prevented him from doing so. Instead it had become a battle of attrition that Anderson was winning hands down. The final obstacle, Hayward, had been given the kind of bonus that would ensure total victory and signal the dawning of a more professional investment-banking age.

Hayward had been informed of his executive compensation in December of the previous year. The paltry amount of fifty thousand U.S. dollars was, for someone of his level of experience, an insult, moreover, for his company, it was a way of saying that they would like him to leave. The writing had been on the wall after his bonus meeting with Anderson. He had read between the lines and had called a head-hunter friend immediately upon receiving the news of this goodbye bonus.

As Hayward emerged from the crush at Liverpool Street Station, he glanced momentarily at his watch. It was 9.32. The branch of Barclays Bank at Moorgate would be open. He pulled his cellphone from the depths of his overcoat, spilling used tissues onto the pavement as he did so. He pushed the memory key which dialed the number for his executive banker at Barclays.

The phone was answered on the third ring. 'Barclays, Rowena Smythe speaking.'

'Rowena, James Hayward here. How are you, my dear?' Hayward had that annoying habit of addressing every woman as 'dear' or 'love'.

'Fine, James. And you? What can I do for you today?'

'Well, I was wondering if you could check my offshore account to see if a sum of money has been credited this morning.' Hayward queried in an expectant tone as he dodged the other pedestrians.

'Sure, just bringing it up now.'

The seven seconds of silence that followed seemed like an absolute eternity to Hayward who was by now panting as he walked up the small flight of stairs towards the main entrance of the London offices of Nelson Smith in the Broadgate Center.

'Okay, I have a credit for twenty thousand odd pounds this morning. Is that the one that you are looking for?'

'Yes, Rowena, that's the one. Thanks ever so much for your help. Bye.'

'No problem, James, bye.'

Hanging up, Hayward swore under his breath at the faceless taxman who took such a huge bite out of his already paltry bonus.

Hayward swiped his smartcard through one of the many turnstiles in the cavernous lobby of the Nelson Smith building, before crossing the vast open space to the liftwell. The imposing lobby, with all its clean lines, metallic shapes and exposed ducting pipes, owed its existence more to the design whim of a modern architect than to a calculated attempt by feeble investment bankers to intimidate their customers. Either way, thought Hayward to himself, it was a complete waste of space. But he would soon be out of here.

Hayward exited the lift at the fifth floor. Turning left, he waved the smartcard in front of the sensor. Momentarily, the loud and familiar 'click' indicated that the door was open. He took a deep breath and stepped forward through the door onto the trading floor of Nelson Smith.

The trading floor housed close to four hundred traders set in an open plan arrangement. Just about everything was traded on this floor: equities, bonds, currencies and commodities. Row upon row of computer monitors and trading screens dominated the landscape, along with the oversized digital clocks on the wall telling the time in New York, London, and Tokyo. Hayward headed for the commodities area in the corner. In doing so he passed the foreign exchange desk with the tacky little Swiss, German, American, British, and Japanese flags on top of the screens to denote the currency pairs in which the trader specialized. No one noticed Hayward, despite his obese frame, as he passed through their area. They were too engrossed with the markets, their eyes caught in a state of hypnotic trance with the Reuters or Telerate screens, clutching two phones and catching up on the latest gossip or sharing views with other traders.

'Hayward, where the hell have you been?' boomed Simon Anderson's voice across the room, as he saw Hayward's figure looming at the end of the trading desk. The desk now resembled the shape of a battleship, much to Anderson's pleasure.

'Um-er, I need to have a word with you, in private, Simon,' came the stuttered reply from Hayward, who despite his conviction only moments before had been rattled by the volume of Anderson's public address.

'Sure, just step into my office. I'll be with you in a second.' Anderson looked intently at the Reuters screen in front of him without giving Hayward a second glance.

Hayward made a quick about-turn and slipped into Anderson's office.

Anderson took his time before entering his office. He wanted Hayward to sweat it out. He knew what this was all about, but he still looked forward to the psychological warfare of the coming encounter. He closed the door and sat on his desk, his legs set astride the corner. The point of the desk visible, his right hand rested by his crotch for support, in a rather phallic yet intimidatory fashion.

'What can I do for you, James?' asked Anderson curtly, knowing full well what was about to come from Hayward's lips. He was the one who had suggested the goodbye bonus plan and it was working like clockwork.

'Well, Simon, I am giving you my one month's notice as stipulated in my contract,' came Hayward's reply, the relief of the statement immediately noticeable on his face.

'Are you sure this is what you want?' Anderson calmly rolled up his sleeves, trying to hide his elation at the events unfolding in his office. He resisted the strong temptation to jump up and high-five himself in the mirror.

'Yes. I have accepted a senior sales position at the brokerage firm Newton Harding.' Hayward struggled to adjust himself from an uncomfortable position on the soft leather couch.

'I see. Well, I guess there is nothing more I can say to keep you here,' said Anderson, lying through his teeth with the convincing illusion of sincerity. 'I'd better get the wheels of bureaucracy turning. Just bear with me a moment.'

Anderson picked up the phone and dialed the personnel department, still gazing at the Reuters screen on the other side of his desk.

'Hello, Kathy, Simon Anderson here from commodities. I am sending someone down to go through the exit procedure motions. Are you free now? Okay, great, I'm sending him down now.'

Looking back at Hayward, managing to conceal his joy exceptionally well, Anderson continued in a rather matter-of-fact tone. 'Okay James, you know the routine. Kathy Stern, from personnel, is waiting for you down on level three. I'll have Erica go through your desk and we will mail you any personal items that might be left there. Any company pagers, mobile phones, or personal digital assistants, and, of course, security smartcards you still have, you can hand in to Kathy on your way out.'

Hayward nodded in agreement, he knew the routine all too well. Go directly to the exit, do not go to your desk, do not say farewell to your colleagues. The inevitable frog-march to the door was common practice in the security-sensitive world of trading.

'Here, let me walk you to the lift.' Anderson motioned towards the door of his office with his left hand, a wry smile of victory lighting his generally stoic visage.

March, 1993

The Piper Navajo touched down with a heavy bounce on the small island airstrip. The twin propellers buzzed loudly into life as the pilot quickly thrust them into reverse pitch, the dust blowing up into a hazy cloud around the wings. Richard Wilmont relaxed his grip on the armrest of his seat. He hated flying and he definitely hated small planes but his partner Alan Bridge had convinced him that it was a key to their anonymity on this occasion. He glanced briefly at Bridge, who gripped the black leather case on his lap tightly with both hands, giving him a quick nod of approval. Apart from the pilot, the six-seater plane was carrying only the two Englishmen and their cargo: a large leather attaché case which contained one million U.S. dollars in crisp, new, hundred-dollar bills.

The two men had formed their company, Wilmont Bridge Securities – an introducing brokerage firm, only two years ago. They had worked together at both Carter Lawrence, the U.S. Securities house, and Newton Harding, the LME brokerage firm in the Eighties, before branching out on their own. It was a perfect, symbiotic match. Richard Wilmont was the consummate salesman: charming, with an air of confidence that stemmed more from his old school tie than any innate abilities. Visually, they were an unlikely couple. The style and finesse of Wilmont contrasted greatly with the rough exterior of his much shorter South London partner, Alan Bridge, who was the brains of the operation. Where Wilmont had been born with a silver spoon in his mouth, Bridge had to settle for a wooden one. His classroom had been the streets, life his university, or that was how he liked to think of it. His cunning and meticulous planning skills combined with Wilmont's sales ability in a recipe for success.

Theirs was a simple business. They were an introducing broker, an intermediary. They brought together buyers and sellers of copper. Their cut was supposed to be one-sixteenth of the value of the trade paid by both the buyer and the seller, but because the buyer and seller were never aware of who was on the other side of the transaction, they were able to take that little bit more. The buyer would trade at a price a few dollars a metric tonne higher than the seller with Wilmont Bridge taking the difference along with an already fat commission. On top of this, they took no credit risk whatsoever because that was underwritten by their clearing bank, Credit Commerciale, who extended Wilmont Bridge's customers' credit lines in the hope of securing all their clearing business. For Wilmont Bridge it was a win-win situation.

The pilot released the stair latch on the left side of the plane and the stairs fell forward onto the runway below with a dull thud. The oppressive heat immediately invaded the air-conditioned confines of the airplane. Richard Wilmont emerged first, wiping the already beading sweat from his brow with his silk handkerchief. Alan Bridge followed closely behind, still clutching the precious cargo tightly in his arms, the bright sunlight causing him to squint in order to see the Jeep Cherokee waiting for them some fifty yards off to the left.

Wilmont turned back to face the pilot. 'We'll be back in about an hour,' he said, gesticulating wildly at his watch. 'We'll meet you back here.'

The pilot nodded nonchalantly, lit a cigarette, and rested up against the left wing of the plane despite the obvious dangers.

The two Englishmen, looking very much out of place in the tropics with their Savile Row suits, made their way across the searing tarmac to the Jeep that was waiting for them.

'Mister Carter, Mister Lawrence?' came the inquisitive tone from the old black man behind the wheel, as he wound down the window of the Jeep.

'Yes, that's us,' replied Wilmont without hesitation.

The use of the names of their former employer brought a slight grin to his face. The old man, Carter Lawrence, founder of the Wall Street firm Carter Lawrence Securities, had built his company on the time-honored principles of fortitude, trust and integrity. He would turn in his grave if he knew of the impropriety for which his name was now being used. The irony was not lost on Bridge either – a smile graced his generally sour countenance as well.

Bridge had assured Wilmont of the necessity of using aliases. They had booked the charter flight out of Miami using the same aliases and paid for everything in cash in order to leave no trail should anyone ever come looking. They had been in New York on business and, both men being avid golfers, had taken a three day excursion to Florida. There was nothing suspicious in that.

'Well, climb aboard then.' The old man commanded in a broad Jamaican accent, slapping the door of the Jeep casually with his left hand.

The two men piled into the back of the Jeep quickly. The air-conditioned oasis it provided was an instant relief from the harsh heat of the midday sun outside.

'So, where to today gentlemen?' The old man gazed inquisitively into the rearview mirror at the two suited figures seated behind him.

'The head office of the National Bank of the Caymans in Georgetown, if you please. Do you know it?' Wilmont's brows came together as he asked the question.

'Sure, I am banking there myself, man.' A broad smile crossed his sun-worn face, revealing a mass of pearl-white teeth. With that he hit the gas pedal and the Jeep lurched forward. Speeding off towards Georgetown they left a trail of flying rocks and dust behind them. All the while Bridge clutched the case tightly.

★

The two Englishmen sat in the white wicker chairs that comprised the lobby of the National Bank of the Caymans. A rickety old ceiling fan swooped tirelessly above them. Its lopsided trajectory managed to disturb the immaculate parting in Richard Wilmont's hair, much to his annoyance. Wilmont gazed thoughtfully at his surroundings. The building's great long verandas with wrought iron lattice work, its high ceilings with massive exposed beams, and the gleaming sandalwood floors all harked back to the glory of the old colonial days, evoking memories of Britain's once vast empire.

Suddenly, the door at the other end of the lobby flew open, breaking Wilmont's nostalgic trance.

'Gentlemen, sorry to have kept you waiting,' proffered Winston Patterson, chairman of the National Bank of the Caymans, apologetically. His arms outstretched in a pre-hugging fashion. His open-toed sandals, khaki Bermuda shorts, and oversized red Hawaiian shirt made him look more like a tourist than a banker.

'No problem at all, my good fellow.' Wilmont arose and shook Patterson's right hand vigorously. 'Good to see you again.'

'Yes, no problem,' chimed in Bridge, not wanting to be left out of the proceedings.

'Awfully hot today!' remarked Wilmont in typically English fashion, all the while running his long bony forefinger around his collar to alleviate the stifling heat.

'Yes it is. Like this all the time I'm afraid,' retorted Patterson. His neutral transatlantic accent gave no hint of his origin. 'Would you gentlemen like a cold drink?' He motioned them towards his office.

Patterson's office looked more like the trophy room of a fishing club than the habitat of the chairman of a bank. Pictures hung randomly around the office depicted Patterson the victor, with a variety of big game fish on weighing scales. The overtly tacky stuffed-head of a black marlin perched ominously above the desk. Patterson had a passion for game fishing. This was what he did, except when interrupted by people such as the two men who now sat in the chairs facing him.

'What can I do for you gentlemen today?' Patterson asked, pouring three large glasses of iced tea.

'We have a deposit to make,' replied Wilmont, who had a masters in the blatantly obvious. Bridge just rapped his fingers across the case.

'Sure. Which account will it be today?' Patterson inquired, directing them to take a glass of iced tea each.

'We would like you to credit the account of Servicio de Negocios with the amount of one million U.S. dollars,' Bridge took over. 'I think you'll find it's all there,' he said, placing the leather case on top of the desk.

This little payment would ensure that their boutique brokerage firm would receive the lion's share of the business done by the Chilean copper giants, Codelco and Enami. In the long run, these inducements would yield them commissions far in excess of the costs of their little expedition. And besides, Bridge thought to himself, in the world of commodity trading it was just the simple cost of doing business.

February, 1995

For Michael Kelly and the foreign exchange team at Henderson Meyer it had been a monster night out on the town. Mike had crawled into bed at 3 a.m. knowing full well that he would be in a world of hurt the following morning.

He had been asleep for barely three hours when he was rudely awaken by the phone. His hand shot out to the table on the right-hand side of the bed, fumbling about, searching for the intrusive piece of technology, face still buried under the pillow.

'Hello?' he coughed. The raspy timbre of his voice the product of one too many beers in a smoky nightclub.

'Mike, Simon Anderson here.' The voice boomed on the other end of the line. 'We met last year at the Foreign Exchange charity ball at the Waldorf. A mutual friend suggested I call you.'

'Uh huh,' Mike replied instinctively, hoping he would go away and let him sleep.

'I run the commodities trading desk at Nelson Smith Securities in London,' continued Anderson. 'I am looking for a young aggressive trader to join my team. I'll be in New York later tonight. Maybe we can hook up for a beer when you finish work and discuss this at greater length?'

'Sure, whatever,' Mike mumbled semi-consciously.

'Okay, great, I'll call you when I hit town. Speak to you soon.' And with that the annoying intruder into Mike's drunken slumber disappeared.

It will be a while yet before the sun graces the Manhattan skyline, thought Mike to himself as he did up his new Zegna tie. The pulsating feeling in his left temple was a curt reminder of the festivities of the previous evening. He continued to gaze out the massive floor to ceiling windows of his apartment on the forty-second floor of the recently built TriBeCa Tower. He was always mindful to keep his eye on the Colgate Clock, which dominated the foreshore on the Jersey side of the Hudson River, just to make sure he wasn't late. He took a long swig from a bottle of Evian before returning it to its perch on the air-conditioner. He would need a lot more fluid as the day went by if he was to have any hope of countering the effects of the dehydration he was suffering. He made a mental note never to drink again. But he knew that come five-thirty that evening, whatever notepad the message was stored on in his brain, his words would be as empty as a politician's after an election. The cycle of destruction would begin again. He grabbed his jacket and overcoat from the back of the chair near the door, feeling the pockets to make sure he had the essential trader's paraphernalia: the mobile phone and the pocket Reuters. Satisfied, he bounded out the door.

Emerging from his apartment block onto Duane Street, the chill of the wind forced him to pull the collar of his overcoat up to protect his ears. Mike made his way across the street into the warmth which was Zoe's deli.

'The usual, Mike?' asked Zoe in a melodic tone.

'Yep, and a large Evian to go,' Mike admired the slender form of the Korean girl behind the counter. Her long, jet-black hair, perfect skin, and pert breasts made Mike fantasize briefly.

'Heavy night, huh?' she quizzed him pleasantly, Mike's bloodshot eyes having already answered the question for him. 'That'll be two fifty.' She shot him an inviting smile as he put the money on the counter. 'Thanks, Mike. See you.'

'Thanks, Zoe, you're a lifesaver.' Beautiful, intelligent, and a good cook to boot. Mike made another mental note: marry Zoe. So what if she was engaged to another guy. That was just a minor detail.

Mike wolfed down the bacon, egg, and cheese roll as he made his way down Broadway. He hoped that the grease might soak up some of the alcohol in his system. As he did this, he called his good friend Stan McCabe, the dollar yen trader on the forex desk at Bankers Trust, London.

'Bankers, Stan here.'

'Yo, Stan the man,' Mike yelled so as to be heard over the din of the passing cars. 'What's up? Anything going on in London today?'

'Not much, brother. Pretty much everyone in Europe's waiting for the U.S. jobless figures due out this morning. The dollar has been in a twenty pip range all morning, around ninety-seven even. Jack-shit, I'm afraid, till the figures come out, my friend.'

'So what's the consensus your side of the pond?' Mike asked, stepping sideways to avoid a vagrant sprawled obtrusively on the pavement near the Chemical Bank cash machine. The urine stench was so overpowering that he was forced to hold his breath. The delicate nature of his stomach made him fearful that the food he had just consumed might attempt the return journey. He cupped his hand over his nose and mouth as a precaution.

'The general consensus is an increase of 150,000 to 170,000 for non-farm payrolls. Anything close to that range and we have a sleeper. That's what the market's priced in,' came Stan's answer with authority.

'What are you thinking?' Mike prodded.

'Well, I've got a small short position. I'm bearish the dollar near term as you already know. This whole war of words on Japanese tariffs and import restrictions on U.S. goods has the market spooked. The U.S. government seems set to fuck the Japs by letting the dollar free fall. I think that no matter what the figure is today, the market will go lower. Apart from that, I'm looking forward to the weekend.'

'Aren't we all?' Mike concurred immediately.

'Do I detect the pain of a big night out in your voice, Mike?' Stan's tone lacked sympathy.

'I'll tell you all about it when I get to the office. I'm almost there now. Take care big guy.'

'Later, Mike.'

Crossing the open expanse around the World Trade Center, Mike fumbled as he tried to put the phone away. His coordination still left a lot to be desired. He tried to piece together the events of the previous evening as he dodged the zombie masses that made up the forecourt. He remembered the obligatory beers down at Moran's with the boys after work. He remembered meeting up with his mate Warren who worked for Chase. Then vague recollections of kissing his boss's secretary, Cindy, who although ordinarily a six had looked like a mighty fine eight with his beer goggles on. Definitely not a good move.

Then kamikazes at some bar on the Upper West side. Ouch. The very thought of this made his head throb uncontrollably. Beer was okay. But shots? Shots were just silly. What could he have been thinking? The rest of the evening was a blur. His tongue brushed probingly across the roof of his mouth. The bits of burnt skin were a poignant reminder of the searing slice of pepperoni pizza he must have picked up on the way home. He decided to avoid Warren in future. Then he remembered a phone call from London. He grabbed the pocket Reuters from the inside of his jacket. He looked at the ranges of the dollar overnight. That's odd, he thought, the dollar had not traded outside the call levels he had left with Stan. Must have been a dream, he thought to himself, pushing through the heavy revolving doors of the World Financial Center. It was going to be a very long day.

Mike had been with the boutique Wall Street investment bank, Henderson Meyer, for four years. He had started there as an analyst straight out of Harvard. Although highly gifted, his grades were unremarkable – they certainly bore a direct relationship to the amount of time he had spent partying. Mike was an opportunist. He had prided himself on the fact that he had passed with a minimum of effort, but with grades such as his, the likes of Goldman Sachs, J.P. Morgan, and Merrill Lynch would not hire him. In fact, he would have been lucky to get a first interview with any of the major players on the Street. Had it not been for the fact that a close friend of his father was a senior partner at Henderson Meyer, Mike might never have got a foot in the door. Now he had and the rest was history.

If his university career had been unremarkable, Mike's rise to prominence in the small trading room at Henderson Meyer was, by contrast highly remarkable. Starting out on the foreign exchange desk as a junior economic analyst at the tender age of twenty-one, Mike found out very quickly that number crunching was not his station in life. The one thing that Mike wanted more than ever was to be a trader. The fast-living, fast-talking, adrenaline-pumped lifestyle he observed on the trading desk appealed to his sense of adventure. Here were guys in their late twenties and early thirties pulling down huge salaries with what seemed like a minimum of effort and a maximum of fun. Here he was busting his ass to produce economic reports that the traders threw in the trashcan without even reading, and for it he was paid peanuts compared to them. Mike spent as much time as he could in the trading room, always asking questions, always offering assistance. In the end, his enthusiasm and persistence had paid off.

Well liked by the trading manager, Leo Epstein, Mike was given his big chance. He was offered a junior trading role as the dollar yen trader's lackey. Mike took to trading like a duck to water, his passion for it was unrivaled. He read just about every book that had ever been written on the subject of trading. He became the guru of technical analysis. He began to eat, sleep, and breathe financial markets. The discipline that had been sadly lacking as a student at Harvard was now his most potent weapon. All this effort combined with his amazing gut instinct had made him stand apart from the crowd. Then the Darwinian nature of the business worked its magic. Dismissal, defection, and promotion became his greatest allies as he rose swiftly through the ranks. Through a combination of raw talent, results, and attrition Mike had become the youngest vice-president in the history of Henderson Meyer.

Mike stared thoughtfully out the window while he waited for the machine to dispense his second coffee. The view from the South Tower of the World Financial Center was breathtaking at this time in the morning. Lady Liberty bathed in the beauty of the winter daybreak as she directed the morning traffic making its way from Staten Island to Manhattan. Mike spared a thought for the cargo that the ferries carried – an army of workers, trudging their way through life in some boring nine-to-five office job. He pitied them as he sipped the hardly palatable black syrup. Here he was, barely twenty-five, earning close to two hundred and fifty thousand dollars a year. More over he was being paid to do something he loved. He gazed back at Lady Liberty. 'Home of the brave, land of the free, baby,' he mouthed to himself.

'Call for you on line five, Mike,' came the painful cry of Carol's voice snatching Mike away from his tryst with Mrs.

Liberty and causing him to spill the remainder of his coffee. That nasal Brooklyn accent always made him cringe.

'Who is it?' replied Mike, as he went for the three pointer with his now empty foam cup, only to have it bounce off the rim of the wastepaper basket.

'I think it's that English guy, Warren.'

Shit, Mike thought to himself. It isn't even eight o'clock yet. 'Tell him I'm... oh, don't worry, I'll take it,' Mike said, changing his mind mid sentence. He knew he was going to have to avoid Warren if he wanted to have a quiet Friday night, but at this point the chances for that seemed slim.

'Hey, Warren, what's up dude?' Mike asked.

'Allo, shag,' came Warren's distinctive East End reply. 'How did you pull up this morning?'

'Pretty ordinary to tell the truth. And you?'

'I must say I have felt better. But it's nothing a couple aspirins and plenty of water can't fix.' Warren said in a matter of fact tone. For him the recovery process after a big night was a minor detail. 'So, tell me,' he continued, 'How did you make out with that cute blonde number you were dancing with at the Zoo Bar?'

Mike hesitated. He didn't remember even being at the Zoo Bar, let alone dancing with some blonde girl. Alcohol amnesia. The kamikazes always did it. 'Must have struck out, matey,' Mike replied with total honesty, ''cause I woke up alone this morning.'

'Too bad, matey. So you had to settle for Mrs. Palmer?' Warren goaded him.

'Huh?' The innuendo was totally lost on Mike in his current state.

'You know. Mrs. Palmer and her five lovely daughters.' Warren answered crudely.

'You're the only wanker around here, mate,' Mike retorted.

'So I take it you'll be backing up again tonight then, big boy?' Warren asked with a hint of joviality in his tone, trying to bring the conversation back to matters at hand.

'Ask me again at five and the answer might be yes. But right now, you must be out of your fucking mind.' And with that Mike hung up the phone. He had work to do.

The global trade in foreign currencies is amazing. Trillions of dollars are sent spinning around the world each day in a fantastic game created by speculation and necessity. Companies raising offshore finance or investing in foreign projects and companies with overseas sales or offshore subsidiaries all make use of the foreign currency markets. Mutual and pension funds investing in overseas stocks and bonds are also major players in the currency markets. All these players combined with the speculative might of the trading and investment banks across the globe merge, forming the international currency markets.

It's a twenty-four hours a day game lasting five days a week. It kicks off in Sydney on Monday morning around 8 a.m. and does not stop until New York blows the whistle on Friday. Between those hours it's non-stop action. It's a high-tech game played out on screens and over phone lines. Making its way around the world from time zone to time zone the game is played across geographical barriers. As Sydney breaks for lunch, the Far East takes up the slack with Tokyo, Singapore, and Hong Kong all bursting into life, before they are relieved by players from the big arenas in Frankfurt, Zurich, Paris, and London. On and on throughout the longest day the game continues, with London finally giving way to the players in New York who, once exhausted, pass the ball back into the hands of the combatants from Sydney, all eager to play again after a restful night's sleep. And so it continues.

The incredible flow of money is rivaled only by the flow of information that constantly bombards the front-line players in this high-stakes game. The high-tech information systems supplied by the likes of Reuters, Telerate, Bloomberg, and Knight-Ridder tirelessly pump out the latest political, financial, and economic news from around the globe, keeping the traders up-to-date with important events as they happen. Along with the news come the prices of every stock, bond, currency, and commodity known to man. CNN is their eyes and ears. Nothing escapes the information hungry world of the trader.

Surrounded by computer wizardry that would make an astronaut comfortable, Mike immersed himself in his familiar environs. His was a world of screens, phones, figures, and prices. His desk resembled something out of *Star Wars*. Directly in front of him was a touch screen phone bank with hundreds of dedicated direct access lines. On top of it a Reuters machine displayed the prices of all the major currencies of the world, some bond prices, and the all important Dow. It was flanked by Telerate and Bloomberg terminals displaying various news items from around the globe. To his immediate right a Reuters Dealing 2000 system beeped annoyingly to alert him of an incoming call. The Dealing 2000 machine was a handy tool. It allowed him to hold up to four conversations on a screen simultaneously and in real time with other Dealing 2000 users. Everyone in the forex business had one. Mike's was in constant use. As a result his typing skills had improved dramatically. I am the fastest two finger typist in the East, he thought to himself, as he tapped away furiously on the keyboard to a trader friend in Zurich. It was almost surreal. But it was his domain. He loved it.

Mike glanced quickly over the front page of the *Wall St. Journal* before throwing it carelessly at his feet. As he looked up he recognized the silhouette of Cindy Bellini in his monitor. Mike resisted his initial temptation to ignore her.

'What can I do for you, Cindy?' He inquired politely, without bothering to turn around. He pretended to be busy. He didn't want to turn around. He was too embarrassed. How could he have done that? How could he have kissed her last night? He knew she had a crush on him. It was the beer, a little voice inside reminded him. He touched his pulsating head. It was definitely the beer.

'Is there anything I can get you, Mike?' She asked expectantly.

Cindy was Leo Epstein's secretary. That made her the desk secretary. She lived in Queens with her parents. She was part of the bridge and tunnel crowd that each day made its way into Manhattan to work. She was exceptionally sweet but her looks were rather ordinary. She came across as quite conservative. It was her Catholic Italian upbringing, Mike thought. Either way, she was not his type.

'A couple aspirin and a glass of water would be lovely, thanks,' replied Mike, not wanting to crush her totally. His eyes were cast steadfastly at the screen.

'Sure. Is there anything else I can get you? A bagel with cream cheese perhaps?'

She was starting to annoy him. He was going to have to bite the bullet and nip this in the bud.

'Look, Cindy, I...' Mike said, spinning around in his chair as he did so.

'What, Mike?' She interrupted, her tone reminiscent of a child being denied an ice cream on a hot summer's day.

Mike said nothing. He couldn't. He was stuck. His eyes transfixed by Cindy's bust which now invaded his personal space.

Cindy stood above him and repeated her question. 'You sure there is isn't anything else I can get you?' She beamed. Her plan was working.

Her normally conservative demeanor was gone. A tight, white blouse barely contained her breasts and the conservative trousers she usually wore had been replaced by a short black skirt. All for Mike's benefit, no doubt.

'Look, Cindy,' Mike regained his composure. 'I have a thumping headache. The aspirin will do me just fine.' He tried to look her in the eyes but he was powerless against the gravitational pull of her breasts.

'Okay. I'll be back in a jiffy.' Cindy headed for the exit, a slight bounce in her step.

Mike swung back around to face the row of monitors on his desk. I sure handled that well... not, he thought to himself. Anyway, he had more important things to think about. The non-farm payroll figures were due out in five minutes. He really would need that aspirin.

September, 1993

Bryan Murphy drew the curtains and peered out the window. The setting sun cast an ochre haze over the buildings in the distance. Below him the streets of Lusaka were abuzz with cars, trucks and people all going about their business. He didn't open the window. He peered out, the quiet humming of the air-conditioning unit now a welcome relief. The double-glazed windows kept the noise of the bustling rabble safely outside. He liked that.

The cab ride from the main airport at Lusaka had taken a good thirty minutes. The poverty had always unnerved him. He wondered how many AIDS victims had stared in at them as they drove along the noisy, dusty streets of the Zambian capital before arriving at the welcome sight of the Intercontinental Hotel on Haille Selassie Avenue. It was an oasis in a world of despair. The five-star hotel, with all its modern charm, contrasted sharply with the stark realities of life outside. The ostentatious display of wealth by the few was more than compensated for by the pathetic display of the poverty-stricken hoards. But that was Africa.

After gaining independence from the British in 1964, Zambia had maintained one of the highest standards of living in black Africa. But after almost three decades under the United National Independence Party's socialist rule, the economy was in ruins. A nationalization program had placed the bulk of productive resources under state control. The economy suffered from an over-dependence on a single commodity, copper, and the country had deteriorated into one of the poorest countries in the world in a relatively short space of time. Africa is a god-forsaken place, Murphy thought to himself as he pulled shut the curtains.

The newly elected Movement for Multi-party Democracy had won a landslide victory in the country's first ever free and open elections. The new president, Frederick Chiluba, had set about a privatization program to reverse the damage done by the previous socialist government. The Zambian Privatization Agency had been set up to sell off state-run assets, the state-owned Zambian Consolidated Copper Mining (ZCCM) being the jewel in the crown. ZCCM was the fourth largest copper producer in the world and made up somewhere close to ninety percent of all Zambia's exports. ZCCM was being courted by the big foreign multinational companies like Anglo American. But this was not what had brought Murphy to Lusaka.

Murphy was in Lusaka for a meeting. Murphy's company, International Metals Trading, (IMT) was a customer of ZCCM. They bought copper concentrates and cobalt from the mining giant. Murphy had started out in the world of physical commodities trading back in the days when Marc Rich was the king at Philip Brothers. When Rich had left Phibro in the late Seventies to set up Clarendon, his private trading company, the young Bryan Murphy had gone with him. In the years that were to follow Murphy learned the business secrets of the master. He learnt, in particular, how bribery greased the wheels of bureaucracy of any developing nation. He spent time buying oil from the Nigerians, gold and platinum from the South Africans, and copper, cobalt, and manganese from the Zambians. He knew Africa well and had developed an array of contacts in his business dealings.

When Rich had fled to Switzerland to avoid U.S. tax evasion charges in 1983, the majority of the ex-Marc Rich traders had formed a new trading company. But Murphy decided to set up on his own. His company was called International Metals Trading or IMT. With the contacts he had in the commodity underworld and his reputation amongst the legitimate consumers, his business thrived. IMT supplied the bulk of the copper consumed around the world. They had contracts for the physical delivery of copper concentrates with the Chilean giant Codelco and ZCCM. On the other side of the equation, IMT's biggest customer was the mighty Yamamoto Corporation of Japan. Yamamoto was the largest trader of copper in the world. They supplied the majority of the lucrative Japanese market and had the rest of the Asian market sewn up as well.

Murphy decided to take a quick shower before his meeting. He really needed to freshen up. As for the number of hours he had been traveling since he had left New York on Tuesday he had lost count. He wanted to get this meeting over and done with. It is, after all, a mere formality, he reminded himself. But his meeting was not with any of the official representatives of the state-owned ZCCM. His meeting was with his insurance company. He would pay the bribes to the relevant person and be on his way. Quick, clean, and tidy. He liked doing business that way.

As Murphy dried his hair with one of the hotel-monikered towels, there was a sharp rap on the door. Momentarily startled, he threw on the hotel-supplied bathrobe and opened the door fractionally, making sure the chain was still attached. Through the gap he saw a tall young soldier of the Zambian Defense Force, his AK-47 slung casually by his side.

'Yes?' asked Murphy in an inquisitive tone.

'The general is waiting downstairs, Mr. Murphy,' the soldier greeted him in perfect English.

'Tell the general I'll be down in a minute.' Murphy replied, still rubbing his hair with the towel.

'The general does not like to be kept waiting,' came the soldier's machine-like reply.

'Tell him I've just stepped out of the shower and I'll be down as soon as I can.' With that he closed the door and proceeded to get changed. The fat bastard can wait, Murphy thought to himself, he is going to make enough money out of the evening.

Fifteen minutes later Murphy found himself in the lobby of the Intercontinental. The lobby was populated by businessmen from Germany and various other parts of the world, but Murphy couldn't discern their accents. There were no tourists. But then again, who would want to come here on holiday, Murphy wondered to himself, as his eyes searched quickly about the room for the hulking frame of the general.

'Over here, Murphy.' A voice boomed from just behind him to his right.

Murphy spun around to see his old friend, General Valentine Matongo, dressed in full military regalia, wallowing in a big leather couch. Murphy had known the general for years. Matongo had been the right-hand man of the former president, Dr. Kenneth Kaunda. After the election in 1991, in which Dr. Kaunda was ousted, the general's share of the profits from the state owned ZCCM had dried up. He had had to turn his hand to a new business. A rather lucrative one. He was now in the protection business or the *insurance* business as he liked to call it.

'Come sit, my friend.' The general beckoned, his arms outstretched. Two young soldiers flanked each end of the general's couch.

'How are you, General?' inquired Murphy, leaning forward to shake the big man's hand.'

'It's been a long time,' he continued. 'So good to see you.' All the while smiling, pretending to be glad to see him. In fact it hadn't been a long time. Murphy had made a similar journey to Lusaka earlier in the year, but he was a master of pleasantries. It was good for business.

'Fine, fine,' came the general's reply. 'Can I get you a drink? Johnny Walker, Black Label, if my memory serves me correct.'

'Yes, on the rocks would be lovely.' Murphy answered briefly, casting his glance over the menacing soldiers that protected the general.

The general barked out some orders in Bantu. Immediately, one of the soldiers who was standing guard disappeared in the direction of the bar. The general leant back into the comfort of the leather couch once again.

'So what is it that I can do for you, Murphy?' The general inquired as he lit a fat Cuban cigar. 'Aren't all your copper supplies reaching the railyards for shipment? Aren't you getting all your supplies on time?' He inhaled stiffly before blowing smoke in Murphy's direction. 'I pride my operation on the timely departure of all the cargoes that are fully insured,' he finished in a slightly unsettled tone.

'Yes, General, everything is just fine.' Murphy said, attempting to reassure him.

'Then what is the problem that you have come here to see me about?' The general looked suddenly perplexed.

'You see, General,' Murphy continued, as the soldier arrived back from the bar carrying their drinks, 'I have a competitor who is using your wonderful insurance service as well. His cargoes are all arriving in a timely fashion. This is doing a great deal of damage to my business, as you can well imagine. I was wondering if I could take out an insurance policy to prevent this from happening in the future. Let's say a sum of roughly double what they are paying you.'

'I think we can come to some arrangement,' said the general, as a broad tobacco-stained smile crossed his face. 'But first, let us drink to the good old days, my friend.' He held up his glass in salute and the two men drank.

February, 1995

Mike stared at the clock on his screen. In two minutes the U.S. jobless figures would be out. The all important non-farm payrolls figure would flash across his screen. His pulse started to race. He could feel the adrenaline surging through his body in an anticipation. He prepared himself for the coming battle. This was what he lived for.

'Here's your aspirin, Mike,' came Cindy's soothing voice over his shoulder, as she placed a large glass of water beside him on the desk.

'Thanks,' he replied, almost unconsciously swallowing the aspirin she had placed in his hand.

He had hardly registered her presence. He was far too engrossed in his own world. He flicked the switch on his desk to turn on the broker squawk boxes. These boxes provided him with a constant flow of information. They told him where someone was prepared to buy and where someone was prepared to sell the U.S. dollar against the Japanese yen. He pushed the call button on his board. 'Morning, team,' he bellowed into the speaker.

'Hi, Mike,' they replied in chorus.

'Freddy? You there?' Mike inquired. 'I hope you're not fucken sleeping on me. I need you today.'

'A very good morning to you, gentlemen,' Freddy's voice came over the box in his unmistakable Staten Island accent. 'Welcome to the sport of kings, gentlemen.'

'Thank you, Freddy.' Mike countered.

'No, thank you, sir.' Freddy retorted with a slightly lyric touch.

They went through exactly the same banter every single morning without fail. Neither he nor Mike tired of it.

'Sixty seconds and counting,' Freddy continued, 'Sixty seconds to the sport of kings.'

'What's the last, Fred?' Mike's tone lacked humor now. He wanted to know the last price that the dollar was quoted against the yen.

'Three bid at five,' Freddy fired straight back. 'Thirty seconds and counting.'

Mike gripped his two phone handsets tightly. He held a big short position. He was short over fifty bucks, or fifty million U.S. dollars in layman's terms. He was heavily short the dollar and long the Japanese yen. He had been for ages. He was betting that the U.S. dollar would decrease in value in relation to the yen. But this was by far the biggest position he had ever taken. Sweat started to bead under his armpits. A trickle of water ran down his side. It made him shudder. Then suddenly there it was. The non-farm payrolls figure flickered instantaneously into life on his screen: 150,000 it blinked, almost taunting him. It was within the lower range of expectations. Stan was right again, he thought. It would be a sleeper.

'Taken at five,' Freddy's familiar voice echoed. Someone had just paid 97.05. 'Five bid at eight.' The market was sitting short. Mike could sense it. 'Six bid small at eight.'

The phone bank started to flash.

'Meyer,' Mike answered abruptly, there was no time for pleasantries in the world of trading. His own mother now refused to call him at the office because of this.

'Mike, it's Stan.'

'Yo, Stan the man, right again. Calling to gloat I suppose.' Mike watched the dollar edging higher against the yen on his screen. It made him shift uncomfortably in his seat.

'Look, Mike, I've gotta run early today,' Stan continued, 'so I need to square up before I go. I don't want to run a position over the weekend. The markets are too nervous, too choppy for my liking. This trade-war talk even has me rattled.'

'I hear you.' Mike said in agreement.

'So, do you have a good offer for me?' Stan quizzed him.

'What size you looking for?' Mike was already short. He didn't really want to sell any more.

'Twenty bucks,' came Stan's reply.

It made Mike wince. If he sold Stan twenty million he would effectively double his own already large position. He would be short seventy million dollars in a market that was nervous and experiencing periods of extreme volatility. If the market rallied sharply he might not be able to get out without a serious loss.

'Eight paid,' Freddy's voice was clear above the general din of screens beeping, phones ringing and people talking. 'Seven bid at ten.'

'It last traded eight,' Mike relayed the information to Stan. 'Market is now seven bid, the best offer is at ten. I'll cover you at ten for your size.'

'Okay, done. I'll call you on the dealer in a second to confirm the trade.' Stan added.

'Thanks for the trade, big guy.'

'Have a good one, Mike.'

'You too, Stan.' And with that Mike clicked out.

Putting down the phone, he glanced over at the Reuters Dealing 2000 screen on his right. He saw the familiar four letter code of Bankers London flash up on the screen. He hit the accept key and proceeded to confirm the deal he had just done with Stan.

'I sold you twenty dollar yen at ninety-seven ten,' Mike said to himself as he typed away.

The Reuters Dealing 2000 is a really amazing machine. Not only does it enable traders to hold real-time conversations on screen and trade, it also keeps a record of whatever is typed onto it. It cannot be erased. Everything that is sent goes onto the screen, including typos. It is highly useful, therefore, for the back office in confirming trades or, rarely, when a dispute arises.

Then the beeping sound alerted Mike to another incoming caller. He looked at the call box on the right of the screen. There was the four letter code for Chase, under it the words 'MRS. PALMER'. Mike smiled. It was Warren. Didn't he have anything better to do? He didn't accept the call. He didn't want a warts-and-all record of this conversation. Mike just typed Chase's code and then typed 'WANKER', hitting the send key as he did so. Warren flashed back 'MORANS?' Mike just laughed. Then Warren flashed up '5 P.M.' 'O.K.', Mike replied, but get off my case, he said to himself as he typed it. 'C U THERE' came the reply.

'Mike, call for you on seven,' that whining voice of Carol Stetson sent a shiver down his spine. It removed him from his playful interlude with Warren. Carol was the junior dollar Swiss trader. How she had got the job he would never know. Mike thought she was a moron, though her grades told a different story – she had graduated from N.Y.U. with flying colors. Wonders will never cease, he thought to himself, but trading was not about grades and intelligence, it was about thinking on your feet. The kids who were good at Nintendo and Sega would succeed in this business. Reaction was the key to success.

'Meyer,' Mike fired out like an automaton.

'M! K!' came the booming voice down the line.

It was Mike's friend John Templeton. They had been at Harvard together and always addressed each other by their initials.

'Big J.T.!' came Mike's reply. 'What's up brother?'

'Not much, my man, how the markets treating you?' John asked.

'So, so. Can't complain. Got a dollar yen short on at the moment. It's giving me more pain than joy though.' Mike watched the screen intently, the dollar still edging higher. 'I can feel my balls slowly working their way up to the back of my throat.' Mike swallowed hard, the dryness in his throat evident.

'That's what I like to hear, my man. A position that makes you sweat.' The comic allusion was certainly not lost on John.

'Say, big guy, are we still on for dinner tomorrow night?' asked Mike, Freddy still bantering on in the background.

'Yes, Luger's at eight. We're going to get some raw meat. Man I love their steak.' John salivated in the background.

Suddenly all of Mike's news screens started beeping wildly. Mike read the message they all beamed.

U.S. TRADE REPRESENTATIVE MICKEY KANTOR SAYS DOLLAR YEN AT 80 IS REASONABLE LEVEL.

'Shit!' Mike let out a yell. 'J.T., you see that?'

'Yes, brother,' J.T. replied dead pan.

'Gotta hop!' Mike dropped the phone. The phone bank lit up like a Christmas tree. Lights flashed everywhere. The pandemonium that Mike reveled in was about to begin. A cacophony of shrieks filled the room.

'Given at five, figure offered, no bid.'

'Freddy?' Mike screamed into the box. 'Where's the bid?'

'There's no bids, everyone's a seller.' Freddy sounded frantic.

'Offer twenty at ninety-five Freddy,' Mike's voice resounded with authority.

He was short and the market was going lower, into the hole, on the back of the statement by the U.S. trade secretary. The U.S. government was going to punish the Japanese for their import restrictions by letting the dollar slide. Here was his chance to put his foot on the gas.

'Where are you for Morgan in ten?' Carol shouted with excitement as she danced on her tiptoes to see Mike over the myriad of screens.

'Eighty eight, ninety eight,' Mike screamed back at her. 'Out! Out! Out!' He waved his arms frantically above his head. 'Now eighty-five ninety-five.' He figured everyone would be a seller.

'Yours,' she patted her chest to indicate that Mike had just bought ten million dollars from J.P. Morgan at eighty-five.

A seller. His instinct was right. He was already short seventy million coming into this so with the ten Morgan had just sold him he was still short sixty. He was still in good shape.

'Get me prices,' Mike shrieked, rising to his feet, beckoning others to do the same. 'Sell eighty-fives or better.'

A buzz filled the room as all the traders called the other trading banks. They were going on a liquidity run. Everyone had a predesignated bank to call for prices in the event that one of the traders needed to move a position in a hurry.

'Ninety bid at ninety-five, your offer,' Freddy came over the box.

'Hit the ninety bid,' screamed Mike. 'Hit it!' His heart pounded. His breathing was short. He was now standing. Two phones in his hands. Veins popping out of his head.

'He was out, Mike, I missed it.' Freddy's tone appeared apologetic.

'Just hit any fucken bid, Freddy! Do it! Sell me twenty!' Mike cried with excitement. This was what he lived for. This was the battle. This was what the game was all about. Mike smelled blood. He was going for the jugular.

Mike looked about the room. 'Did anybody get eighty-fives?' The other traders shook their heads in unison.

'Seventy bid here,' one of the juniors shouted excitedly.

'Nothing. Forget it.' Mike's tone was stern. He was clearly annoyed.

'You sold ten at seventy.' Freddy's voice came over the box. He sounded pleased with himself.

'Is that the best you could do, Fred?' Mike sounded angry now. 'Cancel the balance.'

'But its trading fifty now,' Freddy countered.

'All right, let's go baby.' Mike let out a hoot. He started doing a war-dance as he watched the prices changing on the screen, each price quoted lower than the one before.

'Figure given.' Freddy sounded incredulous.

'Figure bid for fifty, Fred,' Mike boomed down the box, his finger on the speaker button, checking the market's pulse. 'Show it!'

'Whatever you say, sir,' came Freddy's glib response. 'You got 'em. You bought fifty at ninety-six even. Now trading ninety-five.' His tone was now sarcastic. Mike had just bought fifty million dollars at 96.00 and the market was lower.

'Shut up, Freddy. I was short coming into this.' Mike had detected the sarcasm in Freddy's last comment. 'I'm just cleaning up my position here.' He clicked out.

'I am sure you were, sir. I never doubted you were short for a second.'

Mike did a quick mental calculation. He had been short seventy bucks coming into this move at an average of 97.15. He had just bought the bulk of the position back around 96.00. That was a profit of around three quarters of a million dollars. He would stay short ten million dollars. It was a free ride from here. He let out another loud hoot. It was barely 9.30 a.m. and he here was up three quarters of a buck. Not bad for fifteen minutes' work, he thought to himself. This was the beauty of the business. Instant gratification. Those guys up in investment banking didn't know what they were missing, with their leveraged buyouts, red braces, eighteen-hour days and cold Chinese. This was what markets were all about. Who cared about financing arrangements or mergers and acquisitions? His hangover had somehow vanished in the excitement. Adrenaline the cure. He was going to have a wild time tonight. He glanced up at the big clock on the wall and wished it forward to 5 p.m. It was time to celebrate. Come 5 p.m. the spirit of the invincible drinking man would rear its ugly head.

The day seemed to move quickly from that point on. Mike looked up at the clock. It was ten to five. The dollar had continued to slide during the course of the day. Mike had stayed short the ten million dollars. He had a profit of close to a million dollars to show for his day at work. Not bad at all really. He deliberated on the course of action for the evening. He would avoid Cindy at all costs. But given the white blouse and tight skirt she was wearing, he was going to have difficulty. A few beers down at Morans and she would look awfully tempting. It would be hard.

The phone bank started to flash. It was the Chase direct line.

'Warren, dude, what's the plan?' Mike's Southern Californian upbringing showed in his speech now.

'Well, mate, it's a pretty simple one,' Warren continued. 'We go down to Morans, have some beers, and try and meet some nice chicks. If we strike out, well then, we just get absolutely slaughtered.'

'Sounds good to me,' Mike agreed with him. He wanted to celebrate, hard. His was a high pressure world. The work hard, play hard attitude dominated his psyche.

'I'll see you down there in ten,' Warren said, his tone resounding in anticipation.

'I've got a few things to tidy up first,' Mike replied, 'but I'll be down there shortly, dude. Later.'

'Catch you there shortly then, big boy.' And with that, Warren was gone.

'Mike, you coming down to Morans tonight for a drink? Cindy said, as she wandered past Mike's desk, her expression full of expectation.

'Um, er...' Mike fumbled, caught, once again, in the act of staring hopelessly at her breasts. 'Um, yeah, I'll be down there soon.'

'Great, I'll see you there.' She shot him an uncharacteristically wicked smile as she departed.

Mike shuffled all the trade tickets on his desk into an out tray. He was terrible at the day to day details of the business. That is someone else's job, he thought to himself, I'm here to make money, not shuffle wads of paper about. He was lucky that his back office guys were detail beasts. He ran off a couple of profit and loss reports before checking his e-mail. Having done this, he grabbed his coat, once again patting it down to make sure his phone and pager were still there. He turned to head for the exit. Passing Leo Epstein's desk, he paused to place the profit and loss reports on his keyboard. He was bound to see them there. Mike felt a wave of pride course through his body. He had made a million dollars today. Leo would be proud too. Just as he was about to turn and leave. He heard the phone ringing. I bet it's Warren, calling from Morans to see where the hell I am, he thought to himself, picking up the phone.

'What?' he answered, so sure was he that it would be Warren he didn't even say 'Meyer'.

'Hello, I'm looking for Michael Kelly please?' came the voice over the top of some public address system in the background.

'Speaking.' Mike replied.

'Mike. This is Simon Anderson from London. We spoke this morning,' he said with military precision.

Mike froze. Then the penny dropped. It was this guy who had called him this morning. He hadn't dreamt it.

'Yes, I remember,' his reply was short. He started to remember parts of their prior conversation.

'Look, I've just arrived at JFK. Do you have time to meet up for a drink a little later?'

'Sure,' Mike said.

His mind raced. Where could they meet for a quiet drink? Where could he go without fear of bumping into someone he knew from the market? Then he remembered a small bar not far from his apartment block in TriBeCa.

'How about Yaffas?' Mike asked. 'Do you know it?' Knowing full well that the guy on the other end of the line wouldn't, but he asked the question anyway.

'No. But if you give me directions I am sure I can find it,' came the reply.

'Sure. It's downtown. It's on the corner of Greenwich and Harrisson. It's in TriBeCa, near Robert de Niro's restaurant, TriBeCa Bar and Grill.' Mike assured him.

'Yeah, I know the one.'

'Let's meet around nine.' Mike continued. ' It'll give you time to get to your hotel and take a shower.'

'Fine.' Simon responded. 'But how will I recognize you?'

'Easy,' Mike said with a bit of a chuckle. 'I'll be the only guy there wearing a suit.'

'Okay. See you then. Bye now.' And the caller was gone.

Mike glanced at his watch. Shit. It was a quarter past five. Warren would be three drinks ahead already. He would have some catching up to do.

Morans is situated below the World Financial Center, facing the Hudson River. In summer time it's a great place to go for a drink because you can stand outside. The setting sun over New Jersey provides a plethora of red, orange, and yellow tones in sharp contrast to the hard lines of the glass canyons of the business district. The breeze from the river is refreshing. It makes a change from the stifling heat which is summer in New York City. Mike loved summer. Mmm... short skirts. He reminisced momentarily, until the biting wind of the Hudson gripped him, forcing him to hurry his step a little.

Mike pushed his way through the winter crowd at Morans, almost dragging his overcoat behind him in the crush. It was a rather homogenous crowd. Wall Street types; forex traders, bond dealers, stock brokers, commodity traders, their trading assistant incumbents, hangers-on, and wannabes. A veritable gaggle of bullshit and bravado filled the air as Mike headed for the bar. And of course there were the ubiquitous investment bankers or investment wankers as Mike liked to call them. What did they know about making money? Mike asked himself as he pushed past another one of their type, resplendent in blue striped shirt and red braces. Didn't these guys know that braces had gone out in the Eighties? He shook his head in disbelief, grinning as he did so.

He spied Warren across the crowded room. How could he miss him? Warren was a bear of a man. Well over six foot tall and broad shouldered, he was an imposing figure. His drinking skills and escapades were legendary in the forex markets. He must have spent a lifetime collecting jokes and stories to tell at the bar, for his yarns were endless and most entertaining. He kept his audience gripped as he held court. As Mike arrived he caught the tail-end of the story of one of Warren's latest conquests. It was of epic proportions, even Cecile B. DeMille would be proud.

Apparently, last summer, Warren had picked up a married woman in the self-same bar in which Mike found himself now. The woman's husband had been out of town on business.

Warren had scored, which wasn't unusual in itself given his batting average, but what had impressed Mike was the way in which he had scored. He had gone back to the woman's apartment on the Upper East side and had made love to her all evening. It was so humid that day that all the physical exertion had made him sweat from head to toe. This had caused him to slip all over the place as he stood at the edge of the bed whilst he served it to her. He had tried standing on a towel to soak up the sweat, but to no avail. He still kept slipping all over the place. Then, purely by chance, he found a pair of golf shoes in the cupboard. Fortunately the woman's husband was about the same shoe size as him. They certainly did the trick. The thought of Warren standing at the edge of a bed, in all his glory except for a pair of golf shoes, furiously humping away was too much for Mike. He was in hysterics.

'Allo, big boy!' Warren acknowledged Mike's arrival to the circle. 'How did you fare today?' He turned to face the bar, waving his hand as he did so to attract the barmaid's attention.

'Dude, I had a kick-ass day today.' Mike replied. 'Man, I love it when it's busy.'

'Three Heineken, a vodka and orange, and two Molsons for the big girl's blouse on my right.' Warren shouted his order to the barmaid, turning back to face Mike as he finished. 'You are way behind, big boy!' Warren said, as handed out drinks to each member of his court like the lord of the manor.

'Good thing I'm ambidextrous.' Mike said, holding aloft the two beers Warren had just passed him.

'I've heard it's not that big, matey,' said Warren seizing the opportunity that Mike had left him.

'Fuck you!' Mike laughed. 'Cheers!' They clinked bottles and drank.

Then all of a sudden, Cindy appeared. Almost like magic she had arrived at Mike's side like a lost puppy. Mike turned his back to her. He tried his best to ignore her, hoping she would get the hint, but to no avail. Finally, Mike relented.

'Warren, I'd like to introduce you to Cindy. She's from the office.' He winced slightly as he said it.

'Yes, I work with Mike,' she added reassuringly.

'Well, pleased to meet you, darling.' Warren said, leaning forward to kiss her hand.

It was an action that you would never have expected from him. Mike looked shocked initially. But then he realized that from that angle Warren had a perfect view of her voluptuous breasts. He just laughed, shooting Warren a sly grin in the process. Warren just rolled his eyes.

The beers and tall tales flowed thick and fast for the next couple hours. They spoke of wild markets, wild nights, and wild women. Time flew by as they reminisced. Before he knew it, Mike was incredibly late for his appointment with the mystery man from London.

'Shit!' Mike exclaimed, as he took a peek at his watch. 'Dude, I gotta rush. I am way late for an appointment. I mean, I was supposed to be somewhere else about twenty minutes ago.' It was also the perfect excuse for him to rid himself of the lame puppy, Cindy. Warren would look after her he reassured himself. 'Sorry, Cindy I have to go.'

'Okay, Shag. We'll be here till they roll us out. Have a good one.'

'See ya.' Mike said, grabbing his coat and heading for the exit.

'Bye, Mike. I'll see you Monday.' Cindy said forlornly, with a half-hearted wave. But Mike hadn't heard her. He was already gone.

Simon Anderson looked around the room. The decor was strange. Tiger-striped couches, pale green laminex tables, a long wooden bar with a big old clock covered in Roman numerals behind it. A pool table lay conspicuously dormant at the end of the room. Small groups of drinkers clustered quietly together, chatting. The barmaid flew up and down the bar at a furious pace, in complete contrast to the very mellow patrons. She must be coked to the eyeballs, he mused to himself as he sipped on his second bottle of Rolling Rock. It sure was a strange place, but the crowd was even stranger. Artisan types. No suits to be seen. It was deep in the warehouse part of TriBeCa, the area formed by a triangle beneath Canal street, the cutting edge of living in Downtown Manhattan. The façades of the grimy old warehouses in the area concealed lavish apartments and expensive restaurants.

Anderson again glanced briefly at his watch. The third time in two minutes. He was a compulsive punctualist. He expected the same from everyone else. He had been sitting in the bar, studying this diverse crowd about him, for the last twenty-five minutes, waiting for Michael Kelly to arrive. Then he observed a suited figure getting out of a taxi just across the road. It had to be Mike. 'About time,' he mouthed to himself before shaking his head and downing the rest of his beer.

'You must be Mike.' Anderson said authoritatively as he raised himself from his seat.

'Yes, sorry I'm late!' Mike said, shaking the larger man's hand. 'I got a little delayed by some drinks after work.' His beer breath answered for him.

'No problem at all,' Anderson lied. 'Only been here a few minutes myself. Can I get you a beer?' He inquired rhetorically, sensing the answer would be a resounding, 'yes!'.

'Sure. Heineken will be fine thanks.'

'I'll be back in a sec. Take off your coat in the meantime.' Anderson motioned Mike towards a table in the corner. 'Grab a seat over there!'

A minute later, both men were seated in a secluded corner, far from the prying eyes of Wall Street and the business district, beers in hand. Nobody would know them here. No one would overhear their conversation. Mike felt safe.

'So, Mike, let's cut straight to the chase.' Anderson started immediately in a very gruff, businesslike manner. He was a straight-up kind of guy. 'I took over the commodities department at Nelson Smith at the end of last year. It's an exciting business that is growing by the day. What I am looking for is a young aggressive guy like yourself to run the copper book on the base metals desk.'

'But I'm a forex guy.' Mike cut in.

'So was I until last October.' Anderson retorted. 'But what I need is a really good flow trader. I understand you are one of the best. You can learn the metals business three months max. I figure you'll be the best trader on the block by the end of the year, if you give it a shot. You've got to think big, Mike. I am offering you a chance to be a major player.'

'But I am a major player,' Mike replied in his defense. His ego slightly dented.

'You want to be "big" and "real" Mike? To be big and real you have to piss in the tall grass with the big dogs. I am offering you the chance to run a book that made over sixty million dollars last year. That was almost by default. The guys running the business thought they were legends when in fact they were morons. But those guys are all gone now. With a guy like you running the books maybe we could have made five times that. The value of the information that was derived from the natural business flow was worth at least three hundred million.' The sheer exasperation of the situation showed in Anderson's tone as he finished.

'Sounds interesting, but I am perfectly happy right where I am now.' Mike looked up at the ceiling and took a quick sip of his beer. Anderson had shown his hand. 'Why should I want to move to London of all places?' Mike knew how to play the game too. He was a master poker player. He kept a very straight face as he asked the question.

'What did Leo pay you, all up, last year, Mike?' Anderson looked serious. His eyes drew together in a menacing glare.

'Three hundred,' Mike lied, upping the ante. In fact he had only been paid two hundred and fifty thousand dollars in the previous year. But he was being hunted, the rules of engagement were clear.

'Well, I am thinking that you could earn at least double that in your first year at Nelson Smith.' Anderson dangled the words in front of Mike like a carrot on a stick.

Mike could hardly believe his ears. 'Get that to me in writing,' Mike continued, as he slouched back into his chair arrogantly 'and you may just have yourself a new trader.'

February, 1995

Yoshiro Sutoku scratched his head, he was obviously irritated. It was Saturday morning. He was fast losing his weekend. He wanted to get this finished as fast as was humanly possible, but this was the fifth time he had gone over the figures. Every time he got the same answer, but it didn't add up. Somehow a payment of thirty million U.S. dollars had arrived in a Yamamoto account and he had no explanation for it.

Yoshiro was a dedicated back office man, conscientious to the utmost. A young man, he had been with Yamamoto Corporation for three years, since graduating from the prestigious Tokyo University where he had majored in electrical engineering. Yamamoto Corporation was one of the major trading *keiretsu* in Japan. The *keiretsu* had developed in U.S. occupied Japan after the Second World War. They were major trading concerns with close links to banks and finance companies in much the same form as the pre-war *zaibatsu* whose power and influence the U.S. occupational forces had tried to dismantle with little success. The likes of Yamamoto, Mitsui, Mitsubishi, and Sumitomo had all developed into powerful, global conglomerates with incredibly integrated businesses operating in both vertical and horizontal monopolies. These major trade houses were the backbone of Japan's post war recovery and growing global financial dominance.

He grabbed the stack of white papers from his desk and reshuffled them quickly before placing them back into his tray. He hoped that this action would somehow solve the problem, but he thought it unlikely. The end of year audit would start soon. If he didn't have things in order, well, he would just have to sort things out. There was no question of failure in this situation. He was in line for promotion soon. With a young wife to whom he was recently married, he was already slipping into the Japanese corporate way of life. The never-ending chasm of service to the corporation into which he had fallen meant he hardly ever saw her. When he did manage to see her, it was very late at night and he was far too tired for any display of affection. Besides, he was usually too drunk to perform, having gone for a few beers with his colleagues in one of the ubiquitous bars in Ginza. Like so many Japanese, he was a veritable corporate slave. But he wanted his next promotion ever so badly.

Far below the air-conditioned comfort of the Yamamoto Corporation headquarters, the Saturday shopping crowd bustled its way out of the Ginza 4-chome crossing, the heart of Ginza. The subway station is serviced by three subway lines – Hibiya, Ginza, and Marunouchi. Masses of shoppers spew forth from this station into the area that is Ginza – without doubt the most chic and sophisticated area in all of Japan. It's the Fifth Avenue or Champs-Elysées of Tokyo, except that rather than a single street its a whole area of shops and offices. The big department stores like Seibu, Hankyu and Mitsukoshi along with the electronic giant Sony are to be found here. Equally famous are its private bars, the so called 'gentlemen's' clubs, replete with western hostesses and heinous prices. This world is strictly in the realm of the expense accounts of Japanese businessmen like Yoshiro's boss, Satoru Fujiyama.

Yoshiro stared out the window and pondered the antlike masses winding their way through the Ginza area far below. Unless he sorted out this problem, he would have the proverbial window seat for the rest of his life. There was nothing more feared than a sideways promotion in corporate Japan. A window seat for life. He desperately wanted a job on the trading desk. He wanted that corporate expense account to be used in Ginza and all the kudos that went with it. He tried to snap himself out of the trance. Back to work, he told himself. Let's fix this problem.

He flicked through the swift messages piled high on his desk. The swift system is the means by which trillions of dollars is transferred around the world between banks. There it was, staring straight back at him in black and white, a payment from Nelson Smith Securities of thirty million dollars. He had called the young girl whom he knew in the Nelson Smith back office to double check that it was correct, that no mistake had been made in this payment, something which was not at all uncommon. But the reply came that there had been no error. The payment was the premium due to Yamamoto on account of options granted by his boss, Satoru Fujiyama. The only problem was that he had no record of the sales. He had all the trade tickets from all the trades done during the week. Surely the great Fujiyama would not have forgotten to give him the trade ticket for such a sizable deal, would he? Yoshiro feared the worst, he feared that he must have lost the ticket. A shiver went throughout his body as he contemplated having to tell his boss that he had lost an important deal slip. Why can't everything be computerized in Japan like in American firms, he wondered. Then I wouldn't be in this mess. Despite the dominance of Japanese electronic goods on world markets, Japanese offices were archaic when compared with those of their American counterparts. Paper, paper, and yet more paper was often substituted for computer systems in corporate Japan. Yoshiro just stared at his paper-clad nightmare.

Then a thought struck him. Maybe he hadn't lost the deal slip. Maybe, just maybe, his boss had forgotten to give him the deal slip. Maybe it was still in his briefcase by some mysterious quirk of fate. After all, Fujiyama was a very busy man. It had to be the case. There was no other rational explanation. Yoshiro knew in his heart that he hadn't ever received any such deal ticket. He relaxed momentarily into the comfort of his chair, breathing a quick sigh of relief as he did so. Fine. He knew the answer to his problem was a simple one. Fujiyama had simply been too busy to hand him the trade ticket. Simple. But how does one tell one's superior that he has been remiss in his duties? How does one point out a mistake to one's boss when one is hoping for a promotion? How could he accomplish this feat without appearing disrespectful? He was terrified of the possibility of a permanent window seat. He decided on his course of action. It would have to wait till Monday.

★

The yellow cab pulled up outside Peter Lugers's Steak House in Brooklyn. Mike Kelly passed the driver a twenty before stepping out from the cab. Mike didn't venture into this part of town too often – there was no reason to, Manhattan had everything he needed, well, pretty much. Anyway, this area was skanky. It smelled rancid. He figured the steam that billowed out from the sidewalk vents was probably radioactive in this part of town. He reckoned that even the sky was lower in this part of New York. He was an island snob, damn proud of it. The people in this part of town were generally poor. Even the randoms on the streets looked poorer than their Manhattan counterparts. But that was what made America great.

It's a land of opportunity, he thought to himself, as he crossed the road dodging the rubbish and the stretch limos that blocked his path. He even started to wonder for a second what he was doing there. The only redeeming quality, the one thing that had brought him to this part of town, in fact, the only reason he would even think of venturing into this god-forsaken place: Peter Lugers's Steak House beckoned him like a beacon in the night. Who would want to put a top restaurant here anyway? Maybe Lugers's should move into Downtown, he thought to himself as he pushed through the doors. Yeah, now that would be an idea.

'Can I help ya, sir?' An old Italian man leered at him from behind the wooden front desk.

'Yeah, table for Kelly.' Mike said, screwing up his face. Man, he hated that Brooklyn accent. His eyes darted in all directions around the room for the imposing physique of his friend John Templeton, with whom he was supposed to be having dinner.

'You was supposed to be here at eight,' he paused. 'Kelly, table for two, right?' The older man snarled as if the words 'service' and 'friendliness' were foreign to him.

'Yeah, that's right, I got a little delayed in the traffic... err... the cab driver.' Mike started some bullshit excuse for his tardiness and then stopped abruptly. Why the fuck was he trying to justify his lateness to this old guy? He would save the apologies for John, whom he knew was punctual.

'Dis way, follow me,' the old man replied.

Mike followed the old man up a flight of wooden stairs. He had kind of hoped John would have been at the bar having a drink, but he knew John would already be at the table, drinking, salivating, preparing for the feeding frenzy that would ensue upon Mike's arrival.

As Mike appeared at the top of the landing the room resonated with the unmistakable South Carolina boom of John Templeton's voice. 'Yo! M.K.!'

'Yo! J.T.!' Mike replied, and the two men embraced more like a football tackle than an embrace.

It must have been a peculiar sight really. The hulking American football physique of the six foot six inch tall John

Templeton bear-hugging the much smaller, fragile-looking frame of Mike Kelly. Mike had more the physique of a spectator than linebacker but he had a heart the size of a lion, which was what counted. It didn't count enough to win him a place alongside his good friend and flatmate J.T. on the Harvard football team, but his tenacity and aggression had won the respect of the big man who now towered above him.

'Man, it's good to see you!' J.T.'s voice roared. It was a noisy place, but the wooden floors and walls made it echo around them.

'Dude, likewise!' Mike returned fire in a San Diego refrain.

J.T. spun around to face the old man who was standing a couple feet away by now, more for his hearing than anything else, 'Waiter! Get us some beers, fast!' he demanded.

The two men sat down at the table which was covered in a tacky red and white checked tablecloth. You didn't come to Lugers's for style and finesse. You came for steak. Red, raw, bleeding meat, straight off the bone. Any rarer and you would have to carve it yourself. Mike often had visions of John carving his own steak straight from a mooing cow before riding the leftovers back to his apartment on the Upper West Side.

'So man, tell me how you been doing?' J.T. inquired, leaning his upper body over the table, beaming, obviously very happy to see his old friend.

'Dude, I've been having a dream run lately. Kicked some serious butt on Friday thanks to Mickey Kantor's statement.'

Mike didn't even bother to explain his tardiness. John wouldn't have cared, and besides they had roomed together at university. If anyone knew Mike, John did. He had seen Mike pull every excuse from the book and more to explain to girls why he would be late for a date. The extremely creative bullshit that flowed from Mike's mouth made John laugh. What made him laugh even more was that chicks bought it. He had to hand it to him though, Mike was smooth.

'Yeah, I figured you musta nailed that sucker on the head, given the kinda short you were running.' John said in agreement. Although Mike had never told him the exact size of the short position he was running, John had understood it to be a major one.

Mike and John had met for the first time in their freshman year at college. They came from similarly privileged backgrounds. It was a strange match. The tall Southerner and the tanned surfer from the West coast. Their love of football had brought them together, though only John had donned the crimson colors and played for Harvard. In their second year they had moved into an apartment together in Boston, not far from campus, on Putnam Avenue, with two other guys from the football team. It was the quintessential guys' place. Women feared to tread there. Clothes migrated there to die. Six months of home delivered pizza boxes blocked the passage to the kitchen. Beer filled the fridge at all times while ESPN and MTV played a loud cacophony of sport and music in the background. Books and study were a rarity. No wonder Mike had just scraped by at college.

Since leaving college both men had embarked on careers in the world of trading. Mike had started straight away with Henderson Meyer, with a little help from his father. John, on the other hand, had had an even bigger boost. His stepfather ran a large and highly successful commodity fund. He had been able to get John in the door at one of the largest hedge funds in the world, the Icarus Fund, which managed over nine billion U.S. dollars, making it of gargantuan proportions especially when a high degree of leverage was employed. It was in the same league as George

Soros's flagship Quantum Fund or Julian Robertson's Tiger Fund.

Hedge funds were powerful in the financial markets. Their clout held international renown. They were not constrained like the many mutual funds or money market funds that sucked the money from the 401K savings plans to which most Americans now contributed. They weren't limited to buying stocks or bonds, forcing them to be exposed to the markets in all circumstances. No, these were opportunistic funds. They were able to be long or short of any stock, bond, currency, or commodity in the world. Their trades took the form of cash, futures, or options. They played the world's commodity, currency, bond, and stock markets with all the gusto of a newly arrived Texan oil millionaire in Las Vegas wearing a ten gallon hat and white snakeskin boots. But their bets were rational bets. They won more often than they lost, unlike the poor Texan. Sure, they took risks. But they were calculated risks, huge bets placed on the directions of markets based on a combination of political, financial, and economic scenarios from which they derived their fundamental view of the world.

It was every *real* trader's dream. To be a hedge-fund manager. They were paid more than god himself. Some earned more in a year than the G.D.P. of some African nations. Of the top paid one hundred men on Wall Street, the majority were fund managers. In 1993 alone, George Soros reputedly paid himself over a billion dollars, not bad for a year's speculation.

John ran the commodity portfolio for the mighty Icarus Fund. The fund's founder, the legendary investor Steven Richmond, had long since retired. Shit, he never needed to work another day in his life. Forbes's top five hundred rich list could attest to that. He was just a figure-head these days. The young Turks whom he employed ran the day to day activities and investments of the funds that his flagship Icarus Fund managed. But every now and again, old man Richmond had a view and the fund threw its might into that investment.

The commodity portfolio that John managed comprised a mere five percent of the net assets of the fund, as modern portfolio theory indicated was required for a balanced portfolio. But five percent of nine billion is four hundred and fifty million. Multiply that by ten times leverage and John was managing close to four and a half billion dollars worth of funds. It was pretty impressive for a twenty-six year old. Even Mike paid homage to his best friend's awesome power.

In 1994, John had been long aluminum. The price of the metal had almost doubled in the year. John had made over one hundred percent return on his investment, all net of incentive fees for the shareholders. In the process he had saved the Icarus Fund from what had been a disastrous year on the world's bond markets. He alone had kept the fund from reporting its first negative return since its inception some twenty years before. Old man Richmond had rewarded the big Southerner handsomely. Mike figured he had collected somewhere in the region of ten million dollars for his efforts.

Not bad for a simple Southerner, thought Mike. Here was a guy of simple pleasures. Reasonably educated – he had attended Harvard for Christ's sake – but definitely a man of simple pleasures. He loved beer, steak, and football. His C.V. listed his hobbies as, 'hunting, shooting, fishing'. It should have read, 'eating, drinking, fishing,' as he didn't own a gun these days. Twenty-six and a multi-millionaire many times over. He had more money than one could reasonably expect to spend in a lifetime. He was more highly paid than the protector of the 'free world', the President of the United States himself. Only in America.

They talked markets, college football, and girls. The stories were the same, only the boys were now older. Mike sat back in his seat and sipped his beer. As his steak arrived he could smell the blood coagulating under the surface of the seared creation, waiting, preparing to ooze forth from the carcass as he tucked into it. Both men readied themselves with their utensils like soldiers about to enter combat. All of a sudden conversation ceased. It was every man for himself.

'So, did Anderson get in touch with you, big guy?' John asked, his mouth half full of food as he proceed to demolish the thirty-two ounce steak in front of him. He really did lack a lot of refinement.

'Yeah. But how did you know?' Mike looked perplexed.

'I'm the one who gave him your home number, man.' John finished chewing his steak and took a large gulp of beer. 'Remember back in college I went out to Chicago for a summer vacation.'

'You worked down in the wheat pit for Cargill on the Board of Trade, didn't you?' Mike asked rhetorically.

'Well, guess who was my boss during that summer vacation in Chicago?'

'Anderson, of course.' It was a no-brainer. Mike peeled the label off his beer bottle subconsciously.

'Yup, Anderson was a grain guy at Cargill for years before he moved to the forex desk at Nelson. Good man. Solid.' John took yet another long gulp from his beer. 'Yep, definitely a good man.' He nodded with himself in agreement.

An empty plate was all that was left of the massive thirty-two ounce steak that John had devoured. Mike was still way behind, lagging badly, and he was only attempting the bronze medal sixteen ounce event. John looked quietly satisfied with himself. He placed his hands across his ample girth as he slumped back into his chair. Then he belched loudly. The thunderous noise filled the room. The wooden floor and wall paneling caused it resonate throughout the restaurant. Diners shook their heads in disgust. Mike just laughed at the crude antics of his buddy. It was as if they were back in college.

'So, dude,' John deliberately made fun of Mike's surfer-speak, but with his Southern accent it just made him look stupid, 'hurry up and finish that sad excuse for a cow on your plate and let's get some "white metals" trading done tonight.' As he said this he caught the waiter's eye and made a quick hand movement, which meant, in internationally recognized sign language, 'please bring me the check.'

Mike continued to chew his food. He knew exactly what John was alluding to, 'white metals' was their code for a certain table-dancing joint. One of those places where men sit in comfortable lounge chairs, drinking beer, whilst amazingly beautiful girls disrobe down to a G-string. Most of the girls have plastic breasts anyway. At twenty bucks a pop it can become an expensive habit. As far as Mike was concerned, it was all harmless fun. He liked to laugh at the fat, middle-aged, balding men with wives and kids at home, sitting there entranced by it all. Tongues out, wallets out, trying to relive some sort of youthful fantasy. Now they were sad.

Mike usually went to these sort of places only on weekdays, and with clients. On his expense account of course. But definitely not on Saturdays, and no way on personal account or P.A. as they called it. But since John had put him in touch with a guy who could seriously elevate him in the world of trading, he felt obliged to go for at least a couple beers with the big guy. His arm didn't need much twisting. Beer and silicon, Mike thought to himself. What a way to spend the weekend. What harm could it do? Tomorrow was Sunday, he could catch up on all the sleep debt he had acquired during the week and be fresh for Monday.

The waiter arrived back with the bill and John flung a wad of cash on top of it. Without even stopping to read it, he shoved it to the edge of the table in one deft maneuver.

'Ready to trade some "white metals" on the P.A.?' John's eyes lit up with excitement.

'Okay. Done!' Mike snapped, as if confirming a forex deal. 'But let's go to Scores on the Upper East Side instead.' He wiped the bits of steak from around his mouth with a gaudy red-checked napkin. 'I'm sick of Stringfellows, and the chicks are better at Scores anyway.'

'I hear you.' John rose. He looked back at Mike and grinned like the Cheshire Cat, 'Let's get this Scores thing done!'

*

BARINGS COLLAPSE The front page of the *Financial Times* glared at Fiona Bolton as she sipped her coffee alone. The vast empty space of the boardroom at the Serious Fraud Office in London would soon be filled to capacity. The director of the SFO had called a meeting of all the investigators to discuss the plan of action for the Barings debacle. Fiona had made an early start on this crisp morning after seeing the CNN financial news. She followed the same routine every day. She ate her bowl of muesli topped with skimmed milk while watching the business news, then showered and made herself ready for work. Routine was easy. Routine made sense. Alas, she was a true accountant.

She sipped her coffee again and stared distantly out the boardroom window and pondered the Barings crisis. Here was an institution that had financed the Panama Canal, the Louisiana purchase by the United States, and even floated

Guinness on the London Stock Exchange in 1886. Here was a firm that had been adviser/banker to the royalty and governments of Europe. Here was a company that now lay in ruins with over eight hundred million pounds in losses. Exactly how could a British merchant bank that sailed the seas of high finance for hundreds of years be sunk by a marauding young pirate from Watford armed only with futures and options contracts and an affinity for deception? It was the SFO's job to find out. No doubt Fiona would be involved.

Since joining the SFO just six months before, Fiona had been involved in a lot of the dogsbody work on the Robert Maxwell case. It was an interesting assignment, but she craved more responsibility and a hint of adventure. The daughter of prominent Conservative M.P., Sir Peter Bolton and his socialite wife, Fiona had been the recipient of a very privileged upbringing. Private schooling, a country house, skiing in St. Moritz, a villa in St. Tropez, Fiona had a life that most people only dream about. The SFO was a far cry from her schooling at Wickham Abbey and reading classics at Cambridge. It was almost contradictory. Here was this stunning, leggy blonde who looked as if she would be at home on the catwalks of Paris and Milan in an occupation that one associated with tedium, repetition, and boredom. It was her methodical and thorough nature that had led her into the world of accounting. She enjoyed the challenge, and was determined to make it on her own. From her early days at Coopers and Lybrand when she was fresh from Cambridge she had known that accounting was for her. Then a six month secondment to the SFO had led to the offer of a permanent position.

The room began to fill rapidly. A din cluttered the air as people discussed the latest turn of events in the financial world. The scene abounded with the stereotypical accountant types, those interesting individuals who used their personalities for contraception. Faceless to a man, Fiona was the only brush of color in this gray landscape.

The director entered the room and a hush of anticipation settled like a net over the crowd. In his early fifties, the director had a graying band of hair that wrapped around a shiny solar-panel bald spot on his head like a ski headband. He had a regal nose that he used as a weapon of intimidation, staring down on his underlings. He began in a very deliberate tone.

'You have all heard, no doubt, about the situation at Barings P.L.C. I am led to understand that the management believe that fraud and deception by one or more of their employees in the Singapore office is responsible for the current state of affairs. To that end I am setting up three teams. The first team will coordinate everything here in London and liaise with the Bank of England and Ernst and Young, the appointed liquidators. The second team will investigate Barings P.L.C. here in the U.K., and the third and final team leaves for Singapore tomorrow to liaise with the Singaporean authorities. Your individual assignments and team pairings are being handed out now.'

A faceless gray suit moved around the crowded room handing out dossiers randomly. Fiona peered expectantly at the white stapled stack in front of her. Her eyes scanned the front page, looking almost frantically for her name. Group three. Yes! Her blue eyes lit up magically. A tingling sensation shot through her body. She would be off to Singapore tomorrow.

*

Yoshiro shuffled the papers on his desk once more. The missing deal slip had not mysteriously appeared over the remainder of the weekend as he had hoped it would. It was the end of what had probably been the longest Monday of his life. He had spent the whole day staring into space, wondering how exactly he was going to confront his boss, Satoru Fujiyama, and ask him for the missing trade ticket which would account for the thirty million dollars he was out. He dreaded the prospect.

The day was drawing to a close. Yoshiro looked up across the open-plan room which now resembled an empty stadium, desks piled high with papers and no one in the driver's seat. He spied Fujiyama sitting in the corner alone. He looked as if he was reading some document. Here was his chance. Yoshiro took a deep breath and swallowed hard. It was do or die. He must bring this error to Fujiyama's attention.

Yoshiro strode across the room with as much confidence as a child about to tell his mother that he has broken her favorite vase. There sat the man, Satoru Fujiyama, the most powerful copper trader on the planet, engrossed in a report. Here, just inches away from Yoshiro, was a man whose presence in the marketplace made traders tremble from Tokyo to New York. The sweat started to bead on his forehead. He wiped it off quickly with his shirtsleeve. Yoshiro stood there awe struck. Fujiyama continued reading away, oblivious to the underling in his personal space.

Yoshiro cleared his throat. 'Excuse me, Fujiyama-san.' All the while bowing most respectfully. 'So sorry to interrupt your reading. But I have a question to ask.' The fear in his voice was as noticeable as the nervous tapping of his left foot.

Fujiyama, his peace disturbed, gazed inquisitively at the man in front of him. He placed the report that he was reading on the table and peered at Yoshiro over the top of his steel-framed glasses. The most powerful copper trader on the planet looked anything but powerful. He was short, graying, and in his early forties. He looked like a benevolent uncle, yet his standing in the marketplace had elevated him to a godlike status at Yamamoto Corporation, a status similar to that enjoyed in Japanese society by the Yokozuna, the sumo wrestling grand champion.

Fujiyama relaxed back into the comfort of his leather chair, 'Yes? Go ahead.' He beckoned the underling, Yoshiro, with a disarming wave of his right hand.

'Well, Fujiyama-san, I must report that I have a problem. I have a thirty million U.S. dollars receipt from a counterparty for which I have no trade record. I checked with the counterparty who told me that it was payment for options sold by yourself. But I found that this could not be the case as we have no trading authorization to sell options to this counterpart and I have no trade ticket. I am confused, Fujiyama-san.'

Fujiyama looked back at the trembling underling. He lit a cigarette, paused to exhale and started speaking in a very soft manner.

'This is a mistake made by the counterpart. I shall personally resolve this situation this evening. Well done, my young colleague.'

A wave of relief swept over young Yoshiro Sutoku. The man was not angry, far from it, he seemed pleased with him.

'Thank you, Fujiyama-san.' Yoshiro bowed three times in complete deference to the master.

'Just one question before you go,' Fujiyama took on a more serious tone and his brow furrowed. 'Did you come to this conclusion alone, or did you have help from someone else in the department?'

Yoshiro held his head high now, 'No, Fujiyama-san,' he said brimming with confidence, 'I worked completely alone.'

'Excellent,' Fujiyama clasped his hands together. 'I will see that you are handsomely rewarded for your *aisha seishin*, your devotion to the company.'

Yoshiro's face lit up with a big smile, the smile of triumph in adversity.

'Here,' Fujiyama leant forward and held out a card that had come from his jacket pocket. 'Go to my club in Ginza and tell them that I sent you, they will take good care of you my friend.'

Yoshiro thanked him profusely, bowing over and over again as he backed his way towards the elevator shaft. This was truly an honor. He could see that his promotion would be a certainty now.

Yes my young friend, I will take care of you Fujiyama thought to himself as he puffed away on his cigarette. The old man laughed shaking his head and reached for the phone.

*

The dollar had continued its slide in the Far East and Europe overnight. The Barings fiasco had sent the markets into a panic. The Japanese Nikkei share price index futures had been limit down in Osaka. The lead article carried by the *Wall Street Journal* that morning was on Barings and its rogue trader, Nick Leeson, who was now a fugitive. Mike looked up from his copy of the *W.S.J.*, he spied the short, robust frame of Leo Epstein heading towards him. Mike smiled. Leo would have been ecstatic with his performance last Friday.

'Well done, Mike, you really nailed that sucker last Friday.' Leo said, as he slapped Mike across the back. 'We are well ahead of budget for the desk this month, thanks to you.'

'Yeah, it's like shootin' fish in a barrel.' Mike replied, holding his arms up as if he was firing a rifle. 'I'm up another quarter mio this morning before New York opens, I think I owe that Nick Leeson guy a beer when they catch him.' Mike tried to downplay his feat whilst simultaneously reveling in the accolades.

'What's your position now?' Leo asked, with just a hint of concern.

'Don't worry, Leo, I was only short ten thousand Nikkei contracts over the weekend.' Leo's expression showed how impressed he was at Mike's sad attempt at humor so early on a Monday morning. 'But seriously, Leo,' Mike continued, fully aware of Leo's demeanor, 'I'm pretty flat now, I'm just short ten million bucks.'

'Just be careful, Mike. This Barings collapse could prompt some sort of concerted central bank intervention. The Fed may try something major to stop the slide of the dollar. Some sort of concerted central bank intervention could rip you a new asshole Mike, so watch out.'

Leo was the voice of wisdom and restraint. He had long since ceased active trading himself. He just managed the desk these days. He made sure that they met budget and watched the risk profile of the desk like a hawk, so that if the world blew up they wouldn't have their asses handed to them on a plate. The Barings incident would have managers all over the world reviewing their risk profiles. No company would want something along the lines of this disaster happening to them. Henderson Meyer had a strong risk management team, but whenever there was a blow-out in the financial markets you were bound to have management looking for holes in the ship, it was only natural.

'Understood, Leo. I'll be careful.' Mike sat back slightly and watched Leo make his morning round of the desk. He wondered if Leo had any idea about his conversation with Anderson last Friday night.

'Morning, Fred.' Mike fired the first salvo of the week's repartee into the voice box.

'A very fine February morning to you, sir.' Freddy chirped back. 'How was your weekend?'

'Fine, fine. Just the usual beer and silicon weekend. And you?' Paper rustled in the background as Mike searched for his M.I.A. bagel under the remains of the *W.S.J.* that now lay sprawled across his desk. The bagel seemed lost for good.

'Ranger hockey, gentlemen, you can't beat it.' Freddy blurted out his Monday morning mantra. He was a big ice hockey fan. 'Hey, did you hear about that guy in Hong Kong who blew up the Bank of England where the Queen keeps her money?'

'Fred, listen up!' Mike was not known for his patience. 'I'm only going to say this once. It's Barings, a British merchant bank, not the Bank of England that is going down the gurgler, and the guy who put them in the shit was based in Singapore not Hong Kong.'

'Like I said, sir.' Freddy replied, oblivious to the distinction. 'So what do you think it means for the market? Are we gonna be busy today?'

'Yes, Fred. So pay attention.'

'Whatever you say sir, you're the man.'

'Thank you, Fred.'

'No, thank you, sir.' Fred continued the banter.

The phone bank flashed. It was Warren. That guy was like fiber, he called so damn regularly.

'Yo, dude. What's up?' Warren's East End London accent still made Mike laugh.

'Not much, my man. How was your weekend?' Mike asked.

'Not too bad, matey. Bit of this, not much of that. But you remember that girl from your office who was down Morans on Friday?'

'You mean Cindy?' Mike prompted him.

'Yeah, the one with the monster set of wapps.' Warren continued. 'Well, mate, I have some good news for you. After you left the pub on Friday all this chick wanted to do is talk about you. I tried to put in a good word for you but I don't think I did very well. I couldn't help myself, I just got drunk and stared at her breasts. But mate, I'm telling you, she is as keen as mustard for you.'

'She's yours, dude.' Mike said bluntly. Mike was not interested. He would set Warren straight right here and now.

'What, ain't you interested in her?' Warren sounded puzzled.

'You catch on fast, brother.' Mike scoped the room for any signs of Cindy.

'Why not? I'll agree she's not the prettiest girl I ever seen, but she's got a great personality.' Warren came to her defense.

'Personality isn't everything,' Mike retorted.

'I know, but she has two rather large personalities. Come on, Mike, on a scale of one to ten, surely you'd like to give her one.' Warren was a base guy, Mike knew it and loved it.

'Maybe,' Mike relented.

'You sly dog, you!' Warren exclaimed. 'I bet you already been shaggin' her and didn't even bother to tell me.'

'Whoa, hold on there big guy, I have not touched her. I swear!' Mike sounded concerned now.

'Don't worry, big boy, I won't tell anyone.' Warren consoled him. 'It's best to keep it quiet when you're playing a home game with one of your colleagues.'

Mike gave up his protestations. It was useless. He knew the more vehemently he denied sleeping with Cindy, the more Warren would believe that he was. He was in a no-win situation. So he tried to change the subject.

'What do you make of the Barings situation?'

Warren replied with some bullshit Far East global economic outlook that would have made the Chinese Minister for Propaganda and Orwell's Ministry of Truth both equally proud. He crapped on for about five minutes before he ran out of breath.

'Gotcha,' Mike said, sounding rather impressed with Warren's professional fundamental spiel. 'But what does all that mean?'

'Fucks me, to be honest. But it sure sounds good.' Warren was nothing but frank. 'I got no fuckin' clue, big boy. That's why I called you. What do you reckon?'

'Lower.' Mike was monosyllabic at times. 'It's a bear market, dude. No man should buy the dollar unless he's sold it already.'

'I agree, big boy. People who try to pick bottoms just get dirty fingers.' Warren really did have a way of describing markets like no other trader Mike had ever met.

Mike saw Cindy appear to his left, almost like magic, beside him. She was doing her utmost to catch his attention.

'Look, Warren I gotta hop, got another call coming. I'll catch you later, okay?'

'Sure, big boy, see ya.'

Mike looked up into the inviting stare of Cindy. She smiled at him.

'Mike, so how was your weekend?'

'It was pretty quiet.' Mike glanced briefly at the Reuters screen. It was a nasty reflex action, he always liked to see where the market was quoted in the screen, even though he could hear Freddy droning on in the background with an endless string of prices. It was comforting for him, the screen was his safety blanket. 'I had dinner with an old college buddy of mine on Saturday night.'

'And you?' Mike returned the question out of politeness. He really didn't give a fuck what Cindy had done with herself on the weekend, but felt it only fair to ask.

Whilst Cindy rattled off a string of completely mind-numbingly boring activities that she had accomplished over the weekend, Mike stared at her ample bust. He couldn't have missed it. Cindy was wearing a top that was designed to catch men like a Venus flytrap. As Mike gazed into her cleavage, he remembered Saturday night with John at the table-dancing joint. He remembered handing out twenty dollar bills to see five minutes of silicon. Here it was for real, right in front of him. He must be crazy to turn his back on it. Maybe Warren was right. Maybe she wasn't so bad after all.

'So, Mike, I was wondering if maybe you wanted to do dinner tonight, that's if you don't already have plans?' Cindy stumbled through the invitation, having finally summoned up the courage.

'I guess so. I don't think I've got anything planned. But double-check with me around five tonight to reconfirm and, provided the market is not too busy, I would love to have dinner with you.' Mike felt pleased with himself. He hadn't crushed her with an out and out rejection and he hadn't committed himself either. He left that last proviso hanging as an escape clause.

'Great,' Cindy beamed. 'I'll come back and see you at five.' And with that she skipped off.

Mike had till five o'clock to come up with a plausible excuse. 'Nick Leeson,' he said to himself, 'maybe I'll owe you two beers by the end of the day.'

★

Yoshiro Sutoku stumbled out of the train station at Urayasu. He was visibly drunk. He had spent the whole night drinking at Fujiyama's club. The hostesses had flocked around him and plied him with sake. They were obviously under instruction from the his boss. He had enjoyed the time of his life. Fujiyama had rewarded him handsomely. His wife, Masako, would be proud of him too. He had just managed to catch the last train on the Tozai line, which was an impressive achievement given his current state of intoxication. He didn't really stand out from the crowd at this time of the morning, as the majority of the people on the train were drunk businessmen on their way home to their wives and families. They had all swayed to and fro in unison as the train carriage shunted along. Many were asleep, the rest were on auto-pilot.

Yoshiro steadied himself on the handrail at the top of the stairs and prepared for the arduous descent of the five flights of stairs to street level. Even the great Sir Edmund Hillary had not faced such a high degree of difficulty when he stood atop Everest and prepared to descend. He looked down at the task ahead. He took a deep breath and concentrated hard. One foot forward, then the other, one foot then the other. It was easy. Despite the alcohol factor, Yoshiro was making easy work of the stairs. He felt good as he reached street level. Yoshiro was drunk enough not to notice the two men in black seated in the Nissan that he passed as he left the station.

Boy was he thirsty. He had started dehydrating on the train. By now the dryness in his throat had reached critical levels. He stood in front of one of the millions of vending machines that dot the landscape of Tokyo. He reached into his pocket for some coins. He swayed left and right as he wrestled with the fabric, struggling to get the correct change. He managed to get two coins into the machine before dropping the last one, which rolled noisily underneath the machine. Yoshiro put his hand into his pocket to get another coin. All he had left were his car keys. He kicked the vending machine out of frustration – a very un-Japanese display of emotion. He would have to wait until he got home.

He looked at the car keys. It was not far to his home. He normally drove to the station. Sure, he could walk it in about twenty minutes, but he didn't feel like walking right now. That twenty minute walk would take him about half an hour in his current state. He was far too thirsty to wait. Too drunk to walk, Yoshiro decided he had better drive.

At the parking garage, Yoshiro located his car without any trouble. He got the keys into the ignition on the third attempt. The console of the steering column of his little Toyota was riddled with scratches, testimony to the fact drink driving was not a new experience for Yoshiro. Slowly but surely he negotiated his way out of the parking garage and into the street.

Parked across the road was a black Nissan four-wheel drive with heavily tinted windows which obscured the two men in black inside. No one could have seen the gold rhombus-shaped pin that each man wore on his lapel. As Yoshiro's car left the parking garage, the engine of the Nissan roared into life and they followed Yoshiro's car at a discreet distance.

*

Fiona Bolton's day was drawing to a close. The director of the SFO had given her leave to go home early to pack for her Singapore trip. She had been told to expect to be away for a minimum of three weeks. She had not done much in the way of preparation for her latest assignment because she had spent most of the day calling her friends to tell them the good news, that's how excited she was. There would be little time to organize herself for the trip as her flight left from Heathrow the next morning.

Now she was in a dilemma. She threw her suitcase onto the bed and opened it. She stared thoughtfully at her wardrobe which was almost bursting with clothes. What should she take? What was she going to wear? Singapore was a tropical climate, that much she knew. All her favorite clothes were winter ones. All her summer clothes were last season's, and heaven knows, she had probably put on some weight over Christmas and they wouldn't fit anyway. She held a light summery dress against herself and checked her appearance in the mirror from all angles. It was hopeless, winter is never kind to a girl's figure in London. Fiona would need to get some shopping done soon after arriving, but she knew that the chances of that would be slim, at least until Saturday. She had to get through four days between now and then. This assignment was proving to be a nightmare even before she left London.

Then Fiona was startled by a noise.

*

'Meyer.' Mike boomed rudely into the phone. It had been a rather uneventful morning but his current state of anxiety over what to tell Cindy didn't allow him time for pleasantries.

'Mike Kelly, please.'

Simon Anderson hadn't even finished his request before Mike butted in, 'Hey, I thought I asked you not to call me at work.' Mike looked around the desk furtively to see if anyone close by had heard him. Even though all conversations were taped for regulatory reasons, not all of them would be listened to.

'I'll be brief.' Anderson replied. 'I have Fed-Exed you a package which should meet with your approval. If it does, call me at the Millennium Hilton tonight.'

'Okay. Sounds good to me.' Mike concurred. 'Speak to you then.'

Mike cleared the line with vigor and called the concierge at TriBeCa Tower.

The phone answered on the first ring. 'TriBeCa Tower, how may I help you?'

'Hi, this is Mike Kelly, I'm in apartment 42C. I was wondering if a package has arrived for me at all today.'

'Just one moment, sir, I'll check for you,' came the reply.

The waiting time was excruciating for Mike, who had picked up a major adrenaline rush from his previous conversation.

'Yes, sir a Fed-Ex package arrived at ten-thirty this morning. You can pick it up at the front desk anytime. Is there any thing else I can help you with, sir?'

'No, that is fine. Thanks for your help.'

Mike put the handset down and sat on both his hands. He was trying desperately to control himself. He wanted to leap and jump and scream for joy. He knew that he couldn't. He would have to wait till five-thirty tonight when he got home. That would be torture. He now had a serious excuse as to why he couldn't have dinner with Cindy, but one that he couldn't tell her. Damn.

★

Yoshiro's confidence grew with every gear-change as he drove along the street. The road was empty at this time of the morning. The lights beside the road emitted a dim hazy light. Yoshiro's slight swerving motion as he drove would not be noticed by anyone. Anyone that is, except for the two men in the four-wheel drive who were shadowing the Toyota at a short distance. They were very aware of his driving action and his state of intoxication.

Yoshiro pulled a cigarette from his top pocket. As he did so, he tried to wind down the window and the car swerved violently to the right. He didn't smoke usually, but after a large amount of beer and sake, he always felt compelled to do so. He placed the butt in his mouth and leaned forward, pushing the cigarette lighter button in. Twenty seconds later he held the car lighter aloft between his thumb and forefinger and tried without much success to light his cigarette. His hand swayed about as he tried to get the end of the cigarette into the lighter.

Then, in the rearview mirror, he glimpsed a flash of metal. A large vehicle approaching at speed without its lights on. He dropped the lighter onto the floor, attempting to grab the wheel in the same instant. It was too late. The crash of steel upon steel shunted Yoshiro and his Toyota off the road at speed. Before he could react, Yoshiro found himself completely out of control. A stationary lamp post seemed to approach at incredible speed. Instinctively he hit the brakes and pulled on the wheel, to no avail. The car just skidded sideways. The world seemed to slow down as the car careened towards its impending doom. Yoshiro had thoughts only of his wife, Masako. He couldn't remember the last words he had said to her. He wondered if he had told her that he loved her. The impact with the post ripped the car in two. Glass fragments flew everywhere as the metal twisted. As Yoshiro flew sideways towards the passenger door, the blast from the passenger airbag shot him backwards at immense speed into the lamp post. Dead!

Yoshiro would not have felt a thing. His decapitation was swift. The force of the impact had torn his head from his neck. If he had been wearing a seatbelt then the outcome might have been different. If there had been no passenger-side airbag, he might have survived, but being forced back into the pole was more than his body was designed to take.

The first man in black looked at the carnage, the tangled mess of Yoshiro's car, through night-vision goggles from the comfort of the Nissan, which was idling close to the scene of the wreckage. You would never have guessed that only moments ago this had been a Toyota. It looked more like an artistic impression of a metallic spaghetti Bolognese, but the man in black was not here to admire his artistry. His eyes searched quickly for the body, scanning the wreck for signs of movement. Then he saw the gruesome sight. Yoshiro's upper body lay against the passenger side door. Steam rose from the lacerated flesh around his neck. Blood spurted from his jugular like a garden hose let loose. There was no sign of his head. The first man put down the night vision goggles. He was unmoved by what he had seen. It made no difference to him. He was a professional killer and had seen much worse than the fate that had befallen Yoshiro. He had inflicted worse. He didn't even speak to the other man, not a word, he just nodded. The other man slipped the car into first and they moved forward.

Yoshiro Sutoku need not worry about his promotion now. He had been rewarded for his diligence, his boss Satoru Fujiyama had seen to that.

*

Fiona coiled back against the wall.

'Imogen, you bitch!' Fiona cried, as lithe figure of Imogen Worthing-Brown leaped onto her bed from the hallway. 'You startled me!'

'Sorry, darling, I got your message that you were off to Singapore. I was ever so excited, so I quit the shoot and came back to celebrate with you. There's a bottle of Bolly in the kitchen. Fancy a drink?' She shot Fiona a mischievous grin.

Imogen was Fiona's flatmate. They had met back in their school days at Wickham Abbey. Fiona was always the studious one whilst Imogen was always getting into trouble. Imogen was trouble. A tall lithe blonde with a serious attitude, Imogen had fallen into the world of fashion, not as a model but as a shoot coordinator. She traveled the world looking for exotic locations for her company's latest collections to be modeled and photographed. She was an aggressive girl, a trait she got from her father who was a commander in the Royal Navy. But Imogen didn't really need to work, she was a Chelsea T.F.K. – a Trust Fund Kid – the Nineties version of the Sloane Ranger. Her grandmother had died a rather rich old lady and left her entire estate to Imogen on her twenty-first birthday. She had all the right clothes, shopped in all the right places and ate at all the right restaurants. She drove the little black Golf GTI that she had received from mummy and daddy on her twenty-first birthday. Imogen had it all, and she knew it. It made her a serious bitch at times.

'Yes, that would be lovely.' Fiona said, and she placed her hands up over her face.

'What's wrong, Fee?' Imogen asked, sensing that something was not right.

'It's this packing.' Fiona wailed in exasperation. 'It's doing my fucking head in!'

'Don't tell me,' Imogen said with a bit of a smirk, 'the girl with the world's largest collection of clothes has nothing to wear. Am I right?'

'It's easy for you to be smug. You don't have to go to bloody Singapore tomorrow morning.' The novelty of going to Singapore was quickly wearing off on Fiona.

'I tell you what. Let's have some champagne and I'll give you a hand.' Imogen leaped off the bed and headed for the kitchen.

Fiona just looked into her cupboard in dismay. She really did need that drink.

*

Mike looked up at the clock. The day had gone slowly, the markets had drifted in a Monday malaise all day, drawing the day out in an excruciating manner. The minute hand was hovering just before five o'clock on his watch, torturing him. He knew that the minute it struck five, Cindy would be all over him like a cheap suit. He prayed that his watch would stop. Here was the man of a million excuses finding himself short of a plausible one for not having dinner with a girl. Sure, he had a very real excuse, but not one that he could use safely without alerting Cindy to the deal he was concocting with Simon Anderson and Nelson Smith Securities. That would be bad news.

The digital clock on the wall showed five. Sure enough, as Mike had expected, Cindy bounded into his area.

'So, are we on for dinner tonight, Mike?' She said in a rather upbeat, expectant tone. Her hands were clasped behind her back. It was a dead give away that she was really nervous. It also had the added advantage of launching her breasts right into Mike's line of sight.

With an offer like that, how could Mike refuse? He really found himself lost for words for almost the first time in his life. There was no excuse that he could use with any hint of plausibility. He thought about the call he would have to make to Simon Anderson when he got home. What was he to do?

'I forgot that I have an doctor's appointment at six tonight I'm afraid, I'm sorry, Cindy.' It just rolled off his tongue without any coaxing. He was Mr. Smooth, especially in a time of crisis such as this. He was truly a man who could perform under pressure. It's better this way, he thought to himself.

Cindy's whole frame wilted under the weight of Mike's excuse. Her shoulders slumped and her face fell into a look of utter despair. Mike saw this and immediately sought to rectify the situation. He didn't want to do this. After all, she was a nice girl. Then his conscience, that little guy up in his head, woke up for the first time since he began his hibernation many years ago when Mike entered college.

'Look, I'll be home around seven o'clock this evening. If you like I'll call you when I get home and we can arrange to go out to dinner then.'

Mike knew that Cindy would go straight home to Queens and the chances of her coming back into Downtown Manhattan at seven at night were very slim indeed. He felt pleased with himself for this masterstroke.

'How 'bout I come home with you now and while you are at the doctor's, I'll cook you up a feast?' Cindy asked.

'Umm... er I haven't got any food in the house.' Mike replied in defense. He was on the back foot now. Cindy had forced him into a corner. He was helpless.

'That's okay,' Cindy replied gleefully. 'We can pick some up on the way.' Checkmate.

'Sounds great to me.' Mike said, knowing full well that he would probably regret this in the morning.

Walking up Church Street, Mike thrust his hands deep into his overcoat pockets. It wasn't just the late February chill, Mike didn't want there to be any chance that Cindy might grab a hold of his hand. But his thoughts were not of Cindy, but of Simon Anderson, and the package waiting for him at the front desk of his building. He wondered what deal Anderson had been able to get him so quickly. Had Anderson come up with the sort of money that Mike was looking for? Or had he fallen way short? If he had come up with the money Mike wanted so quickly, was he going too cheap? He knew he shouldn't accept the first offer. He knew he should bargain. Mike formulated all sorts of strategies and plans as he wandered along, almost oblivious to the form of Cindy walking beside him, following like a puppy.

A burst of steam shot up from the subway through the grill beneath their feet. In unison they cupped their mouths and held their breath, looking at each other as they did so. It was a thick, vile, warm urine smell that pervaded the air. The stench was so rank that it destroyed Mike's train of thought.

'You see, Cindy,' Mike pointed with a pejorative stab at the grill below them as they walked, 'That is why you'll never catch me riding the subway. Give me a cab any day, and if I can't find a cab I'd rather walk than take the stinking subway.'

Mike was renowned in the office for having lived in New York for years without ever having taken the subway or ridden in a bus. He had this aversion to public or 'mass' transit as he called it. He would walk fifty blocks rather than take the subway, but mainly he took cabs or limos. Cabs were so cheap anyway. He reckoned that he would be a fool not to take them even if your chances of fatality were way higher in a cab that had bald tires, no brakes and Mario Andretti's love child behind the wheel. You had to live on the edge to be a superior trader, that was how Mike rationalized it.

As they turned right into Duane Street, Mike turned to Cindy and said, 'See that building over there?' He pointed at the only tower block in the street. 'That's TriBeCa Tower, that's where I live. And see that deli across the road?'

'Yes,' Cindy replied, with a touch of sarcasm in her voice. She was obviously not blind and resented being treated like a child.

'Well, that is Zoe's deli. I have to pick up my dry-cleaning and collect some mail. While I do that, how 'bout you get the stuff we need for dinner, just tell Zoe to put it on my account, it won't be a problem. Okay?' Mike started off in the direction of TriBeCa Tower.

'Sure. But where will I meet you?' Cindy shouted. She wondered if Mike was now about to do a magical disappearing act.

'I'll meet you in the lobby of my building in ten minutes.' Mike shouted back to her as he ran off towards the entrance to his apartment block.

Cindy just shook her head. She really couldn't figure this guy out.

Mike arrived at the front desk of TriBeCa Tower in a lather of sweat. His face was bright red and the perspiration beaded on him, making him look like a Christmas decoration.

'In a hurry for something, Mr. Kelly?' The concierge inquired at the sight of Mike panting away by the desk.

The man behind the desk had immediately recognized Mike, although Mike couldn't remember his name for the life of him. Why is it that everyone behind the front desk always knew his name but he never knew theirs? He wished now that they wore a name badge like the people at McDonald's did. Instead, they wore this military-style uniform. Blue jacket with gold braiding across the shoulders and big gold buttons down the tunic front, worn with a gray trouser with a single gold stripe. All they need is a hat and a gun to complete the look, Mike mused to himself.

'Yes,' Mike said, trying to compose himself and breathing deeply. 'There should be a package for me here.'

He leant onto the counter and peered behind the desk expectantly.

'Sure, I think it's down here somewhere,' replied the concierge. 'Ah, here it is, a Fed-Ex package. This what you're looking for, Mr. Kelly?' He held the parcel above his head from the kneeling position that he had assumed below the counter.

'Yes, that's it!' exclaimed Mike, his voice full of excitement and anticipation. His hands clutched forward snatching the package.

'You'll have to sign here first, sir.' The concierge said, holding up a bright red clipboard and pen.

'Sure, no problems.' Mike said, as he scrawled his signature on the board. 'Thank you.'

'You're welcome, sir, have a nice day.' Mike heard behind him as he bolted for the elevator.

Mike dived into the elevator. He was alone. He pressed the button for the forty-second floor and started pushing the door close button frantically. He wanted the lift to be his alone. He saw a woman with her shopping arrive at the doors and try to get in just as they were closing. Normally he would have put his arm out to stop the elevator, but right now he wanted some privacy, so instead of pressing the door open button, he continued to jam the door close button. The elevator doors shut and only the muffled wail of the woman could be heard.

Alone, Mike started to rip the Fed-Ex package apart. Bits of plastic and cardboard fell to the floor as Mike tore at the contents like a child opening a Christmas present. Then he had it in his hand. The offer letter from Nelson Smith Securities Limited. He held it aloft like a trophy, before peering at the details. There was the amount in big bold letters. A base salary of 250,000 U.S.D. and a guaranteed cash bonus of 250,000 U.S.D. with respect to the next financial year. Mike flicked through the various other pages which contained notes on healthcare and superannuation plans. Here it was in black and white, a job offer that would guarantee him over 500,000 U.S.D. for what would amount to about nine months' work.

'Waahoo!' Mike screamed in victory as he danced about in the elevator.

The elevator doors opened. Turning right out of the lift he rushed for the door of his apartment. He fumbled with the keys briefly before bursting into the room in a heightened state of excitement. He threw his coat over the back of the chair, its usual resting place, and tossed his keys and the contract onto the glass table, the keys making a loud scratching jingle as they landed. He launched himself onto the couch and grabbed the cordless phone. He called the operator and asked for the number for the Millennium Hilton on Church Street. Then he dialed the number.

'Millennium Hilton, how may I help you?' came the robotlike answer.

'Yes, Simon Anderson's room, please.' Mike replied, trying to compose himself.

'One moment, please, sir, putting you through.'

'Anderson,' came the gruff voice at the other end of the line.

'Anderson, Mike Kelly here, I got your package.'

'Do you like what I sent you?' Anderson inquired.

'It seems adequate.' Mike chose his words carefully. 'So what's the next step?'

'Do you have time to meet up for a drink this evening?' Anderson asked.

'Sure, I'm free for the next hour or so?' Mike replied, knowing that he had told Cindy that he had a doctor's appointment at six o'clock.

'How 'bout you swing by my hotel now and we'll have a drink at the bar downstairs?'

'Done.' Mike replied emphatically. 'I'll be round in about fifteen minutes.'

'See you soon then. I'm in room 802.' Anderson said, hanging up the phone.

Just as Anderson hung up the phone, Mike's intercom buzzer went off. He shot over to the small handset by the door.

'Hello.'

'There is a Miss Bellini down here to see you, Mr. Kelly,' came the concierge's familiar voice.

'Send her up.' Mike looked around the room quickly to make sure that it didn't resemble a demolition site. Lucky for him it was Monday. On Monday, Wednesday and Friday he had a cleaner who came and like magic his mess was transformed into a clean apartment. He let out a sigh of relief before scrambling across to the table to hide the remnants of the Fed-Ex package.

Moments later there was knock at the door. Mike opened the door only to be greeted by the sight of Cindy laden with shopping bags. As she struggled through the door Mike offered assistance.

'Here, let me help you,' he said, grabbing two of the bags from her right hand.

'I didn't know what you had here, so I just got everything I would need.' Cindy said, holding the rest of the bags in her left hand.

'Good thing,' Mike said, placing the bags on the kitchen counter. 'You'll find that when I said I had no food at home, I wasn't joking.'

'I figured as much.' Cindy said, grinning widely.

'Look, I've got to run to the doctor's, I'll be back in an hour.' Mike started putting on his coat, checking for his mobile phone and pager in the inside pockets as he did so.

'Is there anything wrong?' Cindy asked, with just a touch of concern in her voice.

'Nah, just the usual check-up stuff. Nothing to worry about.' Mike shouted, pulling the door shut behind him.

The Millennium Hilton on Church Street is a modern, skinny, dark glass building with wonderful views. Views of the twin towers of the World Trade Center and views into the New York Mercantile Exchange, enough to give any futures trader a woody. At six in the evening it was dark. Mike threaded his way back through the Downtown crowd as they made their way for subway entrances, buses and cabs. An endless sea of headlights shone in Mike's face as he made his way down Church Street to the hotel which was no more than eight blocks from his apartment. It was a brisk, ten-minute walk, but Mike's ears and nose were already starting to feel the bite of the evening wind off the Hudson. He pulled his collar higher up around his ears and gripped the front of his coat together tightly with his right hand.

He pushed through the revolving doors at the Millennium with ease, the porter doing all the hard work, and made his way to the front desk.

'Good evening, sir, how may I help you?' The cheery female face behind the counter greeted him with that false, feel-good, page forty-seven of the staff manual greeting.

'I'm looking for Simon Anderson in room 802.'

'Sure just one moment,' she said, picking up the phone and dialing. 'And your name, sir?'

'Kelly.'

'Mr. Anderson, this is Rachel at the front desk, you have a Mr. Kelly in reception here for you.' She stood there smiling at Mike all the while. He wondered if there was a device that she had implanted in her lower jaw to produce this all-seasons smile. 'Send him up to the fourth floor, sure, no problem, sir.' She turned back to Mike and continued, 'Mr. Anderson requested that you meet him at the bar on the fourth floor, sir. The elevator on your left over there will take you to it,' she said, pointing to her right. 'Have a nice day.'

Mike could have guessed that was coming, 'Thank you,' he replied, still amazed by her unwavering smile.

Mike exited the elevator on the fourth floor. Immediately he caught sight of Simon Anderson, whom he had met just last Friday. He recognized him straight away, how could he miss him with that army buzzcut and polo shirt.

'Mike, good to see you again.' Anderson held his hand out.

'Likewise.' Mike replied, shaking hands with Anderson, whose vicelike grip Mike felt instantly.

'I thought we might grab a quick bite to eat and a couple beers, I'm famished.' Anderson exclaimed, placing his hands on his hips, legs astride. It was another one of those subconscious intimidatory stances that he generally took.

Mike, still in a state of euphoria, forgot completely about Cindy slaving away in his kitchen, ' Sure,' he said, 'I could go a quick meal.'

'Great, this way then.' Anderson led the way to the restaurant which was nothing but functional. Hotel food is rarely exceptional, except in the fact that it is unexceptional.

They sat down to eat, ordering burgers and beers, the meal of champions.

'So,' Anderson said, kicking off the business part of their encounter, 'I take it you are happy with the package that you received today.'

'It seems reasonable.' Mike said, trying to sound as non-committal as possible.

'Mike, you have to look at the bigger picture here. This is your chance to be a major player. The figures set out in the documents you received are by no means the limit of what you could make this year. They are just the starting point, the ground floor. If you are as good as you think you are and you perform, the sky is the limit.' Anderson's tone rose sharply with excitement.

'So, what's the next step?' Mike asked, peeling the label of his bottle of Heineken, flicking the bits onto the side of his plate. Old habits die hard.

'Well, sign the first copy of the contract you received today and deliver it to our offices in the World Trade Center. The woman you want to see is Eva Black in Human Resources, she'll be expecting you.' Anderson now sat back in his chair, it seemed clear to him that he had hooked the young gun. 'Then all you need to do is hand in your resignation to Leo and take the mandatory four-week break that I expect is stipulated in your current contract, in which time we will hopefully have sorted out a work permit for you in the U.K. Sometimes these things take months, the Home Office decides to flex its muscles against a big American multinational corporation and there is nothing we can do about it.'

'Well, that won't be necessary.' Mike sat back and smiled.

'Why is that?' Anderson looked slightly puzzled. 'Do you have an English parent?'

'Better still,' Mike replied with glee, 'I was born in Italy. My father was a diplomat, I only lived there till I was three, but I still have the passport.'

'Well,' said Anderson, clasping his hands together, 'that makes life a whole lot easier.'

'So how long does this offer stand for?' Mike asked.

'Seven days from today.' Anderson replied, giving Mike an uncharacteristically warm stare 'But I get the feeling we'll be hearing from you before then. You would be crazy to pass this opportunity up.'

Mike finished the beer he was drinking and glanced at his watch. Shit! It was almost seven-thirty and he had already eaten. What was he going to tell Cindy? He excused himself from the meeting, citing his prior engagement with Cindy, and made haste for his apartment.

Opening the door of his apartment, Mike was met by a rush of smells. Fried garlic was the most overpowering one that met him as he entered. He saw Cindy's shirt and bra draped over the couch and his interest peaked. Was he going to find her naked in his bed? His heart started to race, he could feel it pounding underneath his overcoat, which he removed, throwing it over Cindy's clothes on the couch. He unfastened his top button and started to undo his tie as he made his way into the lounge room. Then to his left he spied her.

Cindy bounced into view from the kitchen. 'I hope you don't mind,' she started, 'but my bra was killing me and I didn't want to get food all over my new shirt.'

Mike saw that she was wearing one of his old T-shirts, it was almost threadbare and kept purely for sentimental reasons. It was particularly tight on Cindy.

'No, that's fine.' Mike said, admiring her slender figure, 'I'm sorry I took so long at the doctor's.' He was careful not to breathe too closely on Cindy before he could grab a beer from the refrigerator, lest she realized that he had not been at the doctors.

'Fancy a drink?' Mike said already bent over in the refrigerator.

'Don't tell me, Mike?' Cindy chimed in quickly, 'I've got a choice of beer, beer or beer? I've already had a look.'

Mike looked up. He felt kind of embarrassed. A big Homer-style 'Dough!' he thought, he should have bought a bottle of wine on his way home but the three beers he had consumed in his brief dinner with Simon Anderson had been more than enough to cloud his romantic judgment.

'It's okay, Mike,' Cindy said, in an attempt to assuage his fears, 'a beer will be fine.'

'Might I recommend a bottle of the finest house 'Molson Dry', Mike held up a bottle of beer, but Cindy just wrapped her arms around his neck and proceeded to give him a long and passionate kiss. Mike saw her erect nipples through the tight T-shirt. He took this as the signal to hit the nude button. They stumbled their way toward Mike's bedroom, losing articles of clothing along the way. The guys in the office are going to give me hell when they find out about this, Mike thought to himself, struggling to get his trousers off, but fuck them, I'll be resigning tomorrow anyway. Never look a gift horse in the mouth.

April, 1995

The air hostess was going through her final motions before take-off. She looked like a gameshow hostess, from some sad, second-rate gameshow, one that could only afford to hire ugly, stroppy bitches. As if you would have time to find that little yellow mask and put it over your face and tug gently to get the oxygen flowing, in the event a hole was ripped in the plane. Your head would probably be ripped off and your spinal cord separated from your brain stem by the impact of the decompression. Mike just sipped on his orange juice and looked at the inflight entertainment guide. He felt contented with the fact that at least he would get to see an episode of *The Simpsons* as the plane plummeted from the sky.

March had been a really long month for him. Being a bit of a major workaholic, not working had been like punishment for a heinous crime. Mike craved the action of the financial markets. He was like a drug addict being denied his fix. He constantly found himself calling up friends for a random chat about markets. They were really the only thing that mattered to him.

Resigning to Leo was hard. It was made harder by the fact that Leo gave him the whole disappointed patriarch routine and used words like loyalty and commitment. It was all bullshit, Mike knew that for certain, all it took was a bad year or two, or a major loss, and the knives would come out. Mike had already seen a corporate downsizing. Left and right people got the chop. The bottom line was the most essential part of the balance sheet in any corporation, but especially at an investment bank. People were expendable. It is never anyone's fault, it is the company's, that's the great cop out that is used when people are being fired. The faceless, heartless entity, the company is to blame. Mike knew that his Ides of March would come one day and they would all be waiting for him, knives sharpened, to stab him unceremoniously in the back. But that was the nature of the financial markets. That was the law of the jungle. That was life.

But resigning to Leo wasn't the hardest part for Mike. For him, the hardest part was handing over those essential pieces of trader's paraphernalia that were like his umbilical cord to the financial world: his pocket Reuters and his mobile phone and, more importantly, the company Amex card. How could he live without them? It was hard. He found himself ringing Warren more often than ever before just to check where the markets were. He spent more time socializing with traders at the bars Downtown on their company accounts. He loved to talk financial markets. The war stories that all traders revel in became his favorite subject of discussion.

The stewardess arrived with a plastic cup filled with ice and a smattering of single malt scotch whisky. Mike smiled and said thank you, placing the cup on the oversized armrest between him and the other male business passenger beside him. Mike rarely made conversation with anyone on a plane, unless it was a drop-dead gorgeous blonde. Then he might be tempted to make an exception, but he was never that lucky. Otherwise, for him it was like being in an elevator. You just stared at the numbers till it was your time to get out.

'You're welcome, sir,' came the predictable response from the stewardess. Hadn't anyone taught her that four kilos of foundation was a bad look? And maybe someone should tell her about the lipstick smudge across her teeth? It wasn't going to be him.

Mike pulled the headphones onto his head and played with the console to his right, on the side of the armrest. The personal television in front of him whizzed into life and he flicked through the channels till he found a movie that he had not seen before. He puffed the small blue pillow and placed it behind his head, snuggling himself into as comfortable a position as is possible on an aircraft. He took a sip of his drink. This really is the life, Mike thought to himself, as he reclined in the business class seat.

It was his third trip to London in the last month, even though he wasn't yet officially on the payroll of Nelson Smith Securities. Contractual obligations to Henderson Meyer meant that he could not work for a calendar month from the date of his resignation. In England they called it gardening leave. Mike had no interest in gardening, instead, he had made a number of familiarization trips to London to acquaint himself with his new environment and the people with whom he would be working.

All the time he was in London he had stayed at the Savoy Hotel on the Strand. Mike loved the place. It was full of crusty old rich people and ridiculous rules, rules like he had never seen before. You had to wear a jacket and tie if you wanted a drink at the bar. That sucks big time, Mike thought to himself. But the beds, with their 836 spring mattresses, now they were fit for a king. The other thing that Mike loved was the way that all your washing came back in individually wrapped packages, boxers and socks included. Now that was insane, but Mike loved it. It was so anal, so stuffy, so typically English.

Mike looked out the window of the Boeing 747-400. Staring into the cold, dark night outside, he contemplated his new life in London. He would get off the plane, clear British customs and immigration quickly. He was lucky to have a European passport. It saved him having to stand in line with half of the third world. Surely they could make a special lane for U.S. citizens. Once he had forgotten his Italian passport and had to queue. He hated the wait, and the smell, hadn't any of these people heard of washing and deodorant? After the customs ordeal he would head to his hotel, where he would shower and make haste to the offices of Nelson Smith at Broadgate. The Savoy would be his home for the next month or so, until he found a place to live. He would be on expenses for up to two months. Now there was an opportunity that he would not let slip by. He took another long sip of scotch. Yes, he thought to himself, I'm truly living the life of Riley now, whoever the fuck Riley is.

September, 1991

Smoke filled the corridor. The ceiling was low, the walls literally paper-thin, the corridor narrow. Bryan Murphy slipped off his shoes at the beckoning of the hostess. That was the done thing in Tokyo. A rice-paper door slid sideways to reveal a small room. In the center of the room there was a small table with an ornate Japanese tea pot sitting on it. Either side of the table were tatami mats, Japanese reed mats. Two westerners sat, legs crossed, on the mats. Murphy immediately recognized the men as Richard Wilmont and Alan Bridge, the principals of Wilmont Bridge in London. They both gave him a slight nod, registering his entry into the inner sanctum.

In each corner of the room stood a rather well-built man wearing a black suit, white shirt, black tie and dark sunglasses. Each man wore a gold rhombus-shaped pin on his lapel. They all stood, motionless, expressionless, almost devoid of life. There was a third mat on the same side of the table. The old woman, dressed in traditional kimono, with her face painted white and hair done in an elaborate twirl above her head bowed, deferentially to Murphy and gestured to the tatami mat. He sat down in silence. They were all awestruck. No one said a word. No one dared speak. Here they were in some hole in the wall in Asakusa at the beckoning of Satoru Fujiyama, the most influential copper trader in the world. Then another rice door slid aside.

From behind the wall appeared the mild-mannered Fujiyama who proceeded to sit down opposite the three westerners. The old woman started to pour each man seated around the table a cup of Japanese tea. Still the men sat in silence. Fujiyama said nothing.

When the woman had finished pouring the tea, she bowed to each of the men and made her way backwards to the rice-paper door which opened. When she was gone the door slid back into place. Fujiyama held his hands out face up in a welcoming gesture, at this signal all four men in black bowed and stepped backwards through the rice-paper doors behind them, leaving the three westerners and Fujiyama alone in the room. The westerners eyed the men in black with a certain amount of discomfort.

'Thank you, each of you, for coming to visit me here so far out of the way.' Fujiyama finally spoke, breaking the ice. He had a soft voice but spoke in a very deliberate manner. It had the desired effect as people strained hard to hear every word he said. He could rest assured that they were concentrating. 'We can be assured of total privacy in this building. It belongs to my Yakuza friends. Don't let the men who were standing in the corners of the room unnerve you. They are Yakuza, of course, but they are here only to protect us.' He didn't bother to introduce the men sitting opposite him. Introductions were not necessary in this situation. All the men had known each other through their various business dealings for close to ten years.

Fujiyama took a long slurp from the cup of Japanese tea, motioning the others to do so as well. Murphy sipped his tea, constantly eyeing the other men around him suspiciously: it was his nature. Richard Wilmont slurped his tea gracefully, although he didn't like the taste at all, it was nothing like Earl Grey. Bridge guzzled his like a beer before slamming the cup triumphantly down on the table as if it were some sort of race.

Fujiyama began once again in a very soft, very precise manner. 'Now, you may be wondering why I summoned you all here?'

Bridge felt a sudden urge to scream 'No shit, Sherlock!' but managed to restrain himself to a gentle nodding like the other two men.

'Well,' Fujiyama continued, 'I have a proposal to put to you gentlemen which I think you will all find rather favorable.'

'Fire away,' Murphy said, clearing his throat.

'Yes, let's hear it,' Wilmont chimed in.

'Well, I have known each of you gentlemen for some time now. I know you all operate within the bounds of good business practice,' Fujiyama chose his words deliberately. It was a euphemism for saying that he knew they were all involved in some form of bribery to win business contracts. In Asia it was common business practice. In Africa and South America it was the only way to win lucrative contracts from state-owned enterprises, 'gratitude payments' they are called. In the U.S.A. and Europe this practice was illegal. They had all offered Fujiyama these so called 'incentives' to trade with their respective companies over the years. 'I have a plan that will make us all very wealthy men. Wealthy beyond your comprehension.'

All three men sitting opposite him were mesmerized by the quiet charisma of the Japanese man. He saw their eyes light up at the prospect of money. He knew that they would all respond favorably to what he was about to put to them. He would never have invited them to his inner sanctum if he had a smidgen of doubt that they would accept his proposal. Rejection would mean certain death anyway, but he had read these men well. They would bend and sway in the breeze for money. Greed was their motivation.

Over the course of the next half hour or so, Fujiyama revealed his plan to the three gentlemen, who sat there silent and spellbound. It was a simple plan really, nothing too complex. Together they would execute what would be the biggest fraud in human history. With no victim, and no evidence of a crime being committed, no one would ever come looking for them. It was the perfect crime.

When he finished detailing the plan to the other men in the room, Fujiyama clapped his hands together. The rice-paper wall slid open and the old lady shuffled in once again. This time she carried a bottle of sake and four glasses, which she placed on the table before shuffling back out of the room and sliding the wall shut.

Fujiyama poured four glasses of sake and distributed a glass to each man. Throughout the proceedings they had all sat and listened in stoic silence. They all had plenty of questions that would need answering, but they knew that Fujiyama would fill them in on the finer points individually at some later date. None of them needed any convincing whatsoever that this was the greatest opportunity ever to present itself to them. Fujiyama had been correct in his assumption. They were all driven by greed. He raised his glass into the air.

'Gentlemen, let us drink to our success in this venture.'

In unison they all raised their glasses and drank.

Fujiyama removed a small case from his inside jacket pocket. From it he produced three gold, rhombus-shaped pins. He got up and walked around to the other side of the table.

'I have a gift for each of you, gentlemen. Wear it on your lapel always as a symbol of our unity.'

As Fujiyama said this, Murphy saw that the Japanese man was wearing one on his lapel. It was the same one that the men standing in corners of the room had been wearing when he arrived.

'It is the symbol of my Yakuza clan.' Fujiyama continued, 'You are all now members of the Yamaguchi-gumi syndicate. As long as you wear this pin you will be safe. You men are now all members of a very special club.'

The Copper Club was born.

April, 1995

'Would you place your seats in the upright position and secure your tray tables for landing.' The voice came over the intercom. 'The temperature in London is a mild five degrees Celsius and the local time is 6.45 a.m.'

Mike sat upright and prepared himself for landing. He peered out the window, hoping to catch a glimpse of something, but the dull, gray, cloudy weather, which is London, prevented him from seeing anything.

If Mike was asked to describe what London was like to anyone back home he would in all honesty reply with a single word – *gray*. The weather was gray. The people were gray. The buildings were gray. The service was gray. The overcast, often drizzling, weather has a lot to do with the miserable attitudes of most Englishmen, Mike thought to himself. Well, that was his first impression at least. London was gray.

Mike arrived at the Savoy around 9.30 a.m. The traffic coming into London on that Monday morning was not particularly heavy, but all the same it took him close to two hours to get to his hotel in the peak traffic. The one good thing about England was the cabs. The black cabs were big and generally clean, but most importantly, the cab drivers in London knew where the hell they were going and spoke English even if they had a cockney accent that was hard to understand. They had to do a two-year course called 'The Knowledge', and pass it. Now, New York cabbies could learn a lot from them.

Mike liked the forecourt of the Savoy as it was the only street in London where cars drive on the right-hand side. It made him feel at home, right up to the point where the top-hatted attendant opened the taxi door for him.

The porter showed Mike into his room on the second floor. This was going to be his home for the foreseeable future, as Mike never planned his life more than a few weeks in advance. That way he would not have trouble changing his mind. It was pointless to plan things too far in advance, he figured, as you always ended up having to change them anyway. The porter opened the door and ushered Mike into his new abode.

The room was huge, a suite no less. Either way it was much bigger than any of the rooms in which he had previously been housed at the hotel. He thought it must be a mistake, but kept his mouth firmly shut. The company is paying, he rationalized to himself. One of the big 836 spring mattress beds dominated the far end of the room. The furniture looked old, the sort that you would find at your grandparents' place. Two chairs and a coffee table sat on one side of the bed. On the other side sat a chair by a mirrored table. It must be a dressing table, Mike guessed. Beside it, a long table ran the length of the room. On it sat a phone. Mike could see the spare phone jacks into which he could plug his computer. In the other corner of the room a television sat atop a mini-bar cabinet. At least Mike had the essentials, a refrigerator full of beer, a phone, MTV, CNN and room service. Along the length of the other wall ran a set of wooden cupboards. Mike didn't own enough clothes to fill even half of them and he liked to travel light. Mike was not fond of collecting rubbish. At least once a year he would rid himself of all the clothes that had not been worn more than three times in the previous year. It was a disciplined way of keeping himself uncluttered.

The porter had placed Mike's bags on the small fold-out luggage table. Mike continued to familiarize himself with his new surroundings, oblivious to the porter who was waiting like an obedient dog for a biscuit. He flicked the light switch at the end of the room and proceeded through the doorway into the bathroom. It was massive. It had a bath/shower with a huge watering-can style showerhead. Beside the bath were two identical marble basins. A *his* and *hers* bathroom, thought Mike to himself, how quaint. Mike made his way back into the main room and passed the expectant porter a five pound note. Mike stared briefly at this strange currency, it was much more colorful than the greenbacks he was used to, but still it was going to take some getting used to. The porter thanked him and quickly removed himself from the room, closing the door behind him.

Mike didn't bother to unpack, instead he dived across the bed and grabbed the phone. He immediately called Simon Anderson in the office. Mike was as keen as mustard to get a handle on this new market. He had never traded base metals before, but Anderson had convinced him that he would take to it like a duck to water. Mike was going to attack this new arena with gusto.

'Simon. It's Mike here.'

'How was your flight?' Anderson asked.

'The usual red-eye, nothing much to report.'

'So where are you now?'

'I'm at the Savoy.'

'Doing it tough I see.' Anderson jibed.

'Yep, roughing it to the max.' Mike laughed. He carefully eyed the various call buttons that existed on the wall beside the bed. 'I'm going to take a shower and then come straight into the office.'

'Take your time.' Anderson responded. 'It's a very quiet Monday morning market here. Tell me, have you been down to the LME floor yet?'

'No. Not yet'

'Well, rather than coming straight into the office, I want you to go down to the LME. It's off Leadenhall Street. I'll have one of our guys, Mark Thornton, go down there to meet you at midday. It is a good opportunity for you to see the floor before you get stuck up here in the office all day. It will help you visualize what is going on down there.'

'Okay cool.' Mike replied.

'See you this afternoon.' And Anderson hung up.

Mike felt a little deflated. He was raring to go straight to work. Maybe he could catch a catnap before heading out. At least he would be fresh for the afternoon. But try as he might, there was no way that he would drift off to sleep. He was far too pumped for that to happen.

Mike was early, something that was totally out of character for him, but he was excited. It would be about twenty minutes before the guy from Nelson Smith arrived to meet him. But Mike didn't want to waste time. Instead, he made his way up to the visitors viewing platform at the London Metal Exchange. The guy meeting him, Mark Thornton, would find him easily enough.

Mike pressed his face up against the glass and peered down into the LME. From the raised viewing platform he could see everything that was going on below. The trading floor was dominated by a huge, circular, red leather couch upon which all the ring dealers sat. Behind them stood the floor clerks who relayed the prices to the phone clerks who, in turn, relayed the current prices to the traders sitting in offices near and far. It was the strangest form of open outcry trading Mike had ever seen. He had been down to the floor of the NYMEX, the New York Mercantile Exchange, and to the CBOT, the Chicago Board of Trade.

Both these exchanges were open outcry, but all the traders stood in a pit with various tiered levels that looked like the bleachers at a football game. They were never seated on big leather couches. Only in England, thought Mike. But the contrasts didn't end there. On the LME all the traders, clerks, and phone clerks had to wear a full suit and tie at all times which, when compared to the slovenly dress of the traders on the U.S. exchanges, seemed a touch excessive. Either way it seemed to work in an orderly fashion.

The modern-day LME can trace its origins back to the 19th century. The Industrial Revolution meant that the U.K. was the most advanced country in the world. Vast quantities of ores were being imported from around the globe. Merchants were faced with not knowing what the price of the ores that they had purchased would be when their ship reached England many months later. This placed them at considerable risk. The advent of the steam ship and intercontinental communications via telegraph meant that arrival dates of vessels became more predictable. Merchants were now able to sell their cargo of metal for a forward delivery date at a fixed price, thus protecting themselves from price fluctuations during the intervening period of the voyage.

The opening of the Suez Canal in 1869 cut the delivery time for tin from Malaya to three months. This matched the time for delivery of copper from Chile. From this developed the unique concept of trading for three-month forward delivery. The three month contract that exists today on the LME is the most widely traded.

The LME is located in the heart of the city of London on Leadenhall Street. Trading in LME deliverable contracts takes place on a twenty-four hours a day basis through the Far Eastern, European and U.S. timezones. None the less, the lion's share of trading takes place during the few hours a day that the Exchange floor itself is open in London. The whole world waits with baited breath to see what happens during the 'rings', the five minute bursts of trading in the various base metals that take place on the exchange floor.

The day is divided into the morning and afternoon sessions in which all the base metals are traded. Copper, aluminum, lead, tin, nickel, and zinc are all traded on the LME along with aluminum alloy. There are two rings traded for each metal in the morning session and two rings in the afternoon session. Each session is finished with a 'kerb' trading session, when all metals are traded simultaneously. Mike was used to the U.S. exchanges, where the contracts were traded constantly across the whole day, not just in five-minute bursts. As a copper trader on the LME floor, you sit on your ass for five minutes, four times a day and get paid like a king. What a life, Mike thought to himself, only Mike Tyson is on a better deal.

The LME provides an arena where producers, consumers, traders, and speculators can trade futures and options on the various base metals. Producers and consumers 'hedge' their future metal exposures, by establishing a price for forward material and thus protecting themselves from price fluctuations in the interim. The concept of 'hedging' is the reason for the existence and development of the futures markets around the globe. Mike liked this aspect of his new job. For the first time in his life he was going to be trading real commodities, not financial futures. Raw commodities that could be delivered and made into useful objects.

He looked back down into the Exchange, pressing his face right up against the glass and cupping his hands around his face to reduce the glare. He could see the traders in the ring, arms waving, trading books in hand, the clerks behind them making signals with their hands to the phone clerks in the booths. It looked like some bizarre mating ritual being made by backhand, overhand, double underhand gripped wankers. It was a familiar yet foreign sight to behold. It brought a smile to his face.

'You must be Mike?' An inquisitive voice came over Mike's right shoulder.

'Yeah, Mike Kelly, pleased to meet you.' Mike peeled himself away from the glass and turned around to face the rather robust frame of Mark Thornton, his right hand outstretched. Thornton was not what Mike had expected. He was a tall, balding fellow with round-framed spectacles which made him look like a schoolmaster, not a trader. His mannerisms made him come across in a very shy and retiring fashion. Mike guessed that he was in his mid-thirties.

'Pleased to meet you,' Mark answered, gripping Mike's hand and shaking it vigorously. 'I run Nelson's floor operations here in London. We don't have a floor operation here on the LME but we have staff on the LIFFE, IPE and the LCE here in London.'

'Great, I'll have to check them out some time then,' Mike replied with all the keenness of a newlywed. He turned back to face the glass and looked once again onto the trading floor of the LME. 'Can you explain to me what is going on here?' Mike asked.

'To tell you the truth,' replied Thornton, 'I am not really too sure myself. Obviously you have the copper ring trading right now and on that screen on your left you can see the prices that are trading in cash and three months.'

Mike realized from that moment that the man in front of him was definitely not a trader but a career manager. Mike had seen that so often in his very short life as a trader – managers who were not traders, who had no idea about trading. But on the flip side of the coin, a lot of traders could not manage their way out of a wet paper bag. Either way it is a recipe for disaster, Mike thought, managers who have no idea of the real risks that their traders are undertaking. That was the reason for the Barings debacle, no doubt, and the Joe Jett scandal at Kidder Peabody. It was like a time bomb ticking away in a lot of trading operations around the globe.

Trading on the floor reached a fever-pitched crescendo as the morning's second copper ring came to a close. The noise, a gaggle of nonsensical screaming to the uninitiated, such as Mike, was perfectly understandable to the ring dealers who made records of the trades that had just completed in the little notebooks on their laps. A bell sounded the cessation of trading for the ring. The clerks checked that they had all the trades done by their trader, then scuttled around the outside of the ring, confirming these trades with the clerks of the other trading houses. The people on the phones relayed the closing stages to their listeners and confirmed the deals done with them during the course of the ring. The ring dealers met in committee to decide the official closing prices for cash and three months on which much of the world's trade in metal is based.

Mike turned back to face Thornton. 'I think I'll head back to the office now? I've seen enough for one day. Thanks for taking the time out to come done here and show me about.'

'No problems, Mike, and welcome to London,' replied Thornton.

'Thank you,' Mike smiled, a warm broad smile.

Mike sat down in his new chair. It would be his home for a good twelve hours a day, so he was fortunate that it was comfortable. He fiddled for a few minutes with the height adjuster to get the chair to the right position. Directly in front of him was a relatively new Pentium P.C. Through this P.C. he was able to access a multitude of information services such as Reuters, Knight-Ridder, and

Telerate. Also at the same terminal, he had access to Word and Excel along with an e-mail tool. To Mike's right there was a dedicated Reuters terminal showing the 'ring' page which displayed the last three month prices shown by various trade houses for each of the base metals. To his left there was a space big enough to fit another Reuters terminal. Mike would ensure that there was a Reuters dealing 2000 system installed in that space, then he could rap with his friends as well as conduct business from his new station.

He looked along the length of the desk. Screen after screen after screen dominated the landscape. Bits of paper and keyboards littered the desktops in a form of chaotic order that was repeated on every trading desk across the trading floor. Mike had already been given the grand tour of the place a couple of weeks before when he was on one of his familiarization tours. Across the sea of screens he could see the hives of activity and inactivity. Some traders read newspapers, others ate their lunch, some stood waving and screaming. The usual stuff.

To Mike's left sat his new boss, Simon Anderson. Anderson liked to sit on the desk despite the fact that he had a comfortable office about thirty feet away. He wanted to be close to the action and the information flow which was vital to his business's success. He was a hands on manager, something with which Mike felt very comfortable. On Mike's right sat Steve Faulkner. Steve was a fair bit older than Mike, his graying hair and steel-framed glasses made him look older than he really was. It was the product of too much stress. Steve ran the base metals option books at Nelson Smith. He had joined in the week prior to Mike so he too was still finding his feet. Steve had an engineering degree from Princeton and an M.B.A. from Wharton. He had spent four years working as an actuary before entering the world of investment banking. Hell, he had even been an amateur chess champion during his college days. What a geek! Mike shuddered at the thought. Steve was a very analytical type, almost risk averse, Mike had summed him up on their first meeting. It would be a very good match for the desk. Steve would temper Mike's enthusiasm to dive in at the deep end on certain trades, which in the long run would save them a lot of money. Steve was a good risk manager but too indecisive to be a great trader.

On the other side of the desk sat the guys involved in structured marketing and trading sales. They were a mixed bunch. The structured products marketers were primarily a combination of rocket scientists and the smoothest of talkers. The trading sales staff consisted of two 'LME geezers'. The LME geezers were an undying bunch. They inhabited the exchange floor, the brokerage firms, and the offices of many of the investment banks that had recently tried to gain a foothold in the world of base metals. The more senior of the two LME geezers was Roland Walker. Rolo as he was called came from the Jurassic era of base metals. He had done the full LME merry-go-round having worked at just about every shop there was in the market. He knew everyone in the market and drank with them all regularly. It was the typical LME existence. They tended to work for a firm for no more than two years before moving onto the next. It was a world of mates, incompetence, and ignorance. But this was not apparent until the investment banks started to enter the market and decipher their language. They passed themselves off as 'LME experts' but some of them even made fruit truck drivers look like nuclear physicists. It turned out that these LME experts really knew very little at the end of the day. Mike knew that the days of this undying breed of LME geezers were indeed numbered. Natural selection would run its course eventually. He would just have to bide his time and nature would do the rest.

Rolo sounded extremely knowledgeable on the base metals markets to the uninitiated, but under the surface he was a Neanderthal clinging onto the old LME way of life like so many of the other geezers in the market. Resistant to change in the extreme he, like the rest of the geezers, blamed all ills on the investment banks who were killing the commission system in the market and trading with people at either reduced commissions or for free. They were going to kill the fattened cows of the LME and take away their livelihoods. Rolo's value lay in his connections in the market. He had been around for ever. He new everyone in the market and for a new kid on the block like Mike he was a source of invaluable information.

Beside the geezers on the sales side of the desk sat the structured products guys. They were an eclectic bunch. Rocket scientists, now popular with all investment banks, were there to create new and wonderful derivatives products to sell to clients. These products were impressive pieces of work indeed. They seemed to give the customer a great deal and, provided they were priced correctly, they had handsome edges built in that would fatten the purse of any investment bank. Along with the rocket science geeks sat the smooth talkers. These guys would stroke the egos of the customers, wine them, dine them, and accompany them on golfing days out and other corporate piss takes. Theirs was a lifestyle of indolence, as they were hardly ever in the office doing any tangible work.

There was one guy whose nickname was Air Miles, for obvious reasons. Air Miles was never in the office, he was always off on one of his many junkets to exotic locations. It always amazed Mike that no one ever volunteered to go to conferences in Brussels, but the trips to Venice, Rio, the Bahamas, and Miami were always booked solid. As far as

Mike was concerned, going to a conference in Venice or the Dubai Open golf classic was the furthest thing from working that there was. These guys were just another mouth for his trading revenues to feed. Why on earth did they need so many of these structured guys?

The head of the structured products group, Paul Watson, was the smoothest talker of them all. This guy could really sell oil to the Arabs and ice to the Eskimos. His reputation was huge. He had just signed a commodity-linked finance deal that would net the firm a cool thirty million dollars over the next five years provided that the traders could manage the risk effectively. This was the only reason for the existence of the structured guys. If they could pull off even one or two big deals in a year then the rest of them could feed off of the carcass for years to come – such is the nature of the jungle.

Watson was the kind of guy who could pull a deal out of thin air, but his sincerity seemed fake, he came across as smarmy. Mike was always wary of Watson because of this. You had to be wary even in polite conversation. Mike had seen these guys in action before at Henderson Meyer. Watson was a shark and you could never be sure of when or where he was setting himself to strike. For that reason Mike would always keep his distance in a conversation. He was forever mindful that Watson could play one of those *jedi* mind tricks on him like he did to so many clients and he wouldn't even know it until it was too late.

The first day flew by rather uneventfully for Mike. He spent much of the day down in personnel filling out various forms, signing declarations, and taking care of all the admin. and paperwork that is necessary for any new job. Mike hated this type of stuff, he just wanted to trade. Nelson Smith was a behemoth with tons of red tape and for Mike this was to be very trying indeed. He also took the opportunity to find out what he had to do to get his corporate Amex card, mobile phone, and pager – the essentials in life. Life without them had been tough, but soon they would be back in his possession and he would be able to relax again. He felt naked without them.

As the time drew nearer to the copper contract's close on Comex in New York, which was 7 p.m. London time, Simon Anderson walked out of his office and wandered across to the desk.

He turned to Mike and Steve, 'Hey, guys, you got any plans for tonight?'

Both Mike and Steve knew that Anderson knew the answer to this question. When asked by your new boss, the answer is always, no, and both replied, 'No!' almost in unison.

'Great, I'll book us a table at La Pont de la Tour, just down by Tower Bridge, we can go there straight from work and grab a bite to eat.'

'Sounds good to me,' Steve added.

'Yep, fine by me,' Mike chimed in. He figured it would be better than going home to his hotel and ordering room service, as room service was always far from anything to write home about.

The three men stepped out of the cab down by Butlers' Wharf. The area surrounding the wharf comprises mainly warehouse apartment conversions and offices. Trendy, but devoid of much real nightlife, Mike thought to himself. He would strike this area off his list of suitable accommodation right there and then. The lights of the city flickered across the water, illuminating the Thames. Anderson paid the cab driver whilst Mike and Steve milled around by the side of the cab waiting for him. As the cab pulled away Anderson motioned the other two down the cobblestoned alley way in front.

They stood waiting for their table in the bar area of La Pont de la Tour. With its clean lines, vibrant colors and poor acoustics, this was not the place for an intimate dinner but it had a good menu none the less. The maître d', impeccably groomed with classic Scandinavian looks led them to their table in the more sedate restaurant area. Mike and Steve looked at each other for a second, and smiled, before they took their beers with them and followed the girl, almost entranced.

When they were all seated with their menus and had ordered another round of drinks, Anderson began.

'So what are your first impressions of London, Mike?'

'Well, the maître d,' Mike began flippantly, 'she's passable.'

Anderson smiled.

'Yeah, she's pretty cute.' Steve concurred.

'Maybe we should wave her in for the boys later on,' Anderson laughed. 'What did you think of your trip down to the floor today?'

'Well, I must say I have never seen a floor like it before. I mean they sit down for one thing, and they wear suits. Could you imagine the guys down on the Comex or the Board of Trade wearing full suits and sitting on their butts to trade? And I can say with all honesty that I couldn't understand a damn thing this afternoon when I was listening to the floor commentary, it was all Greek to me.'

'Yeah, I wish they would speak English,' Steve added.

'You'll get used to it soon enough,' Anderson consoled them, 'but it may take a few months. Just be patient.'

'This market offers amazing opportunities for smart guys like yourselves,' Anderson said as eased himself into his seat. 'These geezers down on the floor are clueless. Once you get a handle on the lingo then you'll be able to find so many ways to make money out there. The market is volatile and the spreads are wide still. There is a lot of fat out there on the cows that we are going to slaughter. There are also a few structured deals in the pipeline which will take the profit and loss pressure off you guys whilst you find your feet.'

'I agree with you there,' Steve chimed in, 'these geezers are clueless, but the same clueless guys have left us with a ticking time bomb in our option book and most likely in every option book in the market.'

Anderson nodded in agreement, 'Why don't you explain the scenario to Mike to bring him up to speed.'

'Well, it's simple. These geezers have been selling downside puts to U.S. copper producers, which give them the option to sell copper at around $1.10 a pound, although that in itself is not the problem. The problem is that they have sold so many of these options and have been giving them away for basically nothing. They are all revaluing their books with a flat volatility curve at fourteen percent, which is ridiculous. The real volatility is somewhere around twenty-one percent, these guys aren't recognizing the massive skew on the downside, they aren't using vol. wings. No one will sell these strikes inter-bank, they will only sell it to their customers so there is no way to cover the position. If the market were to take a dive, all the option traders would have to sell the market to hedge their positions which would send the market into a tail spin. The potential for a catastrophic move is enormous. As I said, the guys who sold these options before I arrived left a ticking time bomb in our book. I am still trying to assess the best way to try and immunize our book, but we are going to take a massive hit, somewhere around seven or eight million dollars. If the markets were to move dramatically lower it could be way more than that.'

Mike stared, his face aghast.

'But we have about fifteen million in reserves slated away for such a situation,' Anderson added quickly to placate the worried look on Mike's face.

'The bottom line is, we are going to take a serious hit because of these Johnsons who worked here before us. They were a bunch of fucking morons!' Steve started to sound a little agitated.

'What you have to understand is that these guys had almost exclusive access to a client from whose business they made about eighty million bucks. They had access to the buyer in the biggest bull market that had been seen in years. You didn't have to be Einstein to make a buck in a bull market. They made so much money that they didn't care what they were doing,' Anderson tried to calm the situation.

'They had no idea what they were doing,' Steve retorted.

'You're right, they thought they were legends because the money was rolling in, when in actual fact they were completely clueless. That's why I hired you guys. If these guys can make eighty million bucks and be completely clueless, imagine what a couple of smart guys like yourselves could do in this market,' Anderson's face glowed with excitement.

'Yeah, but we would need the same bull market and the same type of business that they saw to replicate the conditions.' Steve fiddled with his cutlery, 'That bullish round table article in Barron's surely marked the top in the market earlier this year. You had the top guys at Goldman, Stanley, and J.P. Morgan talking about base metals going to the moon. Whenever people start going on record saying that this commodity or that stock is going to go to the moon, then you should be getting out. The only person not in the market yet is the fool and if you don't know that, well you are the fool. I figure that the best the market will do this year is go sideways to lower.'

Mike nodded in agreement, 'Technically speaking too, the charts seem to point to much lower prices over the next year since that major uptrend line was broken.'

Anderson straightened himself in his chair, 'Okay, since we all seem to be in agreement that the market is headed lower. If the market does go lower we are going to suffer the most pain in our option book, so what are we going to do to hedge ourselves against this possibility. That's what I want you guys to think about. I want you to come up with a plan to clean up this mess we have been left with. In the meantime, let's order some dinner, I hear the steak with Béarnaise sauce is awesome.'

The three men ordered and over the course of the meal and a couple of bottles of red wine, Anderson tried explaining the dodgy nature of the market of which they were both now a part. He was frank and pulled no punches. Everything he was going to tell them was strictly off the record. It was between them and to go no further.

Anderson began his tale. He went over the history of the desk in detail. The commodities department of Smith Brothers had always been a retail brokerage outfit. The guys were just desk jockeys. They filled orders, had long lunches and schmoozed and boozed frequently with clients, trying to get some scraps of business. The desk numbered close to thirty for what was essentially a six or seven-man operation. For many years the desk had just scratched its way through covering salaries and expenses, never turning any real profits.

All this had changed when they started to deal with Fujiyama and the immense Yamamoto corporation. Then the money started to fall from the sky. A physical trader who had worked for a German operation came to them with a proposal. He would bring them Fujiyama's business on a commission basis. It was a slam dunk. They made money hand over fist. The desk made close to eighty million dollars in the space of a year. These guys thought they were legends when in fact only two or three guys were doing any real work. The only problem was that there was very little regulation of their activities and no one to watch over them.

The head of the desk, Clive Palmer, was a consummate bullshitter. He could schmooze clients like no one else. He was prepared to go one step further than anyone else to get the business, he was prepared to bend the rules a little to get things done. Operating in that gray area much of the time, he was able to secure a lot of business as the metals market was full of dodgy characters. Well respected in the marketplace, he had retained his position during the merger of Nelson Prescott Securities and Smith Brothers and was made head of the newly formed Nelson Smith Securities commodities department in London. The move took the brokerage operation out of the private client area and into the arena of investment banking.

The problems for Palmer started almost immediately. The risk management team for Nelson Smith moved in to look at the systems in place in the commodities division. They were appalled at the situation that presented itself. There were virtually no controls in place. Palmer had been running the show like some cowboy in a spaghetti western. The possibility of a disaster was huge. Then some irregularities with the year-end position reporting were brought to the internal auditors' attention. The gray, not to say, nefarious, business practices that had made Palmer such a hit with some of his customers had finally caught up with him. Apparently he had parked some of his positions with a client over year-end to inflate the balance sheet. He was promptly fired for cause.

Anderson had been brought in to rectify the situation. His task was immense. The commodities department had to make the leap from the filling of orders to commodity-linked financing and exotic products. Entering a virtually systemless environment, he had a most uncooperative team with which to work. To a man they remained loyal to

Palmer. It was an uphill battle from day one. Anderson saw the business from their biggest client wane very quickly as he refused to do any of the gray transactions that Fujiyama requested. The old crew blamed the downturn in business on Anderson's inflexible attitude. Anderson did things by the book and could not be swayed for one second from that path. A man of integrity, a man not prepared to bend or stretch the rules for anyone at any time, Anderson was not the type of person who Fujiyama wanted to do business with. In fact, Anderson said he was sure that Fujiyama had tried to discredit him in the marketplace.

One by one the old crew started to leave. Anderson would have gladly nuked the lot of them on day one. Starting with scorched earth would have been a much easier task for him than trying to pander to a bunch of useless morons such as those who worked on the desk. He wouldn't have given fifty cents for the lot of them. The only thing that had prevented him from firing them all was some archaic clause in their contracts. Most of the geezers on the desk had been there for ever and it would have cost a fortune to fire them all. So for Anderson it was a war of attrition, General Westmoreland and Field Marshall Haig would have been proud of both his tactics and results, for within four months he had achieved his objective. The last of the old crew was gone and all had been replaced by people of his own choosing. The ranks had thinned to seven from the original thirty. The seven new guys could do the job of the thirty who had worked there prior to the Anderson era. The big plus was that the new guys could do a whole lot more.

Anderson had completed his campaign with the acquisitions of Steve Faulkner and Mike Kelly. Now it was time to turn his attention to a new battle. To build his business around the new team that he had assembled. He would now be able to take this business unit to the next level without hindrance. He had assembled like-minded guys who would be loyal to him and fully focused on the prime objective of building a world-beating base metals business. Anderson was very bullish for the prospects of their business.

'I don't get it,' said Mike inquisitively, as he sipped a glass of port, 'If Fujiyama hates your guts, why does he have a forty thousand odd lot position with us?' Mike had seen the position report on all their major customers earlier in the day and the monstrous copper position held by Yamamoto Corporation had amazed him. It represented over one million tonnes of forward copper. The total LME stocks on warrant in warehouses was less then three hundred thousand tonnes.

'It's simple,' Anderson's eyes surveyed the box of cigars held by the Scandinavian maître d' before he chose a big fat Cuban, 'one reason: credit. We have a two hundred million dollar credit line in place with Yamamoto. How many of those LME bucket shops do you think can afford a two hundred million dollar exposure when their paid up capital is only about twenty million bucks? You see, he needs our credit so we have his business here still, but not directly.'

Anderson sat back and the girl flicked a lighter to enable him to light his cigar.

'What do you mean?' Mike asked, as he surveyed the Scandinavian girl more than the box of cigars as she stood beside him.

'Well, the business we see comes directly through International Metals Trading, IMT.'

'I don't follow you,' Mike butted in as he sat back in his chair with his piece of Havana, quickly biting the end off it.

'Let me explain,' said Anderson through the corner of his mouth, as he puffed away happily on his cigar. 'The guys who were here before you arrived, namely Palmer, put together this bizarre deal back in 1993 with IMT and

Yamamoto where IMT would trade in the name of Yamamoto and utilize their credit line.'

'You mean Yamamoto gave IMT power of attorney over their account?' Steve sounded bewildered. 'That doesn't make any sense. Why would a global Japanese trading house let a two dollar start-up company use its credit lines?'

'Exactly!' Anderson sat forward and ashed his cigar into the ornate glass ashtray that the girl had placed beside him. 'What would the Japanese trading house gain by doing this? It seems that the answer they came up with was that IMT has a relationship with producers of physical copper that Yamamoto was not able to trade with directly, such as the Zambians. But IMT didn't have the capital to pull off the deals. So IMT, Palmer, and Yamamoto came up with this power of attorney arrangement. It was signed off by Fujiyama and one of the directors of Yamamoto Corporation who is senior to Fujiyama. Our legal department have been over the whole thing with a fine tooth comb and it's all kosher.' Anderson leaned forward, beckoning the others to do the same. He looked carefully about the room before continuing, his voice lowered to a whisper. 'But between you, me, and the gatepost, I don't like the smell of it. I think there was something dodgy going on with the whole deal, but as I have no proof I can't be seen talking about it on the desk. Yamamoto is a big customer of Nelson Smith in areas other than copper. They do huge business in the bond market, so it's not worth rocking the boat. As long as the legal people say everything is okay, I don't have any choice but to go ahead and trade with them no matter how bad it smells to me. But I tell you it smells. This whole market smells. These guys in the copper business are as bent as a three dollar note. The LME geezers are a bunch of barrow boys and thieves who would just as soon as rob you blind first time out as develop a relationship to get your business. I mean, this whole market stinks. Look at Fujiyama, he trades primarily now with two start-up bucket shops which basically have him as their only customer. He seems to do about seventy percent of his trading through IMT and another group here in the U.K. called Wilmont Bridge. Why, I ask you, would the biggest copper trader in the world choose to trade the bulk of his business through two bucket shops? Why wouldn't he use the big investment banks? I mean, I just don't get it.' Anderson's brow creased with concern, 'The only reason I can see is that there are big brown paper bags going his way.'

Mike looked at Steve, who was looking straight back at him, and wondered if it was the red wine talking. They had drunk quite a bit that night and it was clear to Mike that Anderson was not a seasoned drinker. If drinking was a sport, Anderson would have been a serious benchwarmer.

Anderson took another gulp of his port and continued his tirade. 'It's just my theory and you will never hear me saying anything to that effect on the desk and I don't ever want to hear you saying anything similar. I just wanted you to know my feelings on this market. I am sure there are plenty of opportunities in this market for an honest business run by a group of smart, like-minded guys. You just have to look at the geezers on the floor, their stupid haircuts and their penchant for a beer at lunch to know that none of them knows how to run a serious business. That's where you guys can really add some value, in building a serious business with none of this dodgy shit. Frankly, I couldn't care less if we didn't see any business from Yamamoto if it involves anything that could even be remotely construed as less than one hundred percent kosher.' Anderson stubbed out his cigar forcefully with his thumb and forefinger as he finished. Then he slumped back into his chair like a man relieved of a serious burden.

Both Mike and Steve nodded in agreement with their new chief, but secretly Mike was already harboring fears about what he had got himself into. An uncomfortable feeling filled the pit of his stomach. Maybe he really had made the wrong decision in leaving the relative security of Henderson Meyer. What had he been thinking? Only time would tell.

May, 1995

Stanley Wong sat back in his chair, which squeaked loudly, the broken left armrest hanging limply, a testament to its age. Like so many things in Beijing, his chair needed replacing, but who was Stanley to complain, he had the best that life in the growing capital could offer. A senior trader for the Chinese National Metals Trading Authority, C.N.M.T.A., an arm of the government Chinese National Import and Export Corporation, Stanley was responsible for managing the non-ferrous metal requirements for the Chinese government. With this position came a salary, poor by western standards especially when measured against his counterparts at the U.S. investment banks, but none the less a salary which enabled Stanley and his young wife Lee-Nah to live a life of comparatively decadent luxury in the Chinese capital.

With a population of 1.2 billion, China is increasingly a key player in the global commodity markets as it aims to improve housing and business conditions. The Chinese economy uses an astounding one million metric tonnes of copper per annum, making it a major net importer of the red metal as it produces only half that amount locally. A booming Chinese economy means increasing reliance on imports of raw materials such as copper in order to cope with the enormous demand created by the rapidly expanding infrastructure. A better economy means more income and an improved diet and thus massive amounts of grain are needed to feed the livestock, hogs, and poultry to satisfy the rising middle class's new culinary appetite.

Rumors of Chinese participation in a market can send it into a spin. The grain markets and cotton tend to move violently whenever there are whispers of Chinese buying or selling being bandied about in the pits. China is set to become the world's biggest consumer of a whole range of raw materials. With that power their trades are carefully monitored by the rest of the world for hints on price direction. Copper was no exception.

These import needs gave Stanley an awesome power in the copper market. Exactly how much copper he would need to import this year was known only to him and a handful of others at the C.N.M.T.A. The rest of the world would be kept guessing as to what he was going to do next. Although speculation was not officially a part of his job description, Stanley was expected to make short-term profits from market fluctuations under the auspices of hedging China's physical needs. He was also expected to guarantee a steady supply of metal to keep up with local demand. Stanley had been bullish on copper prices during the bull market run of 1994 and had amassed a sizable long position at much lower prices, which he had stockpiled along with other strategic metals. By the time the market had topped out in early 1995, Stanley had sold out most of his excess copper requirements, making a tidy profit in the process and elevating himself to the most senior trading role at C.N.M.T.A. By April of 1995 Stanley had turned particularly bearish for copper prices and had started to amass a reasonable short position which he hoped to cover at lower prices as the market headed lower.

Being a consummate trader, Stanley knew how to use China's reputation to influence market psychology. Despite his sizable short position, he was not overly worried about covering his position. He would let it be known through various channels that China was vastly overstocked with copper and would be selling material from its strategic stockpile to take advantage of the current high prices. He would deliver some twelve thousand metric tonnes of physical copper to the LME's Singapore warehouse later that month, the boat was already at sea. The increase in copper stocks and associated rumors would send the market into a freefall as traders around the world would anticipate further arrivals of stockpiled Chinese copper. In the ensuing mêlée he would have no trouble covering his short futures position before the world was any the wiser. It was a masterstroke. A student of Sun Tzu's classic manifesto on the Art of War, he was fully versed in the tactics of deception. To appear weak when strong, to be seen to be retreating when advancing, Stanley could play this game of poker better than anybody.

He sat back in his one-armed chair and gazed out over a hazy Beijing sunset. Despite a decided lack of motorized transport in the Chinese capital, a thick veil of pollution covered the city, choking the last rays of the day's sunlight. A few floors beneath him, an apparently endless sea of black-haired individuals massed its way home in a clutter of bells and bicycles. For Stanley, his long day was far from over. As much of Beijing headed home, the LME's pre-market session in London was just getting under way. Stanley's life of privilege meant spending many lonely nights in a poorly vented office, often sleeping under his desk when the markets were busy. Stanley and two other traders were all that was left in the offices of the Chinese National Metals Trading Authority, the rest of the staff were already a part of the thronging mass below. That was the price of success in the new China and it was something Stanley understood all too well. Besides, he was a born capitalist. Stanley loved the markets and he loved the game.

*

As the masses made their way home in the People's Republic, back in London Mike Kelly ruminated carefully over what to have for breakfast. Would it be the bacon and brown sauce sandwich or would he be healthy and go for the fruit salad for once? It was the most important decision that he had made every morning since coming to London. English bacon was so very fatty, not crispy like American bacon and coupled with the stodgy food and beer that Mike was consuming on a daily basis, London was helping him to pile on the pounds fast.

Having been in London for just over a month, Mike was beginning to find his feet. He had found a flat to rent in Old Church Street in Chelsea, which would be vacant at the end of the month. Despite his initial joy at being able to live in one of the best hotels in the world, Mike had tired of the Savoy rather quickly. The romantic notions of living the high life and being waited upon had faded gradually with each knock at the door and some staff member wanting to turn down the bed or check if he needed clean towels. Mike craved some privacy, some personal space. He wanted to be able to throw a shirt on the floor when he came home and have it lie there for at least twenty-four hours before finding it hanging neatly in the cupboard.

Mike was really looking forward to having his own place again, especially since his new flat was just off the famous King's Road. Within walking distance were great pubs, restaurants, a cinema, and some of the finest shopping in the world. This was the biggest lure for Mike, for with fine shopping came mighty fine women and his numerous jaunts down the King's Road had revealed a bountiful supply. Best of all, the beauties in London were natural, unlike those of the West Coast of the U.S.A. where most were surgically augmented.

London certainly had its advantages, but it surely had some major disadvantages for a trader like Mike. For one, the hours that Mike worked were grueling. At his desk by 7.30 a.m. Mike would be there until the Comex copper contract closed at 7 p.m. He would be there all day, he would consume lunch at his desk. In New York he was always out of the office by 5 p.m. unless it was very busy going into the Asian market. He didn't mind the extra hours but the long days were a constant drain on his body. The other thing that Mike particularly disliked was that the bars shut at 11 p.m. Being a pseudo New Yorker, that was to him the stupidest law of all, but it was probably good for his health.

Mike placed his hands around his stomach and cupped his newfound girth. 'What do you think I should call it?' Mike lay back in an easy rider position with his feet up on the desk as he pondered this rhetorical question.

'Piss or wind,' Andy interjected.

Andy was the desk junior. A very likable fellow with the gift of the gab and a jovial spirit, he had been given an opportunity on the trading desk having worked his way up through the back office support area. Andy was Mike's offsider. Mike had taken him under his wing and would attempt to teach Andy as much as he could about trading. In return, Andy got Mike's breakfast and lunch and he ran Mike's errands as well as taking care of all the paperwork that Mike needed done. It was a symbiotic relationship that Mike didn't abuse.

'Breakfast?' Andy asked in the general direction of the desk. 'Let me guess, Mike. By your unshaven appearance and red eyeballs it's going to be a bacon and brown sauce day.'

'You read my mind, Andy. Whenever you are ready.' Mike pulled a twenty pound note from his top pocket and flicked it casually onto the desk.

As Andy picked up the money and made his way toward the liftwell, Simon Anderson wandered out of his office and over to the desk. The sight of Anderson caused Mike to straighten up immediately and pull his feet off the desk.

'Mike, do your tie up properly! You look like a slob!' The order was fired from Anderson's lips. His expression was grave. He looked more serious than usual. The difference was subtle but Mike had picked it up very quickly.

Mike fumbled about with his tie briefly as Anderson took up a chair beside him.

'What do you think from here?' Anderson inquired in a softer tone, only for Mike's ears. The tone served only to heighten Mike's suspicion that Anderson was troubled by something.

Mike understood immediately that he was being asked about his views on the future direction of the copper market, so he quickly pulled up a copper chart which showed graphically the open, the high, the low, and the close for copper over the past few years. Placing his finger on the screen Mike began, 'You see this line here, which comes in around 2910, well if you break that I can't see any technical support until 2820 and through that level the next stop is 2700. Get through 2910 it's sayonara baby.'

'Where is the market now?' Anderson sounded concerned.

Mike flicked back the page on his screen to Reuters 'ring' page. 'Wolff's showing 2940 at 2960. He's such a Johnson, I bet it's only good for two lots. Whenever you call that guy he says, sorry we just traded there, it's lower now. The real market is more like 2930 bid at 50.'

Anderson looked up across the desk to Steve. 'Steve how long are you if we trade down to 2700 today?' His concern was what would happen to their option book if Mike was right and the market plummeted some two hundred dollars a ton.

Steve glanced down at his reports. 'I would be long four hundred lots if I didn't do anything.'

'What do you think, Mike?' Anderson turned his attention back to Mike who was seated beside him.

Mike could feel the pressure being placed upon his call. 'I'm bearish. If we get through 2910 it will be messy.' Mike could sense where Anderson was going with this.

'Should we have a shot at it.' Anderson seemed almost in two minds for a second. 'I tell you what, let's sell eight hundred lots down to 2900. Let's see where this market wants to go.'

'Okay,' Mike said as he stood up. Although not particularly tall, Mike had a commanding presence when he raised his voice. 'Guys, we are going to go on a run.' His voice boomed across the desk. 'We are going to be selling some copper here. Rolo, any customers of yours likely to be buyers?'

'I'll see, but I think most of them are sellers a little higher up. What level are you looking to sell at?' Rolo replied.

'Try 2920.' Mike fired back. He was now like a general marshaling his troops before the battle would begin. His calm demeanor gave no hint of the storm that was to break.

'Steve, can you get Stanley on for fifty lots?'

'Dave, can you get Rothschilds on for forty lots?' Dave was one of the support guys who sat directly behind the desk.

Andy walked straight into the fray having just returned with Mike's breakfast. 'Andy, put that food down. Get J.P. Morgan on for forty lots of copper.'

'Anderson, can you get Refco on for fifty lots?'

'Who are you getting?' Anderson asked, as he picked up the phone handset to ready himself.

'I'm going to ask Goldman in a hundred,' Mike said sternly, 'and MG in fifty.'

'Nicole, get off the phone and get Rouse on the line for forty lots.' Mike cried out to Steve's new option assistant. Despite being a stunning French blonde, the guys on the desk didn't cut her much slack when it came to business.

'What are we doing? Copper?' Nicole asked timidly, with her unmistakable French accent.

'Yes!' Steve shouted at her. 'If you would stop yakking on the phone to your friends you would know.' You could feel the tension in his voice.

'When I say GO everyone sell copper down to 2920.' Mike picked up his two handsets. 'Okay. Everyone, let's GO!' Mike yelled at the top of his voice.

Simultaneously everyone on the desk hit the button that corresponded with the counterpart they had been assigned to call. A buzz filled the room as they all called out. You could feel the energy level rising.

Mike punched the Goldman line then the MG line. The Goldman line rang only twice before it was answered.

'One hundred copper please?' he said calmly into the Goldman handset before clicking the mute button.

'Hello, fifty copper please?' he said just as calmly into the MG, line all the while listening for the reply from the Goldman line.

'20... 30,' came the reply from Goldman.

'Yours,' Mike said firmly to indicate that he was selling, and he promptly hung up.

'25... 30 for fifty copper,' the MG line replied.

'Yours,' Mike cried again before hanging up. 'Okay. What did everyone do? Make sure you write it down.'

'I sold fifty,' Anderson picked up a writing pad.

'I sold one fifty,' Mike said to Anderson who was scribbling furiously.

'Fifty here,' Steve held up his hand.

'I sold forty lots copper to Rouse at 2927,' Nicole said proudly.

'Andy? Dave? What did you guys do?' Mike cried out.

'I sold forty lots,' Andy said, as he brought Mike's food across to the desk.

'Rothschilds would only do thirty lots,' Dave said despondently.

Rolo shook his head. 'I couldn't find any buyers.'

'Okay.' Anderson was busy tallying up the sales. 'We are in good shape. We got off three hundred and sixty lots. Should we go again? Should we throw some wood at it?' Anderson could smell blood a mile off. He had that unexplainable sixth sense that all great traders have.

The idea of throwing some wood at the market made Mike smile. He imagined Anderson throwing pieces of four by two about the room.

'Let's let the market settle for a second,' Mike cautioned.

After about five minutes Mike rallied the troops once more. 'Okay! Everyone get ready, we are going to sell copper again. This time we are going to sell down to 2910.'

At that moment the outside line that the Chinese traders used started to flash. Rolo answered it immediately. Customers phones never ring twice, well, not for the big guys at least.

Anderson saw the line flashing. 'Wait a second Mike. Let's see what the Chinese want, they may be buyers here. We don't want to run into a wall of buying.'

'One hundred copper for dragon?' Rolo asked as he clicked mute button. With his free right hand he pulled the flesh at the corner of his right eye up at an angle to make a slanty eye, just like cruel children do, just in case Mike wasn't aware of who was on the line. Dragon was their code name for the Chinese. They generally used code names for their customers just in case someone had left a phone line open. You could never tell who might overhear a conversation.

Wolff showed 2920/30 on the 'ring' page on Reuters.

'2910/15' Mike went really low because he was a seller. If the Chinese were really a buyer they would snap his offer up, but Mike had a hunch the Chinese guy would be a seller.

'He says he can see 20/30 in the screen,' Rolo passed on his customer's protest.

A seller, Mike was right. 'Sorry, 2910 is my best bid.' As Mike said this the phone board started to light up. 'I'm out!' He screamed loudly back to Rolo. The Chinese were pasting the market, they were selling everywhere. The market was set for a tumble as dealers scrambled to get out of their position. 'Sell everything you can down to 2890!' Mike screamed to the guys on the desk.' He saw the Goldman line flashing.

Steve picked it up immediately, 'One hundred copper?' he shouted frantically.

With the Chinese selling and stops under 2910 in the market Mike would have to go much lower.

'85... 90' Mike quickly spat out the price.

'Nothing there!' Steve shouted back.

'If you are still there, Dragon can sell you one hundred lots at 2910?' Rolo asked.

'No chance!' Mike shrieked. 'The market is now 2885 at 90. Forget the screens, the market is much lower now.'

'He wants to know who is selling?' Rolo asked with a smile on his face.

'Just say stops being triggered under 2910,' Mike replied. Did this Chinese guy take him for a fool? He knew that the Chinese had probably just pasted about five hundred lots across the market. Mike knew how the Chinese operated and he knew they could not be trusted. How can you trust people from a place where they drove tanks over their own citizens? These guys would sell their grandmothers if they thought they could turn a profit.

Anderson turned to Mike. 'How much did you get off?'

'Looks like we got off another one hundred and forty lots, so we've sold a total of five hundred lots.'

'Okay. Put four hundred lots in the option book and you can run the rest of the short position in the copper book.' Anderson stepped back a few paces and rolled up his sleeves. 'It's time to get down in the three-point,' referring to the American football line-up position. He bent over, placing his clenched fist on the floor, legs astride. 'I can feel a big move coming.'

Anderson was right. Over the course of the day the market saw an onslaught of fund selling as discretionary traders sold copper short and signals went off on computer based trading systems giving sell signals to their traders to exit their stale long positions which added weight to the landslide in prices.

Every time someone called, Mike went low when he made a price. Whenever someone sold him, he made sure he sold it straight out into the market. In doing this, Mike managed to keep his short position which he had initiated around the 2920 level. The market made its low at 2800 before short covering from dealers and a large buyer in the market helped stabilize the price around the 2820 level. The rumor in the marketplace was that Fujiyama was the buyer.

On his short copper position, Mike had made roughly a quarter of a million dollars and Steve's option book had made close to half a million dollars. The desk was up a little shy of three quarters of a million dollars for the day. Cause to celebrate. There would be a large amount of beer today after work, of that Mike was sure.

Just before the end of the day, Anderson called Mike and Steve into his office. He shut the door behind them. With the door closed the room was almost soundproof. He motioned them both to take a seat on the leather couch. Steve sank into the leather couch, but Mike propped himself against the edge of the desk.

'There could be a problem with the Yamamoto account,' he began slowly, his tone grave. 'The guy has a forty thousand odd lot position with us. At twenty-five metric tonnes per lot that is roughly a one million U.S. dollars swing for every one dollar move in the copper price. With the market down close to one hundred and fifty dollars today, Fujiyama has lost close to one hundred and fifty million dollars and that is just with us. Who knows what positions he has on elsewhere?' Anderson's concern filled the small office.

Both Mike and Steve were silent. In all the confusion and excitement of the trading day, they had both forgotten about the sizable position of their and the market's biggest customer.

'What is their credit usage? How close are they to their two hundred million dollar limit?' Mike asked, fidgeting with his hands.

'Well, I have to see the end-of-day report, which we should get in about thirty minutes from the back office, and see how the forward curve pans out, but I think that we will be making a margin call of roughly thirty million dollars. That shouldn't be much of a problem for them. But the problem is that we don't know what their exposure is at other houses and whether they will have to liquidate some of their longs. The danger still remains on the downside. Markets generally move in the direction that will hurt the most people. We have to be wary of a meltdown. In the meantime we will not be taking any new buy orders from Yamamoto Corporation, management here have set a forty thousand lot position limit for their account. I suggest that we play everything from the short side for the time being. How did we do today?'

Mike looked at Steve and then shifted his attention to Anderson, 'We were up roughly three quarters of a buck today.'

'And what's our position now?' Anderson queried with a matter of fact tone. It paid to be rigorous when managing a trading desk's risks.

'The copper book is short one hundred lots and the option book is short two hundred and fifty lots,' Mike answered succinctly.

'So we are in good shape? Anyone for beers?' Anderson posed the rhetorical.

'I thought you'd never ask,' Mike said. Boy did he need a beer.

Over the course of the next week the market did indeed move lower. The copper price moved another 100 U.S.D. lower till it stabilized around the 2700 region. Yamamoto continued to meet its margin calls. There were rumors of massive sales of July put options with 2700 strikes. This had two immediate effects. First, it created an artificial floor for the market as the purchasers of the puts had to buy copper in order to hedge their positions. Second, it crushed volatility in the market causing copper to trade in a thirty dollar range. Yamamoto was rumored to be behind the massive option sales which were routed through the brokerage firm Wilmont Bridge.

Although Nelson Smith saw none of the business directly from Yamamoto and did not deal with Wilmont Bridge, Steve's option book eventually saw a fair slab of the business second and third-hand via other traders in the marketplace looking to get out of some or all of their position. Mike and Steve were left in no doubt as to who was behind the massive option sales or what was the motive behind the sales. Fujiyama was defending his long position by getting longer. Right now he was just holding on against the funds who were short. It was indeed going to be an epic battle.

★

At Singapore's Changi airport, the two men waded their way through to the baggage collection area with the mass of Japanese tourists. Unremarkable in slacks, blazers, and polo tops, they looked like any other Japanese businessmen replete with briefcases, suitcases, and golf clubs. The thing that differentiated these two Japanese businessmen from the crowd was that they both wore small, gold, rhombus-shaped pins on the lapels of their blazers. But the wearing of a small gold pin was not going to draw any undue attention to them. They passed through customs and immigration without drama and were met by another Japanese man who also bore the rhombus-shaped gold pin on his lapel. None of them spoke a word, they just nodded and bowed to each other. The three men made their way to a waiting car and then to the Mandarin Hotel on Orchard Road. It was here that they would wait for further instructions.

The Yamaguchi-gumi clan is Japan's most powerful organized crime syndicate or *Yakuza* clan, as they are known. The Yamaguchi-gumi syndicate controls over two thousand five hundred businesses which have revenues close to a half a billion dollars per annum. Apart from a multitude of legitimate businesses, their interests cover a whole spectrum of nefarious activities ranging from sophisticated gambling and loan-sharking, to narcotics, prostitution, smuggling, pornography, and illegal weapons. They are also involved in political blackmail, extortion, and racketeering by causing trouble at stock holders meetings in a practice known as *sokaiya*. The syndicate is also involved in the rigging of baseball games, horse racing, and public property auctions.

The Yamaguchi-gumi clan operates under a hierarchy that has existed for the Yakuza for over three hundred years. It is based on a *oyabun-kobun* or 'father-child' relationship, which controls the day to day management of the syndicate. The *oyabun* is the 'father' providing advice, protection, and help, while the *kobun* acts as the 'child' swearing unswerving loyalty and service whenever the *oyabun* needs it. This relationship is the basis for the management hierarchy. The most senior *oyabun* is the *kumicho* or supreme boss. Under him are a number of senior advisors, or *saiko kumon*, who manage a number of gangs in the major cities of Japan. These *saiko kumon* have advisors or *kumon*. These men manage a number of gangs in that city and have *shingiin* or counselors who, in turn, manage sub gangs, and so on. The *kumon* have a number of secretaries, accountants, and underlings. In all the Yamaguchi-gumi crime syndicate is comprised of over seven hundred and fifty gangs and has thirty-one thousand members.

Steeped in tradition, the Yakuza operate in a 'noble' fashion. They have a code of chivalry similar to *bushido*, the way of the warrior, which calls upon them to defend the interests of society's weaker members. In the initiation ceremony, the Yakuza exchange cups of sake to symbolize the entrance into the Yakuza and the oyabun-kobun relationship. The ceremony is usually performed in front of a Shinto altar, giving it a religious significance.

The symbol of the Yamaguchi-gumi syndicate is a rhombus-shaped gold pin which is worn on the lapel of their suits. Such is the power of the Yamaguchi-gumi syndicate that the simple showing of this pin can get a member almost anything they want.

*

Fiona Bolton leaned forward, placing her empty glass on the table. She eased herself back into the wicker chair clutching a handful of peanuts that she had taken from a bowl on the table. The Long Bar at the very colonial Raffles

Hotel was abuzz with expats. The Raffles Hotel is one of the more prominent reminders of Britain's once mighty empire upon which the sun never set. Automatic fans in the ceiling swayed slowly from side to side above Fiona's head with monotonous repetition. It had been a long day but her job in Singapore was almost done. Initially she had been told that she would be in Singapore for at least three weeks. Those three weeks had turned into three months. Fiona disliked Singapore immensely. Hot, wet, and so humid, Singapore is an equatorial country with a relatively uniform climate which roughly translates into a one hundred percent chance of uncomfortable weather. You don't go anywhere in Singapore unless there is air-conditioning.

The team from the Serious Fraud Office had almost finished its investigation into the Barings collapse and Nick Leeson's involvement. It turned out that Nick Leeson had control over trading operations and the back office settlements in the Barings Singapore office. This lack of segregation of duties had been responsible in part for the Barings collapse, in addition to upper management's complete incompetence. The method behind his deception was rather simple. An error account, which is not uncommon in most brokerage houses for genuine mistakes, was used as a cover for Nick Leeson's unauthorized trading. The 88888 account held all the errors and the trades that Leeson had done in an attempt to recoup the losses in the error account. Leeson had started with a small, justifiable loss and through dishonesty and incompetence was able to turn this simple error into the eventual collapse of the whole bank. The bigger the loss was, the more he had to win back to get to square one, the more he traded, the more he lost, and so on until he had brought down the whole bank.

The massive margin calls of Lesson's positions on the Simex, the Singapore Futures Exchange, had led Leeson to represent the 88888 account as a client position each night when he called his head office in London to ask for funding. As the positions got larger and larger he had to resort to other ways to finance his positions. He started to sell options, puts, calls, anything that he could gain a decent premium from selling. This had a number of effects. Firstly, it increased his exposures immensely, multiplying his original positions over and over. Secondly, he had crushed the volatility in the market which made selling the options follow a path of diminishing returns in terms of the premium he was receiving. Finally, the sales of these options helped him garner enough cash to cover the ever-growing hole in his balance sheet and keep it concealed from upper management. There was no proof that he had made any personal financial gain from his unauthorized trading. If this was the case, then Nick Leeson was the dumbest man to ever walk the planet.

Fiona had gone over thousands of documents in the past three months. She would be happy to see the back of the Barings case and Singapore especially. There is only so much shopping a girl can do. Apart from shopping, there really isn't that much to do in Singapore. Sure, Sentosa Island, with its dragon park and sandy beach, is fine for a day trip, so is the zoo, but Fiona was really looking forward to returning home to London on Sunday. One of her colleagues brought her another drink, a tall glass of gin and tonic. It was Friday evening at the end of a long week and a very tiresome three months. The fourteen-hour days, poring over countless documents, were starting to take their toll on Fiona. Although she was doing the investigative work that she loved, she was definitely sick of being in Singapore. Maybe it was homesickness, maybe it was the heat, whatever it was she wished she was back in her own apartment in Fulham. She couldn't wait until Sunday.

While Fiona pondered her future back in London, a black Lexus pulled up opposite the Tanjong Pagar container terminal and dimmed its headlights. Tanjong Pagar is one of six terminals operated by the Port Authority of Singapore. At any one time there are eight hundred ships in port as Singapore is the busiest port in the world in terms of shipping tonnage. The men in the Lexus knew this was the terminal at which the cargo would be arriving.

The two men surveyed the area intensely from the comfort of the car. Heavily tinted windows meant that no one could see into the vehicle. Both men wore a pair of AN/PVS-5s, state of the art night-vision goggles. These image intensifying goggles allow the user to see close to one hundred and fifty meters under moonlight conditions. Casting their attention to the main gate opposite them, the men made a note of the terminal's security systems. They noted the ten-foot high wire fence, the video camera mounted on one of the poles at the main gate, along with the guard stationed at the front gate. They also noted the two armed guards in the main office just inside the security gate. When they had finished making their observations, the first man started the ignition and they drove off unnoticed, as they had arrived. Phase one of their mission was complete.

They had completed their reconnaissance of the Tanjong Pagar terminal. They had secured ample warehouse space in one of the Yakuza-owned warehouses located in the tax-free zone at the airport and had assembled a team of dock workers and truck drivers to do all the work. Everything was set for them to complete their mission should it be required of them.

It was now time to wait for phase two.

*

Friday in summer was 'dress-down' day at most investment banks in New York. This tradition had carried itself across the Atlantic to London and the trading floor of Nelson Smith. The guys on the commodity desk were able to wear 'casual' clothes on a Friday. This ostensibly meant a polo shirt or shirt, jacket and trousers. Jeans, T-shirts, and shorts were a definite no-no. This led to a muted, almost cloned look. A blazer, Polo Ralph Lauren shirt, khaki trousers and Timberland boat shoes became their uniform. But on this particular day Mike couldn't find any clean trousers. He hadn't done any dry cleaning or washing in a number of weeks and had run out of clean clothes to wear. Other than wearing a suit he had nothing to wear to work. There was no way he was going to wear a suit to work on a 'dress-down Friday', so Mike, pushing the boundaries as he always liked to do, wore jeans and a T-shirt with a jacket. Besides, he was up close to a million dollars that month already. What were they going to do? Send him home? Hardly likely.

Mike sipped his coffee slowly as the various LME brokers called up to give their predictions for that morning's copper stocks announcement. Twice a week, on Tuesdays and Fridays at 9 a.m. London time, the LME reports the movements of physical metal into and out of its warehouses around the world. Traders speculate prior to the announcements what the numbers will be and position themselves accordingly. As Nelson Smith was not involved in the physical business, Mike didn't care much for the figures themselves, but used the activity of various market participants as his barometer for that morning's price direction. He liked to fade certain geezers and go with others. In his short experience he had worked out who was in the know and who was completely clueless. It was not rocket science. Mike was sure that one of the brokers with whom he traded was slipping brown paper bags to some guy who worked in the warehouses in Rotterdam as they almost certainly knew the stock numbers for aluminum at least one hour ahead of the market. Either way, the dealers and the physical trade followed the stock numbers carefully for hints as to future price direction.

Throughout its history the LME has been a trade-based market with contracts for tangible deliveries. In order to meet this physical aspect of the trade, large stocks of metal are held in various warehouses which are approved by, but not owned by, the LME at selected locations around the world. The delivery of LME contracts is in the form of warrants which are bearer documents entitling the holder to take possession of a specified tonnage of metal at a specific LME-approved warehouse. There are over four hundred approved warehouses and compounds in forty-three locations spanning the U.S.A., Europe, and the Far East.

Warrants are issued by the warehouse companies on receipt of metal. These warrants state the brand, the exact tonnage, the shape, and the location of the metal. They are issued by the warehouse companies once they are satisfied that the metal conforms to the exact specifications set down in contract guidelines by the exchange and is of a brand or production of a producer named in the LME approved list. The choice of warrant for delivery against an LME contract is at the seller's discretion.

Despite the physical nature of metals trading, only about five percent of all LME contracts traded result in physical delivery. The vast majority of contracts traded prove to be of a financial nature in the form of hedging or speculating which are closed out before coming to maturity. As a result, deliveries that do take place either into or out of warehouses strongly reflect the physical market supply and demand.

As Mike sipped his second cafe latte of the morning, the positively obese frame of Nelson Smith's Pat Wagner shuffled its way across the dealing-room floor towards the metals trading desk. Mike looked at his watch, there were twenty minutes till the stock numbers. Heaven help him.

Pat Wagner was Nelson's well respected metals analyst. An affable chap in his late forties with thinning wisps of white hair and thick coke-bottle glasses, he was often quoted in *The Financial Times* and the *Wall Street Journal*. Customers loved to talk to him. Exactly why, Mike couldn't work out. To Mike, Pat was a geezer, and a big fat one at that. His incredibly successful lunching career was evident in his extreme rotundity. His penchant for striped shirts and thick red braces to hold up his trousers was a sickening look. None the less, clients loved to know his ideas on the market, not because he had any real insight into price direction but because he specialized in the geezer-filled world of rumor-mongering. Mike didn't care one second for Pat or his rumors. He figured that if Pat had been a trader he would have been fired long ago as he was incredibly successful at getting the price direction wrong at just the right time. He was the penultimate anti-Midas. It took a certain gift to be wrong so consistently.

'Morning, chaps.' Pat's voice echoed about the desk.

'Morning, Pat,' came Andy's cheerful response. Being the most garrulous person on the desk, Pat tended to migrate towards him in much the same way that the rest of the guys on the desk avoided him.

'So, what are you guys hearing about Chinese copper deliveries into Singapore?' Pat's voice rose slightly as he posed the question.

It was rare for Mike to air his views openly to Pat like this, but this particular Friday he couldn't help himself.

'The whole market is awash with rumors of massive deliveries from the Chinese strategic stockpile. I figure it's all bullshit. The Chinese do this sort of thing in the grain markets all the time. Watch what they are doing not what they let leak. I figure they are really looking to buy. It's a classic head fake.'

'No, I have it on very good authority that the first delivery will take place next Tuesday in Singapore. Somewhere in the region of twenty thousand metric tonnes and that over the next month they will deliver close to one hundred thousand metric tonnes to take advantage of the high price and domestic overstocking.'

'Well, we will see Pat, we will see.' Mike's voice faded away. He remained highly skeptical. He figured the Chinese were heavily short and would deliver a small amount of metal to cause a panic. In the ensuing free-fall they would simply cover their short futures position without delivering any further material. It was as plain as pie to Mike.

*

Back in Beijing, Stanley Wong ate some noodles while he waited for the stock figures to come out. He had been rather nervous over the last couple of weeks owing to the sizable short copper position that he had amassed. The one consolation that he had was that the whole market was awash with the false rumors that he had cleverly disseminated. Stanley was totally confident that the market would panic when the copper started arriving in Singapore. They were not aware that this was the only boatload of copper that would arrive and by the time they found out that it was all a ruse, Stanley would be out of his positions and laughing all the way to the bank.

Just as Stanley finished his noodles the phone rang.

'Hello?' Stanley answered sheepishly, expecting some joker from the LME to be calling him asking about copper deliveries.

The voice at the other end of the line was soft but deliberate, 'Stanley Wong, please.'

'Speaking.' Stanley sounded more than a little confused. It certainly wasn't one of the Essex boys from the LME.

'Hello, this is Satoru Fujiyama of Yamamoto Corporation.'

Stanley knew the name and the reputation of the copper legend, but had never met with him personally. 'Hello, Mr. Fujiyama, what can I do for you?'

'Well, I understand from talk in the marketplace that you are shipping physical material into Singapore as we speak.'

'Yes, that is correct.' Stanley started to wonder where this was leading. He would try to play his cards close to his chest.

'I have an interest from a customer of mine to purchase one hundred thousand tonnes of physical copper in Singapore and was wondering if this might be a perfect fit for your current requirements.'

Stanley's pulse began to race. What was he going to say? Fujiyama was calling his bluff.

'Well, Mr. Fujiyama,' Stanley began slowly, choosing each word carefully, 'I would like to help you out, but the copper that I am shipping into Singapore is set for delivery against short contracts that were entered into many months ago. Unfortunately, I am afraid that at the moment I cannot help you.'

'I see,' Fujiyama replied, although it sounded to Stanley more like 'I see through you.'

'What sort of time frame are you looking at?' Stanley asked, in an attempt to sound more convincing. 'There is a chance that I may have some excess production at the end of this month that I could have shipped to Singapore, or anywhere for that matter.'

'My client is looking for more immediate supplies. But I would be interested in discussing this matter further with you after I have had a chance to speak with my customer. I thank you for your time.'

'I look forward to speaking with you again soon,' Stanley lied.

With that the conversation ended. It had left Stanley with a very empty feeling in the pit of his stomach. Was Fujiyama just trying to suss him out? Did the Japanese trader really have such a large buyer of physical material or was he calling Stanley's bluff? The thought of that made Stanley very uncomfortable. He would rest much easier next Friday when his copper hit the warehouse in Singapore and was reported in the LME stock figures. Then he would be able to cover his short position and breathe easier.

At his home in Tokyo, Fujiyama lit a cigarette. The red tip of his cigarette glowed in the darkness of his room. I've got you, Stanley! he thought to himself, I've got you right where I want you. As he exhaled a billow of smoke filled the room. He reached across his desk for the phone and started to dial.

The phone in the Lexus rang only once. The first man picked it up immediately. 'Hai,' he replied, bowing in deference even though the caller could not see him. The order had just been given for phase two to take place.

★

Mike Kelly and Simon Anderson generally shared a cab to work each morning. Anderson lived in Chelsea about three minutes by car from Mike's flat. As was almost always the case, when Anderson arrived, Mike was furiously trying to get himself dressed. Mike could see the cab outside through the front window. His phone rang. Mike grabbed the phone as he hastily threw on his shirt.

'Hello?'

'The phone in my limo is busted.' The voice came slow and steady over the line. 'But you would not understand that. That is why I cannot call my bitches!'

Mike got the joke, it was Eddie Murphy, *Trading Places*. 'Dude where are you?' Anderson continued, 'I am out the front of your place.'

'I'll be out in two secs.' Mike replied grabbing his tie and jacket to put on in the cab.

'Okay. See you then.' Anderson hung up.

Just as he reached the front door, Mike did a quick double take. Shit! He had forgotten his pager and mobile phone. He dashed back into his bedroom where he had seen them last. He scanned the room frantically. Aha! They were on the table beside the bed. He quickly tucked them into the inside pockets of his jacket before rushing once more to the front door.

Struggling, almost breathless, Mike climbed into the cab. His tie hung loosely around his neck, the top button of his shirt undone.

'How was your weekend?' Anderson inquired, before turning his attention to the cab driver. 'Liverpool Street via the Embankment please.' He turned back to Mike. 'It was a beautiful weekend. Did you go anywhere?'

'Yeah, I took the Eurostar to Paris. It was awesome,' Mike replied as he finished dressing himself. It was not often that you got a three day weekend and Mike was determined to see as many European cities as he could whenever the opportunity arose.

'Been to Paris before? It's a wonderful city isn't it? My wife and I love Paris, we are taking our daughters to

EuroDisney next month. Do you think we should take the train?'

'Oh yeah, the train is fantastic. You leave Waterloo and arrive in Gare du Nord right in the center of Paris. You don't have to worry about getting out to Heathrow and all the customs and immigration queues. It is a fine service.'

'Yeah, I think we will be taking the train. So what do you think will happen today?' Anderson turned his attention to business.

'I guess everything will hinge around today's stock figures. With the market awash with these rumors of Chinese deliveries in Singapore I guess the pressure will be on the downside.'

'I agree. What do you think our plan should be?'

'Do nothing much and go with the flow. I really don't have any strong views except that I think this whole Chinese deliveries bullshit is a ruse.'

'I think you might be right, but the biggest danger for us is not on the upside but on the downside so we have to be careful.'

Mike looked up at the big clock on the wall. It was five minutes to nine, five minutes until the all-important stock figure came out. The market had inched its way lower all morning as people readied themselves for the fabled Chinese copper deliveries into Singapore. Mike had squared his position up, figuring the market would pop after the stock figure came out as every man and his dog was short ahead of it. These situations almost always proved the old adage of 'buy the rumor, sell the fact' which in this case was the inverse 'sell the rumor, buy the fact'. He pushed the cold remnants of his coffee to the side of the desk to make space for the coming battle. He gazed intently at the screens with the voice of Rolo babbling crap to some customer or other who was on the line for the stock figures.

With baited breath the whole market watched the screen. Then came the stock numbers. 'COPPER STOCKS up 1250mt.'

It flashed as plain as day on the screen in front of him. He wondered if it was a mistake as can sometimes be made. The Chinese were supposed to be delivering at least 12,000mt into Singapore. He waited for another ten seconds to see if there was a correction. So was the rest of the world, for not a phone rang. It was eerily quiet.

Mike stood up, picking up both phone handsets out of habit. The screen said 2720/30. Then it changed 2725/35. He glanced at Anderson who was sitting beside him.

'Well, what are you waiting for?' Anderson looked puzzled.

'Buy everything you can up to 2740!' Mike screamed at the top of his lungs, the tendons in his neck straining under the volume. 'Go! Go! Go!' Mike looked down at his phone board which was already starting to light up. 'It's a light show!' He cried with glee. Boy did he love this stuff. Today was going to be wild.

*

In Beijing, Stanley Wong sat dumbfounded in front of his screen. The smell of stale cigarettes filled the air, his ashtray overflowing with butts and ash. He could not believe what was happening in front of his eyes. He gripped his forehead tightly about his temples before running his hand through his hair. He let out a huge sigh. Dazed, distraught, he looked more like a deer in headlights than a powerful copper trader. The copper price was ticking up, not going down as he had expected. And where was his copper?

He started to dial his shipping company. His heart pounded at a frenetic pace, fear and anger were starting to choke him. His breath was short. He hung up. Of course, it was too late. They would already have gone home for the day. Damage control. That is all he could do for now. He had to cover some of his massive short position. He had to save his skin before it was too late. Or was it already too late? He frantically called one of his trusted London brokers.

Satoru Fujiyama relaxed on a soft leather couch in his lounge room. He didn't need to see a screen, he knew what the stocks would be well in advance of the marketplace. He had seen to it. He looked at his pocket Reuters with a smirk of satisfaction. The copper price was starting to move higher as he had planned. He picked up the phone beside the couch. He dialed the number for the Mandarin Hotel in Singapore and congratulated the man at the other end of the line. The operation had gone very smoothly. They had done well. They had slipped into the Tanjong Pagar terminal and removed all the copper that had just arrived and spirited it away to a Yakuza warehouse under cover of darkness. They had been in and out without a trace. Fujiyama was now about to reap the rewards of his Yakuza brothers' work. Phase two was indeed a success. Now for phase three.

When the conversation was finished, Fujiyama hung up and hit his speed dial for the offices of Wilmont Bridge in London.

Alan Bridge answered the line immediately. No one else called on that line. It was the Batphone.

'Fujiyama-san, what can I do for you?' Bridge asked in an almost sycophantic manner. He knew all too well on which side his bread was buttered.

In his familiar but precise manner he began to give simple but concise instructions. 'When the Comex opens in New York I want you to buy all the copper you can up to 2800. When the market gets to 2800 call me at home.'

'Yes, Fujiyama-san. We will buy everything we can up to 2800 and then call you at home.' Bridge repeated the instructions just for good order's sake.

'Yes, that is correct.' Fujiyama replied, before ending the call.

Fujiyama hit a second speed dial for the home number of Bryan Murphy in New York. This time he used a secure scrambler to code his conversation. Murphy had a similar terminal at his home. This way they could be assured of absolute privacy.

*

It was four-thirty in the morning in New York, but Bryan Murphy was still awake. He had been for the last forty-five minutes, since he had awoken to see the stock numbers. Unable to get back to sleep, he had been tossing and turning in the dark. He reached across the bedside table, flicking on the lamp, as he heard the phone ringing. He answered the phone a little sheepishly as he was still rather tired.

'Hello?' he spluttered, trying to clear his throat.

'Bryan-san?' Fujiyama queried.

'Yes, Fujiyama-san, what can I do for you?' It was rare for Fujiyama to call him at home at this time in the morning. It had to be something important. He sat upright in bed wiping the sleep out of his eyes with his thumb and forefinger.

'Bryan-san, on the open of Comex today I want you to bid for two thousand lots at two cents over whatever the London price is just prior to the open. The whole world will no doubt fill you in. When the order is filled I want you to bid for another two thousand lots one cent higher than your first order. Do you understand these instructions?'

'Yes, Fujiyama-san, perfectly.' He grabbed a pen and paper from the drawer under the bedside table and jotted down the instructions.

'Good. I will call you after the open.' Fujiyama hung up.

Whilst reaching for his cigarettes Fujiyama flicked the remote on his television on to catch the last part of the NHK Tokyo news. He lit a cigarette and slouched back into a comfortable position on his couch. He had finished the groundwork for phase three of his plan. All there was left to do now was wait.

*

Stanley Wong had started to cover some of his copper position but had held off as prices started to stabilize. He had held himself together quite well after the initial shock had worn off. With a bit of luck, the market would settle down for the rest of the day and Stanley would be able to establish what had happened to his copper shipment. If it had just missed the cut off point for inclusion in Tuesday's stock figure then it would surely show up in Friday's stock numbers and the market would once again head lower. Of that he was certain. There was no point in panicking right now. The best thing for Stanley to do was to stay calm, not push the market against himself and not let on to the market that he was worried. If he kept his cool, everything would be okay, that's what he kept reminding himself.

*

Back in London, the copper market had stabilized around the 2740/45 region. It hadn't taken off as Mike had expected and the initial adrenaline rush at the release of the stock figures had quickly dissipated into a Monday morning malaise, even though it was Tuesday. There had been rumors of some light Chinese buying, but as Mike had seen nothing directly he had discounted it as market scuttlebutt. Mike relaxed in his banana chair, feet up on the desk, lying in a supine position. He threw a blue stress ball up into the air with his right hand and caught it repeatedly. He looked at his watch. It was two minutes to the Comex open. As the market was quiet, he didn't even bother to look at the screen. Instead he continued tossing the ball into the air. As he did so he called out to Andy.

'Andy, where did Comex open?'

Andy, who was busy taking down some orders from a customer, fumbled with his mouse to get the Comex screen up.

'July is trading at 1.2650' he shouted out, whilst simultaneously clicking the mute button so the customer could not hear what he was shouting.

Mike continued to flick the ball up into the air whilst he did a quick mental calculation of the equivalent London price. Comex copper was quoted in U.S. cents per pound whereas London copper was quoted in U.S. dollars per metric tonne. Mike threw the ball up in the air once more, but then the penny dropped. He caught the ball and sat bolt upright. In the same motion, he punched into a line that went straight to Stampleman brokers on the Comex floor.

'Hey Larry,' Mike shouted down the line in order to be heard over the din in the pit. 'What the hell is going on down there? Are they bad prints?' It was not uncommon for a bad print or two to be thrown up by the locals on the open.

'It's Ralph,' came the indignant reply.

'What?' Mike shouted incredulously. He didn't give a fuck who was on the other end of the line, just as long as they could give him the information he needed.

'Larry is busy in the pit. Do you want me to get him for you?'

'No, Ralph, it's fine! Just tell me what is going on down there.' Mike spoke calmly and clearly into the receiver. All the while he was thinking, shit I've got some kid on the line who doesn't know his arse from his elbow.

'Well, the market came in two cents higher than expected. J.G. is bidding for two thousand lots. All the locals sold him and so did some of the trade from London. He is still bidding.'

Right then the direct line from Goldman flashed.

'One hundred lots of copper for Elvis,' Steve shouted. Elvis was their code name for Goldman. The commodities arm at Goldman Sachs was called J. Aron, and by word association Mike and Steve had come up with Elvis as a code name for them. As in, Elvis Aaron Presley.

Mike looked at the screen. It said 2775/80. It had rallied in a vacuum, without trading in London. The price just went up without touching the sides.

Mike winced. He had no idea what to do. There was something strange going on down on the Comex floor. Was Elvis covering his short from the morning session? Or was he going to get pasted and have the market fall away? He closed his eyes for a millisecond hoping for some divine inspiration.

'J.G. is filled, he bought two thousand lots at 126.50! He is stepping out of the ring.' Ralph shouted excitedly. 'Locals now on the offer.' Mike heard this in the background.

He looked back at Steve for help. Steve could only shrug his shoulders for support.

'72/77,' Mike said sheepishly, closing his eyes and screwing up his face as he waited for the reply. It was the safe option, he thought.

Steve pointed his finger in the air, indicating that Mike had sold one hundred lots of copper to Goldman. So, he was covering his short as Mike had suspected. The Comex was bound to come off now that this mad purchase had been made. Mike felt comfortable sitting short at 2777. He figured the market would start to fall back and he would have no trouble covering this short.

Just then, he heard another voice on the phone. It was Larry.

'Mike you there?'

'Yeah, Larry, I'm here. What the hell went on down there on the open?'

'Well, J.G. came in and bid for two thousand lots two cents above London.'

'No shit.'

'Locals and trade from London all sold him. Then when he was done he left the ring.'

'Any idea who he was buying for?' Mike asked. What he really was thinking was, who would be that stupid to bid way over the offer?

'I think it was some fund.' Larry answered. He was obviously making it up. It was the stock reply when your floor broker had no clue who was behind some business. Trade or fund buying, it was a simple cop out.

'Wait a sec. J.G. is back in the ring. He is bidding for another two thousand lots at 1.2750.'

'Shit!' Mike cried. 'Larry, gotta hop.' Mike slammed down the phone. He had to cover his short position and fast.

'Guys!' Mike screamed across the desk. 'Get me prices!'

The whole desk started calling the counterparts that they had been previously designated. Mike stood up, listening to the prices being called out by the people around the desk. He made eye contact with each person calling out the price and waved his right hand towards himself signaling that they were to take the offer being shown. With his left hand he had dialed Goldman. They read him way too high.

'Ouch. Nothing there thanks,' he responded with a jovial tone. They shared a friendly rivalry.

'Mate, I was just covering the copper that you took from me this morning. This market is way too skittish to hold a short position,' came the sympathetic reply from the other end of the Goldman line. The market was now trading above 2800 in London and stops were being touched off everywhere as market makers and fund managers alike scrambled to cover their positions.

'Agreed, Brother.' Mike concurred. 'Oops, gotta hop.'

He had acted quickly, but not quickly enough. He had just dropped close to 100,000 U.S.D. in the space of seconds. It had cost him close to 35 U.S.D. a metric tonne to cover his short position. The market had moved up at a pace he had never seen before. It was like a huge vacuum cleaner had been shoved into the market and hoovered up all the copper before he could get a price. There were rumors of Wilmont Bridge buying all the copper they could lay their hands on up to 2800. Mike was sure that this was Fujiyama defending his long position by jamming the shorts. It was a master stroke. Hats off to the guy. He had surely kicked the Chinese's butt and even Mike's today. Sure, Mike had dropped some wood, but it could have been worse. Much worse.

*

Stanley Wong sat, mouth agape. He stared blankly at the screen. He felt the awful feeling in the pit of his stomach somehow drop even lower. On the screen in front of him his whole life seemed to be flashing before him. Powerless to cover his positions he knew that banks would be calling at the end of the day, making margin calls that he didn't have the cash to cover at this point in time. He had not foreseen this series of events. What had gone wrong? He had planned this whole maneuver perfectly, or so he had thought. Someone was conspiring against him, of that he was sure. But his superiors would not see that. All they would see would be the requests for immediate margin payments on the outstanding short positions that he had, which were well under water by now. Every dollar the copper market rallied was costing him a fortune. The move today had probably cost him his job, his career, maybe even his life. Who knows in communist China? He grabbed a phone and started to buy back part of his position.

The Fujiyama hotline in the offices at IMT was answered on the second ring. Bryan Murphy took the call personally.

'Fujiyama-san. We have filled the orders that you left. You bought two thousand lots of July Comex at 1.2650 and a further two thousand lots of July Comex at 1.2750. Is there anything else I can work for you?'

'Very good work, Bryan-san,' Fujiyama said, sounding more than a little pleased with the outcome of the proceedings so far. 'Call me on my mobile at the beginning of the last hour of Comex.' It was now 11 p.m. in Tokyo and Fujiyama was off to one of the Yakuza's hostess clubs for the rest of the evening.

*

The market continued to rally into the London close at 5 p.m. It was a hectic market which went out at 2815/20 up against a major resistance level. It felt to Mike as if some major hedge fund was serving the market in the afternoon, which was keeping a lid on the price rally. Then, in the last hour of New York trading, the market started to tick up again. The volume on Comex was thin and whomever was buying was trying to ramp the price higher. Mike had a good idea who that might be. A good close which would force further short covering and induce some of the systems-based traders into the market on the long side, pushing the market up even further on Wednesday. It was a clever ploy that he had seen Fujiyama use before. Most of the London and European players had gone home for the day by 6 p.m. London time and it was only a handful of London players who kept their desks fully staffed after 5 p.m. London trade was thin during this time, as was Comex, an ideal time for some manipulation to take place.

Rolo was putting on his jacket to go home for the day. Most of his customers were European or Middle Eastern and had long since finished for the day.

'What do you think of this move on Comex?' Mike asked, hoping for some words of wisdom from his more experienced colleague.

'Well, it's maximum piss hour,' Rolo said with a grin, placing his briefcase on the desk in front of him as he did up his coat. 'It's about 3 a.m. in Tokyo now and Fujiyama is probably mindless on scotch in some hostess bar buying the shit out of Comex from his mobile.' Rolo grabbed his briefcase and bade everyone farewell for the night.

Mike laughed, but knew it wouldn't probably be far from the truth. It was the way the LME geezers had explained these last hour moves on Comex to him in the past. He wondered how much truth there was in the theory and how much it was a blatant manipulation of the closing prices. These closing prices could revalue positions to the tune of millions of dollars. That was a huge redistribution of wealth when you thought about it. The interest alone on these overnight cash balances could be worth millions of dollars. It was a scary thought.

Anderson made his way out to the desk in a very purposeful fashion. He had just left Julio Rodriguez's office. Julio, a Brazilian American in his late thirties with a distinct Spanish accent, was the global head of the Nelson Smith commodities department. As the 'big kahuna', the 'head honcho' of the commodities department, Julio was

Paul Watson's (head of the structured products group) and Simon Anderson's boss and therefore by extension he was Mike's boss too. A career manager and academic, Julio had been the head of European swaps before his current posting. Prior to that he had been a lecturer at Yale in quantum physics. His many years in the impractical world of academia were well-suited to managing the ideas of the structured products group, but not a trading desk where the improbable and the highly illogical were prone to happen with more than unnerving regularity. Julio, although based in New York, made frequent visits to the London office, so much so that he had his own office not far from the trading desk in London.

'Mike, where's Steve?' Anderson asked with just a slight hint of concern in his eyes as he gazed into the empty place where Steve always sat.

'It's pretty quiet here, so he's just popped out to the bathroom,' Mike replied. When it was busy there was no time for bodily functions to take place, so they had to grab the opportunity when it arose, and right now the market was in a comparative lull for the day.

'Okay. Can I see you both in Julio's office straight after the close.'

'Sure. No problems. I'll tell Steve when he gets back.'

Anderson turned and walked back into Julio's office, slamming the door shut behind him.

When the Comex had closed and Mike and Steve had finished checking their trades and running their seemingly endless end-of-day reports, they made they way into the inner sanctum which was Julio's office. Both Mike and Steve made their way tentatively into the office. Julio beckoned to them to take a seat. Anderson was already seated in a chair opposite Julio's desk. Apart from the usual photos of the wife and the kids, the shelving behind Julio's big desk was adorned with the types of tombstone plaques that are posted after most new bond issuances.

Julio lounged in his huge leather chair. 'So, how did we do today?' he asked, with his obviously Spanish accent.

'We got nicked up in a little copper,' Mike replied.

'But apart from that we did okay.' Steve added, as he knew that it could have been much worse.

'I see. Well, I have called you both in here as we think we might have a problem with our Chinese friends.' Julio sat forward and placed his forearms on the desk and clasped his hands together tightly. 'Do you guys remember last year there was a problem with Citic Shanghai?'

Mike and Steve both nodded.

Citic, the Hong Kong subsidiary of Citic Shanghai, had run up losses to the tune of one hundred and twenty million dollars with a number of institutions before they defaulted. Citic claimed that the people who had been executing the trades were not authorized to do the trades and thus they were not liable for the losses incurred. They promptly arrested the traders and spirited them away. The likes of Nelson Smith, Merrill Lynch, and Lehman Brothers took Citic to court and eventually negotiated a settlement which was just a fraction of the losses incurred by the subsidiary. With China's increasing financial importance, no institution wanted to anger the Chinese government and fall out of favor. It was one of those growing pains issues that they were prepared to write off in the pursuit of longer term profits and opportunities.

'Well, our friends at the C.N.M.T.A. have called us today to advise us that they might have some problems with working capital until the end of next month. They told me that it was due to some delayed payments for some physical material sold internally.'

'What's the size of their problem?' Steve asked, shifting uncomfortably in his seat as he fiddled with the height adjuster.

'At the moment it's about thirty million dollars,' Anderson cut in quickly.

'There goes our bonus,' Steve mumbled to Mike under his breath.

Julio picked up the change in mood very quickly. 'Guys, it is not going to be a problem for us. Lee Wei Han who runs the parent group has personally assured me that it will be sorted out in the next month. Lee is the son in law of Deng Xiao Ping so there is little chance of them defaulting like Citic did.'

Anderson added to the upbeat tone. 'Anyway, we are way ahead of budget at this point in the year and Watson's group are very close to closing two structured deals in Eastern Europe. One is with a Polish national oil concern and the other is with the Siberian Natural Gas Company. Each of those deals should kick about ten to fifteen million into the commodities bottom line before the end of the year. So there is really nothing for you guys to be concerned about at the moment.'

'If everything is fine, then what does concern us?' Mike asked bluntly.

'Well, for one,' Anderson continued, 'we won't be accepting any new positions from the Chinese until they are able to meet all their margin requirements. We will only be liquidating existing positions.'

'Are they aware of that?' Steve asked.

'Yes, we have advised them that this will be the procedure until further notice.' Anderson added reassuringly.

Julio stood up. 'Any other questions?' he asked as he grabbed his jacket from the coat stand.

Both Mike and Steve shrugged their shoulders. They were mentally exhausted from the day's proceedings. Everything had been covered that needed covering for the moment.

'Good,' Julio said with a smile, as he put his right arm, then left into his jacket sleeves before pulling it up and over his shoulders. 'I am going to go home now and see my wife and my son. It has been a very long day.' And with that the meeting finished.

*

In New York, John Templeton sat high above the stinking hustle and bustle of rush hour. From his air-conditioned sanctuary in mid-town he was well immunized against the 85 percent humidity outside. He had popped downstairs for a quick walk at lunchtime but as he had ventured through the revolving doors of the building he had been hit by a wave of oppressive heat and he quickly decided against it. He was hoping that the weather would be more favorable when he left the office in a couple of hours' time. He had spent the day watching the copper market with great interest. He had started selling copper short about three weeks ago and was not at all phased by its latest short covering rally. He looked at it as a great opportunity to sell yet more copper. The Icarus fund looked for opportunities at the macro level and took into account the longer term fundamental picture. They were looking for the big moves.

All of John's latest research indicated that the market was way over-priced relative to the amount of new supply coming on stream later in the year and this fact, coupled with the relative lack of hedging by a number of major copper producers, and the price must eventually go down. It was a simple equation. Supply would exceed demand and hence the price would fall to an equilibrium point somewhere around ninety cents per pound. The market had traded up to $1.28 on the close today. John sniffed an opportunity to make some serious money. He had a keen eye for the bigger picture. That was his strength. He could see the big move coming, and it was down.

Tomorrow morning when he came into the office, John would start selling copper again. He didn't want to crush the market so he would sell a little bit each day as he built up his short position. This selling program would take place over the next few weeks. He was going to create a massive short position which, if his projections were correct, would make him hundreds of millions of dollars for which he would be rewarded handsomely. John was methodical. He had done his homework and was now ready to put his plan fully into action. He would need the approval of Steve Richmond but with the weight of evidence that he had amassed that would be little more than a formality. Little did John Templeton know it, but he had unofficially declared war on Satoru Fujiyama and the 'copper club'.

*

The next morning, as Mike had expected, all the systems traders came into the copper market heavily on the long side. Their computer signals had been triggered by the previous night's closing price and they came in buying from the start of trading. As the market rallied hard, the Chinese were also seen scrambling to cover their short positions. On the other side of the market, selling, were the macro hedge funds including Mike's friend John Templeton who saw that copper was fundamentally overpriced and sought to profit from its inevitable move lower. Fujiyama was also on the other side of the market, taking profit on the copper he had bought the prior day in juicing the market to its current level. He often did this to place a lid on the market, keeping it within the range which best suited his options positions.

About 11 a.m., Rolo went through a stack of faxes that had just come from the overflowing in-tray beside the fax machine. He began scrunching each fax into a little ball before filing it in the bin. Most were junk, but one particular fax caught his eye. He stood up and read it aloud to the desk.

'Listen up. It says here that Stanley Wong is no longer an authorized trader for the C.N.M.T.A.' He couldn't hold back a slight chuckle as he read it. The whole market knew that the Chinese were getting killed by this move and were currently blowing out of their highly unprofitable short positions.

'Wow. Stanley Wong is no longer an authorized trader.' Mike repeated what Rolo had just read. 'And you can find his organs on sale in the lobby.' He said in a jovial tone, putting his feet up on his desk.

'Dude. It's not a joking matter.' Anderson, the voice of reason, addressed Mike softly. He turned to face Mike from his seat beside him. He tried to keep a straight face, but his grin was all too obvious. 'For all we know, this guy's wife is getting the bill right now for the bullet. China is an evil place. You never know what might happen. Dude, it could be real nasty for this guy. The Chinese really got 'gaffed' by this move.'

The image of a huge fish hook being ripped across your midsection, gaffing you, so that your entrails fell all over the deck, was immensely poignant.

Mike stopped and pondered the gravity of the situation. One minute you're hot, a copper trader on top of the world, the next minute you're an organ donor. The markets were brutal, especially in China. But that was the

Darwinian nature of the game. You played hard, you knew the risk. If you didn't manage your risk properly, then you lost and you're out. No cry babies, no organ donors. Simple, brutal, effective. Capitalism doesn't fuck around!

June, 1995

The ride into Manhattan from JFK is not a particularly pleasing one, at least, not visually. Traffic, exhaust fumes, pot-holed roads, crowded filthy streets, and an ugly hotch-potch of structures mar the journey. The growing disparity of wealth in America is highlighted from start to finish. Inside the air-conditioned safety of a Lincoln Towncar, Mike flicked through his metallic filofax, which had been a birthday present from his parents. He was notorious for losing numbers, forgetting appointments, and generally being late for everything. The disarray in his life stemmed from his inattention to details. The diary had been part of a last-ditch attempt by his family to make him a little more detail conscious, but to no avail. As he flicked through the diary, countless scraps of paper with phone numbers and appointments scrawled hastily on them fell onto the back seat of the car. Mike fumbled through them trying to collate them into some sort of order. They represented his schedule for the week, and what a busy week it would be.

Anderson had suggested that Mike spend some time in the New York office getting to know some of the sales staff a little better. With perfect timing, it would coincide with the Comex Copper Week, which included a cocktail party at the Tavern on the Green and a black tie function for industry participants. The 'copper club' functions, as they were referred to, would have traders, brokers, fund managers, consumers, and producers from all over the world present. It was really just a huge piss take and an excuse for people in the industry to go to New York and drink it up while their wives went shopping. Mike relished the opportunity to return to New York and party with his friends on an expense account. He had only been away for a couple of months, but already Mike sorely missed his beloved city.

What he didn't miss was the traffic. Mike had forgotten about the long delays on the Long Island Expressway going back into Manhattan on a Sunday afternoon in summer. Every man and his dog with a weekender in the Hamptons was making his way back into the city. He realized that he should have flown in on Saturday. He made a quick mental note never to fly into JFK on a Sunday summer afternoon again. The traffic was barely crawling along in the sweltering humidity outside. Mike finished arranging his scraps of paper into a week of appointments. He was to meet with the New York sales team and visit a few clients with them, easy enough, he thought. Then a couple of dinners, a cocktail party, and a black tie function. A pretty hectic week confronted him but he had the added advantage that the copper market was all but closed by 2 p.m. New York time, which left him plenty of time to catch up on some much needed sleep and a spot of shopping before his business appointments in the evening. Mike had kept Sunday night free to catch up with Warren for a few beers and Thursday free for dinner with his good buddy John Templeton. Although he doubted the prudence of having a few quiet beers and a couple games of pool with Warren on a Sunday night before a hectic week, it was an event that could not be missed. All too often a few quiet beers with Warren on a Sunday evening had turned into a night of heavy drinking followed by a big fry-up of bacon, eggs, and home fries at the Moondance diner before showering and heading into the office all bleary-eyed and smelling like a brewery.

For this very reason, Mike was staying downtown at the Millennium Hilton Hotel, opposite the World Trade Center. He liked the modern rooms and its proximity to Wall Street. It was close to the office and a short cab ride uptown to the various meetings and dinners he had planned across the course of the week. He figured it was better to have a short stumble to work in the morning than a tortuous rush hour cab ride. That extra half hour of sleep in the morning was worth its weight in gold.

In the distance, through the heat haze, Mike spied the monstrous silhouette of Manhattan. It was a majestic sight, awe-inspiring in its enormity, like a massive battleship run aground. Tall spires at each end dominated the skyline, and a concave midsection cleverly disguised the chasms that ran its length. Pure, raw energy – this was what New York was all about – an overpowering presence of strength and vitality. Mike figured he would have enough time for a quick nap to recharge his batteries before venturing out into the fray to meet up with Warren at their favorite haunt, Yaffas, a rather funky bar in TriBeCa.

While Mike was psyching himself up for the main event that night with Warren, a slightly graying and very unassuming Fujiyama slipped through customs and immigration at JFK. The flight from Tokyo to New York was not unfamiliar to the copper king because he had made the journey on countless prior occasions, as had his minders, who had slipped into New York on the previous day.

In one corner of the noisy, crowded arrivals hall, Fujiyama, carrying an old black briefcase and garment bag, was met by a solitary man in black, his golden pin gleaming against his dark lapel. The man bowed reverently to Fujiyama, who merely nodded his head in acknowledgment. They knew each other well but rarely spoke in public. Without a word, he took Fujiyama's garment bag. All the while, Fujiyama retained his precious briefcase which contained all the details of his latest plan. The man in black led the way outside, Fujiyama followed. Waiting for them was the second man in black, seated in the driver's seat of a black Humvee wagon, the engine idling.

The first man opened the door for Fujiyama before placing the garment bag in the back. Fujiyama greeted the driver with a curt nod which was returned accordingly. When the first man was in the front passenger seat, the man behind the wheel shifted the Humvee into drive and the big six liter V8 engine roared into life as they drove away. Their destination was the Waldorf Astoria Hotel in Midtown, where they and Fujiyama were staying for the week. Fujiyama lit his habitual cigarette and started to puff away. As he did so he contemplated the course of action on which he was set to embark. It was his most ambitious plan yet. If successful, he would transform himself from the 'copper king' into a 'copper god', of that he was sure.

Mike's evening with Warren had been, as expected, anything but a quiet affair. He had managed to stumble back to his hotel around two in the morning. The two empty bottles of Evian beside the bed were testament to the dehydration that his brain was suffering. Twice he had hit the 'snooze' button on the alarm clock. He was pushing it to the limit, he knew that if he didn't get up soon he was going to be late. Fuck it! He had had a good month last month and it was his first day in the New York office. He could be a little late. He was only meeting with the guys on the sales desk. He continued to rationalize to himself. He didn't have any specific appointments until the afternoon and he wanted to be fresh for them. But he did decide that he had better avoid any more sessions with Warren that week. Well, at least until Friday. Warren never changed.

Mike really liked that and the fact that the pain of the morning after was always large and highly predictable.

By the time Mike was making his guest appearance in the New York offices of Nelson Smith, Richard Wilmont and Alan Bridge were just arriving at JFK from Heathrow. They had been summoned by Fujiyama to a secret meeting of the 'copper club' at the Waldorf, set for that afternoon. It had been almost four years since they had been inducted into this elite and clandestine world. In those four years each of them had amassed fortunes far beyond anything they had ever thought possible. Their company had gone from a tinpot brokerage house to a powerful trading concern with basically one major client. Their other major client, Codelco, had disappeared when it was discovered that their head trader, J.P. Davila, had lost two hundred and seventy odd million dollars trading copper. They had made good money from Codelco's business, but now that cash cow was gone, they relied almost totally on Fujiyama's business although they both had more money now than either of them could spend in a lifetime. Still, they were curious as to the purpose of this meeting. They had only been summoned on half a dozen prior occasions. Each time a strategy was outlined by Fujiyama which would net them tens of millions of dollars. They assumed that this meeting would yield similar results and thus were both in good spirits despite the long flight across the Atlantic.

To save time, Mike hadn't bothered shaving. He figured he could pop back across the street to the Millennium at lunchtime, take a quick nap before showering, shaving, changing, and heading uptown for the first of his merry appointments for the week. He would arrive fresh and clean for the real meetings. He strode across the massive cauldron of space which made up the trading floor of Nelson Smith's New York operations. Five or six hundred traders and support staff filled this frenetic space, concocting deals and making trades. A ceiling two stories high and massive air-conditioning ensured there was enough air-flow for this ego-filled room. Row upon row of trading desks and screens lined the room with elevated bleacher seats for the sales staff, all on two phones at once. The New York trading floor had more raw energy than its London cousin, but then again it had more New Yorkers. It was that simple. It would have been a truly intimidating site for the uninitiated, but Mike took it all in his stride.

Mike located the commodities area without much hassle. It was in the far corner of the room almost hidden beside the forex desk. It was well away from the massive bond desk which was the epicentre of the arena. With the whole room facing it like Mecca, the bond desk was Nelson Smith's shrine to capitalism. It was a machine. All day long it cranked out profits like a cash register in a supermarket. The budget for the whole commodities unit for the year was made by the bond desk in a week. Its money-churning ability was phenomenal. The bond desk was staffed by hundreds of traders and salespeople sitting in rows like a Viking longship. Even when the captain of this marauding Viking boat had jumped ship earlier in the year to go to one of the big German banks, the longship had continued to power on, undaunted by its task. The guys on the trading desk thought they were in control of the ship, but no single person had power over it, it had power over them. It was like the Terminator of trading desks. It positively would not stop making profits, ever, making it the perfect franchise.

Mike watched the spectacle as he sauntered casually past the bond desk. Despite the aura of the desk and the massive profits it generated, he held no reverence for the traders who worked there. They certainly weren't the demi-gods that they thought they were. If you have a golden goose and it lays golden eggs, you don't need to be Einstein to make money. Any fool could tell you that.

He made his way across to the commodities desk, grabbing a cup of water from the water cooler as he did so. Still in need of rehydration, he swiftly gulped it down. Pulling his thumb and forefinger from the corners of his eyes, across to the bridge of his nose, Mike carefully checked for crusty bits of telltale sleep. Phew! None! He steadied himself, straightened his tie, took a deep breath and prepared himself for the coming bombardment which would be his introduction to the desk.

Having spoken to all the commodities sales staff in New York previously over the phone, fitting faces to voices would be pretty easy, but as he had not yet met any of them in person, the pictures he had conjured up in his mind as to how they looked would be very different to the reality. They were all typical New Yorkers, fast-talking, fast-living individuals. Born hustlers, they were all very efficient in extracting business from customers even when there was none. That meant that Mike would get on well with them. He was in the business of making money and the more business these guys brought in, the more money he made. The more money the traders on the desk in London made, the bigger the bonus pool at the end of the year, the more everyone got paid. But Mike's mission to New York was to stress the importance of 'value' business as opposed to 'volume' business. Value-added business was important because no matter how much volume the salespeople brought in, if the trading desk didn't make money on the trade, no one would get paid. So all the anal attention to sales credits and who got credited with bringing in what business was a waste of time at the end of the day unless there was some profit on the bottom line. It was a simple, symbiotic relationship that many of the salespeople didn't get. New York is such a 'me' culture sometimes that people miss the fact that there is a 'me' in 'team'. This kind of attitude ran contra to the smooth and profitable workings of a trading desk much of the time. That was part of the reason for Mike's visit to New York. He was there to help create better relationships with his own sales team so that the business they would bring him would be more profitable. This would engender a win-win situation for all concerned. Or so Simon Anderson hoped.

*

Bryan Murphy hailed one of the ubiquitous dented yellow cabs just outside his offices in Water Street, Downtown. He would normally have called for a limo to collect him but he knew they kept records of journeys. Having been summoned to a meeting of the 'copper club' he had told his secretary that he was just going out for lunch. He didn't tell her where or who with – you could never be too careful. Big Brother was always watching, which was also why he never used a cellphone. You could never be sure who else was on the line listening. That was why all the important conversations he held with Fujiyama were via the portable scrambler terminal he had in his office, or the permanently scrambled line from his home. Anyway, at this time of day the traffic going uptown wouldn't be too bad. The windows were up on the cab. That was the reason he had hailed it. He had figured that in New York's sweltering heat a cab with its windows up had to have air-conditioning. He wasn't wrong in that assumption. As he stepped into the cab he felt sudden cool climatic change. Then, seconds later, the stench hit him. The body odor of the cab driver was almost overpowering. He was left in a catch 22 position. Windows up, cool and smelly. Windows down, stinking hot. The journey wasn't that far. He elected to tough it out, windows up.

'The Waldorf Astoria on Park,' he barked at the driver. 'Take F.D.R. drive, please.'

Big Hank Mitchell, the head of commodities sales in New York, showed Mike around the desk. Hank was another man of good Southern stock whose genteel nature had all but been erased by the stark urbanity of New York City. The trading jungle had done the rest. Mike greeted each person on the sales desk, in turn, and had a short rap with them as he made the rounds. There were no surprises for him. He had spoken to them all on the phone before so it was just a case of putting a face to a name. Mike was set to go with Hank to visit one of the big hedge funds that afternoon in a bid to get their business. This was serious stuff and Mike wanted to be at his best, so once he had finished his circuit, Mike excused himself, electing to snatch a couple hours' sleep before heading uptown. He needed the rest.

In a suite in the Waldorf Astoria, high above the noise of Park Avenue, Richard Wilmont and Alan Bridge had already made themselves comfortable with their drinks on two of the couches that were gathered in a circle at one end of the room. Satoru Fujiyama sat quite relaxed in a big red chair. The room was tastefully appointed with a slightly art deco feel, but it retained a regal feel. Fujiyama lit another cigarette as he glanced wistfully at his watch. Murphy was barely five minutes late but Fujiyama was keen to get on with proceedings.

There was a swift tap at the door. One of the men in black moved to open it, the other stood expressionless, facing the group at the other end of the room. They had swept the room the day before and were quite satisfied that the room was secure. The only intrusion or interruption could come through the door. The first man peered through the peephole. Having recognized the familiar face of Bryan Murphy he unslid the latch and opened the door, beckoning Murphy to join their private gathering. Once Murphy was safely inside, he shut the door again, fastening the latch. They didn't want any uninvited guests at this meeting.

Fujiyama, upon seeing his final accomplice, stood up immediately.

'Ah Bryan-san. So good of you to join us today. Come, have a seat.' He said pointing at the remaining chair in the circle with an open hand, 'Would you like a drink?'

'Scotch on the rocks would be lovely,' Murphy replied, nodding an acknowledgment to both Wilmont and Bridge as he did so.

Fujiyama gave a quick look to the other man in black, who had already made his way to the drinks cabinet, before resuming his comfortable position on the big red chair.

'Gentlemen,' Fujiyama began, leaning forward, ashing out his cigarette. 'As you know, I am already engaged in a battle with the major macro hedge funds. Yamamoto Corporation is heavily long of copper and they have gone short copper recently with the view that the market will head lower over the course of the next year as new supply hits the market, induced by these high prices. Whilst this is inevitably true in the long run, in the short term we have an opportunity to squeeze them out of the market and make massive profits in the process, thus giving Yamamoto a chance to exit its long position. The situation as it stands is very simple. Copper stocks on the LME are very low, in fact they are the lowest they have been in years. If we were to disrupt the flow of new material into LME warehouses and even take some material off warrant, we could create such a severe backwardation in prices that the shorts would be begging for us to let them out. We could name our price. Gentlemen, in this venture we will certainly make a killing.' His voice tailed off as he finished.

'What about the regulators?' Murphy asked, quite pointedly.

'Don't worry about them. They are merely a big white elephant.' Fujiyama grinned. 'Besides, ever since the 1991 LME investigation into my dealings in the copper market, I have had one of the directors of the exchange on my payroll. Sure, there will be a lot of noise, but they will report that normal market forces are at work. Supply and demand. These general conditions, gentlemen, are our greatest allies.'

It was true. In 1991 the LME had investigated Fujiyama's alleged manipulation of the copper market and found that normal market forces were at work. He was only one of a handful of Japanese people to have been featured on the front page of the *Wall Street Journal* and he had made it there twice. They had referred to him as MR Five Percent as they postulated that he controlled about five percent of the trade in world copper. They were so far off the mark, it was not funny. He really controlled about thirty percent of the physical supplies of copper. In the coming months it would be more, much more than that. But despite the copper market's interest in the 'copper king', he remained an enigma to all but a select few.

Over the course of the next few hours the four men plotted and planned the strategy that they would employ to corner the copper market and squeeze the short hedge funds out of the market. The opening of LME warehouses in Longbeach, California in late 1994 to compete with the Comex in the U.S.A. provided them with the perfect propaganda machine. Longbeach warehouses were perfectly located for transportation to Japan. Thus the use of Longbeach warehouses would be the cornerstone of their plan. Fujiyama would visit the U.S. producers with stories of massive physical commitments in China and buy up whatever physical material they were thinking of delivering into Longbeach so that the new supplies would never hit the warehouses and thus the stock figures. Murphy would travel to Chile to ensure disruption by mineworkers so that fresh supplies leaving the copper producing giant, Codelco, would be a trickle. He would also visit his old friend, the general, in Zambia to ensure that shipments leaving Zambia were conveniently delayed. Fujiyama would not lend to the market any of the material he held on warrant, thus creating an artificial tightness in supplies and finally, the nail in the hedge funds' coffin would be driven in by Wilmont Bridge who would use their vast knowledge of LME trading to ramp up the nearby spread prices on Yamamoto's behalf. Nearby spread prices would explode, forcing shorts to cover at great expense and, being the holder of the material they needed to get out, Fujiyama would make them pay through the nose to get out. They were sure to succeed in their plan. They had covered every base possible, it was almost infallible. 'The Copper Club' was now set to embark on its greatest and most daring mission. 'Operation Longbeach' was ready to commence.

*

One of the highlights of the Comex Copper Week was the cocktail party at the Tavern on the Green. Located on the west side of Central Park, the Tavern on the Green is a perfect spot for such an event. Mike accompanied Hank Mitchell to the function. Mike despised these kinds of events. They were a stupid, back-slapping excuse for industry participants to get drunk. He could do that any time. Why immerse yourself in a room full of wankers?

As Mike walked down the corridor which was glassed on one side and heavily mirrored on the other, he mentally prepared himself for the coming banal banter. Anyone truly important and influential was bound to avoid this sort of event like the plague. Sure enough, when Mike reached the large room where the reception was being held, he was not disappointed. Surveying the room quickly he could see LME brokers, Comex brokers, and other associated vultures circling their prey, namely the investment banks, the miners, and the producers. The investment banks courted their own prey – the weaker miners and producers. In all, this savannah courting ritual was rather comical. Mike decided that he needed a beer. He turned to ask Hank if he wanted one too, but Hank was already engaged in aimless conversation with one of the copper producers from Arizona. How quick is that? Mike thought to himself as he scoped the room once more, looking for the bar.

He located his objective and started to make his way across the crowded room. He hoped that he could get there without being engaged in conversation by anyone. He had deliberately placed his name tag in his pocket. He didn't feel particularly sociable at this point in time and figured it was easier if you didn't leave the door open to conversation.

'Mike?' came an English-sounding voice from behind him.

Shit! Went the little alarm at the back of his head.

'Mike. How are you doing?' The hand was thrust forward to shake his.

'Fine, thank you. And you?' Mike knew the voice and the face but had momentarily forgotten his name. He knew him as I.B.M. and on the LME that was good enough. The funny thing was that I.B.M. thought he was so named for his computerlike brain, when really it was an acronym for the 'Incredible Bullshitting Man'. Here was a man who had always bought the low and sold the high and no matter how cheap you had bought something, he had always bought it cheaper elsewhere. Mike couldn't help but smile broadly.

Mike looked down and saw I.B.M.'s half empty beer. 'Another beer?' he inquired, making a drinking motion with his empty right hand.

'Love one.' I.B.M. replied.

'Be back in a minute then.' Mike said, once again making his way through the crowd in the direction of the bar.

On his way to the bar, Mike spied more of the LME characters. There were a bunch of Refco people off to the right boozing it up with other LME geezers from Lehman. The LME was full of colorful characters always out for a laugh. Essex boys come good. A serious piss take like Copper Week and they were all there, the whole crew, Monkey, Fridgey, Doley, Des, Compo, and ALF, which was an acronym for 'Arrogant Little Fucker' and suited him well. It was like a curtain call for *Snow White and the Seven Dwarves*, all they needed was boozy and sleazy and the cast would be complete. Mike was certain that without the multi-ringed circus known as the LME there would be a serious oversupply of fruit truck drivers in the East End of London. But then again, the world moves in strange cycles.

As Mike finally reached the bar and ordered his beers, he caught a glimpse of a slightly retiring Japanese man who had just entered the room through a small door behind the bar standing just to his right. He stared momentarily at the man holding the glass of what he guessed was scotch.

'Fujiyama-san?' Mike asked hesitantly.

'Yes,' came the reply from the Japanese man, who was now trying to light a cigarette.

'Mike Kelly of Nelson Smith.' He held out his right hand. 'Pleased to meet you.' He said politely, shaking the outstretched hand of the older Japanese man. He hadn't planned on meeting the 'copper king' under such circumstances, but figured he would make the most he could out of the encounter.

'So what do you think of the copper market?' Mike asked, fumbling to make conversation. What a stupid question? Mike knew the guy was long forty thousand odd lots. Surely he wasn't bearish. Mike felt like a complete fool. The guy was just going to talk his book.

'I see very good physical demand from Asia for the next quarter.' Fujiyama replied in a clear soft voice.

Just as Mike was about to ask another question, a flock of A.I.G. vultures who had been circling Fujiyama for a few minutes made their move, saving him from any further embarrassment. The whole room would be sticking to this guy like flies to shit. It made Mike sick, but the reality of the situation was that Fujiyama was the biggest trader in the market. For the brokers he was a cash cow just waiting to be milked of commissions, and for the investment bankers he was a seam of gold just waiting to be mined via exotic structured products and commodity-linked financing. His business kept them all in highly paid jobs. He was the source of the bulk of the business done on the LME. Everyone quite rightly wanted a piece of his business. Fujiyama stood, unfazed by all the attention like the 'copper king' that he was, with all his loyal subjects jockeying to kiss his ring.

Mike was impressed by the spectacle. Although, so much had he heard of this legendary trader that his first impression was a little bit of a let-down. He had expected to meet some kind of superman but he was faced instead with a softly spoken, slightly graying man from corporate Japan. He didn't strike Mike as a market wizard like a Soros or Tudor, yet there was something else about him that Mike could not quite place. He seemed very relaxed and confident, but with all that sycophantic attention, who wouldn't? Fortunately he hadn't made himself look like too much of a fool in front of the copper legend. He had kept his dignity, at least he hadn't knelt at the feet of 'the man', as they called him, like the rest of those useless oxygen pirates.

Mike's Thursday dinner with John Templeton was going to be a rather casual affair, even though John was now technically Nelson Smith's and therefore Mike's customer. The sales guy in New York who had been assigned to cover the Icarus Fund would have been hopping mad if he known that Mike was meeting with one of its senior traders without him. But Mike didn't care, John had been one of his best friends for years and no amount of banking protocol would ever interfere with that.

They had decided to meet at the bar of the very chic restaurant, I Tre Merli. Situated in a vast renovated warehouse on West Broadway, I Tre Merli was a great place to go for people watching. The girls behind the bar were all aspiring models and actresses, as was much of the clientele. It was quite a scene. It was a show that Mike didn't want to miss. He broke with tradition and was on time for once in his life. Rather pleased with himself, Mike stood there patiently, a bottle of Corona in hand, quite happily sipping it from time to time, watching the world go by, while he waited for his big Southern friend to arrive.

Mike spied the hulking presence of John as he entered the restaurant and half waved his right arm in the air to grab the big guy's attention.

'Dude, good to see you.' Mike said hand outstretched.

'M.K., my man, how are you doing?' John replied, shaking his hand with a great deal of force. 'I didn't expect to see you here so early.' John jibed. He knew why Mike was on time for once in his life. The spectacle behind the bar was clear to see.

'Yeah.' Mike smiled. 'We all have to make sacrifices for our friends once in a while. Can I get you a cold one?' He asked as he turned around to face the bar.

'Twist my arm a little more,' John replied.

'Sam Adams?' Mike asked over his shoulder.

'Done bro!'

For the next two hours they drank and chatted away, always keeping an eye on the multitude of babes coming and going from the bar or the restaurant. Mike kept a running commentary going on the talent. If you lost your concentration for a moment, you could miss something great. The conversation revolved around drinking stories, women, and sport – the three staples of any guy's repertoire – before moving onto business and the financial markets. Mike was very candid when it came to business, especially when there was no conflict of interest or matter of confidentiality at stake, more so than John, who was slightly more coy. Mike figured that John was heavily short copper even though he had not seen the business, but he was not going to place his friend in an awkward position by asking him any direct questions. That would have been plain rude. He hoped that his presence on the desk at Nelson would facilitate more business being done with the big Icarus Fund, but now was not the time to push the matter.

The beers flowed thick and fast into the evening, as did the stories. Dinner was placed on the back burner. Then they got onto the topic of the great financial debacles of recent time. They started to compose a top ten list of financial markets losers. Top of the list was Nick Leeson who brought down Barings, followed by Toshihide Iguchi who lost about a billion dollars trading bonds at Daiwa before anybody noticed. Also high on the list was Bob Citron, another billion dollar loser, who almost bankrupted Orange County. Then they gave out the minor placings. Juan Pablo Davila who lost two hundred and seventy million trading copper for Codelco after a supposed computer error. Then they added Joe Jett, the bond trader from Kidder Peabody, and his three hundred odd million in phantom trading profits. It was amazing how much money had been lost in the previous year by so-called 'rogue traders'.

But really, when you thought about it, these guys could not have done it alone. Someone superior to them had to be culpable. Someone must have been negligent in their duties for these things to be able to happen, to go unnoticed or, in some cases, encouraged. It boiled down to the fact that management were seriously ill-equipped at many institutions and companies to deal with the rapidly changing landscape of financial products that were being dreamed up by the quants, and the rocket scientists. You had Procter and Gamble and Gibson Greetings suing Bankers Trust for loses incurred using derivatives. Derivatives had become a dirty word. The media had made it so. Derivatives weren't evil, they were created to reduce risk. Derivatives were great if you used them correctly. It was kind of like the argument in favor of guns. Guns don't kill people, people kill people. It was that simple. But how many times was this going to happen again before people realized it? It was the clueless individuals higher up the corporate ladder who were the ones to blame. Lax management was the danger man.

It was with unnerving regularity that these debacles had occurred in the past few years. The frequency and size of these disasters had been increasing. It was scary. Who was going to top Nick Leeson's amazing feat? Who would take his crown? Who would assume the mantle of the greatest fool in financial history? Only time would tell.

July, 1995

Satoru Fujiyama sat calmly opposite John Jacobsen, the C.E.O. of Copra, the largest copper-mining conglomerate in North America. The plush, air-conditioned office of the C.E.O. was a far cry from the hundred degree plus heat in the shade outside. Phoenix, Arizona was hot at the best of times, but in summer the dry heat was unbearable, unless you were a lizard. The cool office was a welcome respite from the tour of Copra's Arizona operations. Copra was the second largest producer of copper in the world, owning mining operations all around the globe. From the U.S.A. to Indonesia, the Philippines, Australia and joint venture projects in Chile and Africa, Copra was a truly global mining giant.

With production of over half a million tonnes of copper annually and revenues in the billions, Copra was a major force in the global copper market. Jacobsen had built this Arizona-based mining company into a global concern in the space of twenty years. Starting with just the single mine just outside of Phoenix he had single-handedly taken on the world. A family man at heart, he was married with five children ranging in age from thirty-seven down to twenty-four. He even had three grandchildren. Pictures of the Jacobsen clan adorned every surface in his office. On the side of his big desk, in a gold frame, was a picture of his wife of the past forty years, Ethel. In his weary early sixties, Jacobsen was now looking forward to retirement and spending more time with his beloved Ethel.

He looked long and hard at the man sitting opposite him. He didn't care much for the Japanese or 'harbor bombers' as he referred to them. At the tender age of seven, it was hard to comprehend what being killed on active duty in the Pacific really meant. To a boy of seven the only thing he could understand was that his daddy would never return home. The past was the past, and business was business, but somewhere deep down inside, Jacobsen hated himself for doing business with the 'harbor bombers'. He gently pulled his white goatee beard and repeated what the Japanese man sitting opposite him had just proposed.

'Now let me see if I understand you correctly. You want to buy two hundred and fifty thousand metric tonnes of copper from us, almost all of our production over the next six months, and you want to store it on our mine site here in Arizona? And for this you are prepared to pay us a premium over the daily LME settlement price?'

'That is correct,' Fujiyama replied slowly. After taking a sip of water from a glass he continued, 'I have just concluded a one year contract to supply China with close to half a million metric tonnes of copper over the next year. We will ship the material from Longbeach directly to Shanghai when it is needed by my customer. By shipping copper from Arizona by rail to Longbeach only when we need it, and not before, we will save much in warehousing fees and expenses. Thus, in saving money on our storage costs we are able to pay a premium to ensure a guaranteed source of copper supply for our customer.'

'I see. Well, it looks like you have yourself a deal, Mr. Fujiyama,' Jacobsen said, as he stood up and held out his hand. 'I'll have our legal department draw up a contract straight away.'

'That is wonderful,' Fujiyama replied, shaking his hand.

Operation Longbeach was now in motion.

*

Mike had slipped back into London life with relative ease. Comfortable with his surroundings, he soon began to get used to the slower pace of life. The lack of New York urgency and aggression that had at first irritated him, he was now beginning to find agreeable. He also enjoyed working with the team of guys that Anderson had assembled, which always made things easier.

Over the course of the rest of June, the copper market had continued to rally on the back of declining stocks on the LME. The macro hedge funds like Tiger, Soros's Quantum, and Icarus must have been sucking some serious wind as the copper price headed back up to the 2900 region. But it was only a matter of time before new supply hit the market and drove prices back down. The big hedge funds were in good shape, they were looking at the bigger picture.

It was toward the end of July that Anderson had become further concerned about the Yamamoto account. Each month Yamamoto, through IMT and their power of attorney agreement, had been rolling their massive copper position forward into the next trading month. This month no such rolling forward had been done by IMT at Nelson Smith. It was entirely possible that they were rolling the position elsewhere and that Nelson would receive a 'give-up', which would either reduce their position or liquidate it. But as the month-end drew closer and no such give-ups were in sight, Yamamoto's cash position started to grow larger and larger.

Mike answered the phone. It had been a long day. He punched the flashing button. 'Nelson.' He barked into the phone. During the day his phone manner became less and less inviting, especially when it was busy.

'Hello, this is Satoru Fujiyama, of Yamamoto Corporation. I would to speak with Simon Anderson, please.'

Mike changed his tone quickly. 'Sure,' he said, as he quickly scanned the room for Anderson, whom he located off to the left near the coffee machine. 'One moment Fujiyama-san.' He put the Japanese copper trader on mute and, waving his hand in Anderson's direction, shouted, 'Anderson. Line one for you. It's Fujiyama.'

'I'll take it in my office.' Anderson said, raising his hand in acknowledgment as he made his way across the room.

'Fujiyama-san, Mr. Anderson will be with you in one moment.'

'Thank you.'

Mike put line one on hold when he saw Anderson was settled at his desk and ready to take the call. He was curious as to why the Japanese man would be calling at this time of day. It must have been about four-thirty in the morning in Tokyo. He didn't sound intoxicated, so it wasn't going to be a maximum piss hour trade from some bar. It must be something rather important. Mike's mind raced at the possibilities. He knew he would have some form of answer soon enough when Anderson emerged from his office.

After what seemed like a long phone conversation, Mike noticed the little red light on line one switch off. He saw Anderson open his door and wander into Julio's office shutting the door firmly behind him. This only served to heighten Mike's curiosity. What had just transpired? He was eager to know.

After what seemed like an eternity, Anderson emerged from Julio's office and strolled over to the desk where Mike and Steve were seated. Steve was reading that morning's paper and Mike was busy bullshitting with Warren on the Reuters machine. The market had died in the afternoon session and both were just killing time, waiting for the market to shut for the day before going home.

'You guys busy?' Anderson inquired.

'Market's dead,' Steve replied gloomily. Slow markets tended to do that to all traders.

'Okay. Can I see you both in my office now.' Anderson, said making his way back to his office.

Mike and Steve ensured that their subordinates were well-versed in what to do if anyone called and they courteously told the New York sales guys via the open box that they would be off the desk for a few minutes. That done, they headed into Anderson's office.

Once inside the privacy of his office, Anderson recounted the telephone conversation he had had with Fujiyama and the subsequent conversations he had had with Julio and the legal department via conference call from Julio's office. Fujiyama had called to esquire about commodity-linked financing. This was one of Nelson Smith's strengths, lending money using the underlying physical commodities as security. Anderson had discussed it with Julio and the legal department and seemed quite bullish on the whole idea. Nelson would lend Yamamoto Corporation money against physical holdings of copper at an interest rate just slightly above the London Interbank Offered Rate, or LIBOR as it was known. Anderson said it would be in the region of fifty to one hundred basis points which would amount to some easy money for the desk. It was a legitimate form of secured lending which made Anderson very happy. He hoped that it would pave the way for Nelson to secure more of Yamamoto's business and herald a new era in relation with the Japanese client. Both Mike and Steve were delighted at the news. July had been a tough month for them profit wise and they welcomed any new business that would take some of the profit-making pressure off their shoulders. There were a lot of mouths to feed come bonus time on the desk and the more revenue that hit the bottom line, the better it would be for all concerned. Mike was extra delighted as Anderson revealed a plan to head to Tokyo for a couple of days in early August to have dinner with Fujiyama and hopefully win some more business from the giant Yamamoto Corporation. Anderson was excited at their prospects.

'Fuck the Jap,' Mike thought to himself as he left Anderson's office, he was just excited at the news of his first trip to Japan.

*

In the bar of the Intercontinental Hotel in Lusaka, flanked by AK-47 toting goons of the Zambian Defense Force, Bryan Murphy placed the briefcase he was carrying on the ground beside him and greeted the hulking frame of his old friend General Valentine Matongo with a bear hug.

'General. So good to see you.'

'That's brigadier general now.' The general replied, pointing at his lapels with a wide, trademark, tobacco-stained grin. 'A drink for my old friend.' The general demanded, waving his left hand which held his unlit cigar. 'Two scotch on the rocks.' He turned back to face Murphy. 'Come, let's sit.' He motioned towards two empty couches on the other side of the bar. Murphy picked up the briefcase and made his way across the room.

When they were settled, Murphy placed the briefcase on his lap. 'General. I have a present for you,' he said, as he fiddled with the combination locks. He flicked open the briefcase and removed a fine wooden cigar box.

'My favorite,' the general exclaimed with glee. 'Now what is it that brings you back to lovely Lusaka, Mr. Murphy?' The general was a busy man. He knew Murphy needed his help and it was better to cut the formalities and get straight down to business. That would leave more time for socializing later.

'Well, my associates and I would like to purchase some further insurance.'

'Insurance is very costly these days,' the general sighed, rolling his eyes.

'My associates realize the high costs of insurance these days,' Murphy continued, swiveling the briefcase to face the general before popping the lid open for him to inspect the contents, 'and they are prepared to pay high premiums provided they receive the necessary cover.'

'I see,' said the general, peering inquisitively into the briefcase, marveling at the diamonds it contained. 'Just exactly what sort of cover would your associates like to take out?'

Closing the briefcase with a snap designed to grab the general's full attention, Murphy proceeded to outline his insurance needs. He wanted the general to ensure that no copper whatsoever left Zambia until further notice. For the full disruption of supply leaving the African nation, the general would be rewarded handsomely. It was a simple proposition.

The general nodded rhythmically, 'I think we can provide the sort of cover you are looking for, Mr. Murphy. I am sure we can come to some sort of agreement.'

'Great,' Murphy concurred, patting the briefcase twice, 'Consider this a down payment for your service.'

August, 1995

The red-eye from London to Tokyo must be one of the longest and most debilitating flights in the world. Mike and Anderson had arrived at around nine in the morning at Narita airport. No wonder it had been voted for the third year in a row as the world's worst international airport. Arriving at Narita was like taking a vacation to hell. Mike was more than slightly dazed by the whole journey and Narita just compounded his delirium. He would need a good six hours' sleep at his hotel before the round of scheduled meetings with Yamamoto Corporation. Thankfully Anderson had not scheduled anything for them until later in the afternoon. It was sure going to be a whistle-stop. The next day at noon they were booked to fly back to London. Another thirteen hours or more in the air. Mike certainly wasn't looking forward to the journey home.

The two men took the J.R. Narita express train into Tokyo and made their way to the Imperial Hotel. It was almost 10 a.m. by the time they checked in. The Imperial Hotel was within walking distance of Ginza and the offices of Yamamoto Corporation which was an added bonus for the two Americans. Anderson suggested that they get some sleep and meet up at 3 p.m. in the lobby to prepare for their afternoon appointment at Yamamoto. Anderson was sure that the dinner they had scheduled for that night with Fujiyama would probably run into the wee hours of the morning. If that was the case, both he and Mike would need a good sleep.

As space ran at a serious premium in Tokyo, Mike's room was small despite the exorbitant price that Nelson were paying for it. It had a bed – he needed some sleep. It would do. He only needed it for one night.

Despite his overtiredness, Mike was not really able to get to sleep easily. It seemed like ages before he dropped off. Then the phone rang. It was his wake-up call. It was already 2 p.m. He had been asleep for hours. Mike's body clock was all over the place. He was going to struggle today.

Mike met Anderson in the lobby and the two made their way across Hibiya Park to the offices of the mighty Yamamoto Corporation. They were greeted by a security guard at the front desk who directed them up to the fifth floor where the metals trading department was located.

They were met by a very apologetic young woman who showed them into a meeting room. On the way to the meeting room they passed the trading floor, which the petite young lady proudly pointed out to them. Mike was surprised to find a serious lack of screens in the trading room. It was strange. Rows of desks in an open-plan arrangement. Piles of paper, in-trays, out-trays, and a few computer screens dotted about the landscape. It was in stark contrast to the rows of multi-layered screens that he was used to finding in dealing rooms around the world. He had thought Japan was a technologically advanced country but here was a trading room that would have looked Third World compared to his London or New York office.

They had been seated for only a few minutes before the woman returned with a tray. It had coffee, tea and assorted soft drinks on it. She placed it on a table in the corner and bowed to them before leaving the room. After about ten minutes, but what seemed like an eternity, the door opened once again. This time it was Fujiyama.

Anderson stood up and approached him. 'Fujiyama-san, good to meet you again,' he said, shaking the Japanese man's hand, 'May I introduce my colleague, Mike Kelly. Mike runs our copper book in London.'

'Yes. I believe we met last month in New York,' Fujiyama replied.

'That is correct. Fujiyama-san,' Mike said with a half bow. He really had no clue as to the correct etiquette but hoped he would not make a fool of himself. This time he would let Anderson do all the talking. That way he would be safe.

'Gentlemen, please take a seat,' Fujiyama said as he placed himself in a big leather chair at the head of the table. 'Let's get down to business, shall we?'

'Shouldn't we wait for Okimura-san?' Anderson inquired. Okimura was Fujiyama's direct superior at Yamamoto. He was on the board of directors.

'I am afraid that Mr. Okimura had an urgent meeting to attend, but he shall be joining us later for dinner. He sends his deepest apologies,' Fujiyama lamented. It was a lie. Okimura was in Los Angeles on business for the week, but the men opposite him would never know that.

'Well, we have the legal documents for him to sign in relation to setting up the commodity-linked finance arrangement with Nelson Smith,' Anderson placed a manila folder on the table. It contained all the legal documents necessary for the facility to be put in place. It would give Yamamoto extra finance to the tune of 250 million U.S.D. should the need arise, which would be offset against Yamamoto's physical holdings of copper as security.

Fujiyama explained that he had massive physical obligations in China over the coming year and the loan facility was necessary to finance the deal. He stressed that this was just the beginning of a much expanded role for Yamamoto in the Asian region where the demand for copper had exploded in the past five years as each of the

Asian Tigers had rapidly industrialized, creating massive demand for infrastructure materials such as copper and zinc.

Over the course of the next hour, Anderson tried his pitch to win more of the day to day business from Yamamoto. He stressed the global nature of Nelson Smith's operations, the superior service and greater range of products that they could provide, but really it was all a waste of time. Fujiyama had his circle of brokers and was very happy with their service. His response was very Japanese. Yes, he would consider doing more business via Nelson. It was 'yes' with a capital 'N' for 'no'! But he wasn't going to say it outright to Anderson's face. Especially not while he needed Nelson's credit to get this loan facility in place. Right now, Fujiyama needed Anderson.

About five o'clock, Fujiyama excused himself citing a conference call that he needed to be present on. He told them that he and Mr. Okimura would meet them at a bar in their hotel called the Imperial Bar at seven. He also asked if Anderson could bring the documents for Okimura to sign. Anderson agreed. Mike and Anderson headed back to their hotel.

*

In the corner of a small hotel in Santiago, Chile, Bryan Murphy sat back a little in his chair to aid his digestion. He undid his belt buckle and breathed a heavy sigh. He was full. He had almost finished his bacon and eggs when a man appeared in front of him. 'Ah, Luis, my friend. Please have a seat.' Murphy said, before placing another forkload of food in his mouth. 'Here, help yourself,' he said, holding forward a basket of pastries.

'No thank you Mr. Murphy. I am not hungry, I have already eaten breakfast,' the wiry, dark-haired man now sitting opposite him replied. He wore a tattered old beret which made him look like an aging Che Guevera.

'I see,' Murphy replied. 'Do you mind if I finish then?' He asked rhetorically.

The other man waved his hand for Murphy to continue.

'To what do I owe the pleasure of this visit?' He asked, staring intently at the American.

Luis Orega, in his late forties was the head of the thirty thousand strong C.M.U., the Chilean Mineworker's Union. A former member of Pinochet's secret police, he trusted no one, and at the same time he was both feared and respected by everyone. He was renowned for his bully-boy tactics and there were even rumors of torture and executions of strike breakers. His reputation for brutality had always ensured that the mining companies listened to his demands. The standover tactics he employed had obviously worked. His members had never had better conditions, and men like Murphy were prepared to pay great sums to keep the supplies of copper flowing from Chile. He had only received visits before from Murphy when the powerful Chilean mine workers union was on strike. But this did not puzzle him. Murphy had always had a vested interest in keeping his company, IMT, constantly supplied with copper. What did puzzle him was the timing of the meeting. None of his members were on strike. All the mines in Chile were open and production was once again reaching near capacity levels.

'I have a simple request,' Murphy said, taking a gulp of orange juice, before moving closer to the union official.

'Yes, go on, I am interested to hear,' Luis prompted him.

Murphy took a quick look to make sure no one was watching them before continuing. 'Well, I want your members to go on strike. I want you to close down every mine in Chile in a dispute over pay and working conditions.'

'It can be done,' Luis said, sitting back in his chair. 'Like that.' He snapped his fingers. 'But why?' He asked incredulously.

'Don't you worry about that,' Murphy replied sternly. 'All I want to know is can you arrange it?'

'Yes, for sure. But, of course, there would be a fee for such a series of strikes.'

'But of course,' Murphy said with a smile, as he stood up, wiping the bits of food away from the corners of his mouth. 'Against the right leg of this table I have left a briefcase. You can take the case as your first installment. Each month you will receive a similar payment. I hope you will find it more than ample for your services.' Murphy threw his napkin down on the tablecloth and walked off. 'Goodbye, Luis. I look forward to hearing of your progress.'

*

Back in Tokyo, in the impressive Imperial Bar with its Frank Lloyd Wright originals, Fujiyama and Okimura of Yamamoto Corporation met Mike and Simon Anderson of Nelson Smith. Sitting in a private booth, Anderson produced the documents for Okimura to sign. Once signed, they could activate the loan facility for Yamamoto. Okimura duly signed the papers and the four men drank a toast to further business.

The four men left the Imperial Hotel and made their way across Tokyo for a traditional Japanese dinner. Crossing a small wooden bridge, over a meandering, carp-filled pond, the four men made their way to the gate of a traditional Japanese building. Around them was a meticulously landscaped Japanese garden, replete with bonsai and stone lanterns. A woman in full kimono greeted them at the entrance. She bowed with deference to each of them. Fujiyama explained that they must take off their shoes. Mike realized now why Japanese businessmen never wore lace up shoes. He didn't know if it was the jetlag or the six beers and sake that he had consumed at the Imperial, but it took him a while to get his shoes off, which was in itself quite embarrassing. Having placed a pair of plastic slippers on their feet, the woman then led the way down a narrow wooden corridor. At the end of the corridor she slid a rice-paper screen aside to reveal a tatami room almost devoid of furniture. The woman bowed and pointed into the room with her right hand. In the center of the room there was a low table and around it four floor cushions. An antique-looking scroll hung in a slight alcove to one side of the room. Beside it, a simple flower arrangement. The room oozed traditional, finite simplicity.

Fujiyama and Okimura removed their plastic slippers and stepped into the room. Anderson and Mike did the same. What followed was a number of courses of traditional Japanese food, and mountains of sake. Mike had always been a big fan of sushi. New York had great sushi restaurants. But he had no idea what was being served to him this evening. He figured it would be rude to ask. Everything tasted fine, so he just went ahead and ate everything that was placed in front of him.

It was a very serene atmosphere, far removed from the choking crush of Tokyo, yet in its heart. It was amazing that a place such as this existed in such an immense urban sprawl. It was so peaceful, so spiritual.

Anderson broke Mike's spiritual mood by once again talking shop. He was determined to win more of Yamamoto's business. Mike, who had said very little in the past four hours, was a mere observer. He was patiently watching everything that was going on. He watched the woman bringing in their food. The small steps she took. The delicate care she took placing their meals on the table. He had noticed that both Okimura and Fujiyama wore a gold, rhombus-shaped pin on their lapels. He figured it must be a corporate emblem as he had seen Fujiyama wearing the same pin in New York. He noticed that Okimura had a very poor grasp of English and had to be guided by his subordinate, Fujiyama. He also noticed that one of Anderson's socks had a hole in it by the big toe. Another thing to watch out for. Never wear a pair of holey socks to dinner in Tokyo. It could be embarrassing when you took off your shoes.

Anderson was glad that he had met with the powerful Okimura-san and had clinched the financing deal arrangements. It would be another feather in his cap. Anderson was very politically astute. He was aware that sealing this type of deal could only enhance his standing within the company.

Little did they know that the real Okimura was still on business in Los Angeles. The man whom they had met was one of Fujiyama's Yakuza minders who had been briefed to play the part. The Yakuza man played the part well. He didn't say much. A poor grasp of English was his cover. He even smugly handed out Okimura's business cards that Fujiyama had spirited from Okimura's top draw earlier that afternoon.

Fujiyama saw the wonderful irony in the situation. He smiled as they drank another toast to increased business relations. The upstanding Anderson was now, although unwittingly, aiding and abetting his plan. He had no clue whatsoever.

Operation Longbeach could now move into top gear.

September, 1995

Once the commodity-linked financing deal was in place, Yamamoto Corporation just kept accumulating more and more warrants. By not rolling their position forward, and refusing to lend it to the market, the amount of nearby copper began to dry up and a major backwardation started. Usually commodities markets are in *contango*, where forward prices are higher than nearby prices which reflects the costs of storage and finance of the material. In a backwardation, nearby cash prices of a commodity are higher than the prices for further forward delivery, which reflects a shortage of near-term supply.

All the hedge funds like Icarus and Tiger would have to roll their short positions forward as they would not have the material to deliver. Stocks were at record lows and the scarcity of material pushed the backwardation even wider with each week's stock figures. It had started at a bearable 30 U.S.D. back from cash to three months. By the end of September, it had blown out to 180 U.S.D. back. This meant that to carry a short position for three months it would cost you 180 U.S.D. per metric tonne even if the price didn't move. This was bound to make the hedge funds rethink their position. It might even force them to cover. Both Mike and Anderson wondered how much pain these big funds could endure before cutting their losses and running. It made sense to live to fight another day.

Yamamoto had accumulated a cash position of close to five thousand lots or close to half the LME inventories. They financed this metal each night on an overnight basis rather than lending it to the market. Fujiyama had told Anderson that they might need the material at any moment and did not wish to give up the Longbeach warrants that they had accumulated. Fujiyama explained that it was easier to ship the material to Shanghai from Longbeach than from any other LME warehouse location. Longbeach material was running at a high premium to other LME warehouse destinations. Despite the large backwardation, it was more economical to hold onto the material and pay overnight interest rates than receive the bonanza from lending the material with the possibility that they might not get the right material back. There seemed to be some method in the Japanese trader's madness. Mike thought it was just that. Complete madness. Why pay overnight rates when he could be making a fortune lending the material overnight?

In the familiar privacy of Anderson's office, Mike, Steve, and Anderson all spoke candidly about the situation.

'What do you guys think?' Anderson inquired, both hands on his hips.

'Simple. The bastard is squeezing the nuts off the market,' Mike blurted out, flicking his well-worn stress ball into the air. It had been a long day trying to keep a track of all the spreads inside the three month period. He had neither the time nor the patience to be eloquent.

'Yeah,' Steve concurred. 'I think he is trying to get the hedge funds out. They have to roll their positions forward soon. Ouch. It is going to cost them a fortune.'

'That is if they roll. They might just decide to cover their positions outright,' Mike added.

'Right. So how are we going to make money out of this?' Anderson queried.

'I think we look for anomalies in the spread and lend it,' Mike said with confidence. 'It is getting silly down there on the floor. Some periods cost a fortune, others cost nothing. It makes no sense.'

'I agree. But the danger there is that once you put on a position, you might not be able to get out.' Anderson advised caution. He knew that the key to success in the financial markets was longevity. They were having a good year and, provided they made budget, everyone would get paid. He didn't want them blowing up trying to hit a home run. 'How 'bout we put on a short spread butterfly and buy some upside options as protection?'

'Sounds like a reasonable plan to me,' Steve said, twirling a pen around his thumb and forefinger. 'Vol is cheap at fourteen percent, if the big funds were to cover their positions, vol could explode.'

'Yeah, the real danger is on the upside at the moment,' Mike threw the stress ball into the air. Anderson's hand shot out, catching it.

'Then we'll insure against it,' Anderson smiled contentedly, playing with the stress ball. 'Also, one more thing before you go,' his tone turned grave, 'I don't want to hear any talk about a squeeze on the desk. That sort of stuff is illegal. You never know who might be listening. You have to be very careful out there on the desk. Make sure all the junior guys are aware of it as well. Is that clear?'

'Crystal,' Mike replied. Steve just nodded his head.

*

The considerable figure of Lloyd Cartwright sat back in a big chair in the long bar of the R.A.C. Club on Pall Mall. It was one of the few places that women were not allowed these days. Dressed in a conservative gray suit, he puffed away on his Montecristo number four cigar while he waited for the man he had come to see. In other corners of the room, old men who still thought that India was one of the colonies chatted quietly. The days of the empire were gone and the days of male bastions such as the long bar were numbered as well. It was best to enjoy them while they could.

As director of the LME, Lloyd Cartwright was in a high-profile position. He was responsible for the smooth running of the largest metals exchange in the world. In his mid forties, he had a substantial gambling habit. He couldn't help himself. Every day he had to have his fix at any one of a number of private gaming establishments around London. It had been his downfall. He had taken some loans from a loanshark at one of the casinos. It was only later on that he found out that the loanshark was Yakuza. They had owned him ever since. Fujiyama had summoned him to the R.A.C. Club. He was obliged to go. He had no choice.

Almost from nowhere Fujiyama appeared beside him in a chair.

'I'll make this very short. I have a busy schedule today.'

'Okay.'

Lloyd was sweating. He wiped his brow with his handkerchief. He hated these meetings. It always ended up with him bending some exchange rule or another.

'You will stage an investigation into the copper market backwardation once it gets above 300 U.S.D. per tonne,' Fujiyama stated in a soft clear voice. 'Then, a few months later, you will announce your findings. Do you understand?'

'Yes.'

'Good. You will receive the usual amount for your cooperation.'

Then, just as quickly as he had appeared, Fujiyama was gone.

October, 1995

There was blood in the streets. People were blowing out of their short spread positions in copper as the spread between cash and three months blew out. Cash was trading at three hundred dollars a tonne premium to the three months price. Those getting carted out included traders with short spread positions, short speculators rolling the positions forward and the copper consumers who had neglected to hedge properly. Cash copper was now trading above 3,000 U.S.D. per metric tonne. People were hurting.

When the news of a massive strike in Chile involving the powerful mine workers' union had hit the market, it had only served to accelerate the rally. Across Europe and the U.S.A., consumers were crying foul to the authorities. Rumors of a squeeze, or corner on the copper market abounded. The LME announced that it would conduct an investigation into the backwardation. It would examine all of its members and their positions amidst allegations of market manipulation before deciding what action, if any, to take. The whole world knew exactly who they would be investigating. It was no witch-hunt. The LME would be looking directly at the positions held by Fujiyama and the powerful Yamamoto Corporation.

Meanwhile, on the sidelines, the big copper-mining companies were content to sit and watch the value of their stock increase with each passing day. They were happy to buy downside puts which would insure them against a price move lower. This strategy provided them with the best of both worlds. It gave them downside protection whilst leaving them open to participate fully in any rally that might ensue.

On the other side of the coin, 'the copper club' led by Fujiyama was making a fortune. Yamamoto, IMT and Wilmont Bridge were printing money hand over fist as people scrambled for the exits which they had bolted firmly shut. Fujiyama was very pleased with the way *Operation Longbeach* was going. The squeeze he had created was a roaring success. Fujiyama estimated that it had enabled them to siphon off close to three hundred million dollars from the copper market and Yamamoto.

*

Every year in October, market participants gather in London for what they call 'LME Week.' Like its poorer cousin in New York, Copper Week, LME Week is a week-long excuse for a party. Traders, brokers, producers, consumers, and speculators all descend on London for a week of receptions and cocktail parties highlighted by the LME Dinner, the largest black tie function on the planet. Over three thousand people attend this black tie affair with the majority dining at the massive ballroom in Grosvenor House on Park Lane. Other dinners are held by various brokerage houses at off-site locations.

Mike wondered how many times he would be waking with bloodshot eyes that week. He figured the next time he applied for a passport he would answer 'red' for color of eyes. It would be a truly trying week for his liver and his kidneys. Anyway, the thought of three thousand odd people getting together for a self-congratulatory affair really didn't do much for him. How many times can you pat yourself on the back in a single year? The LME directors would get up and tell everyone how volume had increased and that they set the standard for the world pricing of metal and so on and so on. They would blow all this smoke up their own arses, but they really had little control, if any, over their market. That was obvious. Blind Freddy could see that Fujiyama was squeezing the market. Mike wanted to know when the exchange and or the regulators would step in and curb this market manipulation. Or was the whole industry bent? From the top down? The metals markets were dodgy indeed.

It was a quiet day. Mike was reading a copy of *The Financial Times*. Suddenly there was an interesting headline on the Reuters news service. SECRET DAVILA BANK ACCOUNTS DISCOVERED IN CAYMANS.

'Hey, did you see that story?' Steve called out to Mike across the desk.

'Yeah, just bringing it up now,' Mike said, putting down his paper.

He fiddled quickly with his mouse and clicked on the headline bringing up the article. It appeared that Ernst & Young Asset Recovery, acting on behalf of Codelco, had found accounts in the Cayman Islands that were controlled by their former head copper trader Juan Pablo Davila. Close to $25 million had washed through these accounts in the period before Codelco fired the trader and announced losses to the tune of 270 million U.S.D. Codelco also announced plans to file lawsuits against Sogemin and Metallgesellschaft, both metals brokers were allegedly involved in an illegal kickbacks incentive scheme involving Davila.

'Dude, that's wild,' Mike called out to Steve as he finished reading the article.

Steve started his usual tirade, 'Man, this market is so dodgy. They are all a bunch of criminals. They should all be in jail.'

'Maybe they will be,' Mike laughed. 'And you and I will be the only ones left.'

Minutes later Anderson was at the desk.

'Mike, Steve. My office please.'

He was very matter of fact. In the confines of his office, Anderson explained that they had received a call from the SFO earlier in the day.

'It is nothing to be alarmed about. The Codelco fiasco occurred years before any of us started working. The SFO has asked for access to all the trade blotters and trade tickets and documents for business done with Codelco. Most of it will be archived by now. I'll get Andy to help them out there. But just in case they come out to the desk and ask any questions, well I just want you to be as courteous with the regulators as possible. We don't want them making life tough for us.'

'Do you think they will make life tough for us?' Mike raised his eyebrows.

Anderson was frank. 'Dude, it could be bad. Who knows what dodgy shit Palmer and the old crew did? Palmer was eventually fired for parking a position with Codelco over year end. But if we cooperate, everything should be fine.'

It was only a couple of hours later that the next headline hit the Reuters newswire. SFO TO LAUNCH CODELCO INVESTIGATION, LME BROKERS TO BE TARGETED.

Over on Elm Street at the headquarters of the SFO, Fiona Bolton was summoned to the director's office. Her work on the Barings collapse was almost finished. She had spent seven long months on the case. Countless hours of pouring over documents. Her research had been crucial for certain sections in the final report being tabled to the governor of the Bank of England. The director informed her of her new assignment. She had been assigned to the Codelco investigative team. Starting next week she would be at the offices of the gargantuan U.S. securities firm, Nelson Smith.

The LME dinner was a huge occasion indeed. Mike lay there, dressed in the remnants of his tux, hurting, feet up on the desk. It was his recovery position. He covered himself with the black jacket. He wished the lights on the floor would go off to make it easier for him to sleep. How inconsiderate were the Asia desk traders, working with the lights on. He was just trying to grab a couple hours' sleep before it got busy. But if the whole market was feeling as bad as him he doubted whether much business would take place that day. It was going be a very slow day. Or so Mike hoped.

It had been a huge night. Mike had gone to the dinner, and had been, as expected, bored to tears by the speeches. Luckily, the alcohol had managed to numb his senses enough for him to get through it. He then went on to the after party staged by Merrill Lynch at the roof gardens, which was a so-so affair. After that he had partied on with his brokers, and a large portion of the LME at Chaplin's on Swallow Street. What a heinous strip club it was! Sometime in the wee hours of the morning, he had stumbled out into the street. He had decided to take a cab straight to the office as he and Anderson had made a bet sometime during the night about who would make it to the office first. It was a bet he was determined to win.

Around 9 a.m. he was confronted by a sight to behold. Through his half-closed eyes he saw her. Tall, blonde, beautiful, she was standing there in front of him. Waiting. Patient. He sat up with a jolt.

'Um. Hi, can I help you?' Mike grabbed for words.

'Yes. I think maybe you can,' Fiona replied in a soft feminine voice. 'I am with the Serious Fraud Office. Simon Anderson said that you might be of assistance to me. I was wondering if you could direct me to the trade blotters for the period January through December of '92 and '93.'

'Sure,' Mike smiled. 'They are in the filing cabinet over there.' He pointed to a big steel-cased cabinet on the other side of the desk. I'm Mike by the way. Mike Kelly. I'm the head copper trader,' he hastened to add holding out his hand.

'Fiona Bolton. Pleased to meet you,' she said, as she shook his hand.

'If you need any help, just give me a shout. I mean, anything. It's no problem, really.'

'I'll keep that in mind,' Fiona said as she made her way around to the other side of the desk.

Mike looked up at his screen. There was a fresh e-mail message. He clicked on his mouse to open it. It was from Anderson.

'Dude, you win. There's your payment.'

Mike looked across the room into Anderson's office. Anderson was howling with laughter. Mike smiled. What an awesome payment it was indeed!

November, 1995

October had been a sensational month. The commodities desk was well ahead of budget. Julio was happy. That meant Anderson was happy. The mood translated into a warm, fuzzy feeling on the desk. As Anderson had explained it to Mike and Steve, their bonuses were basically decided by the end of October. Any money they made from here on in, they would try as much as possible to salt away into reserves for next year's budget. It was better to play it safe for the rest of the year. A large loss might be harmful toward their bonus prospects whilst a large win would do them no further good. It was a losing proposition on all accounts to swing for the fences. That meant sound business management and a lower profile in the market. It suited Mike and Steve perfectly. It took a lot of pressure of their shoulders.

The backwardation had almost doubled in the last month since the consumers had started protesting. It stood around 320 U.S.D. per metric tonne from cash to three months. The LME had been around asking infantile questions about Yamamoto's copper positions, but had done nothing as yet about the backwardation. All indications were that they probably would do nothing except limit the back to 25 U.S.D. for any single day. Which, when you worked it out, was a theoretical backwardation of 2,250 U.S.D. for a three-month period. The hedge funds must have been bleeding losses.

All the while Fujiyama and his cronies were busy printing money. They were intent on making hay while the sun shone. And by mid-November, it was shining brightly.

Mike had finally summoned up the courage to ask Fiona out to dinner. He had been watching her, entranced, day in, day out, for weeks. He had developed a coffee machine rapport with her over the past week. He waited till she was alone in her office and casually walked up to the door.

'Busy?' Mike inquired, hanging off the doorframe.

'Not really. What can I do for you?' Fiona asked, closing a manila folder on her desk.

'Well, I was wondering if you'd like to go out for a bite to eat sometime?'

'I guess so,' Fiona replied hesitantly.

'If you don't want to, it's okay. I mean, there's no pressure or anything,' Mike looked down toward the floor.

'No. I'd love to. Is Thursday good for you?'

'Sure.' Mike replied with glee. He wanted to high five himself.

'Mike, copper in one hundred for Elvis,' Andy shouted in the background.

'Sorry, I've got to run. We can arrange this later,' Mike ran back to the desk.

Back at the desk, Steve and Anderson were killing themselves laughing.

'They made me do it,' Andy pleaded.

'Oh ha ha. Very funny,' Mike said, slumping back into his seat. But a smile did cross his face. He didn't care at all. He had finally broken the ice.

★

In a smoky Irish bar in the East Village, Bryan Murphy sat waiting patiently. He sipped a pint of Guinness slowly, carefully eyeing the whole bar. The smell of beer-stained wooden floorboards pervaded the air as he gazed at the long bar with pictures of John F. Kennedy and an Irish flag draped above it. As he gazed at the flag, his mind drifted back to County Fermanagh, to his youth. He was nine again, playing in the rolling green hills, the lush vegetation, in the peace and calm, the tranquillity of his native Northern Ireland. He could see himself climbing over O'Rourke's fence, almost tearing his trousers (for which he would get a thrashing). He saw himself racing with Sean to the front gate beside O'Rourke's barn, sneaking up the ladder into its loft. It was from this vantage point that they spied on their older brother Patrick and his new friends from Belfast. Patrick was nigh on ten years older than his younger siblings. He had forbidden them to go near the barn, let alone enter it. Ever curious, his younger brothers had done just the opposite. They had set a trap for him. They lay waiting in the loft with sticks and rocks, ready to ambush Patrick and his friends. They could see Patrick and three other men sitting in a circle, but they couldn't make out what they were saying.

'Ready?' whispered Sean.

'Aye,' Bryan replied.

'On the count of three,' Sean said raising a rock above his head.

'One... two...'

'Three!'

There was a loud crash as the barn door burst open. Four men dressed from head to toe in black flooded into the room. Rapid bursts of machine-gun fire echoed around the barn. The sound of metal bullet casings bouncing off the wooden floor reverberated off the walls. The boys, filled with mortal terror, held their heads down in the hay, whimpering, praying that the gunfire would end.

It was over in seconds. The terror would last a lifetime. The boys lay motionless, too scared to lift a finger. Too scared to scream, they just lay there.

Summoning up the courage, Bryan had crawled forward and looked over the edge of the loft and into the carnage below. To his horror the four men who had been standing there less than thirty seconds before lay stagnant, a pool of blood swimming about their bodies. Then he saw Patrick's face. Empty. Dead.

He grabbed Sean by the scruff of the neck and screamed, 'Run! Sean, run!' And run they had. The boys ran and ran, faster than they had ever run before. Hearts pounding. Not stopping. No looking back. Never turning, they reached their farmhouse two miles down the road. Breathless.

Neither of them said a word about what they had witnessed. It would be etched on their minds for life. They didn't need to talk about it. Patrick and the three others were given a proper I.R.A. funeral three days later. In killing the four, the S.A.S. had fermented hate in the two innocents. Hate that would come back to haunt them later.

'Bryan. Can I get you another?'

Bryan was startled out of his daydream. 'Sorry?'

'Is that how you greet your only brother?' It was his older brother Sean. Older, that is, by all of seven minutes. The fraternal twins greeted each other with a big hug.

'Yeah, but I find it strange calling my only brother, father.'

Bryan made fun of his brother's clerical robes. Bryan had been sent to live with his aunt in New York at the tender age of ten and Sean had entered a catholic boarding school. Having finished his schooling, Sean had decided to enter the priesthood. He was now the priest for the diocese near their family farm in Fermanagh.

'So, back to my original question. Can I get you another pint of mother's milk?' Sean's Irish lilt was obvious. Bryan's accent had weathered into a New York one, but somehow he slipped back into a more Irish-sounding accent when he was around his brother.

'I thought you had to give it up when you entered the priesthood.'

'Bryan, Bryan. Whatever will we do with you?' Sean threw up his hands in exasperation. 'How many times do I have to tell you? Our Lord Jesus Christ served alcohol at the last supper. So tell me, have you been to mass lately?'

'Yes,' Bryan replied, with just a slight hint of hesitation.

'Liar!' Sean retorted in an accusatory tone. 'Now you'll have to make a trip to confession as well for that one. When will you ever learn? Now what about that beer?'

The two men drank pints of Guinness and Sean filled Bryan in on all the local gossip. Despite living in New York for most of his life, Bryan still dreamt that he would one day retire to his home town. It was a pie in the sky type of dream as he knew he would die of boredom if he moved back there, but through Sean he was able live there vicariously. It was therapeutic for them both.

Just as Sean was about leave, Bryan reached into his jacket pocket. He pulled out an envelope and placed it on the table.

'What's this?' Sean asked, knowing full well what the envelope contained.

It was his regular donation. Inside the envelope was a check for two hundred and fifty thousand U.S. dollars made out to a registered children's charity that Sean Murphy managed. This children's charity acted as both a legitimate children's charity and a front for the I.R.A. Through it the I.R.A. were able to launder millions of dollars from the U.S.A. Proceeds from drugs that were used to buy weapons were all laundered through the charity. For its work, the charity received ten percent of all the money laundered. Many legitimate social schemes had been financed by the proceeds from the money-laundering activities.

'It's for the children, father,' Bryan finished off his pint.

'Bless you my child. The children of Ireland need more loyal sons like you.'

*

Dinner at the trendy Kensington Place restaurant had been a rather noisy affair. The rectangular shape of the premises combined with the highly polished floorboards meant the acoustics left a lot to be desired. Not really the right venue for an intimate dinner, more a place for people watching. But a fine meal and three bottles of Merlot had given the place a really buzzing ambiance. Mike arranged for one of the sales guys in the New York office to call him at least twice during dinner so that he would look more important. He really was a complete wanker at times.

He waved capriciously at the yellow light approaching them down Kensington Church Street.

'Where to guv?' The taxi driver asked deferentially, in a typically East London accent.

'Fulham Road, please.' Fiona rattled off her address as she stepped into the comfort of the black cab. Turning back, she beckoned. 'Come on, Mike, I'll make us some coffee.'

Without hesitation Mike bounded into the back of the cab. He needed no persuasion. Not, at least, when 'coffee' was involved.

Sitting on the back seat of the cab, Mike sidled up close to Fiona. Leaning across he put his right arm around her delicate shoulders. His fingers gently massaged her neck as he kissed her softly on her left ear lobe. Fiona grabbed Mike's hand and guided his fingers up her neck, across her soft cheeks into the moist environment of her mouth. She tantalizingly sucked his fingers one by one in an incredibly sexy, phallic fashion. Mike's hopes rose. He had been out to dinner with her twice before. Twice he had struck out. Twice he had gone home kicking stones. A quick goodbye kiss outside the restaurant was all he had to show for his efforts. He was suddenly gripped with fear. Maybe the third bottle of Merlot was not such a good idea after all. Sure, it had done the trick. Fiona was rather pliant, but what if it had rendered him incapable. That thought terrified him.

'Just anywhere here on the left will be fine, thanks,' Fiona's sweet voice broke his concentration. 'Come on, Mike,' she said, flashing him a wicked grin, 'let's go up for some coffee.'

The door open, Fiona fumbled around for the light switch immediately on the left. A soft white glow lit the entry hall. Mike checked himself briefly in the mirror. He was still in the suit he had worn to work. He hadn't had time to change before dinner. He grimaced for a second, making sure there were no errant bits of dinner still caught between his teeth.

'How do you like your coffee, Mike?' came Fiona's muffled call from the kitchen.

'White with two sugars,' he replied hesitantly, sounding rather perplexed.

'We only have instant. Is that okay?'

'Yeah, sure,' his mind raced. She really *was* making coffee. This was not good.

He hurried to the kitchen. Fiona's jacket hung limply on the doorknob. Fiona was at the sink, her back to him, filling a kettle with water. Mike rested against the doorframe admiring her figure. Her long blonde hair cascaded carelessly down the back of her white shirt, her bra straps almost visible through the fabric. The tight, short, black skirt and black high heels showed off her svelte legs resplendent in black stockings.

He sensed the opportunity to make his move. Without a word, he stepped forward, grabbing Fiona tightly around her slight waist from behind. She stiffened suddenly. He gnawed tenderly on the exposed nape of her neck to allay her tension. She relaxed. Pushing his pelvis against her buttocks he ran his hands slowly, gently up the outside of her thighs. Starting at the top of her stockings his wandering hands made their way up the inside of her skirt all the while caressing her neck with his tongue and teeth. Fiona closed her eyes dropping the now full kettle into the sink with a crash. Gripping the kitchen bench top firmly, both arms outstretched, she thrust her buttocks harder against Mike's pelvis, rubbing him up and down in a rhythmic, sensual pattern. His hands moved confidently from the top of her thighs to her naked cheeks. His heart raced. She's not wearing any underwear, Mike thought to himself briefly, until the lace of her G-string convinced him otherwise. Hands still under her skirt, Mike turned Fiona around to face him. Clasping her arms firmly around his neck, she kissed him passionately. She ran her right hand around his neck to undo the top button of his shirt, loosening his tie in the process. Mike's heart pounded with anticipation. She gently massaged the inside of his thigh with her right foot as they kissed. He felt his pulse quicken. Any apprehension he might have felt earlier dissipated instantly as he rose to the occasion. In one swift move, Mike pulled Fiona up around his waist, her legs wrapping tightly around his back. His face nuzzled in the safety of her breasts. She flicked her heels off.

'Take me into the front room,' she whispered ever so softly into his ear, gently chewing it as she did so.

Mike stumbled slowly into the darkness of the front room, Fiona still wrapped tightly around his waist. Supporting her with his right arm firmly under her buttocks he used his left hand to undo his belt and unzip his trousers causing them to dangle restrictively around his knees. They shuffled forward, still locked in a passionate tongue wrestle.

They bumped into the armrest of the sofa. The impact caused Mike to loose his balance and fall forward. Fiona let out a slight squeal as she fell backwards into the soft cushions of the couch, her limbs flailing wildly, and landed in a rather unladylike position. With her legs spread-eagled her skirt rode up to her waist. Mike keeled forward, face planting into her void, his knees still on the floor, torso resting on the armrest. Seizing the opportunity, Mike ran his wet tongue along her bikini line. Fiona grabbed for Mike's head instinctively but the tingling sensation she was now feeling caused her to run her fingers through his hair rather than push him away. Sensing the time was right Mike fumbled with his right hand, pushing his boxers down around his knees to join his trousers. He climbed over the armrest of the couch, placing his sturdy frame above Fiona. Lifting her buttocks slightly of the couch, he pulled her lace G-string off swiftly and flicked it triumphantly into the far corner of the room. He bent over and kissed her softly on the neck. Fiona's hand gripped his him tightly, guiding him towards her. Mike gushed with anticipation. Then suddenly, she stopped.

'What's wrong, babe?' Mike asked softly.

'Shhh,' she said, 'I think I heard something.'

'Fee?' came a woman's voice down the corridor.' You home?'

'Shit!' cried Fiona as her body went rigid. 'It's Imogen. Quick!' And in one smooth motion Fiona jumped up, pushing Mike off her, and attempted to adjust her skirt. Mike went reeling onto his back on the floor. A blinding light greeted him as Imogen flicked the switch.

'Imogen what are you doing back?' asked Fiona incredulously. 'I thought you weren't due back from Milan till Saturday.' She continued, pretending not to be at all phased by the intrusion.

'I wasn't, but the photo shoot finished early. The photographer fell ill so I'll have to go back next month and do it all again.' Imogen paused, all the while staring at Mike who, although paralyzed with the initial embarrassment of the situation, was now struggling to put his trousers back on whilst he lay on the floor. 'So, Fee, aren't you going to introduce me to your new friend?'

'Ah, yes, sure,' Fiona now struggled for words. 'This is my friend Mike, he's from New York,' she said, gesturing in his direction with an open hand. 'And Mike, this is my flatmate, Imogen,' Fiona continued, her face suddenly turning bright red as she noticed her lace G-string hanging prominently from the Bose speaker in the corner.

'Pleased to meet you,' Mike rose to his feet offering his right hand.

'I can see that,' Imogen smirked, eyeing his still bulging trousers.

Right there and then Mike wished the earth would somehow open up and swallow him whole.

December, 1995

Mike and Fiona had just returned from a sensational weekend in Monaco. It turned out that Fiona's uncle had an apartment in Monaco that was vacant for the winter. They had flown down to Nice on the Friday night, hired a car, and driven to Fiona's uncle's place. After a fantastic weekend of wining, dining, and gambling, they had flown back into Heathrow late on Sunday night. Mike was still buzzing when he got back to work on Monday morning. He had a tell-tale 'perma-grin' smile from ear to ear. He was glowing.

Year-end reviews were taking place. Mike was already deciding how he would spend the money he received next January. It was typical of him. It had been a good year. The desk had cruised past its budget for the year in late October, thanks to the backwardation in copper, so Mike was looking for a new toy. He had a guaranteed bonus of 250,000 U.S.D. in cash for his first year in the contract that he had signed, plus, of course, whatever else Julio would pay him on top of that.

He had always wanted a motorbike. A red Ducati 916 had caught his eye. The Ferrari of motorbikes. Italian. It was fast and stylish. A veritable chick magnet. His mother would have had a cardiac if she had known what he was planning to buy. He knew her views on bikes. But as his family lived in San Diego, they would never find out. And what you don't know can't hurt you, Mike figured.

He also had to buy a present for Fiona. They had only been dating for about six weeks but in that six weeks they had spent so much time together. They had spent a weekend together in Paris, a weekend in Barcelona, and this last weekend in Monaco. And besides that he had been invited to her family's chateau in central France for Christmas. Seeing as he had been back to San Diego briefly for Thanksgiving, he figured it would be okay to miss Christmas with the family this year. Besides, they would understand. You don't get an invitation to spend Christmas in a French chateau every day of the week.

Despite the short amount of time he had known Fiona, Mike was already hooked. He had been smitten with her from the moment he had lain his bloodshot eyes on her. She was so elegant, so refined, so beautiful. And even better, she was rich and she could ski. She was his ideal partner. Still, he didn't know what to get her for Christmas. He had to get her something special but not kitsch. Something to show he was a serious player but not something garish or over the top. He had never felt like this before about anyone. It scared him half to death, but excited him at the same time. He decided to go 'limit up' and buy Fiona a bracelet from Tiffany's for Christmas, provided for, of course, by his bonus.

Whilst waiting for his turn in Julio's office, Mike surfed the Net, looking for his new toy. The Internet was probably the most productivity sapping device that was ever made available to the desk. The commodities area, via Andy's resourcefulness, had got a hold of a Netscape browser and had it hooked up to every terminal on the desk. From that point on, countless hours were spent surfing the Net. Netscape made it so easy. The desk already had access to a plethora of information systems. It wasn't as if they needed any more, but they took to it like ducks to water.

For something billed as the greatest tool for research ever devised, one hell of a lot of time was spent surfing for porn. Andy seemed to stay late every night since they had gained access to the Net. Mike finally worked out why. For the best porn sites to visit, see Andy.

Despite the fact that bonus reviews were taking place, the desk had taken on a fairly morbid tone for what should really be such a happy time of year. It was almost Christmas and they were all being told how much money and or stock they would receive as part of their performance bonus. No one really wanted to get saddled with a lot of stock. As Steve put it, 'you might as well write that part of your bonus off'. It was true. The stock incentive was a kind golden handcuff. It didn't vest for three years and once vested you couldn't sell it for two further years, thus delaying your income for five years. Sure, it paid an annual dividend in the meantime, but unless you had a serious wedge it wasn't worth it.

One by one everyone on the desk was going into Julio's office for their end of year review. One by one they came out. People rarely looked pleased when they left his office. It was one of those unwritten rules. No one talked about what they got but everyone speculated about what everyone else got. Mike would have preferred them to have just published a list and placed it on the noticeboard by the coffee machine. Then everyone could have seen where they ranked in relation to everyone else, rather than bitching about what other people got when they didn't even know the full story.

Steve came out of Julio's office. Mike wondered if he had received any stock. He couldn't tell. Steve's face was blank, expressionless.

'It's your turn, big guy,' Steve said, slumping into his seat.

Steve's stony-faced reaction didn't phase Mike. He was confident that Julio would take care of him. After all, they had made budget easily. Thanks, in part, to Mike's efforts.

'Come in, Mike. Please, close the door,' Julio beckoned. 'Please take a seat.'

When Mike was comfortably seated Julio launched into his speech. 'Look, Mike, I am not going to waste a lot of time with you today. We are happy with your progress and your results this year. Hopefully next year you will continue the good work. Your incentive payment will be 300,000 U.S.D. in cash. No stock for you this year. Any questions?'

Mike was a little taken aback by Julio's direct approach. He was more than happy with the fact that he wasn't receiving any stock, but had actually hoped for a larger cash bonus. Maybe he was just a little greedy.

'How do I get more?' Mike decided to be direct as well.

'I can see that you are a greedy guy,' Julio continued. 'I like greedy guys working for me. But you have to understand that you have only been here for nine months. It will be a different story next year, I promise you. As long as you keep making money you will be fine.'

'I see. I make money so that you can buy a new house,' Mike smiled. He knew that Julio had just bought a new multi-million dollar house in London, it was common knowledge on the desk.

'Mike,' Julio started looking up at the ceiling for inspiration, 'let me ask you a question. Who built the atom bomb?'

'Oppenheimer, of course.'

'Oppenheimer!' Julio exclaimed, pointing his finger direct at Mike. 'That's what everyone thinks. Robert Oppenheimer was good physicist, not a great one. But what Oppenheimer did was that he gathered all these great physicists from around the world and assembled them in the desert in Los Alamos in New Mexico. These great physicists toiled and toiled and created the bomb. Oppenheimer gets the credit.'

'I see,' Mike said thoughtfully.

'I am Oppenheimer,' Julio proudly proclaimed, patting his chest with both hands, 'And you, Mike, you build my bomb.'

Mike went back to the desk. He couldn't help laughing. Julio's Oppenheimer story was really pretty funny. It took the edge off any disappointment he had felt. The fact that he hadn't received any stock was a plus and he guessed he couldn't be entirely unhappy with the result. After all, he had only worked nine months of the year. His mind switched back to the money. How was he going to spend it?

With the market so dead that afternoon, Mike went back to surfing the Net for more information on motorbikes. He was using the mother of all search engines, the metacrawler. For some reason, today his P.C. was really slow. He had ordered a major RAM upgrade but it had not yet been forthcoming. With all the applications he had running his memory was being sucked dry. His Netscape browser kept closing itself down. Finally Mike decided to call the help desk and get someone from the I.T. department to come up and take a look at his machine. It was so infuriating.

Ten minutes later V.J. Singh from the I.T. department was at Mike's desk. Of Indian extraction, V.J. had graduated top in his class in computer science at the University of New Delhi before coming to the U.K. to work. Coming from India that made him one in a billion. He was a whiz at all things computer-oriented. In a flash he had solved all of Mike's P.C. and information systems problems on prior occasions, so Mike was more than happy to sit back while he worked.

'Your RAM upgrade should arrive in a couple of days,' V.J. faced the screen, clicking away furiously with the mouse. 'You know, part of the reason why your P.C. is so slow is that your hard drive is almost full. You should save your files to the network server, not to your hard drive. It will speed up your machine. Gee, you sure have a lot of garbage on your hard drive. Do you want to clean it up a bit?'

'Sure. Do whatever you need to do to stop Netscape from crashing all the time.'

'Do you really need all these old e-mail files? There are close to two thousand e-mails in your inbox. They are taking up a hell of a lot of space.'

'I suppose I could get rid of some of them,' Mike sat forward in his chair.

'I'll leave you to it then,' V.J. said as he left.

One by one, Mike went through his old e-mail files. It was going to take him ages to sort them. There was even a heap of files on the hard drive that weren't his, they were addressed to James Hayward. Mike had inherited Hayward's P.C. when he had started in London. It was the fastest P.C. on the desk and had not been in use since Hayward's departure at the end of January. Mike had seen it lying dormant at the end of the desk and commandeered it for his own use.

Mike started trashing Hayward's old e-mails one by one. Then he came across a peculiar e-mail. It grabbed his attention initially because it was the only e-mail that was unread. What made him even more curious was the fact that he couldn't open it. It had to be encrypted somehow. He decided to call V.J. again for help. This e-mail really intrigued him, especially as there was nothing else of interest going on in his world at the time. He wondered if it would turn out to be a pornographic picture. It had no subject title.

V.J. arrived promptly. It took him all of five minutes of fiddling to break the encryption device. It was pretty primitive, well at least for a guru like V.J. It turned out that the e-mail contained not pornography, as Mike had suspected, but an excel spreadsheet. It had been sent from an America Online address, davidgreen@aol.com. It was quite a large spreadsheet. It seemed to show cashflows from Yamamoto Corporation to IMT and Wilmont Bridge and then via a myriad of companies these cashflows arrived at some company that Mike had never heard of called Metco International. Mike thanked V.J. for his help. It was late now. The market would be closed in about ten minutes. Rolo was already preparing to leave for the day. He was going to dash for the five past seven train home.

'Rolo?' Mike called out to Rolo who was, by now, dressing himself at the coat stand. 'Do you know a guy called David Green?'

'Yes. I did.' Rolo wrapped a Burberry's scarf around his neck.

'Did?' Mike looked slightly bemused.

'Yeah. Did is the operative word. David Green was a trader at IMT in New York until he died in a house fire in Connecticut earlier this year.'

'How awful.'

'Yeah, apparently he had been drinking heavily, gone up to bed and lit up a fag before he passed out. Somehow the curtains caught fire and his whole place went up. He was dead when the paramedics arrived.'

'You ever heard of a company called Metco?' Mike continued his inquiry.

'Nope. Never heard of them. Why?'

'No real reason. Just saw their name and wondered what they do.'

'Anyway, I gotta run. Catch you tomorrow,' Rolo called out as he headed for the elevators.

Mike looked at his watch. It was two minutes to seven. He should really blow out early today. He had arranged to meet Fiona at Bibendum for dinner at eight. Mike loved the place. The stained glass windows of the Michelin tire man were way cool. It was rather funky to have a fine meal in what used to be a Michelin tire store. Anyway, he was going to have to go straight from work. There was no time to go home and change. Otherwise he would be late.

Gazing thoughtfully at the screen he read the title of the spreadsheet to himself aloud. 'The rhombus holds the key.' It was really weird. What the hell did it mean? Was it the password to something? Who knows? Either way, he had better get moving or he would be tragically late as usual.

Mike copied the file onto a floppy disk before erasing it from his hard drive. Grabbing his laptop case he threw the floppy into it. He bid farewell to the stragglers on the desk.

'Don't stay too late, Andy,' Mike jibed as he headed in the direction of the elevators. 'You might just end up going blind.'

'Oh, ha ha,' Andy replied sarcastically as he time-stamped another deal slip.

As he waited for the lift he couldn't help thinking about what the spreadsheet meant. What the hell did that cryptic message mean? Why was the rhombus the key? What was a rhombus anyway? He would have time to look at it later on at home. Anyway, Fiona would be waiting for him at this rate.

January, 1996

Christmas had been a rather warm and inviting affair at the Bolton's family chateau in the Dordogne valley, just outside of Beaulieu. The chateau, with its twenty rooms, original beams, and fully restored turrets, was truly impressive. Fiona's father, Sir Peter, had ensured that the chateau was painstakingly restored to its original condition. Mike had been particularly impressed by Sir Peter's wine cellar and his time at the chateau had been one giant gastronomic and conversational delight. Sir Peter was a self-made man but not affected by his wealth; he remained very down to earth. He had initially made his money as a merchant banker, before selling his boutique firm to a much larger European consortium. Having sold his business, he entered politics on the conservative side. Mike, being a banker and on the right side of the political spectrum, got on famously with Sir Peter, much to Fiona's satisfaction. The three days that Mike had spent with Fiona's family over Christmas was long enough to win their approval and short enough to ensure he didn't embarrass himself.

Leaving the chateau late on Boxing Day, Mike and Fiona had driven directly to Val d'Isère for ten days' skiing. It had been a particularly good start to the season and Mike was very keen to get out and do some serious skiing. Everything was blissful until about the fourth of January.

Mike sat on the edge of the bed struggling to take off his S.O.S. ski gear. It had been a hard day's skiing and he was feeling particularly weary. The powder was deep and keeping up with Fiona had been difficult for him. She was really a terrific skier. She had humbled him. He was none too pleased about it either.

'Mike, there's a fax here for you,' Fiona said, picking up the piece of paper that had just been shoved under the door.

'What does it say, babe?' Mike finally pulled off his ski pants and collapsed backwards onto the bed, exhausted.

'It's from Simon Anderson, he wants you to call him immediately,' Fiona climbed on top of him, straddling his chest and pinning him down on the bed.

'Gee. I'd love to, babe, but looks like I won't be able to call him. I think I'm kinda stuck. You've got me in your tractor beam. I can't move.' He laughed.

'Is that so?' Fiona bent over and kissed him. 'Then maybe I won't let you go,' she kissed him again. 'I have got you under my power now.'

'Oh, have you now?' Mike pretended to struggle.

'It is useless to struggle. Submit to my power.' Fiona started to tickle him. She knew he hated it. He was so ticklish. Mike started writhing all over the place.

'Not fair,' he shouted. 'Stop it!' He cried as he writhed even more. 'That's it! I'm warning you!'

'What are you going to do then?' Fiona laughed as she jumped off his chest. 'Not only am I a better skier than you, but I'm stronger than you too!'

'Okay, fine,' Mike replied petulantly. 'Give me the fax now, please?' He eyed the fax she still held in her right hand.

'Make me!' She challenged him from the other side of the bed.

'Girl, you are so naughty. I am going to have to punish you,' Mike smiled.

'I can't wait,' Fiona flashed a wicked grin.

Mike jumped across the bed and tackled her. They embraced passionately for a few minutes before Mike wrested the fax from Fiona's right hand.

'Aha! I win!' Mike proclaimed triumphantly. He looked briefly at his watch and his voice took on a more serious tone. 'I had better make the call now before he leaves the office for the day. I'll be back shortly.'

'You'd better. Or I'll have to find someone else to play with,' Fiona taunted him.

'Don't worry, babe. I'll be back,' Mike did his best Arnie impression.

Mike took a look at the fax as he wandered down the hall to the front desk. He looked at the time it had been sent. It must have been received the day before, but somehow the front desk had only just put it under the door.

'Typical French service,' he muttered to himself.

The conversation with Anderson was brief. Anderson was annoyed that Mike hadn't taken his mobile phone skiing with him and that it had taken him so long to call. Copper was collapsing. The desk was short-handed. Holiday over. It was that simple. Within minutes Mike was back in the room explaining to Fiona why his holiday was coming to an abrupt end. She elected to stay. There was no point wasting a holiday that they had paid for. Besides, the snow was fantastic.

*

Far above the wintry streetscape of New York, in the warm comfort of his office, big John Templeton eyed the Reuters screen with quiet satisfaction. He had ridden out the largest part of the backwardation. His balls of steel had been tested by Fujiyama's corner, but he had survived so far. Now he could see the light at the end of the tunnel. The long term fundamentals pointed down. No man was bigger than the market. Eventually the economic forces of supply and demand would catch up with him. John picked up the phone and paused. He sniffed twice before dialing his broker in London. He could really smell blood now. It was time to lever into his already monstrous short position. Despite the cost of rolling his positions forward, he had sufficient profit in the trade that he could really put his foot on the gas. It was time to go in for the kill.

In just one week copper had fallen from 2800 to 2600. Option traders had to be getting very nervous. If the market were to fall substantially under 2400 there would be disastrous implications for most players. The chances of a quick fall snowballing into a massive collapse were quite real. Mike prepared himself on the short flight from Lyon back to London for the mother of all collapses.

The first week of January is usually very quiet with much of the world still in New Year mode. Much of the market was still away on the Christmas break. After his brief conversation with Anderson, Mike had understood the urgency of the situation. Steve also was particularly worried about the potential for a meltdown and had flown in, begrudgingly, from his holiday in Nice. They had arrived back in London to find the desk running on a skeleton staff.

Luckily Steve had done a wonderful job over the previous six months, cleaning up much of the nuclear waste that he had inherited in the option book, but still there was a massive hit they would take if the market just dropped off the edge and into oblivion. Anderson was not taking any chances. He wanted all hands on deck. If Fujiyama sank, he didn't want the commodities desk going under with him. At least not on his watch. That was for certain.

Despite Anderson's fears of a meltdown, the market had stabilized around the 2450 mark in the second week of

January. There were rumors of massive physical copper shipments from Longbeach to the Far East. Mike doubted the validity of these rumors. Someone had started selling massive amounts of 'at the money options'. There were no points for guessing who was behind the sales. Volatility was getting crushed. Option dealers were puking out anything they could sell. 'At the money copper' vols fell from fourteen percent down to eleven percent, people were hurting everywhere. In selling huge quantities of 2400 strike puts, Fujiyama was creating an artificial floor for the market.

Meanwhile, back in Tokyo, Fujiyama was busy using the premiums gained from his massive option sales to cover margin payments and hide the holes that were developing in his copper book. He had to be able to hold the market in a 2400 to 2500 range for a while in order to cover up his losses from the recent fall.

Far from the noise of the trading desk, Mike, Steve, and Anderson relaxed over a couple of beers. The venue for their informal meeting was the Front Page pub in Chelsea. High ceilings, wooden paneling, and a warm fire made for a very cozy atmosphere in winter. Antipodean bar staff, the norm for London, were cute as well as friendly. Mike loved the place. He was a regular. Not far from the King's Road it was a world away from its bustle.

In a private corner of the bar the three men from Nelson Smith had a few beers and discussed tactics.

'Guys, I want to thank you both for cutting your trips short. I'll make it up to you somehow, I promise you.'

'Don't mention it,' Steve really didn't want to dwell on the subject. He had left his French fiancée in Nice and was none too happy about it.

'So what do you make of the situation at hand?' Anderson opened a packet of chips and placed them in the middle of the table.

'I smell another Leeson,' Mike stated emphatically, before he took another sip from his bottle of Molson.

'I think you might be right,' Anderson concurred, taking a handful of chips from the opened packet and placing them in his mouth.

'I agree.' Steve reached for a handful of chips. 'But what can we do about it? I mean, the LME is investigating the backwardation, but it looks like they are doing nothing. It's fucken criminal what's going on.'

Anderson placed his beer on the table and leaned forward. He looked about the pub quickly to make sure no one was listening in on their conversation. He took a quick sip of his beer again before lowering his voice.

'That may well be the case, but we have no proof that anything untoward is going on. Until such time as we do, we just have to abide by the rules and regulations of the exchange. You know I am not happy with the situation as it stands, but as long as we play it by the book, we should be fine.'

'I bet they all end up in jail,' Mike downed the last of his beer.

'Maybe. But that remains to be seen. Anyone for another beer?' Anderson asked as he got up and made his way to the bar.

Mike made quick work of the fifty or so yards in the cold from the Front Page to his apartment. It was great to have such a short journey home from a night out. Poor Steve had to make his way back to Hampstead. As Mike walked into his apartment he flicked the hall light on and made his way into the lounge room. Sitting on a table in the corner was his laptop. He decided to check his e-mails before going to bed, as was his habit.

As he unzipped the leather bag which held his Toshiba laptop computer, a floppy disk fell out onto the floor. Picking it up, he stared at the unfamiliar disk for a few seconds before it tweaked his memory. It contained that strange Excel spreadsheet. The one that he had copied just before Christmas and forgotten about. He quickly booted up the computer and placed the disk in the floppy drive before opening the file.

He looked in wonder at this spreadsheet. Doing his best to focus on the numbers, as the handful of beers that he had consumed had gone straight to his head, he grabbed a pen and a yellow legal pad and started to make some notes. It seemed that Yamamoto was entering into seriously disadvantageous trades with IMT and Wilmont Bridge. It was quite amazing some of the trades that Fujiyama had done with these two counterparts. Then, via a series of companies and identical trades, a company called Metco in the Channel Islands received large payments from IMT and Wilmont Bridge. Mike was starting to get very confused. This whole series of payments, if indeed that was what they were, was starting to look very strange indeed.

It got stranger as he read on. Following the list of payments, it turned out that Metco then paid almost all of its revenues to an individual or entity called Wolfgang Schmidt. There were a few random payments to a company called Barter Holdings, but basically it looked like Metco was washing all its profits to some guy called Wolfgang Schmidt. Who the hell was Wolfgang Schmidt?

Mike turned to the next page of legal paper. He jotted down an address in Jersey for Metco. He suspected that it was just a name plate on the wall address but did so nonetheless. There was something fishy going for sure, but this random spreadsheet proved nothing. As Mike tabbed down the screen he found a line of text. There was a message from David Green to Hayward asking him to go to the authorities with this information if anything happened to him.

Mike remembered the brief conversation he had had last December with Rolo. Rolo had said something about Green dying in a house fire in Connecticut. Mike connected his laptop to the phone line and hooked himself up to the Internet. Using Netscape's Navigator to surf his way around the Net, Mike found the *Greenwich Daily Post*, a local newspaper in Connecticut. Using the *Post*'s own search engine, Mike painstakingly navigated the paper's archives. He narrowed his search down to 'Green and/or fire' during January and February of the prior year. He came up with seven matches for his search. The first article, dated February 2nd, contained both 'Green' and 'fire.'

He clicked onto the first article to bring it up on his screen. Bingo! It was the one he was looking for. Metals trader David Green had been killed in a tragic house fire on the 31st of January. The investigating coroner had establish that a drunken Green had gone to bed with a lit cigarette. Green had passed out, knocking over a bottle of vodka and dropping a lit cigarette in the process, which had subsequently caused a fire. The actual cause of death was asphyxiation. The coroner's ruling had been death by misadventure.

Mike sat back in his chair, placing his left hand across his chin, and let out a sigh. Green had sent this cryptic e-mail on the 31st of January. If this was the case, then he had died only a few hours later. Was it a coincidence? Why send it to Hayward? Where was Hayward now? Mike decided he had to find him. Hayward would be able to answer some of his questions.

Mike tore off the top two pieces of legal paper from the legal pad and folded them neatly. He felt around behind him for the inside pocket of his overcoat which was slung casually over the back of the chair. When he had located the pocket, he placed the two slips of folded paper deep inside.

He would speak to Hayward tomorrow. That would be his first step.

Mike put his hands on his head and ran his fingers through his hair. Metco, Wolfgang Schmidt, the rhombus holds the key. What the fuck did it all mean?

Back at work the next day, Mike began his investigation. He seized a quiet moment by the coffee machine to quiz Rolo about Hayward. Rolo knew everyone in the market so Mike figured it was his best bet.

'Rolo. Do you know how I could get in touch with James Hayward, the guy who used to sit at my desk. I found some things of his when I was cleaning up the other day and figured he might want them,' Mike stirred his coffee before placing the spoon in the sink.

'Well, I guess you could send them to his widow,' Rolo said solemnly, as he undid the lid of a jar of instant coffee.

'Widow?' Mike looked shocked.

'Yeah, widow,' Rolo shoveled two large spoonfuls of coffee into his mug. 'He died of a massive heart attack not long after he left here.' Rolo concentrated on filling up his mug with boiling water. 'Think it was the stress and all,' he looked back at Mike. 'Died at his desk you know.'

'Shit,' Mike leant back against the white cupboard in the little kitchenette alcove that adjoined the coffee machine. 'That's awful.'

'Yeah. Well, I can get his wife's address for you if you'd like,' Rolo continued, as he walked back in the direction of the desk.

'Oh, it wasn't that important, really,' Mike's voice trailed off. Fuck! he thought. His best lead was dead. The guy who sent the spreadsheet was dead. Why had Green sent Hayward the e-mail in the first place? What was the connection between the two of them? That, he would probably never know. How was he going to continue his investigation?

Then a thought hit him. Fiona!

Mike dashed back across the room to the coat stand. He grabbed the two folded pieces of paper from his inside pocket and sat back at his desk. He promptly called Fiona who had just arrived back at work that morning from Val d'Isère.

'Hi babe, how was your flight?' Mike asked. 'And I don't want to hear anything about your skiing.'

'Oh, you poor thing, you,' Fiona teased. 'In that case I won't tell you about the fifty centimeters of fresh powder that fell after you left.'

'I'm not listening,' Mike hummed away loudly in the background.

'All right! All right! Enough!' Fiona pleaded. 'It was terrible being there without you. Does that make you feel any better?'

'No. Not even close,' Mike laughed, 'but it was a nice try. Anyway, are you busy?' Mike asked.

'Not really. Why? What do you have in mind?'

'Well, I can think of a number of things, but right now we are on a recorded line. I can show you tonight if you like.'

'You are such a naughty boy!'

'Hey, I try,' Mike looked at the pieces of yellow legal paper in front of him. 'Seriously though, babe, can you do me a favor and find out what you can about a company called Metco and another company called Barter Holdings. Seeing as you are with the SFO it should be a piece of cake.'

'Any particular reason why I should do this for you?'

'I'll tell you tonight.'

'Can't wait. See you around eight at my place.'

'Done,' Mike affirmed as he put down the phone.

Later that evening in the comfort of Fiona's lounge, Mike started to spell out his theory. He opened a bottle of red wine, a nice cabernet blend, allowing it to breathe. Imogen was busy preparing dinner in the kitchen. She was making one of her famous pasta dishes. She loved to cook just as much as she loved to show off. Mike poured a glass of wine for Imogen first and walked into the kitchen to hand it to her. Then he poured a glass for Fiona, handing it to her across the coffee table, before pouring himself a glass and relaxing in the big green couch.

'How was your day?' Mike slung his right arm across the back of the couch.

'Fine. Thanks for asking,' Imogen shouted from the kitchen, bringing a smile to Mike's face. Despite her airs she was really quite good value.

'It was okay,' Fiona pulled a face. 'You know how it is. One minute you're skiing in France, the next there is a pile of paper in front of you.'

'Rough life for some. Tell me, did you get a chance to find out anything about Metco and Barter Holdings?'

'Honestly, Mike, I really didn't have a chance to do much today. I spent most of the morning telling one of my colleagues about my ski trip before catching up on my mail and going through my in-tray. Was it urgent?' Fiona asked apologetically.

'Not really,' Mike sort of shrugged his shoulders.

'Then why the sudden interest in these two companies? Are they involved in something nefarious?' Fiona placed her wine glass on the table.

'Well. It's a long story, one that I don't even understand myself yet.' Mike leaned forward, grabbing the bottle of wine, and topped up Fiona's glass before generously refilling his own. 'I'm not sure, but maybe finding out something about these companies can help me unravel what is going on.'

Fiona sat forward listening intently. 'And you want my help?'

'Yeah, well, I figured you were good at this sort of stuff. I mean, it's what you do for a living, right?' Mike asked rhetorically.

'What are you going to pay me for my services?' A cheeky grin crossed her face.

'Well, I'm sure we can come to some sort of agreement,' Mike lent close enough to give her a long kiss on the lips.

'Enough of that you two!' Imogen boomed as she walked across to the dining table carrying a pot of pasta. 'There is plenty of time for that later. Dinner is ready. Fee, can you set the table please.' Imogen was such a pushy little thing.

February, 1996

The light was on in the rectory. It was long since dark on this cold wintry evening. A small fire burned in the far corner of the room, giving it a warm glow. Father Sean Murphy's silhouette was obvious through the window as he finished up his duties for the day. It had just gone five-thirty and he was keen to get some work done on Sunday's sermon before dinner at the Finegan residence. Old Mrs. Finegan, now in her late sixties, was a fine cook and he particularly looked forward to dinner at her house each Friday. She would be cooking a wonderful roast with three veg. His favorite. It was the culinary highlight of his week. He closed his eyes for a second and inhaled deeply through his nose. He could almost imagine the aroma coming from her kitchen as he warmed himself in the cozy sitting room of her cottage.

Despite the cold February weather, it had been a pleasant week for Father Murphy and his mood reflected the successful nature of it. The new books he had ordered for the children's home would be arriving soon and the repainting of the church hall was going to plan thanks to the kindly donation made by his twin brother Bryan. As he washed his hands in the sink there was a sudden unexpected knock at the rectory door.

'I'll be with you in a minute.' He called out, turning off the tap and shaking his hands twice to get some of the water off them before reaching for the towel by the hand basin. He carefully dried his hands, put the towel back by the hand basin, and made his way to the door.

Father Murphy opened the door. The chill of the wind whistled about his ears.

'Hello!' He called out into the darkness. Silence. There was no one to be seen. 'Must have been the wind,' he muttered to himself as he went to close the door.

Just as he started to close the door he noticed a small brown package at his feet. Pulling his jacket across his chest to protect himself from the biting cold, he knelt down. Stealthily he placed the package under his left arm before shutting the door firmly.

Back in the warm of the rectory he sat at a rickety wooden table. One of the legs was slightly shorter than the others so there was a piece of cardboard shoved under it to stop it from rocking. The package lay unopened in front of him. Brown paper tied with string. He stared at it blankly for a few moments wondering what it would contain. He knew very well what it contained. He had hoped that he would never receive another package like this again. Very slowly he opened the package, his hands trembling. He undid the string. It had been well over eighteen months since he had received a package like this. For the last eighteen months the I.R.A. had observed a ceasefire. Was this to be the end of it? He shuddered at the thought. Carefully unwrapping the brown paper, he found a typed note. On it was a coded message, the number to call, and the time and date to call it. Father Murphy took a quick look at his watch and made the sign of the cross. He had less than fifteen minutes to make the call.

He took the note and shoved it into his trouser pocket. Doing up his clerical collar he reached for his tattered long coat which hung by the door. He pulled it on over his shoulders. Flicking off the light in the rectory, he pulled the door shut behind himself and made his way down the three dark steps at the back of the rectory into the lane. The stiff breeze caught his face. Leaves blew tempestuously in circles. He pulled the collar of his coat up to protect himself. He jerked the rusty iron gate behind him and started his journey. His heart started beating faster. Adrenaline was pumping, coursing through his veins. The payphone that he was going to use was more than half a mile down the lane. He had to hurry.

*

Fiona put down the phone. She looked rather bemused. She chewed the tip of her pen as was her habit and reflected on the strange conversation that had just ended. It turned out that the address that Mike had given her for Metco in the Channel Islands was for a boutique law firm called Turner and Associates. The principal, Frank Turner, had seemed polite and helpful, when she had first called that is, until she had mentioned the name Metco. Then he had turned evasive. After she had mentioned that she worked for the Serious Fraud Office he had turned positively hostile. There was something that Mike was not telling her, of that she sure. But what? What had Mike gotten himself into? She would ask him tonight.

*

Mike kicked back in his chair. Feet up. Belly out. There was a stain on his shirt from lunch, but he didn't care. It was late. It was Friday. He would be leaving soon. The week was almost at an end. And what a trying week it had been. The copper market had died. Volume was scant. Fujiyama had sold so many options that he had created a massive floor for copper around the 2400 level and he seemed intent on capping the market for the short term at 2500. In the middle of this range no one wanted to do anything. The market traded in this listless range, but violently at times. It was choppy and nasty, so much so that Mike wasn't having a good time in it. All too often he was getting whipped out of a position that then proved right later in the day. Losing money when you were wrong was okay, Mike could live with that. But losing money when you were right, now that sucked! It was a bullshit market, he thought, being controlled by an underworld consortium. But he couldn't prove a thing. He was still waiting for Fiona to find out something concrete about the mysterious companies on the spreadsheet. She had established that Metco was a Belize-based trading company. As a Belize-based international business company there was no need to list directors, shareholders, or even lodge annual reports. So far all her attempts to find out more about Metco had been unsuccessful. Barter Holdings was a little less complex. The company was based in Jersey and Fiona expected that soon she would have some further information on them.

Mike looked up expectantly at the clock. In an hour's time New York would be closed and he would head over to the pub with the boys and have few quick beers before heading into the West End to meet Fiona. They were off to see a play tonight, although he couldn't remember what it was called. Whatever. He would be sinking beers in sixty-seven minutes exactly, allowing for time to cross the courtyard to the Corney and Barrow and be served. The countdown to the weekend was on.

*

Frank Turner was a respectable man. He owned a thriving law practice which acted as trustee for many offshore companies in the tax haven of Jersey in the Channel Islands. For many years he had carried on an honest trade in company services. A very sprightly man for his late fifties, Turner had recently beaten the battle of the bulge by running close to five miles everyday before work. It had turned him into a fitness junkie. Strong of mind, strong of body was his motto and he encouraged everyone who worked for him to think the same. He poured much of his energy into his work now. His children had long since left the nest and only visited during major holidays, much to his ire. He had fed and clothed them for close to twenty years and this was how they repaid him, with two visits, if that, per year. His wife was very active in local community groups. She also ran a small store in town which sold handicrafts to hoards of tourists in summer. He had even run for local office once, but other commitments had forced his withdrawal from the race. Turner and his wife were stanchions of local society.

Well, that's what everyone thought at least. No one knew about the dark side to his success. Now one knew that his early success could be attributed to money-laundering. It was really just a form of tax minimization, he rationalized. At the time he didn't know what the Yakuza was. He was just acting on behalf of a client wishing to minimize its tax obligations. The authorities called it money-laundering, he thought it was just hair splitting. Either way, it was only later on, when he was too deeply involved, when it was far too late for him to do anything, that he had found out who his real master was. Ever since then he had just been a willing servant. There wasn't much else he could do. He cooperated fully and they took care of him well. Anyway, he knew the Yakuza penalty for betrayal.

Turner called Fujiyama immediately on a secure line. He had orders to call if anyone started asking questions about Metco, no matter how trivial. This was a worrying situation. What was the Serious Fraud Office doing asking questions about Metco? He cleared his throat as he heard the voice at the other end. 'Sorry to call so late, Fujiyama-san,' he pleaded apologetically. 'But I am afraid that we might have a problem.'

'I see,' Fujiyama said thoughtfully. He was wide awake, the Comex was open for another hour. 'And what might that problem be?'

'There was a young lady named Fiona Bolton from the Serious Fraud Office who called my office asking questions about Metco.' He sounded more than a little stressed.

'How did she find out about Metco?' Fujiyama seemed rather stunned by the news.

'I don't know,' Turner replied. 'I told her I didn't know anything about Metco, but she seemed suspicious.'

'Don't worry,' Fujiyama said reassuringly. 'I will take care of it.' He hung up the secure line. 'Fiona Bolton,' Fujiyama said to himself as he jotted down the name. 'I don't think you will be a problem for much longer.'

Fujiyama promptly picked up the phone and dialed a Tokyo number.

'Hai,' the person answered sleepily at the other end.

It was early in the morning but he was not completely asleep. He had been tossing and turning all night. He knew the only person who would be calling on this line, so he didn't need to ask.

'Go to London immediately and find out everything you can about Fiona Bolton at the Serious Fraud Office. I need to know everything about her.' The voice was clear and concise.

'As you wish,' replied the voice at the other end.

'Good,' he paused briefly. 'I'll expect your report in seven days.' Then Fujiyama hung up.

★

Father Murphy arrived at the lonely phone booth panting. He was not a fit man these days. A little more warning would have been appreciated, but he knew it would not be forthcoming. These men did not mess around. Opening the door to the red phone, he fumbled in his pocket for the note and some spare change with which to make the call. He looked at his watch in the gloomy light of a street lamp a couple of hundred yards down the road. Its faint light was barely enough to read by. Six o'clock exactly. It was time to dial. A car passed along the lonely lane, its headlights caused shadows to run up the walls of the booth. Father Murphy held his breath, standing still, waiting for it to pass. Gone, he started to breathe more calmly. Holding the receiver up against his ear with his shoulder, he began to dial. He didn't need to read the number. He knew the number of the R.T.E., Ireland's state-owned broadcaster by heart. The phone began to ring at the other end. He ran his finger across his clerical collar till he found the button and undid it, giving him more room to breathe. He held the slip of paper up to the light so that he could read the message. He squinted, making sure he could read it correctly.

A young girl answered at the other end. Father Murphy slowly repeated the coded message twice, just to make sure the girl understood it fully. 'This is for you, Patrick.' He whispered to himself as he hung up. Placing the piece of paper in his mouth he started to chew. Northern Ireland's fragile ceasefire was over.

*

Mike hailed a cab on the other side of Liverpool Street Station. He had managed to sneak in three quick beers with Steve and Andy before excusing himself. It was just before eight.

'Covent Garden, please,' Mike asked the driver as he climbed into the back of the cab throwing his laptop case onto the back seat.

'Do you really wanna go there? I mean, there's a bomb scare in the West End at the moment and most of the area around Piccadilly Circus is cut off to traffic. The police ain't taking no chances after that bomb that went off in the Docklands tonight.'

'What bomb?' Mike sounded shocked.

'Here, listen in,' the cabbie turned up radio so that Mike could hear it.

A massive device had been detonated in an underground parking garage in Docklands, east of London, just after seven that evening. Two people had been confirmed dead and at least forty others had been taken to hospital with cuts and bruises from shattered glass. Incredible damage had been caused to surrounding buildings in the Canary Wharf office complex by the bomb, which had been detonated only hours after the I.R.A. formally ended its eighteen-month ceasefire. Apparently the police had been alerted to the presence of a bomb by the I.R.A. and were in the process of clearing the surrounding area when it was detonated.

'Shit!' Mike exclaimed.

He grabbed for his phone to call Fiona. There were two missed calls and one new message. He dialed the number for the message retrieval. It was Fiona. She was caught in traffic on the other side of London. The West End was closed to traffic so she would meet him at home. They could go to the theater another night.

'Forget Covent Garden,' Mike called out over the din of the radio. 'Let's go to Fulham via Embankment.'

'Cheers, guv.' The cab driver replied, as he stopped to do a U-turn.

The traffic in London that night was chaotic to say the least. It took Mike close to an hour and twenty minutes to make what was essentially a thirty-minute journey even in peak traffic conditions. Mike had called Fiona on three occasions, each time he changed the estimated time of his arrival at her place. For once she was more than understanding of his tardiness.

In the comfort of her living room, Fiona cuddled up with Mike on her comfy green couch. She started to relate the latest of her findings on Metco.

'I think I made some progress investigating that company that you asked me about. You know that address you gave me for Metco in Jersey?'

'Yeah, vaguely,' Mike's brow narrowed. 'It was somewhere in St. Helier, as I remember.'

'Well, that's correct, but the address is for a law firm called Turner and Associates.' Fiona sounded pleased with herself.

'That's what I expected,' Mike added. 'I mean, given that Metco is a Belizean I.B.C.'

'Yes, but the conversation I had with the principal, Frank Turner, was really strange. I told him that I was looking for information regarding a company called Metco. At the mention of that name he became very evasive. He demanded to know who I was and why I was interested in Metco. It was really weird, his change in tone. When I told him that I was Fiona Bolton from the Serious Fraud Office in London he said that he had never heard of Metco. It was positively bizarre.'

'Wow, that is bizarre,' Mike looked thoughtfully into space.

'Mike, is there something you're not telling me?'

'Sorry?'

'Don't give me that. I know you're keeping something from me. Now what is it?'

'Well, it's a long story. One that I don't really understand myself, but seeing as you are helping me, I guess I should let you in on everything I know.' Mike pushed her legs off his lap as he got up. 'Let me grab my laptop and I'll show you what I'm talking about. It will be easier that way.'

Mike returned promptly with his laptop. Placing it on Fiona's well-loved coffee table, he plugged it into a socket next to the couch and started to boot it up. Fiona sat beside him, her hands cupped together and resting on her knees.

'You're going to think I'm a complete nut when I've finished.'

'I already do.' Fiona smirked. 'That's what I love about you. You are so unpredictable.'

Over the course of the next half hour, Mike related all his fears and suspicions about Fujiyama and the copper market. He explained the peculiar relationship that existed between Yamamoto, IMT and Wilmont Bridge. He showed Fiona the spreadsheet that he had stumbled across when he was cleaning up files on his hard drive. They went through the series of cashflows from company to company that were on the spreadsheet. Fiona's eyes boggled at the size of the transactions that were taking place. Mike was right. Everything seemed to flow to a company called Metco.

But transactions between trading companies were not sufficient to prove any wrongdoing. Although the size of the transactions and their frequency were enough to raise suspicions of money-laundering in Fiona's mind. Still, this random e-mail and Mike's hunches didn't prove anything. They needed hard evidence.

Then Mike revealed his theory on the death of David Green, who had sent this mysterious spreadsheet just before he died. He figured that somehow Green was blackmailing his employer, IMT or maybe even Fujiyama, and had been liquidated for it. He suspected a link between the spreadsheet and the accidental death of Green in a house fire. He then discussed the intended recipient, Hayward, who had died of a heart attack, although Mike doubted whether it would be possible to induce a heart attack in someone on a trading desk. Mike supposed that Hayward had never seen this e-mail, seeing as it had been unopened when he found it, and given that fact, Mike presumed that Hayward's death might just be coincidental. But in the back of his mind he couldn't rule out some form of foul play.

He related what he had discovered about Hayward and Green's relationship. Fiona sat spellbound throughout. Discussions with Rolo had revealed that Hayward had been Green's LME broker for years. It appeared that there had been plenty of back-scratching involved, possibly even in the form of brown paper bags stuffed with cash in return for business. A practice that was not atypical for the LME so it seemed. Green and Hayward had become good friends along the way and went fishing every year in the Bahamas. Maybe Green was blackmailing someone and going to cut Hayward in on the action. It seemed crazy, but anything was possible. Either way, there were still plenty of pieces missing from this puzzle. Mike was determined to get to the bottom of the mystery.

Then there was the question of who or what was Wolfgang Schmidt? This was the most puzzling question. Hundreds of millions of dollars had flowed to this person or company in the past three years. Of course, Barter Holdings had received a couple million dollars, but Wolfgang Schmidt took the lion's share.

The most puzzling thing was the cryptic statement: 'The Rhombus holds the key.' What the hell did that mean? Was it some password or code? Mike had no clue. Fiona looked as if she was getting rather bored with the whole episode. What Mike had related to her sounded rather far-fetched, some would say the product of a highly imaginative mind with plenty of spare time. Still, he had raised a number of valid points which had piqued her interest. There did seem to be some sort of money-laundering going on if the spreadsheet was to be believed. She would continue to investigate Metco and Barter Holdings for him.

When Mike had finished his conspiracy theory monologue, he gazed back at Fiona.

'I'll leave you with this copy of the spreadsheet,' he said, pulling out the floppy disk from the drive and holding it aloft. 'It should help you with your investigation. So what do you think? Should I be committed?'

'Hardly.' Fiona replied, leaning forward and slowly unbuttoning his shirt. 'The money-laundering I can comprehend. I deal with that each day at work. But all these murders sound a little far-fetched to me. I think you've been reading way too many spy novels double '0' seven.'

'Oh have I now?' Mike started to caress the inside of her left thigh. 'Then you should know that Commander Bond always gets the girl.'

'Is that so?' Fiona kissed him a couple of times on the chest before staring him directly in the eye.

'You'd better believe it,' he giggled, as he started to nibble her ear lobe.

Monday morning started just like any other. Mike had spent Sunday night at Fiona's place and struggled out of bed just in time to shower and head home to change into a suit before Anderson arrived in a cab to pick him up. He was really cutting it fine these days. Each day he was putting more and more clothing on in the cab.

But it wouldn't be happening for much longer as Mike had found his new toy whilst shopping with Fiona on the weekend. His bonus had been paid into his bank account on the second of February. Every day since then it had been trying to burn a hole in his pocket. Mike had to resist the temptation to go nuts. He needed the discipline to stick to his game plan. So far it was working. The majority of the money he had received had gone straight into a couple of big board stocks that Mike liked. It was a bull market in stocks and he could see no reason why he should be left behind. Anyway who wanted to invest in treasuries? Who in their right mind would lend to the U.S. government at six and a half percent? The stocks that he chose were a fair bet, he figured. They all had diversified interests so a downturn in one sector of the overall economy wouldn't affect them too badly.

Another chunk of his bonus money went to Mr. Amex to pay for Fiona's Christmas present and skiing in Val d'Isère. It was a cash flow thing. Mike knew he had the money coming in eventually so he felt safe to spend up in anticipation of its arrival. The final chunk he had saved for his new toy. He had ordered the red Ducati 916 motorcycle which would be delivered the following Thursday. He was so excited. He had bought himself a black Arai helmet just like the one world 500cc champ Mick Doohan wore, and a set of black Dainese racing leathers and black boots to go with it. He had practiced wearing them whilst watching the Simpsons on Sunday night. He paraded around Fiona's apartment like the child that he was with his new toy. He felt like the Terminator when he was all geared up. As soon as he got his confidence up driving in London traffic, he could cut fifteen minutes each way off his traveling time by riding his bike to work. That was an extra fifteen minutes of sleep that he could probably use to his advantage. Right now, he couldn't wait for the bike to arrive.

Mike's euphoric morning was short-lived. His extra energy was wasted on a morning of listless copper trading. The highlight of the day looked like being the announcement of the LME's findings in its copper investigation. It seemed that the market would do nothing until it heard what action, if any, the LME would take.

At midday down on the exchange floor, the chairman of the exchange Lloyd Cartwright read out a press release addressed to all the members. The LME announced that it had finished its investigation into the copper backwardation and that they were satisfied that normal market forces were in operation. No action would be taken and they would continue to monitor the situation in the future.

'What a crock!' Mike exclaimed at the top of his voice. He stood up clutching the bottom of the phone handset with his left hand and pounded it into the palm of his right hand.

'I can't believe these guys are serious,' Steve echoed in the background.

'I wonder how much they got paid to come up with that verdict?' Mike looked directly at Steve.

'I don't know, but it's absolutely ridiculous,' Steve shook his head in disbelief. 'They have spent the past four months investigating the most obvious squeeze in human history and draw a blank. Any moron can see what these guys are doing!'

Anderson returned to the desk a few minutes later. He had just been meeting with the legal department.

'What's news?' He asked in the general direction of the desk.

'The LME have released the findings of their investigation into the copper backwardation,' Steve slumped back in his chair, 'and they are going to do nothing. They said that they felt that normal market forces are at work. Can you believe that?'

'Yes. I could see that coming.' Anderson appeared unmoved by the news. His expression was blank, a million miles away. He seemed to be deep in thought. Opening the door to his office he turned back to face the desk. 'Mike, Steve, can I see you for a moment?'

Mike and Steve hesitated and looked at each other for a second, before making the short journey to Anderson's office. It had to be something important. What could it be?

A few moments later, in the privacy of his office Anderson began to relate the latest series of events in the Yamamoto saga to his traders.

'I figured they would draw a blank.' Anderson had a very cool head. His expression didn't change. 'From now on I want everything, and I mean everything, relating to the Yamamoto and IMT accounts passed by me. That means transfers, payments, the works.'

Mike and Steve seemed rather surprised by this turn of events. Anderson seemed so serious. Something must have happened of which they were not yet aware.

'What has prompted this?' Mike spoke up, not being one to hide in the shadows.

'Well, yesterday the back office received instructions from Fujiyama to accept a payment of one hundred million dollars from an IMT account into Yamamoto's account here at Nelson, which was then to be transferred back to an account at Yamamoto in Tokyo.'

'What does he think we are, a fucking bank?' Steve made a face.

'Exactly. Julio is going to call him later today and tell him that we will not receive the payment. We are not going to launder money for these guys. Not under any circumstances.'

'Why would he want to do this anyway?' Mike scratched the back of his head for a second.

'It's coming up to Japanese year-end, which is at the end of March. For some bizarre reason cash balances that Yamamoto holds with us don't accrue any interest. So if Yamamoto's auditors see a payment for a one hundred million dollar balance that they think has been sitting with us they won't be looking for any interest. The money could have been picking up at least Treasuries making, say five percent. That's five million bucks that they won't be looking for. Five million bucks in IMT's pocket. Now do you get the picture?' Anderson's tone was serious.

Mike and Steve were silent. They understood the gravity of the situation. It was a strange request. It smelt bad.

'My fear is that some back office person has okayed payments like this in the past. We were lucky that this one was brought to my attention because the back office couldn't understand it. That is why we are going to make sure that everything is done by the book from now on. So like I said before, I want absolutely anything relating to the Yamamoto and IMT accounts to pass by me. I'll pass everything by the legal department to ensure we toe the line. I want to make sure that there is no chance that we will be tarred with the same brush as them if they go down. If Fujiyama calls make sure you put him through to me straightaway.' Anderson finished his lecture. 'That is all. And I would appreciate it if you kept this quiet on the desk.'

Fuck! Mike thought to himself. This is serious stuff. There was no way Anderson was going to wash a hundred million dollar payment for Fujiyama and quite rightly so. He wondered if there was any connection between this request and the spreadsheet that he had come across. The spreadsheet was over a year old, so he doubted it. It looked like Fujiyama had slipped up. He was still long some thirty thousand lots with Nelson Smith and who knows how long elsewhere. Not to mention the massive amounts of options he had sold across the market. Fujiyama must be a in a desperate situation to try this. Either that or he figured Anderson for a fool. Anderson was no fool.

*

Mike was comfortably numb. Television blaring, he lay sprawled across his couch. It was late on Sunday evening. Fiona had gone out to dinner for an old friend's birthday.

She had invited him to go with her, but he had declined. He didn't really feel like going out. Instead, he had opted for the couch, home-delivered pizza and his beloved remote.

The phone rang. It rang half a dozen times before he answered. This was despite the fact that the lazy sod had dragged it across the room and placed it right beside the couch almost an hour earlier.

'Hello.' He grabbed the handset and rolled back into his comfortable position.

'M.K. What's up, bro?' John's familiar voice boomed down the line.

'Not much, bro, just relaxing,' replied Mike. 'How's the weekend treating you?' He used the remote to turn the volume down on the television.

They engaged in small talk, the usual chit-chat, for the next fifteen minutes, the television flickering all the while from channel to channel as Mike surfed aimlessly. It was a rude habit, but one that he couldn't shake.

'So what do you think of the LME's findings on the backwardation?' asked John out of the blue. This grabbed Mike's attention. He sat up and turned off the television, placing the remote of the coffee table in front of him.

'Where do I start? Sanitized or unsanitized version?'

'Give it to me straight,' John replied.

'I think it's a fucking crock,' Mike said.

'So what do you think is going on?'

'Truth is, bro, I am not sure. But I know one thing for sure, that this market reeks. I suspect that it's rotten to the core. I wouldn't even be surprised if someone on the LME board was receiving brown paper bags stuffed with cash.'

'I hear you. It sure looks that way.'

'Yeah. Exactly. I would love to be able to prove my theories but without a shred of evidence there is nothing that we can do about it. Until then, brother, my hands are tied.' Mike sounded exasperated.

'You know I am at war with the Jap.' John changed the conversation.

'I'd figured as much, bro. You don't have to be Einstein to work it out,' Mike paused. 'So when am I going to see some business?'

'Don't worry, your time will come. I'll be calling you when it's time to get out. You can unwind the position for me,' John reassured him.

'Cool. I'll be a legend.'

'You're a legend already, big guy,' laughed John.

'You and me both, bro,' concurred Mike.

'So what do you think of the market?'

'Not sure, to be honest. What I do know is that the minute this market shows signs of weakness you should put the foot on the gas pedal. All the downside puts that have been written in the copper market are a Chernobyl waiting to happen. But you have to wait for the opportunity to present itself. If you strike during a moment of weakness you'll start a chain reaction. An avalanche of selling will break out. Even Fujiyama will be powerless to hold it. The cascade of selling will send the copper market over the edge and into oblivion.'

'I like what I'm hearing, bro,' John added.

'Then, when the ducks are squawking, feed it to them. Get out. Take your money and run, and I'll be happy to help you.'

'When do you think the time will come?' asked John.

'No idea. Just be patient. I think the time is approaching. I'll let you know when I think the time is right. One day, Fujiyama will blow up. Just like Leeson and the Hunts found out. No man is bigger than the market.'

'Just be sure to let me know when you think it's time to go duck hunting, bro. I'll have to get the twelve gauge ready.'

'You can be sure of that, bro. You will be the first to know.'

March, 1996

Fiona got up early for a Sunday. Normally she didn't get out of bed until at least noon on the weekend, unless, of course, it was to going shopping with Imogen on Sloane Street. She let out a sigh as she put the kettle on to boil. She would need a cup of tea to get moving. Running her fingers through her long, knotty blonde hair, she squinted to see the clock on the oven in the kitchen. It was still dark outside. Her eyes had not yet fully adjusted to the fluorescent light in the kitchen. It was ten to seven. How rude! She had to be out at Heathrow to pick up Mike, who was returning from what he had called a business trip. She seriously doubted the 'business' part of the trip.

She had been at his apartment on Monday night when he was packing. She had helped him pack. He had packed two suits, a pair of versatile black shoes, a pair of well-worn jeans, a couple of shirts, a couple ties, socks, underwear, and his ski gear. It was when he started packing his ski gear that she became curious.

'A business trip, huh? Where are you going? Who are you going with?' Fiona asked the typical female questions, which he answered, although not to Fiona's full satisfaction. Was Air Miles a man or a woman? Mike told her emphatically that Air Miles was a guy and not to be silly. But with a name like Chris she was more than suspicious. Anyway, she had continued to help him pack. He only took his ski boots because taking his skis would have been cumbersome. Besides, he could hire skis and poles when he got there. To Fiona it seemed more like a fully funded ski holiday than a serious business trip. Nevertheless he had cut it a day short to come back and see her. She supposed she should be grateful.

Mike had been in the States for the last five days on a business junket with Air Miles from the structured products desk. Air Miles had conceived this piss take and convinced Anderson that Mike should go with him, much to Mike's satisfaction. Anderson had relented finally, mainly because he felt bad about Mike cutting his Christmas ski holiday short. He had made it clear to Mike that this was his way of saying thanks.

Their destination was a big copper conference in Salt Lake City, Utah, that was being run by the trade magazine *Metal Bulletin*. It was attended by all the mining fraternity and the usual hotpotch of brokers and investment bankers. The attendance was quite remarkable, but given the conference's location it was bound to be. The setting by the lake provided a wonderful backdrop to the snow-capped mountains that surrounded the town. It also involved a day trip to a big copper-mining operation which Anderson thought would be useful for Mike. Here they were trading commodities that they had really never seen before. Anderson thought it was important that Mike get a better understanding of the nature of their customers' business. Mike was grateful for the break and extra pleased by the fact that Salt Lake City was only thirty minutes from Utah's legendary ski fields. Mike and Air Miles would only have time for a couple of days of spring skiing but it was better than nothing.

As the kettle came to the boil Fiona grabbed the pot from the shelf to her right. She opened the lid and poured some boiling water into the pot. She took two tea bags from the box on the bench, placing them in the pot. Leaving it to settle, she searched for her favorite mug. Her mother had given it to her for her birthday last year. It was one of those

Far Side mugs. A picture on the side of the mug showed a person trying to enter the school for the gifted by pushing on a door that clearly said pull. It always made her laugh. She found it behind a mess of cups and mugs in the cupboard. Imogen had last unstacked the dishwasher, that was for certain. A shower would be nice, she thought to herself as she poured herself a cup of tea. Stirring a pinch of milk into the cup of tea, she picked up the phone and dialed the Virgin Atlantic arrivals number. Mike's plane was expected to be on time. She yawned hard and stretched, pausing before she replaced the receiver on the wall. She made her way into the living room with her cup of tea and climbed onto her comfy green couch, pulling her legs up into her chest to keep herself warm. She pulled the oversized T-shirt of Mike's that she had slept in over her knees for added warmth. Reaching across the coffee table for the remote control, she turned the television on and flicked it over to Sky News. Using the remote again, she turned the volume up. Imogen was away in Paris for the weekend so it didn't matter. Exactly when Imogen would be back Fiona wasn't entirely sure.

Fiona gripped the mug firmly with both hands, warming herself. A smile crossed her face as she was genuinely pleased with herself. Mike would be pleased as well when he heard the news. Her weeks of searching had finally paid off. She had found out who controlled Barter Holdings. It hadn't been easy and she had drawn on all the resources at her disposal to do it. It was a small victory for her as every other avenue had drawn a blank. Still she knew nothing about Metco or Wolfgang Schmidt, but she couldn't wait to tell him about Barter Holdings. She wondered if it might help Mike unravel the mystery. She would only have to wait a couple of hours.

It was now half past seven. She quickly finished off the remnants of her cup of tea and headed for the shower. After showering and blowdrying her long blonde hair, she put on a pair of chocolate-colored trousers, a white shirt, and a jacket and shoes that matched the pants. Holding her left arm out she carefully put on the wonderful gold bracelet that Mike had given her for Christmas. It was really extravagant. At first she had felt that she couldn't accept it, but Mike had convinced her otherwise. Twisting her arm over from left to right she marveled at its beauty for a moment. She quickly dabbed a spot of perfume on each side of her neck. Her eyes darted across her dresser for the keys to her Golf. They were nowhere to be seen. Imogen! she thought. Immediately she headed for Imogen's room.

Sure enough the keys were beside Imogen's bed. She had put her car in for a major service about a week ago and hadn't even bothered to pick it up. She was like that. Always too busy to look after the details in life. Besides, why bother going through all the hassle of picking up your car from the garage when you can take your flatmate's? Fiona didn't mind so much, but she wished that Imogen would put the keys back when she was finished using her car.

Keys in hand, Fiona grabbed a coat from a hook just near the door before pulling it closed behind her. With a bounce in her step she made her way to her car, a black Golf GTI, which was parked about a hundred yards down the road. She started up her car and drove off.

A few hundred yards down the road, two men in black in a Porsche 911 with heavily tinted windows observed Fiona as she exited her apartment. She didn't notice. There was no way she would. She was in a dream world and the Porsche was inconspicuous amongst all the other European cars parked along her street. A second car, a black 3 series BMW also started its ignition. They waited for her to start her car before moving. As she pulled out, a solitary man in black exited the Porsche and started walking towards her apartment. As he walked along he put his hand up to his right ear to make sure his two way radio device was working. He did a quick voice check. The other three men all acknowledged. All systems go. The man in the black Porsche gave the signal. The two men in black in the BMW pulled out from the kerb and followed Fiona at a discreet distance.

The first man in black entered Fiona's apartment block totally unobserved. There was no one about on a sleepy Sunday morning. They had been watching Fiona for close to a week now and had noted all the comings and goings from her flat. He was convinced that it was empty right now, which made it a perfect opportunity for some reconnaissance. The other man in black sitting out front in the Porsche would alert him if anyone approached the flat. It was a precision operation.

He pulled out a pair of latex hospital gloves from a black bag that was slung over his right shoulder and carefully put them on. Then he took a small piece of metal from his left pocket and started to jiggle the lock on the door. It took all of seventeen seconds for the man in black to open Fiona's lock. He had already checked for an alarm system on a visit two days earlier. There wasn't one, which made his task easier. He pushed the door open and scanned the apartment for signs of life. He carefully made his way into the living room. He searched for a computer. He found her laptop in the corner. He pulled out a zip drive from the black bag on his shoulder and attached it to the back of her laptop. He made a copy of everything on her hard drive before reformatting it entirely. There would be nothing on her computer when she returned. It would be blank. In the meantime he went through everything. Removing a small digital camera from the black bag he took photos of bills, letters, cards, post-it notes, and photos. All the while he was careful to make sure that everything was returned to its rightful place. He went through her briefcase meticulously, taking photos of every document he found. He removed two pieces of paper which made reference to Metco and Barter Holdings. When he was finished he placed the rest of the documents back in their original order. He attached a listening device inside the handset of her phone. They would now be able to monitor all her calls.

'Mike!' Fiona waved excitedly with both arms as she jumped up and down.

Mike looked around like a stunned mullet. He could hear her voice but squinting hard through his bloodshot eyes he could not see her. He had just taken a red-eye from New York and was not really with it.

'Over here,' Fiona shouted.

Mike finally found her in the crowd. Fiona threw her arms around him. They embraced for a couple of seconds.

'I really missed you,' she whispered in his ear.

'Same.' Was all that Mike could manage. He was really tired. He tried clearing his voice. 'Can we go home, babe,' he asked. 'I'm beat. I really need some sleep. There was a kid three rows back who wailed all night along. I can't believe they let people into business class with kids. It's ridiculous.' Mike's voice sounded husky. It was obvious that he was coming down with the flu.

'Oh you poor thing,' Fiona hugged his limp body again, kissing him on the forehead. 'Come! This way.' She beckoned. 'My car's parked in the car park just outside.'

When they were in the car Mike leaned across and turned off the radio before slumping back into his seat and closing his eyes. His head was throbbing and he couldn't bear the sound of the radio in the background.

'Thanks for coming to get me, babe. I really appreciate it.' He pulled the seat belt off his shoulder, leaned his head against the door and closed his eyes.

'How was your trip?' Fiona indicated right, checked for cars over her shoulder and entered the flow of traffic. She didn't notice the black BMW behind her.

'It was okay.' Mike was not very talkative which was highly unusual. 'I only got to ski one day. The rest of the time I was busy,' he said despondently, eyes still closed.

Fiona held out her left hand and felt Mike's forehead as she drove, her eyes fixed on the road ahead.

'You're very hot. I'd better get you straight home to bed. You sound like you're coming down with the flu.'

'Yeah,' Mike groaned.

'It's time to pack up.' The passenger in the BMW said slowly into a small microphone in his left hand as they passed over the Hammersmith flyover.

'Acknowledged,' came the reply.

Within minutes the man in black was back in the Porsche. He had everything he needed now. It was time to report back to Fujiyama in Tokyo. He attached the scrambler to the car phone and called Fujiyama on the secure line. He explained that he had gathered the necessary information.

'Good. I will meet you in London tomorrow,' Fujiyama stroked his chin with his thumb and forefinger. 'Until then, please continue to monitor the subject.'

As soon as he had put down the phone, Fujiyama was on the line to London and New York. An emergency session of the Copper Club was called.

Mike lay there, stretched out on Fiona's couch covered in a blanket. She sat to one side of him and felt his forehead again.

'Seems like your temperature has gone down. But here take these cold and flu tablets. They should make you feel better.' She held out her left hand which contained two white tablets. In her right she held a glass of water.

'I feel terrible,' Mike complained as he lifted his head up slowly. He looked like he was dying. It was a great act.

'You are such a baby sometimes,' she smiled as she gave him the glass of water which he used to wash down the tablets.

'Maybe this will cheer you up.'

'What?' Mike snapped.

'I found out who controls Barter Holdings.'

'Really?' He perked up a little.

'Yes. Really.' She chided him. 'Don't sound so astonished. I have my ways.'

'And, so who is it?' Mike was more impatient than usual.

'Barter Holdings is controlled by another shelf-company that is owned by Lloyd Cartwright.'

'Lloyd Cartwright!' Mike coughed in disbelief.

'Yes, Lloyd Cartwright. Do you know him?'

'He's the bloody chairman of the LME for Christ's sake.'

'I thought the name sounded familiar, but I couldn't place it.'

'So that's why the bastard didn't take any action against Yamamoto over the squeeze. He's on the fucking payroll!'

'What are you raving about?'

Mike sat up. 'Look. Last month the LME concluded its investigation into the copper backwardation. They concluded that normal market forces were at work. Which everyone knows is a complete crock. Now I know why. The chairman has been taking back-handers from Metco. Now all we need to do is find out who is behind Metco.'

'That's easier said than done.' Fiona walked across the room and grabbed her briefcase. She sat down on a chair and placed the briefcase flat on her lap. She flicked it open and started riffling throughout the papers in it. 'That's strange,' she said to herself.

'What's strange?' Mike interrupted her train of thought.

'Well, I thought I put everything relating to the spreadsheet in my briefcase on Friday before I left the office. But I can't see it in here.' She paused for a second. 'I guess I must have left it at the office.' She closed the briefcase and set it back down on the floor again. 'Oh well. I'll have to get it for you tomorrow.'

Mike had dozed off. He didn't know how long he had been asleep. He heard movement in the kitchen, and got up to investigate. Feeling a little groggy with fever, he moved slowly. His eyes were heavy and sore. He rubbed them.

In the kitchen he could see her. She had his back to him making a cup of tea at the sink. Her long blonde hair cascaded down the back of her chocolate-brown jacket. He loved her hair. Placing his arms around her waist he moved close to whisper in her ear.

'Hey sexy, don't you want to come to bed?'

'Sure, but don't you think Fiona would mind?' Imogen asked. A smile crossed her face as she turned to see Mike recoil in embarrassment.

'I… I… I…' thought you…' he stammered.

Imogen put her finger on his lips. 'I won't tell if you won't tell.' She grinned. 'Fiona's just popped out to get some milk. She'll be back in a tick. Don't worry, it'll be our little secret.'

'It was the hair, and the jacket,' Mike protested.

'Yeah. It's Fiona's jacket, I borrow her stuff all the time. We're the same size. It's pretty handy really. Double the wardrobe. People mistake us for sisters all the time.'

'I can see why,' Mike agreed.

★

The next afternoon, in a suite at the Park Lane Hotel, overlooking a very drab Hyde Park, which was not yet even close to the beauty of spring, the Copper Club met in seclusion. Their security was tight. The two men in black once again manned the doors. One inside and one out. The other two were still following Fiona.

'Gentlemen. Thank you for coming at such short notice. It seems that we have another slight problem. Similar to the one we had last year.'

'I thought we took care of that problem,' Bridge shuffled nervously in his seat.

'So did I. But it appears that the spreadsheet that David Green stole has resurfaced once again.' Fujiyama pulled a cigarette holder from his jacket pocket. 'Not only has it resurfaced, but it has fallen into the hands of a young woman at the Serious Fraud Office here in London. So far her attempts to discover anything relating to Metco have been thwarted, but documents retrieved by my fellow Yakuza have discovered that she has uncovered the payments Metco made to Lloyd Cartwright back in 1993.' He removed a cigarette from the case and placed it in his mouth. 'Any suggestions on how to handle this?'

'Shouldn't we handle her the same way we handled Green?' Wilmont spoke up for once. He was generally very quiet in these meetings. But it wasn't often that Fujiyama asked for their guidance.

'At first glance that seems the best way to handle the situation, but,' Fujiyama struck a match, 'unfortunately it turns out that Fiona is the daughter of Sir Peter Bolton, the prominent conservative M.P. It makes this a most delicate matter.' He lit the cigarette and took a puff. 'Also it seems she is involved with Michael Kelly, a trader at Nelson Smith. From the files we copied from Fiona's computer, it seems the source of the spreadsheet was Nelson Smith.'

'How did it get to Nelson Smith?' Bridge stood up and started pacing the room nervously.

'Why has it taken a year for it to surface?' Murphy said with astonishment.

'Well, I am afraid I can't answer that.' Fujiyama exhaled, blowing smoke into the air. 'But it seems that our friend Green was in cahoots with James Hayward who used to be at Nelson Smith. Fortunately, natural causes took care of him before he became a problem.'

'The question remains. How do we deal with them?'

'We must recover what information we can from them. Monitor their movements. And then,' Fujiyama twisted his cigarette into a silver ashtray, 'extinguish them.'

Murphy sat back in his chair and rubbed his hands together. 'Gentlemen. I think I have an idea.' He stood up and walked across to the phone in the corner of the room and called his brother Sean in Ireland. He stood there tapping his foot for a few moments until the phone was answered.

'Sean, it's me, Bryan. Fine. Fine. Tell me, can you meet me in Dublin tonight? Yes, of course it's urgent. Paddy's on O'Connell Street at ten-thirty it is. See you there.' Murphy hung up and made his way back to the circle where the others were sitting. 'Gentlemen, leave Miss Bolton to me.'

*

Fiona sat at her desk. She was more than confused. She had looked for the file containing the information on Barter Holdings and Metco but couldn't find it anywhere. She wondered if the cleaners had mistaken it for rubbish and thrown it away. Surely they wouldn't. What was even more concerning was that her laptop had been blank when she booted it up. She had called the I.T. support group. Someone from I.T. support had inspected her laptop and told her that it had been reformatted. Fiona was shocked by the news. Her laptop had not been out of her sight. What had happened to the file? The whole situation frightened her. All the information she had gathered had disappeared into thin air. Maybe she was losing her mind. She was really starting to believe Mike's conspiracy theory.

*

Bryan Murphy sat in a quiet corner of Paddy's, a rowdy bar just off O'Connell Street in Dublin. Most of the patrons were suitably lubricated by this time and were quite loud and jovial as a consequence. Irish folk music played in the background. A smoky haze blanketed the room. Like most Irish pubs in Dublin, you got lung cancer just walking through the front door. Bryan glanced down at his watch. Ten thirty-five. His brother should be there any time. He held the lapel of his jacket up to his nose for a moment and sniffed. He knew it would wreak of smoke. Turning back to his table, he brooded over his pint of Guinness. It tasted so much better than Guinness elsewhere. Bryan figured the Irish kept the best drop for themselves and exported the inferior product overseas.

It had been a long forty-eight hours for him. He had flown on the red-eye from New York on Sunday night into London, met with Fujiyama, taken a quick nap at his hotel and then taken the last flight that evening into Dublin on Aer Lingus. He was very tired now. It showed in his eyes.

Bryan caught a glimpse of his brother across the room.

'Off duty are we tonight, Father?' He called out, trying to be heard above the din of the pub.

Sean spun around to see Bryan holding up a pint of Guinness. Smiling.

'Come and join me why don't you.'

'Aye to be sure,' Sean replied, taking the pint from his hand. 'You certainly owe me. So tell me, what is this emergency that you made me drive all the way down here for?' Sean seemed a little agitated. 'I had to borrow Mrs. Finegan's old Fiat Bambino.'

Bryan just laughed. 'What happened to your car?'

'It's on loan to sister Mary,' Sean spoke through gritted teeth.

'I'm sorry, Sean. But the thought of you driving Mrs. Finegan's little Bambino for hundreds of miles,' he broke into more laughter. Bryan could imagine the hassle that his brother had gone through to borrow Mrs. Finegan's car. She would have made him jump through all sorts of hoops before she gave it to him.

'Okay. Okay. Very funny. Now tell me what is this emergency that you've brought me down here for?'

Bryan's mouth turned down at the corners. 'I need to ask a favor of your charity.'

'I was afraid that was the case.' Sean shook his head, exhaling heavily.

'I see that a number of members of your clergy have become active again.'

'Aye, indeed they have.' Sean rolled his eyes to the ceiling. 'Lord help us.'

Bryan cast a furtive glance across the room and lowered his voice. The background noise would do the rest. 'It is a legitimate political target.' Bryan slid an envelope across the table. 'Make sure they see to it.'

Sean picked up the envelope and placed it in his jacket pocket. 'I'll see that the right member of my clergy gets it,' he said as he patted his pocket. 'We have to keep the financial members of the clergy happy now, don't we?'

'To Patrick.' Bryan held up his pint glass.

'Aye. To Patrick.'

April, 1996

Wednesday morning. 'Fuck!' She was running late. Standing in the kitchen, she brushed her long blonde hair, bent over so that gravity would help her out. Reaching for the keys to the Golf which were sitting on the kitchen bench, she put on a chocolate-brown jacket, grabbed her purse, flung the keys inside it, and rushed for the door.

Out in the street, about two hundred yards away, the two men in black watched from a discreet distance. When they spotted the blonde leaving the building, the first man switched off the radio. Silence. They watched her open the car door and step in.

Behind the wheel she fumbled with the keys, trying to slot them in the ignition. She put her foot on the clutch and shifted the stick into neutral. She turned the keys. The car coughed. It was cold. She tried again. Nothing. 'Fuck! Fuck!' She hit the steering wheel with both hands. Why did it always happen when she was late? She waited a few seconds before trying again. 'Come on. Come on.' She turned the key a final time. The men in the Porsche watched. Waiting. Expectant.

The explosion was massive. Windows shattered everywhere along the street. Bits of metal and glass flew everywhere. The sound of the blast woke the whole street, as smoldering bits of metal hailed down upon the street. The little Golf was torn apart like a sardine can. The roof had been completely blown off, and a fire raged in the wreckage. The force of the blast had thrown the body a good ten feet in the air before it came down to rest on the pavement. She lay there, face down. Dead.

The men in the Porsche witnessed the carnage before them. Debris littered the street. Cars around the epicenter of the blast were alight. Twisted, burning pieces of metal lay everywhere. A second explosion rocked the street as the petrol tank of one of the nearby cars ignited. Screams. Sirens wailed in the distance. Unmoved by the scene, the first man slipped the car into gear, and quickly turning the car around, burned off, leaving two sets of rubber tracks, just as the first emergency vehicles arrived at the scene. It was too late for that.

*

It was the middle of the night in New York, but Bryan Murphy couldn't sleep, tossing and turning more than usual tonight. His conscience weighed heavily on his soul. Pain filled his heart. He had no regrets. There had been no apologies when Patrick had died. They had never apologized for taking away his innocence and filling him with rage and hate.

Then he saw Patrick plain as day. Patrick was older now. He just stood there holding out his hand. Smiling big brother. Caring. A storm. Light flashes! Patrick lying in a pool of blood. Running. Mud. Not going anywhere. Trying. Sinking. The dogs chasing. Closing.

Bryan sat up stiffly. His body was damp with cold sweat. He put his hands up to his forehead and quickly ran them both through his hair. Breathing hard, he reached for the glass of water that he had placed beside the bed, and started to gulp. At night he saw his demons. At night they came to him, the same demons that had been coming since he was nine. He could never silence them. They would never leave him.

The phone rang. It was the secure line. Murphy answered. Problem number one was solved.

*

Mike arrived at the office. He was on time for once in his life, his new bike had made the difference. In the corner of Anderson's office, he took off his leathers, hanging them up triumphantly on the coat stand, before stuffing his gloves in his helmet which he hid in the corner behind the lounge far from view. It was the first time he had ridden to work on his new Ducati. What a buzz! He had ridden rather tentatively in the rush-hour traffic but the adrenaline was pumping through his body. It would be hard to sit still at work today.

He made his way across to the desk. There was no one to be seen. Then he saw them. Grouped around the television in the corner was nearly everyone from his part of the floor. Mike made his way across to see what the fuss was all about. Must be something important. There was no one at the desk taking the first calls of the morning.

'What's going on? Have they re-arrested O.J.?' Mike joked. The last time he had seen the room this quiet was when the O.J. verdict was given. No phone had rung then for about twenty minutes.

'Shhhh.' Nicole turned and frowned at him. 'The I.R.A. set off another bomb in Fulham this morning.'

'What?'

'A young woman was killed.'

'Shit!' Mike started to panic. Frantic, he pushed his way to the front so he could see the screen.

There was a CNN reporter at the end of Fiona's street.

'Please, God, no,' Mike whispered to himself. He swallowed hard. Straining to hear the what the female reporter was saying, he caught a glimpse of the wreckage in the background. It didn't matter what she said anymore. The female reporter's voice blended into nothingness. It was Fiona's car. His stomach sank at the realization. She was dead.

Suddenly Mike felt very ill. The color left his face. Pale. His stare blank. He covered his face with his hands and turned. Pushing his way back through the crowd, he ran for the bathroom. Kicking aside the cubicle door, he fell to his knees and started to dry retch. Nothing came out. His body convulsed. Tears streamed from his eyes. A searing pain filled his body.

There was a bang at the cubicle door. 'Mike. You okay in there?' Anderson's voice boomed.

'No!' Mike spat into the bowl. 'Leave me alone.'

'Well, I think you'd better come quick. Fiona's on the line!'

'What?' Mike's disbelief resonated loudly from the bowl.

'I said Fiona's on the line. You'd better come quick. She sounded very distressed.'

In a flash, Mike was on his feet, almost knocking Anderson over as he bolted through the door. He ran for the desk, wiping tears from his eyes as he ran. Adrenaline coursed through his veins. He reached the desk, panting, and picked up a handset. 'Which line? Which line?' He demanded, finger pointing at the phone board which had half a dozen lights on hold flashing.

'Line one.' Mike heard Anderson calling out over his shoulder. He punched the top line.

'Fiona!' He cried tears of joy. 'You're alive. I thought you were—'

'No, Mike, Imogen's dead.' Fiona coldly cut him short.

'What?' Mike said, stunned by the news, yet over the moon that Fiona was still alive.

'She took my car keys this morning. It should have been me.' She sobbed. 'The police think that the I.R.A. made a mistake. They think that they were after daddy because the car was registered in his name.'

'Where are you now?'

'I can't say. But I'm safe. I'm not even supposed to be making this call to you. I had to plead with daddy and the secret service agents to call you. We're leaving the country this afternoon till they think it is safe to return.' She wept some more.

'How will I contact you?' Mike sounded desperate.

'You can't,' she sobbed. 'But carry your mobile with you. I'll call you when I can.'

'I love you, baby.' His voice crackled. His eyes were all bloodshot and watery. Mike held his hand over mouthpiece and blew a soft dry kiss down the phone.

'I love you too,' Fiona replied.

Mike hit the clear button and put down the phone.

He fell back into his chair. Taking a deep breath, the enormity of the events unfolding around him started to sink in. He exhaled long and hard. It was an exhale of relief and shock. He felt numb. He wanted to dance because Fiona was alive, but the thought of how close she had come to death made him sick. He felt bad about the fact that he was relieved when Imogen had died instead. He didn't know how to handle it. He was still in a state of shock.

Anderson pulled up a seat close to Mike, who just lay there facing the ceiling in a daze, no good to the desk in his current state. What's more, Anderson was worried about him. Anderson was a very intuitive person who cared deeply for his troops, but you didn't need to have any insight to see that there was something wrong. It was obvious. Mike was visibly shattered. He had just been through the whole gamut of emotions.

'Dude. You should take the day off. It's quiet here. Steve and I have got everything under control. You should go home and get some rest.' Anderson's voice echoed paternal care.

'No. I'll be fine.' Mike sat up and tried to focus on the screen. It was blurry. His eyes were sore, dry.

'I really would consider it a wise move if you went home.'

Mike lowered his voice and looked Anderson directly in the eye. 'Look, I would prefer to stay, if you don't mind. I don't think I want to be alone right now.'

'Okay. Then maybe you should go for a quick walk outside to clear your head. You can grab some coffees while you're out. It might be fun to go outside during the day for once. You can see what Andy does each day.' It got a slight smile out of Mike.

'What do you want?'

'A flat white is fine.'

Mike composed himself and stood up. 'Anybody want anything? I'm going outside to grab some coffees.'

Outside in the brisk spring morning air, Mike's eyes adjusted to the sunlight through the protection of his Armani sunglasses, the ones Fiona had given him for Christmas. He went for a walk down to Moorgate to clear his head. He walked like a zombie, the rest of the world simply shut out, the fresh rays of the unfamiliar London sun filling him with the overwhelming joy of being alive. He basked in this joy of life as he walked, the warmth of relief soothing him. He couldn't help replaying over and over in his mind the sequence of events that had unfolded that morning. It had been a roller-coaster ride for his emotions, one that he wasn't keen to have repeated too soon.

As Mike made his way back to the office carrying a box full of coffees, he admiringly passed the sleek black Porsche which was parked outside. From the window seats of a cafe on the other side of the street, the two men in black patiently watched him walk by.

It was around seven-thirty that Mike thought about making a move to head home. The market had closed about half an hour before, but Mike was just marking time. He didn't really want to go home, but he didn't feel like going for a drink either. He was just milling around, waiting for Anderson who was busy on a conference call in his office. Mike's leathers and his helmet were in the corner of Anderson's office and he needed them if he was going to ride home tonight.

When Anderson was finished, he grabbed his jacket from the coat stand and made his way across to the desk where Mike was killing time reading the *Evening Standard*.

'Dude, you should go home and get some rest. I know it's been a long day for you. I'd have you over for dinner at our house tonight, but there's a function on at my daughter's school.'

'That's okay.' Mike closed the newspaper. 'I was just reading about that bomb today.'

'Like I said earlier, feel free to take some time out if you need it. We all need a mental health check every once in a while. I really think it would be a wise move if you took some time for yourself.'

'I'll be fine. But thanks for the concern – I appreciate it.'

Mike made his way into Anderson's office to put on his riding gear. First he removed his shoes, placing them in his backpack, then his suit jacket and trousers, cramming them into the pack. Next, he put on his leathers and his boots, before securing his backpack firmly on his back. He grabbed his helmet and gloves and made his way to the elevator.

Mike looked across the trading floor. What had been a thriving metropolis only an hour ago was a ghost town now. Computers beeped and hummed away by themselves. There was no one around.

Out in the street, Mike made his way down the lane to the quiet street where he had parked his beloved Ducati. He was going to try and do a deal with the guy who was in charge of the car spaces in the building because he wasn't keen on parking his new toy out on the street where it could get damaged or even stolen. Mike put the keys in the ignition and hit the starter button. The Ducati's engine roared into life. He gave it a little bit of throttle for a few moments to get it idling properly, then, standing beside the bike, he placed the helmet on the seat whilst he put on his gloves. After he had finished putting these on, he reached for his helmet.

At this moment, a screeching of tires caused him to turn around and look. The black Porsche was heading straight for him. He tried to jump out of the way, but it was too late. He landed on the hood of the Porsche, bouncing hard and rolling up to the windscreen which he hit face first. The force of the blow caused him to lose his helmet. He held onto the windscreen for dear life as the Porsche went faster and the driver tried to dislodge him. Mike couldn't hold on any longer. Letting go of the hood, he flipped onto the roof before rolling over the back of the car. He hit the asphalt hard. Rolling over and over, he came to a sudden stop when he hit the gutter. In agonizing pain, Mike felt for himself for broken bones. His leathers had done their job; they were a little scuffed and torn but he was in one piece. He looked into the distance and saw the red tail lights of the Porsche disappear around the corner. He got up and started running back down the street to his bike.

He reached the Ducati in a few seconds. It was still idling. He looked for his helmet, which was further down the street, when he saw the Porsche heading straight back for him. He kicked the stand out from under the bike and shot off down the street with the car in pursuit.

Mike roared past the Barbican. With the wind biting at his face, adrenaline pumping faster than ever before, Mike kicked up through the gears. The bike whined as he pulled harder on the throttle. He rode like he had never ridden before. In the side view mirror, Mike could see a passenger hanging out the window of the Porsche aiming a pistol. Bullets whizzed past him. He crouched down on the bike, making himself as small a target as possible. He took a long corner, knee down, rubber clawing at the road for grip. The Porsche driver threw the car sideways through the corner trying to keep up, the passenger nearly falling out in the process. Tears streamed down Mike's face. Without his helmet, it was difficult to see at these speeds. In the mirror he could see the passenger readying himself to take another shot. Mike started swerving from side to side to make himself a harder target to hit. He had to get away, fast! In the corners he had the Porsche's measure, but in the straight Mike knew he would be history. He realized he had to lose himself in the traffic. That was his best bet. Flying through Smithfield market, the Porsche gave chase. Mike made a hard left, right, then left again to come out onto the busy Farringdon road. The traffic was backed up bumper to bumper. Mike shot into the far lane, running beside the traffic jam. The Porsche stopped, and the passenger window went up. Mike looked in his side mirror. His pursuers were stuck in traffic half a mile back. Safe, at least for the moment, he headed home.

Mike parked his bike down Justice Lane, just around the corner from his apartment in Chelsea and far from sight. The pressure off for a moment, he had time to relax. For the first time since the chase had started he became aware of his erratic breathing and pulse. His heart was beating faster than ever before. He started shaking uncontrollably as he stood in a doorway concealed by the shadows. Too scared to move, he watched his apartment for a few minutes. He looked up and down the street. It was empty. There was no sign of the black Porsche. When he was convinced that there was no one waiting, he made his way across the street in the darkness.

As he made his way across the street his mind flashed back to the Porsche. He had seen two Japanese men in the car, both dressed in black. It was dark and he had only seen it for a second, but the face of the driver would be etched in his mind forever. The face was familiar. Where had he seen it before?

Turning the key to open the door to his apartment a chill filled Mike's body. He remembered where he had seen the face. It was Okimura – the man he had met in Tokyo. Why was Fujiyama's boss trying to kill him? It made no sense.

He walked down the hallway and flicked on the lights. He stopped, frightened. His apartment had been ransacked. The place was trashed. Everything had been overturned. Papers littered the room, and his couch had been slashed from end to end, its stuffing all over the room. His laptop was gone, with all his disks and all the pages relating to Metco.

He ran to his bedroom to find the same disarray. Drawers open. Clothes everywhere, although it was hard to tell the original mess from the intrusion which even to Mike wasn't completely obvious.

His mind started racing; he had to get out. They knew where he lived. They knew where he worked. It was only a matter of time before they came back. He had to move quickly. Mike grabbed a sports bag from the cupboard and started throwing in clothes indiscriminately. Still dressed in his leathers, he pulled the backpack off his back. He opened the outside pouch and pulled out his Nokia 9000, his latest electronic toy. He blew on it and rubbed the screen. It was a little scratched, but to his surprise, it worked when he turned it on. It had survived the hit and run remarkably well. He flicked it off, closed it and threw it into the sports bag. He grabbed its charger and threw this into the bag as well as a spare battery and a power converter. He checked the side compartment of the bag. It still contained his two passports – one U.S., one Italian – and some U.S. currency from his last trip to Utah. Thank God for that.

The more his mind raced, the clearer it became. Okimura, Fujiyama, IMT, Wilmont Bridge, Metco, and Cartwright – they all were involved in some big conspiracy. Somehow they had to be defrauding Yamamoto of millions of dollars. With all the copies of the spreadsheet gone, he had no hard evidence. He needed proof. Some one was trying to kill him. Then a thought struck him: someone had tried killing Fiona that morning too. Maybe it wasn't the I.R.A. trying to kill Sir Peter, as everyone suspected. Maybe these guys were behind it. Maybe it was Fiona who was the real target. There was a lot of money at stake. They had to be desperate men. What had Fiona stumbled across in her investigations? If he went to the police with this theory and no evidence, they would send for the men in white suits to take him away. They would certainly think he was crazy. He had to have hard evidence. But they had taken it all. The trail was cold. What could he do?

'Think, Mike, think!' he said to himself, as he zipped up the sports bag and threw it over his shoulder. Then he remembered something. The yellow legal pad!

Mike rushed into the front room. The pad was on the floor beside the couch. He stuffed it into the side compartment of the sports bag and ran for the door, making a dash for his bike. When he reached it he changed his mind. They would be looking for the machine. Better to go on foot. In the darkness, he quickly discarded the torn leathers and put on a rugby top, pulling a baseball cap down hard on his head to help conceal his face. Satisfied that no one was following him, he circled the long way around the back streets of Chelsea to the busy King's Road where he blended in with the bustling Wednesday night crowd.

He walked naturally, but avoided eye contact He made his way down past his own street, crossing the road swiftly. Seeing a Barclays cash machine, he felt for his back pocket. He pulled out the money clip and quickly counted the money he had. Eighty pounds, that was all. He would need more.

When he got to the machine, he placed his sports bag between his legs and pulled out his keycard. Inserting it into the slot, he punched in his four-digit pin number. He had the same number, 6969, on every account. It was a number he knew he would never forget. It always brought a smile to his face when he punched it in, but not this time. He kept looking up and down the road for the black Porsche. Fuck! He could only access five hundred pounds a day. That was his limit. He would have to go into a branch tomorrow to get more. Five hundred would have to do for tonight.

Just as he was taking the cash from the machine, he caught sight of the Porsche again. He froze. His heart skipped a beat. It was two hundred yards up the King's Road. To run would be obvious. Besides, it was unlikely that they would recognize him from that distance in the dark, especially since he was wearing a baseball cap. He watched them turn off King's Road into his street. He relaxed.

Mike thrust his hand out and seconds later was in a cab. 'Earl's Court, please.' He lay across the back seat, exhausted.

'Rough day at the office?' the cabbie inquired in a friendly tone.

'It was a killer,' Mike quipped. If only he knew.

Mike found himself a room in a dodgy hotel just near Earl's Court tube station. As he paid cash up front for the night's accommodation he didn't even have to leave his name with the front desk. That made him feel a little easier.

The room was Spartan to say the least: a bed, a pillow, a rickety cupboard that smelled musty, a small beside lamp mounted on the wall, a television that didn't even work, paint peeling off the walls. At least there were fresh sheets on the bed. He didn't care. He felt relatively safe here. No one knew he was there. He sat down on the edge of the bed, closed his eyes, and allowed the weight of the world to slip off his shoulders for a second. He was thankful to be alive, and even more thankful that Fiona was still alive. He wondered where she was. At least he had his phone so she could call him. Shit! His phone wasn't on. He rummaged through his bag looking for it. Having located it, he turned it on, plugging the charger into the wall and sitting the phone upright in it. It could charge whilst still being able to receive calls, for which he was thankful. He checked for missed calls. Nothing.

Mike unzipped the side compartment of the sports bag, pulling out the yellow legal pad and putting it on the bed. He put his hand deep into the side slit and trawled his hand along the length of the join with the main part of the bag. Ha! He found something. No good. It was a biro. He needed a pencil. He shoved his hand back into the side compartment and started to rummage once again. Then he felt it. He pulled his hand up with glee.

Pressing softly with the pencil, he started to color in the top page of the yellow legal pad, as fond memories of doing this as a child came flooding back. He had always done this when he wanted to write secret messages, when he was a spy playing games. Now it was no game. Slowly but surely, words appeared in front of his eyes like magic. There was a lot of twisted garbage on the page, but soon he was able to make out the address for Metco in Jersey. He tore a page from the back of the pad and scrawled it down.

He had to go to this address and see what he could find out. He thought back to the conversation he had had with Fiona. The address was a law firm of some description. Turner and Associates. That was it. Tomorrow he would fly there and check it out. Now he was exhausted. Physically and emotionally he was shot. His energy spent, Mike fell fast asleep.

*

Around 1 a.m. the men in the black Porsche decided that Mike wasn't coming home that night. They resolved to call Fujiyama and give him the bad news. They told Fujiyama that they had recovered all the evidence, so far as they knew, but that Michael Kelly was still alive.

Fujiyama was furious. 'I want him dead,' he shouted like a maniac down the line. 'When he surfaces, and he will surface at some point, I want him killed. No mistakes this time.'

While Mike was still alive, he was a threat. Fujiyama needed him dead.

*

Mike awoke from his peaceful slumber wondering if it had all been a bad dream. He flicked on the lamp beside the bed. It was real all right. The paint, bubbling and cracking from the rising damp, and the small single bed were a dead give-away. He yawned and stretched, scratching the back of his head, then looked at his watch. He would be late for work. Anderson had told him to take some time for himself, anyway. He decided to call him but then reconsidered. It would be better that way. Anderson would understand. He had decided to go to Jersey to see what he could glean from Turner and Associates about Metco. It was going to be dangerous. He couldn't stop replaying the incident with the black Porsche over and over in his mind. The face of Okimura, if that was who it really was, staring coldly at him. He could see him as plain as day.

The rhombus! Of course. That's what Green had meant. Somehow, that lapel pin that Fujiyama and Okimura were wearing at dinner was the key to it all. It explained that cryptic title of Green's spreadsheet, 'The rhombus is the key'. It was the pin of some sort of secret society, some copper underworld. That gold, rhombus-shaped pin was the key to this whole thing.

Mike showered and put on his suit, which was a little crushed, having spent the night in a pile on the floor. He grabbed his other things, left the dump that had been his fortress for the night, and ventured out into the mid-morning light. It was just after nine. The bank would be open soon. Mike walked along Earl's Court Road, ever mindful, eyeing suspiciously everyone he passed.

As he walked along the street he passed an ex-army store. This sold all types of surplus military goods, camping and hiking equipment, as well as hunting knives and military memorabilia. It was a pin board in the front window housing medals that gave him an idea.

Mike popped inside quickly and bought a Swiss Army knife and a small Union Jack lapel pin which only cost him a couple of pounds. He put them in his pocket and made his way to the bank. On his way there he stopped at a stationery supplier where he purchased a gold paint pen. Finally, he made it to the bank where, after producing his passport, he withdrew three thousand pounds in cash. These tasks accomplished, he got into a cab and headed out to Heathrow.

At the airport, Mike located the British Airways ticket desk and paid cash for a ticket for the midday flight to Jersey. Having done that, he found a disabled persons' toilet and locked himself inside. He put his sports bag on the floor, sat on the toilet, lid down, and took the Swiss Army knife and the flag pin from his pocket. Opening the file blade from the knife, he set to work on the lapel pin. Scratching the paint off the surface was easy, then he set about changing the rectangular shape into a rhombus. It took about twenty minutes of furious filing till he was happy with his work. He blew on it hard to get rid of the little metal shavings, and rubbed it on his sock just for good measure.

Suddenly, Mike was aware of a ringing sound. His reached for his phone, which was at the at the bottom of his bag. He hoped it might be Fiona. Then he saw the number; it was the office calling. He decided to let it ring off. It was probably Anderson. If it was important, he would leave a message. Mike didn't feel like talking to anyone at the moment, and put the phone back in the bag.

Holding the pin up in the air, Mike nodded to himself. Satisfied with his handiwork, he took the gold paint pen from the side pocket of his sports bag and set about coating the surface of his new pin with a lustrous golden color. He applied the paint thick and evenly across the surface, blowing on it from time to time to speed up to drying process, then held it up in the air as far away from himself as he could. It was passable. It was only on closer inspection that you could see the slightly uneven grooves along the edge. Anyway, it would have to do.

Mike left the disabled toilet and made his way to the left luggage area. He unzipped the bag and took out his phone, his passports, and sunglasses, putting them in the inside pocket of his jacket. He checked that he had all his cash and his ticket before depositing his bag for the day. He didn't need the rest of his gear for the moment. Looking inside his jacket, he double checked that he had his ticket, and made his way to the departure lounge.

In the departure area he bought a metallic briefcase. While he waited for the plane, he tried to think up a story that he could use when he met Frank Turner. What was he going to say? He decided that he would pretend to be an attorney acting on behalf of IMT. He really hoped he could pull it off.

On arrival in Jersey, Mike hired a small sedan, a Fiat Punto. It was cute and functional. He drove it to the capital, St. Helier. Mike pulled up the car outside a wonderful old sandstone building. It was positively regal. There were golden plaques all over the wall on the outside. They were all nameplate companies. He took the address from inside his pocket and took a look. Yes, this was the place. Mike took the pin that he had fashioned and fastened it to his lapel. He grabbed the metallic briefcase from the passenger seat, took a deep breath, straightened his tie, and headed inside.

Despite being in an impressive building, the interior was nothing to talk about. The old-world decor fit in with the overall atmosphere, but it really needed some updating, Mike thought as he walked up a grand sweeping staircase to the offices of Turner and Associates, located on the second floor of the building.

Mike walked in through the front door. It was a small office. There was a mousy-looking young secretary at the front desk. She had long, fine, brown hair which cascaded over her right shoulder, a soft complexion and alluring hazel eyes which Mike found rather attractive. She looked barely twenty-one, young and unsure of herself. Mike sensed an opportunity. He walked straight up to the desk and stood in a commanding stance in front of her.

'Hi. I'm Dave Hansen from Lufkin, Hansen and Strong in New York. We act on behalf of IMT in New York. I'm here to see Frank Turner,' he said sternly with a very New York attitude.

'I'm sorry, but Mr. Turner is out to lunch this afternoon with a client.' She looked though an appointment book on her desk. 'I don't even have you listed here, sir. What did you say your name was again, sir?' she asked timidly.

'Damn.' Mike slammed his fist down on the table in anger. 'I've only got two hours till I have to take a flight back to London. I spoke with Mr. Turner yesterday. He assured me he would be here this afternoon to meet with me. But maybe you can help me.' Mike changed his tone.

'He should be back in about an hour – you could come back then. Or I could call the restaurant where he's dining, if you would like to talk to him,' she offered, picking up the phone.

'No. That won't be necessary,' Mike said, placing his hand on hers and hanging up the receiver. 'I don't want to disturb him. If you could just show me to the Metco files I can get to work. I'll see Mr. Turner when he gets back from lunch.'

'I don't think I can—' but she stopped mid-sentence. She had seen the rhombus-shaped pin. Mr. Turner had given her strict instructions to be extra helpful to anyone bearing the emblem, even if to date all the people wearing it had been Japanese. 'If you'd like to follow me, all the Metco files are in this room.' Mike looked down at the pin. It had obviously worked. He followed her down the corridor, passing a photocopying room on the way. 'They are all in there,' said the girl, pointing into a filing cabinet in the corner of a lonely office. On the door was a golden plaque with the name 'Metco' on it.

'Is there anything I can get you?' she added politely. 'Tea, coffee, soft drink, water?'

'No, I'll be fine, thanks,' Mike said.

She turned to leave him, pulling the door behind her as she did so. Mike watched her intently. He saw her slender young legs through a slit in the side of her skirt, which diverted his attention momentarily.

'Just one quick question before you leave,' Mike called out before she had completely shut the door. 'When do you expect Mr. Turner will be back?' As he spoke, Mike placed the metallic briefcase on the top of the cabinet.

'He should be back around two-thirty,' she said, poking her head back around the corner of the door.

'Thank you,' Mike said. Excellent, he thought. He looked at his watch. He had just an hour before Turner returned. He had to get cracking.

Mike poured over the files. Fujiyama controlled Metco: that was the gist of the documents that he read. It appeared that Fujiyama was laundering money that he, Murphy, Wilmont, and Bridge had defrauded from Yamamoto. It amounted to billions of dollars. Along the way, he was washing substantial amounts of money to a Yakuza front company back in Tokyo called Dantotsu. It was all starting to make more sense, but there were still pieces missing from the puzzle. Also via Metco, payments had been made to LME directors, union officials, and politicians. You name it, their brush had touched it.

Mike stealthily made copies of most of the documents, making sure that the secretary could not see him, and always mindful of his time constraints. He had to move quickly. Turner would be back soon. He could make duplicate copies later.

He returned the files to the cabinet, placing his own copies in his metallic briefcase. He looked at his watch. In about fifteen minutes Turner would be back. He had to get out.

Mike walked back out through the reception area.

'I'm just going to pop down to my car and get some more documents. I'll be back in a minute. While I'm gone, do you think you could put on a pot of coffee?' He opened the door and looked back at the poor girl. 'Thanks. I really appreciate your help.' He smiled at her.

In a flash Mike was in his car and heading back to the airport. He patted the metallic briefcase on the passenger seat. 'Fujiyama, you son of a bitch. I've got you now.'

Waiting at the airport for the flight back to Heathrow, Mike checked his phone messages. Anderson had called three times to check how he was doing. Still nothing from Fiona. He hoped that she was all right. The secret service guys probably had them holed up somewhere safe until things died down. Maybe she wasn't allowed to call him. He flipped open the briefcase on his lap and started going over the documents he had copied. What still puzzled him was where a large portion of the money was going. It all seemed to go to some guy called Wolfgang Schmidt. Was this the mastermind behind the whole operation? Was he the Mister Big controlling Fujiyama. Just who the hell was he? There was an address listed in Vienna. Mike took a pen from his jacket pocket and circled the address. He would take the first flight he could to Vienna that night.

'Whoever you are, Wolfgang Schmidt,' Mike said to himself under his breath, 'I will find you.'

At Heathrow, Mike bought a ticket for the last flight of the day to Vienna. He only had an hour to kill till departure. He claimed his sports bag from the left luggage area, went to the bathroom and changed into casual clothes. As he came out of the cubicle, Mike noticed a Japanese man in a black suit washing his hands at the basin. His blood started racing. They had found him. Mike stared at him in terror, frozen. Then he ran for the door. He didn't look back.

The Japanese man looked up into the mirror and caught sight of the terror-stricken face just before the figure ran from the bathroom. He grabbed some paper towels, dried his hands, picked up his briefcase, and casually wandered out, shaking his head, and wondering what was wrong with the young Caucasian.

Mike bolted through immigration and boarded his flight to Vienna.

*

Turner returned from lunch to some distinctly unwelcome news. When he had finished his tirade to his poor secretary, who was weeping profusely as a result, Turner summoned up the courage to call Fujiyama.

'There was a young man here today.'

'American?'

'Yes. How did you know?' Turner sounded surprised. 'Did you send him?'

'No. But I think it is time that I took care of him.' Fujiyama paused. The line went quiet for a few seconds. 'Thank you. I will attend to this immediately.'

The first man in black took the call.

'Hai, Fujiyama-san. Vienna. We will take the first flight available tomorrow. We will pay Herr Schmidt's office a visit.'

*

Mike arrived in Vienna late in the evening. He decided to take a room in a small pension overlooking the pedestrianized Graben in the Hofburg quarter. He walked through a set of ancient gates, across a courtyard, and up a wide, stone staircase. A green-carpeted walkway connected the bedrooms, each newly renovated with Rococo-style furnishings and adorned with crystal chandeliers. He opened the door to the bathroom and took a peek. Rudimentary, but at least it had a real shower. It was late. He was tired. That made the combination of a three hundred year old building and rather dowdy decor strangely endearing.

Mike fixed the power converter to fit the socket and plugged it into the wall. He put his phone on charge and switched off the light. Tomorrow would be a long day.

From his deep sleep, Mike became aware of a ringing sound. He looked across at the clock. It was almost eleven. He had slept like a baby. Still half asleep, he tried to get his bearings. The phone was on the dresser, still in the charger. He leapt across the room. Maybe it would be Fiona.

'Hello,' he said excitedly down the line.

'Michael Kelly?' the voice asked slowly.

'Yes. Speaking. Who is this?'

'You know very well who I am.'

It was Fujiyama. Shit! How had he found his number?

'What do you want?' Mike asked aggressively.

'We are reasonable men. I think we can come to some sort of reasonable agreement.'

What was Fujiyama playing at? Was he trying to buy him as well? He had tried to kill him just the other day. It didn't make sense. What had he stumbled across that was of such value?

'I am sorry about the incident the other day,' Fujiyama continued in a soft, rational tone. 'It was most regrettable. You have my apologies.'

'What about the girl?'

'You have my utmost condolences. It was not my doing.'

Mike sensed that he was lying, but decided to play along with him. 'What about my safety?'

'I can guarantee your safety,' Fujiyama stated unequivocally.

'And what is my silence worth?'

'Ten million dollars,' Fujiyama said without emotion. He was a businessman; this was simple economics. Given that Mike had escaped the other day, it seemed it would be cheaper to buy him than kill him. It made good business sense.

Mike decided to buy himself some time. 'Okay. You have a deal.'

'Good. So we understand each other.' Fujiyama sounded pleased.

'Yes. I'll call you in twenty-four hours with the details of the account I want you to place the money in.' Mike hung up.

Mike doubted the sincerity of a man who only twenty-four hours earlier had tried to have him killed and probably tried to kill his girlfriend as well. Why had he now resorted to this tactic? What did Mike have in his possession that was so valuable? Ten million dollars was a lot of money, even if in the big scheme of things it was spare change.

*

Meanwhile, the two men in black arrived at Vienna's Schwechat International airport. After clearing customs, they made their way through to the arrivals hall where they were met by a third man who handed over a black briefcase before ushering them into a waiting Mercedes 300E.

'Where to?' the third man asked from the driver's seat.

'Shulerstrasse,' the first man barked.

Placing the black briefcase on his lap, he flipped open the locks. Inside were two Austrian-made 9mm Glock pistols which were disassembled. He lifted the top drawer containing the pistols out of the case, and passed it to the second man, sitting beside him. The other drawer contained six full clips of ammunition and two silencers. They immediately set about assembling the weapons.

*

Mike showered quickly and put on his suit. He grabbed his phone and the metallic briefcase and headed outside, making a quick mental note to eat something. He hadn't eaten in almost two days. Airline food didn't count as far as Mike was concerned. He walked out into the Graben and past the impressive Sparkasse bank with its gilt bee on the pediment. Mike wandered his way through the complex maze of lanes, alleys, and courtyards which make up medieval Vienna. Map in hand, he turned right into Kohl Markt and headed toward Stephansplatz and the impressive Stephansdom Cathedral with its mix of Romanesque, Gothic, and Baroque architecture. He had chosen to make for this landmark because it was hard to miss and close to the address listed for Wolfgang Schmidt on Schulerstrasse.

With a little difficulty, Mike found the offices of Wolfgang Schmidt. It was easy to miss, just a little door with a brass name plate on it at the side of a big old building in Schulerstrasse. Mike opened the door and stepped inside. As he pulled the door there was a little jingle from the bell that was attached to it. There were a man and a woman in the room, sitting facing each other at a large desk which took up most of the room in the very small office. There were no computers. An old, rotary-style telephone, an antique to someone like Mike, sat to one side of the desk. The room reeked of tobacco and pipe smoke, and there was an old pipe smoldering away on the desk. The rest of the room was covered in bundles of paper tied with crimson ribbons. It was a mess, even worse than Mike's bedroom. This was not what Mike had expected. He could only see the back of what appeared to be an older gentleman, almost bald from the look of it. The woman sat facing the door. As soon as he had entered the room she had stood up. She was wearing a particularly unflattering, rather frumpy dress. Mike guessed that she was probably in her mid to late forties, but the dress made her look much older.

'Guten tag,' she welcomed him cheerfully with a smile.

'Guten tag,' Mike stumbled. 'Um.' He paused. 'Sprechen ze English?' he asked in his best German, which was still pretty woeful. Like most Americans, Mike assumed cultural hegemony over a world where everyone should naturally speak English.

'Yes. Can I help you?' she asked, her English marked with a heavy accent.

As she asked the question the older gentleman turned around.

'Maybe you can.' Mike took a good look at the older man, a rotund fellow with gray hair, mustache, and beard, a jovial-looking character. Mike thought that Santa Claus might have looked this way in his youth. 'I am looking for Wolfgang Schmidt.'

The older man stood up, pipe in hand. 'I am Wolfgang Schmidt.' He smiled.

'Hi, my name's Dave Rosenbaum. I represent Metco.' Mike held out his hand.

Wolfgang moved forward to shake it. He saw the lapel pin. His eyes lit up. 'Ah. So good to meet you finally. Come. Come. Please sit.' He motioned to the chair that the woman had just vacated. 'Gertrude, can you make us some coffee, please, darling?' he called out after her as she walked down the corridor. 'My wife.' He pointed in the direction of the corridor. 'I hope you like coffee. Mr. Rosenbaum, wasn't it?' he asked, turning back to face Mike.

'Yes. Rosenbaum. Coffee would be fine. Thank you.' Mike was taken aback by the hospitality. Wolfgang Schmidt certainly didn't look or act like the Mr. Big of a crime syndicate. He seemed to be your average everyday attorney. How did he fit into this picture? He would soon find out.

'I was wondering when someone from your organization would come. You will see that I have deposited the monies that I have received over a conservative portfolio of investments as you instructed.' Schmidt looked pleased with himself.

'Could you show me what you've done on our behalf?'

'Sure. Sure. No problems.' He got up and started to sort through some of the piles of paper on the floor. Mike thought it was comical. The thought that the paper trail of billions of dollars was somehow ending here in these bundles of paper on the floor of this attorney's office in Vienna was incomprehensible. 'Ah. Here it is.' He picked up a bundle, blew a light film of dust from the surface, and undid the crimson ribbon that held it together. 'Yes, it's all here,' he said proudly. 'Everything. Everything from the start. It's all accounted for here.'

'Can I take a look?' Mike held out his hand.

'Sure.' Wolfgang handed the file to him.

Gertrude returned to the room with a tray containing a pot of coffee, two cups and milk and sugar. She placed it on the table and went on her way down the corridor.

'Thank you,' Mike called out to her as an afterthought, as he opened the file.

Mike looked over the file. Wolfgang Schmidt was obviously a fastidious man despite the apparent chaotic clutter of his office. He had kept every piece of correspondence that had passed between Metco and himself. Metco had established Schmidt as a trustee for funds that they wanted to invest, and over the past four years had wired him somewhere in the region of a billion dollars that he had dutifully invested over a wide spectrum of investments. These investments had returned somewhere in the region of seven percent on an annual basis, which was not bad. Schmidt had done an amazing job funneling Metco's money into an incredibly diverse portfolio. Most had been invested in an array of international equities, international bond funds, and property. The equity investments had been via U.S. Mutual Funds and European investment funds, and amongst other things, Metco owned a hotel in Paris, an office block in New York, apartments in Hong Kong, and a golf course in Florida.

A large chunk of the money, somewhere in the region of one hundred million U.S. dollars, had been invested in a variety of negotiable instruments. These included bearer bonds issued in various currencies, gold bullion and rare gold coins, physical cash denominated in U.S. dollars, deutschmarks, yen, Swiss francs and sterling or placed into anonymous numbered bearer bank accounts called 'sparbuchs'. All these liquid assets, as they were listed in Schmidt's ledger, were held in safety deposit boxes at the post office savings bank, the Postparkasse.

From his conversations with Schmidt, and briefly reading the correspondences that he had meticulously kept, it was obvious to Mike that Schmidt had never met anyone from this mysterious company, Metco. Everything had been done via the post from a mailing address in Bermuda. There were written instructions for him to hand over anything that was requested by a person bearing the rhombus-shaped gold lapel pin.

Mike finished skimming the documents. He looked up at Schmidt.

'Can you give me a copy of the ledger?'

'Sure, I have a duplicate copy of everything. It's here somewhere.' Schmidt started sifting through the mountains of bundles on the floor. 'Here we go.' He held up another bundle of papers tied together with the customary crimson ribbon.

'Excellent,' Mike said, taking the bundle and placing it in his big metallic briefcase. 'Can you take me to the Postparkasse?'

'Sure. It is just around the corner.' Schmidt opened his desk drawer and pulled out a set of keys on a big circular keyring. 'Come, let's go,' he said, reaching for his jacket which was hanging from a stand in the corner. 'Gertrude,' he called down the corridor, 'I am taking Mr. Rosenbaum to the Postparkasse.'

Walking into the Postparkasse it was hard not to admire its beauty. Spindly aluminum columns supported a huge glass canopy, creating a massive open area which formed the large banking hall. With its polished marble floors and fine oak tables, the bank was one of Otto Wagner's masterpieces. Schmidt marched up to a big oak desk in one corner where a small elf-like man sat at a table, shuffling papers.

'Helmut, I would like to visit the vault.' He smiled.

'Sure, Wolfgang.' The small man's face showed no emotion; he just grabbed a set of keys from his desk. 'Please, gentlemen. Follow me.'

He opened a wooden door behind him which revealed what looked like a 1920s elevator, almost art deco in its design. He pulled apart the sliding metal doors and the three of them stepped inside. He pulled the doors together and pressed a button. The elevator jerked a couple of times before starting to descend slowly.

When they reached the bottom, Helmut opened the door and beckoned them to step out. He then opened a big metal door, which must have been at least two feet thick, Mike estimated, and walked into a vast cavern. As far as the eye could see were walls of steel. Steel safety deposit boxes. Row upon row upon row of metal boxes lined the walls of this immense space. Helmut and Schmidt then walked up to one of the boxes. They both placed a key into one of the two locks that it, like every box, had, then simultaneously turned their keys anti-clockwise, opening the box. They went through the same procedure over and over again with about a dozen safety deposit boxes.

*

The black Mercedes pulled up outside Wolfgang Schmidt's office. The first man opened the door and stepped out of the car. Making sure that his pistol was securely holstered against his right side, he paused for a moment and adjusted his tie briefly before going inside.

Seconds later he was back in the car. Slamming the door he cried. 'The Postparkasse. Quick!'

*

Mike stared in awe at the contents of the boxes. It was like being let lose in Ali Baba's cave. But the spoils of forty thieves were nothing in comparison with this. The first box contained close to seventy million dollars in bearer bonds issued in various currencies. The second contained bearer passbooks and a collection of rare gold coins. The rest of the boxes contained hard currency. Notes of all denominations. Bundles. Thick wads of money held together by elastic bands: yen, dollars, Swiss francs, deutschmarks and sterling.

Opening his big metallic case, Mike started to shovel the contents of the first two boxes inside. There was just enough space to fit it all. There wasn't enough space to put in any of the hard currency. He would have needed an armored car for that. Still he reckoned he had just placed about ninety million dollars in negotiable instruments into this big metallic briefcase. Every single one of them was just as good as cash. Better even, as they were easier to transport.

'I'll just take the contents of these first two boxes for the moment, Wolfgang,' Mike smiled.

'Sure. It's no problem,' Schmidt chuckled. 'It's your money. Do what you like. Are you finished with these other boxes?'

'Yes,' Mike was struggling on the floor to get the metallic case shut. While Mike did this, Helmut and Schmidt systematically closed all the boxes in the reverse order.

*

The Mercedes double parked right opposite the Postparkasse. The second man was just about to get out of the car.

'Wait.' The first grabbed him by the arm and pulled him back. 'It's a bank. They'll have metal detectors in there. We'll wait out here.'

They sat waiting in the car as it idled. The first man kept a sharp eye on the front steps of the Postparkasse. Then he recognized Michael Kelly, carrying a metal briefcase walking beside a rotund, older-looking man.

'There he is!' he said, attaching a silencer to the end of his Glock. 'Let's go.' He opened the door. Simultaneously, the other exited the vehicle and started making his way across the street.

At the bottom of the steps to the Postparkasse, Mike was shaking Schmidt's hand. 'Thank you, Wolfgang. I look forward to seeing you again soon. Thank you so much for your help.' He looked over the shoulder of the shorter man in front of him. About one hundred metros away, he saw the face of the man in black who was known to him as

Okimura. He saw Okimura reaching with his left hand for a bulge inside his jacket.

In an instant, Mike let go of Wolfgang's hand, turned and ran in the opposite direction across the square. Like a startled jack rabbit, Mike scampered through the lunchtime crowd, running into people, knocking them flying, the metallic case weighing more than ever before and hindering his progress. Behind him, the two men in black, pistols still holstered, gave chase. His pulse racing, Mike ran harder and faster, as fast he could. These men didn't muck around. He knew that his life depended on this sprint. Through the main thoroughfare the chase continued. Mike's superior speed and will to live gave him an advantage, and the distance between him and his pursuers increased. He lost sight of them in the crowd. He pushed on, not looking back, running as fast as his legs would carry him.

Running across the busy Biberstrasse Mike tripped on the gutter. Falling to the ground hard, the metallic case went flying. He got up instantly and looked at his hands. Coarse skin, dry blood. He had taken the skin off the palms of his hands, but he was fine. He looked back over his shoulder, searching for a sign that the men had given up their chase. No such luck. He saw Okimura about two hundred meters back down the road. Mike grabbed a hold of the case and ducked around the corner. He kept running, with the men in black, relentless in their pursuit never far behind.

Finally, his lungs bursting, gasping for air, Mike could go on no longer. He stopped to get his bearings for a second. He saw the lofty Stephansdom Cathedral, and the many tourists surrounding the main entrance, and made a dash for it.

Inside, Mike made his way forward toward the altar. Tourists wandered about the vast space created by the lofty vaulted interior. Standing hard up against a big stone pillar, clutching his metallic case against his chest in the cool sanctity of the cathedral, he started to catch his breath. At the back of the church, Mike saw his two pursuers slowly making their way forward, carefully checking each row of seats.

Mike stiffened up against the pillar, trying to make himself as invisible as possible, looking for a way out. He tried to regulate his breathing a little. Amidst the silence, his mobile phone rang. The sound echoed throughout the cathedral, and almost everyone in the cathedral around him looked in his direction in disapproval. Then he saw his way out. Mike bolted for one of the side entrances.

The men in black saw the figure scuttling toward the door and gave chase. Along Rotenturmstrasse they followed him, fresh from their brief rest in the cathedral. Mike bobbed, weaved, ducked, and battered his way through the crowds using the metallic case as a shield. The case, which was starting to feel heavy now was becoming a liability. It started to slow Mike's progress, and the men in black were steadily gaining on him. He thought about ditching it, but immediately decided against this. The case had everything he needed to put Fujiyama and his co-conspirators away, and he wasn't about to let it go lightly. He pressed on, driven only by fear.

Mike burst onto Franz-Josefs-Kai, hesitated, and then saw one of the many red and white trams that dot the landscape of Vienna. He turned. The men were only about seventy or eighty meters behind him. He turned back to the tram – a number two tram which was just pulling out. Mike made a dash for it. He jumped into the side of the car just as the doors were closing. Safe. He looked back through the glass door to see the men in black standing there, foiled.

Mike slumped into a seat and tried to catch his breath once again. He was buzzing from the excess of adrenaline pumping through his body. It felt as if he had drunk a thousand cups of coffee all at once. He had to get off the tram. They would surely be following. He had to get out of Vienna. He couldn't go back to his hotel. His clothes would be recognized. He could buy new ones. They would be sure to find him there at the hotel. He couldn't go through the airport, not carrying close to ninety million dollars' worth of negotiable instruments in his case. The gold coins would set the metal detectors off, anyway. The only option left was rail. Mike got off at the next tram stop, hailed a taxi and headed to the Westbahnhof railway station.

In the relative safety of the Westbahnhof which, as its name implied, serviced train routes to the west, Mike bought a ticket to Salzburg. The trains left every hour. He only had to wait for fifteen minutes. Once he was on the train, he found an empty compartment for the three-and-a-half hour journey.

Mike sat back in the train seat, his feet up on the seat on the other side making a bridge across the compartment. He put the metallic case, now heavily scratched on one side from his fall, on his lap. Mike smelt his armpits and reeled back in shock. Boy, did he need a shower. He needed a change of clothes. He had been in the same suit since Wednesday, and it was now Friday. After a furtive glance to check that no one was watching, he opened the case. He stared in awe at the contents. Gold coins, bearer bonds, and bearer savings accounts. Here in his lap was a fortune, an untraceable booty, close to ninety million dollars' worth. He could disappear with this money and live like a king for the rest of his life. Then again, he would always be looking over his shoulder, because the Yakuza would be after him. He decided against it. But what was he to do? He had to get all the evidence he had to the proper authorities, whoever they were. If Lloyd Cartwright was corrupt, who else was on the Yakuza's payroll? He couldn't fly back to London, as the Yakuza would surely be waiting for him.

Then his phone rang. He had forgotten about his phone. He pulled it from inside his jacket.

'Hello,' he shouted into it, to be heard above the din of the train which was crossing a bridge.

'Well done. I see you have named your price.'

'What?' Mike recognized Fujiyama's voice.

'You may keep what you have taken if you return to me all the copies of documents that you have in your possession. Then you will resign from your job and disappear. I will never hear from you again.'

'And the men who have been following me, trying to kill me?'

'They will be called off. We are businessmen, not assassins. Do we have a deal?'

The line was quiet. Mike thought long and hard. Ninety million dollars was a lot of money. It would be easy to disappear with such a large amount. Then he thought about Fiona. Visions of her car, a burning wreck. Imogen dead.

'Do we have a deal?' Fujiyama repeated himself.

'Yes. This is the deal. I promise to fuck you, you son of a bitch!' Mike hung up.

He quickly flipped open his Nokia 9000 and started typing up a fax. It was addressed to his stockbroker in Lugano, giving orders to sell as much Yamamoto stock as his account would allow on margin. He was going to blow this whole conspiracy wide apart. He was going to bring down Fujiyama. If he brought down Fujiyama, Yamamoto's share price would tumble.

Next, he checked his messages and e-mails. Fiona had left a message. She was safe. She was staying at her uncle's apartment in Monaco. Anderson had sent him a bundle of e-mails. Where was he? Was he okay? Why was Fujiyama asking for his mobile number? What was going on? Mike decided to call Anderson later in the evening, when he got to Salzburg, to explain what he had stumbled across. That was if he could still trust Anderson. Mike was confused. He didn't really know who he could trust. He figured that if he couldn't trust Anderson, then he couldn't trust anyone.

Finally, just before his battery ran out, he sent a quick e-mail to his friend John Templeton. It was simple. 'THE PATH OF LEAST RESISTANCE IN COPPER IS DOWN. IT'S NOW OFFICIALLY DUCK SEASON.' When he had finished, he switched off the phone and decided to try and get an hour or so sleep. If his morning was anything to go by, he would need the energy.

Mike awoke to the jolt of the train stopping in Salzburg. It was now nearly five in the evening, making it four in London. Mike had an idea. He bought a ticket to Zurich and got on the next available train.

*

In New York, John Templeton was at his desk, a little bleeping sound alerted him to the fact that he had new mail. He clicked on the mailbox icon on his screen and saw that he had a message from Mike. His eyes lit up. He had been concerned, as he hadn't heard from Mike in days. Mike's office had said he was at home. John had tried his home and mobile but was still unable to reach him. Instead he had only got Mike's answering machine and voice mail. John noticed that the e-mail was from Mike's personal account and not the usual Nelson Smith address. He hoped that Mike was okay. Maybe the e-mail would give him some clue. He clicked on the unread message with interest, staring at the cryptic message for a few seconds. So Mike thought it was duck season.

John turned and looked at the clock. It was five-twenty. Most people in London would have gone home for the week. Trading on the Comex in New York would be thin at best. The timing sure seemed right. John trusted Mike's judgment implicitly.

Without hesitation, John picked up the phone. With his forefinger he stabbed the direct line to one of his floor brokers in the copper pit.

'Sal?' he demanded.

'He's— he's in the pit, sir,' the young voice stammered. 'Can I help you?'

'Yeah, get me Sal!' John didn't use Sal very often. Sal had a reputation for being a big mouth and for front running orders. John didn't trust him one iota. That made him perfect for the job that John had in mind.

'Actually, he's on the throne.' There was a pause. 'I'll run and get him if you like.'

'Have him buzz me immediately!' John sounded annoyed.

'Yes sir, you got it,' the youngster replied eagerly.

John clicked out. He flicked up an hourly Comex copper chart onto his screen. The chart looked weak. If Mike was right, now was the perfect time to put his foot on the gas pedal.

*

Mike started planning his next move. So far, the bad guys had been one step ahead of him the whole way. He was only just beginning to catch up. How did they know his movements? Had they placed a transmitter somewhere? Surely they weren't tracking him via his mobile phone? He had read somewhere in one of those anti-Big Brother publications that it could be done. For a moment, he thought about ditching his phone, tossing it out the window of the moving train. The thought crossed his mind and left just as quickly. They couldn't be that sophisticated, surely. It was just natural that the bad guys should turn up looking for him in places that they expected he would go next, wasn't it? He was up against simple deduction, he figured, not hi-tech criminals. Everything that Mike had seen so far led him to believe that was the case.

Whatever happened, Mike knew he had to be prepared for them next time. Maybe he should buy a gun? Not likely – he didn't even know how to use a gun. He decided against that course of action as well. Go to the police, right? He wasn't sure of that either. In fact he wasn't sure of exactly what he had uncovered. In any event he had stolen ninety million dollars. What was he going to do, walk into a police station with ninety million dollars?

He tried piecing together the events of the past few months within the context of the information he now possessed. It made more sense, but there were still things that Mike didn't understand. It was confusing to say the least. Mike started to tire. It was all too much. The last few days were a blur. His lids felt heavy and his thoughts started to wander. He started to think about Fiona.

*

The phone line flashed only once.

'Sal?' John barked.

'Yeah, John. Sorry about that, young Tony is new down here—'

'It's fine, Sal, trust me,' John interrupted him. 'Tell me, how does the market feel this afternoon?'

'It's been pretty quiet to tell you the truth. A few nearby spreads traded earlier, but it's really quite dead.'

'Listen up,' John said. 'What if I wanted to sell a thousand lots?'

'A thousand?' Sal asked in disbelief. He couldn't believe his ears.

'Yes, you heard right, a thousand.'

Sal paused. 'If I could work it over the rest of the day, I could probably get it out before the close. There's no paper out there this afternoon. It would be tough but if you leave it with me I think I could do it.'

'What if I went to market on it?' John asked, deadpan.

Silence.

Finally, Sal answered. 'It would be a bloodbath. It would be real nasty.'

Excellent, John thought.

Another pause. 'You're kidding, right?' Sal asked. 'You're just yanking my chain?'

'Sal, listen up. I want you to sell two thousand lots at market. Don't try and work it. I want to hear you hitting bids. Make it noisy. Butcher the sucker. You hear me?'

'Loud and clear, boss.'

'Sal?'

'Yeah?'

'One more thing. If you fuck this up, so help me, I will come down there and crush you like a bug! You got that?'

'Yeah, if I fuck it up, you'll crush me like a bug.'

'Perfect. Now get in there and sell those two thousand lots at market.'

'Gotcha.'

'And Sal?'

'John?'

'Tell them there is more where that came from!' John clicked out.

It was now officially *Duck Season* and John had just pulled out his trusty twelve gauge.

Down on the floor of the Comex, Sal looked across the pit and caught the eye of Jimmy Z., a local pal of his. Sal gave Jimmy the nod. Immediately Jimmy Z. sold forty lots of copper. Twenty lots for him and twenty for Sal's personal account. Sal was as honest as they came down on the floor. That was why John had chosen him for this mission.

Sal stepped into the pit. He raised both arms above his head and began to shout. Locals frantically slammed any bid they could. Then Sal started selling like a wild man. He was going to drive this bus south. You could hear him on the offer.

Upstairs, John heard it all. He could listen to the action in the pit via the Refco floor commentary. He sat back and smiled. His plan was working perfectly. Just as he had suspected, Sal couldn't resist the temptation to give his pals the nod. True to form the locals were front running his sell order. Normally he would be furious, but for once he didn't care. They were adding momentum to the decline. John sat there watching the copper price tick down on his screen with increasing acceleration.

John had just fired a massive salvo in his war against Fujiyama.

*

Over in London, Steve grew more and more concerned with each downtick in price. 'Nicole,' he shouted at his assistant. 'Get off the damn phone and run me some fresh reports. Run them with fifty and one hundred dollar intervals instead of the usual twenty.'

He knew that if the market closed around these levels that he would be very long come Monday morning. If the market continued to slide into the close, his position would be way too big. So, of course, would every option trader in London. Everyone who had sold downside puts to the producers would be experiencing the same ugly negative gamma problem as the market slid lower. The only way to hedge against further losses was to sell more. He feared an avalanche and didn't want to be buried.

Nicole appeared from the printer with the fresh reports. 'Wow,' she exclaimed. 'We are really long.'

'No shit.' Steve was irritated. 'Give them to me,' he said as he grabbed the reports from her.

'What are we going to do?' Nicole asked innocently. Her French accent made her all the more so.

'What do you think?' His tone was sarcastic now. He often became sarcastic when he was under pressure.

'Sell some copper?'

'Yeah. But who are we gonna sell?' he asked. 'Most people have gone home for the week.'

'Oh shit!' Nicole said. 'I guess we are in trouble then. Why didn't we sell some before?'

Nicole was saved from Steve exploding by the arrival of Anderson at the desk.

'How are we situated?' he asked.

'Long and fucked.' Steve sounded despondent. 'We need to sell, but there's not really any liquidity.'

'How much?' Anderson looked concerned.

'In all seriousness, as much as we can.'

'Right.' Anderson paused for a second. He understood the gravity of the situation better than anybody. Steve had just placed the first GMTFO, or 'Get me the fuck out' order. It would certainly not be the last by any stretch of the imagination. He had always feared this type of event. A thin, Friday Comex-driven sell-off. What was worse was that Mike was off the desk. Nevertheless, Anderson knew what had to be done. The only problem was that everybody else in the market was in the same boat. Most would probably try and sit tight till Monday when there would be better liquidity; others would pray for a bounce. It was going to be ugly. That was unavoidable. 'The first cut is the best cut,' Anderson muttered to himself under his breath. People would go under before the next week was out. He wasn't going to be one of them. Not his desk. Not on his watch.

Cool as ever, Anderson picked up the handset in front of him. With a wave of his hands he rallied the troops on the desk. He looked around at their eager faces. Mike, where the hell are you, he thought to himself, I need you now, more than ever. Anderson took another deep breath. He knew there was no real liquidity but he had to do something before it slipped away. Now was time for action. Anderson was decisive.

'Okay, people.' Anderson took on the tone of a general. 'Let's get to it. I want you to sell copper. Sell anything you can. Don't shout it out. Just do it. Go!'

The meltdown had begun.

*

Fujiyama was furious when he took the call from Murphy.

'What do you mean, copper is in free fall?' he shouted. 'What about my scale down buying orders?'

'All filled,' Murphy winced.

'Then buy everything you can,' Fujiyama screamed like a lunatic. 'Whatever happens, don't let copper close—' The phone cut out. Fujiyama had lost reception.

Murphy tried calling him back. Fujiyama was not contactable. In a way, Murphy was glad. He had never heard Fujiyama like this before. He sounded desperate.

Fujiyama was starting to lose his grip.

*

While the train stopped briefly in Innsbruck to pick up passengers, Mike jumped off quickly to call Anderson. Mike's phone was almost dead, and since he had decided to save the batteries, having left the charger at the hotel in

Vienna, he used a pay phone. Mike looked at his watch. It was almost six o'clock in London now. It was Friday. Anderson should be home. Mike dialed the number. It was engaged. Mike looked at his watch. He had four minutes until the train left. He tried the number again. Still engaged. 'Come on,' he said to himself as he tried again. 'Get off the damn phone.' Success. It started ringing.

'Hello. Anderson?' Mike shouted down the phone.

'Mike? Where the hell...?'

'Just shut up for a second and listen.' Mike interrupted. 'I only have a few minutes.'

'Okay, shoot.' Anderson was pragmatic.

'You know how you've been saying that the copper market was crooked.'

'Yeah.'

'Well, I have enough information to sink the boat. Meet me in Zurich at the Hauptbahnhof, the main train station, at midday tomorrow under the big clock.'

'Where are you now?'

'Austria.'

'Austria? What the hell...'

'Look. It's a long story,' Mike butted in. 'I'll tell you tomorrow. Just promise me you'll be there. Zurich Hauptbahnhof. Midday tomorrow.'

'Okay,' Anderson answered, but the line was already dead. Mike dashed for the train which was just about to pull out of the station.

In a nondescript van just outside Anderson's house, a man dressed in black put down the headset. 'Call Fujiyama immediately,' he said to the other man. 'Tell him we have contact. Midday tomorrow. Zurich Hauptbahnhof.'

Mike arrived at the Hauptbahnhof late that night. He took a locker in the left luggage section and placed the metallic case inside. He turned the key and took it. It would be safe for the moment. It was better than having to carry it.

He changed some of his sterling into Swiss francs and set about trying to find a cheap hotel for the night, which was going to be a hard task in Zurich.

Mike got up early next morning. He found a store where he bought a pair of scissors and some hair dye. At another store he bought a long overcoat. Back at the hotel, he went to work. He showered and washed the dye through his hair. When he was finished, he took the scissors and cropped his hair very short. He looked in the mirror. Good, he thought. Then he put on his sunglasses and the long overcoat. Better. He could hardly recognize himself. He checked out of the hotel and headed for the Hauptbahnhof.

Bahnhofstrasse was busy with Saturday shoppers. Mike kicked back at an outside cafe opposite the station. A German-language newspaper obscured him from view. He couldn't actually read a word of German, but it provided good cover. From his seat against the wall of the cafe he could watch both major approaches to the station. He sat back, his phone on the table, enjoying his double espresso in the spring sun. For a moment, he forgot about his predicament. He thought of Fiona. He really wanted to call her, but thought it best to wait until everything had passed. When he could be sure it was safe, then he would call her.

About eleven-thirty, he saw Anderson get out of a cab opposite, look around to get his bearings for a second and make his way into the station. Good, Mike thought to himself, Anderson had come. He knew he could count on him.

Just before midday, Mike paid for his coffee, folded his paper and placed it on the table and got up to leave. As he did so he saw two black Mercedes cars pulling up across the road. Three Asian men in black got out of each car. Mike grabbed the paper and held it up to obscure his face. The men looked well prepared. Mike could see they had walkie-talkie devices. They were probably armed. Then he saw that face he would never forget: Okimura. Shit! How had they found him? Had they bought Anderson? Surely not. Anderson wouldn't sell him out for money. But what if they had threatened his family? Surely if his children's lives were at stake it would be a different story. Maybe they had bugged Anderson's phone? Regardless, Mike was going to have to think fast. He watched as the men fanned out and headed into the station. What was he going to do?

An idea struck him. Mike sat back down at the table, flipped open his phone and started to type furiously. Then he hit 'send'. The phone started to dial. Leaving the phone on the table, Mike dashed down the escalator beside the cafe which led to the underground shopping arcade that linked up with the station and ran past all the shoppers in the arcade, oblivious to their existence. He had one thing in mind – to save Anderson. He had to get to Anderson before the Yakuza did. Anderson would surely recognize Okimura. Okimura would kill him. He had to warn Anderson before it was too late.

Anderson stood in the open area in front of the train departure platforms under the big old clock with its Roman numerals. People were going about their business. A group of Swiss men wandered past him laughing, joking, and smoking, laden with packs and rifles slung over their shoulders, obviously on their way to a week of compulsory military service. A porter struggled with a large cart piled high with luggage. A mail cart was being hastily driven to an awaiting train. Unlike most of Europe, trains always left on time in Switzerland. Anderson surveyed the area looking for Mike. At a nearby cafe, an old woman casually sipped her coffee whilst a young boy, probably her grandson, ran around, making a nuisance of himself. She didn't seem to care. He was having fun. In front of him, a group of Canadian backpackers looked at a train timetable and tried to work out what platform to go to. All around him, shoppers and travelers went about their business. Where the hell is Mike, Anderson thought to himself. Why am I waiting for him at a railway station? What the hell is he doing in Zurich anyway? What is Mike involved in?

The men in black took up positions near the entrances to the station on Bahnhofstrasse, while Okimura and another man started walking purposefully toward the main area under the big clock.

In the main police station, just a few blocks away, a young female police officer took a strange fax from the machine.

'Inspector,' she called out as she read the message, 'I think you should come and take a look at this.'

Mike ran into a burly man who had stepped into his path, knocking him flying. The man abused him in German. Mike didn't care. He just gathered himself together and kept going, pushing and shoving, Mike jumped onto the escalator which went up to the departure level of the station from the shopping arcade. As Mike came over the rise he saw Anderson, but because of his disguise, Anderson did not recognize him. Mike looked right, saw the face of Okimura, and quickly averted his eyes. He hoped that he had not made eye contact. He started off in the direction of Anderson.

Anderson saw the familiar face of Okimura. It struck him as strange that he was there in Zurich as well.

'Okimura-san,' he called out, raising his right hand to draw Okimura's attention.

Mike turned. He saw Okimura placing his hand inside his jacket. He was reaching for his gun.

'Anderson!' Mike screamed. Running.

Both Anderson and Okimura spun around to face Mike, who was now sprinting directly at Anderson. Anderson's face read shock. Okimura pulled out his 9mm Glock pistol, took aim, and squeezed the trigger. A shot rang out, echoing throughout the entire station. Screams. Commotion. People ran in every direction. Chaos.

Mike was still running. Anderson stood there. Shocked, frozen. Bewildered. Okimura took aim a second time. Mike dived at Anderson. Okimura squeezed the trigger. Mike flew through the air, with a burst of muzzleflash, the Glock discharged. The bullet tore through flesh and bone in Mike's shoulder. Searing pain. Blood everywhere. Still flying through the air, Mike crash-tackled Anderson. They fell behind the baggage cart, limbs sprawling everywhere.

The Swiss soldiers hit the ground, dropping their packs. Quickly loading their rifles, they returned fire. The rest of the Yakuza, rushing from the exits, guns drawn, joined the fray. Gunshots and the sound of bullet casings hitting tiles reverberated throughout the cavernous hall like a symphony of battle.

Mike was bleeding heavily. He looked up. One of the Yakuza hit men took a bullet in the chest and went down. Mike lay still on Anderson. He couldn't move. There was blood everywhere, which pooled around them. Mike started to feel faint. He looked Anderson straight in the eye.

'New suit?'

'Yeah. Armani,' Anderson smiled back. It was a surreal question with the sound of gunshots and sirens ringing out in the background. Mike slumped forward.

'Sorry about the blood,' he whispered. Mike's body went limp. Cold. Out.

June, 1996

It was hot. The sun was just making its appearance over the immense caldera of the ancient volcano. The rich reds, browns and blacks of the volcanic structure radiated the sun's warmth. A large white yacht bobbed up and down in the crystal clear waters of the Aegean as the sunlight frolicked patterns across its surface. In the distance a graceful figure, tall, tanned, young and beautiful came into view. Mike squinted. He could see Fiona. Her long tanned legs, her blonde hair glistening in the daybreak. She was carrying a basket. It looked like she had some fresh fruit and bread. 'Mmmm, breakfast,' he thought as he stretched his legs out on the deck.

They had been at sea for almost three weeks now. It had taken them that long to sail to Santorini from Monaco. They had borrowed Fiona's uncle's yacht not long after Mike had been released from hospital. Mike had lost a lot of blood but the bullet had passed through soft tissue mainly and any damage to his shoulder was repairable. The doctors told him that it would be sore for months but that, given the proper amount rest that in time he should make a complete recovery. In the meantime Mike and Fiona were going to holiday for an indefinite period. Well, at least to the end of the summer as Anderson had given Mike the time off, which was only fair under the circumstances.

Mike stood up and waved at Fiona with his left hand. It caused him to grimace with pain, holding his right shoulder. His right arm was still in a sling. It hurt to sleep on it. It hurt to eat. Basically it just hurt. Mike was such a baby when it came to pain. The Swiss Polizei had arrived not long after Mike had passed out. Two policemen, one of the soldiers, and all six Yakuza had died in the firefight. Half a dozen other bystanders had also been injured. The Polizei had confirmed with the Japanese authorities that all six Japanese nationals killed in the mêlée were known Yakuza members. A couple of days later and after multiple blood transfusions Mike had told the Polizei about the locker at the station which contained the metallic suitcase. They had retrieved it and investigations were fully under way by the time Mike was discharged from hospital in Zurich.

'Hey Mike.' Fiona cried as she climbed back onto the yacht. 'I grabbed this.' She held up a copy of the *International Herald Tribune*. 'It's a couple days old but I thought it might interest you.' She threw it into his lap.

Mike held up the paper. He stared at the front page. 'YAMAMOTO ANNOUNCES 2 BILLION DOLLAR LOSS. HEAD COPPER TRADER ARRESTED.'

'It's about time,' Mike said to himself as he read the rest of the article. It said that Yasuo Tanaka, Chief Executive of the mighty Yamamoto Corporation, had announced losses in the region of 2 billion dollars at the hands of a rogue trader in their copper department. The losses had come to light as selling by the Icarus hedge fund had forced the copper market to collapse. The internationally respected head copper trader, Satoru Fujiyama, had been sacked and promptly arrested on fraud charges relating to forged documents. Simultaneous raids by the U.S. and U.K. regulators on IMT's offices in New York and Wilmont Bridge's London office had taken place but no further details were available at this point except that the regulators were investigating irregularities in their trading. Alan Bridge and Richard Wilmont were unavailable for comment. Both had retired to Monaco only weeks before citing lifestyle reasons for the move. A lawyer acting on behalf of Bryan Murphy of IMT said that the charges were unfounded and would be defended vigorously.

Mike looked up at Fiona and threw down the paper in disgust.

'Typical bloody Japs!' he cursed. 'Whenever there is a scandal they just sweep it under the carpet. I wonder who got paid off this time. I should have kept the fucking ninety million.'

'Ninety million?' Fiona asked incredulously. 'I thought it was only seventy million that the police recovered from the locker.'

'Yes, I meant seventy million,' Mike smiled holding up a locker key, 'give or take twenty million in bearer bonds that I kept for a rainy day. I mean you never know when you might need it. Besides it's just compensation.' He pointed at his shoulder. 'Pain and suffering, you know.'

Fiona just smiled.

'Well, I figured this would happen,' Mike continued his tirade. 'I bet nothing happens to Murphy, Wilmont or Bridge. And I bet that son of a bitch Fujiyama only gets two or three years in a country club jail before he walks free to his millions. Well, at least there is one consolation in all this.'

'And what's that?'

'I was short Yamamoto shares,' Mike smiled. 'And on the back of this announcement, Yamamoto shares were limit down in Tokyo. The Tokyo stock exchange suspended trading in the stock until Monday. I guess when trading resumes the shares are sure to be limit down again.'

Mike held out his hand.

'Can you pass me the Nokia?'

'Sure.' Fiona got up and walked across to him with the phone. She put her arms around his waist and squeezed him hard. 'What are you doing?'

'Nothing. Just sending a couple faxes.'

'To whom?'

'Well, the first is to my broker, telling him to cover my Yamamoto short position when trading resumes on Monday.'

'And the second?'

'Well, I'm going to fax Anderson my resignation.'

'Why? You love trading.'

'Ah.' He paused. 'I've had it with this market. It's just way too crooked for my liking.'

'So what will you do now?'

'I don't know. J.T. and I have always talked about starting up our own hedgefund. With the bonus he'll get this year from being short copper and my little windfall,' Mike held up the key again smiling, 'we should have enough seed capital to get us started. Then again maybe I'll just write a book.'

'Sounds like fun. What will it be about?'

'Picture this,' Mike's face became very animated. 'A rogue Japanese copper trader loses two billion dollars. It's going to be a financial markets thriller.'

'Why write a thriller? Why not just tell the truth?'

'The truth?' Mike scoffed. 'The truth? Are you kidding? Who would believe the truth?'